Mysterion 3

Stories from the Plague Years
2020-21

I0636116

Edited by Donald S. Crankshaw and Kristin Janz

ENIGMATIC MIRROR PRESS

Quincy, MA

Table of Contents

Introduction

EARLY IN THE pandemic, when it was still unclear how long everything would be shut down and in short supply, and whether life would ever return to normal, one of Kristin's science fiction writer friends said, "The world always ends faster in books."

Like most science fiction authors, Kristin had her own global pandemic story, which was published in 2019 despite being written years earlier (right around the last time pandemic fears were "trending"). Of course, she got almost everything wrong, finding it impossible to imagine that a disease without at least a 10% mortality rate could have much impact on the global economy, and assuming that everything would have reopened after a month or two. But she wasn't the only one.

We avoided publishing COVID stories during the pandemic, though we did publish four about the end of the world and two in which the world has already ended. It takes time to write a story and then find someone who wants to publish it. By the time a literary work is broadcast to the world, the world may have moved on from the conditions that inspired the work's creation, and nowhere is this truer than with near-future science fiction reacting to current events.

Almost nine years have passed since we published the first *Mysterion* anthology, and about seven since we started the *Mysterion* online magazine. If we're asked to explain what sort of stories we publish, the answer depends on who's asking. The serious answer—when introducing ourselves as panelists at science fiction conventions, for instance—is that *Mysterion* publishes speculative fiction that is about Christianity in some way, but not necessarily from a Christian perspective or by Christian authors. The flippant answer is, "Christian fiction for people who don't read Christian fiction."

The Christian part is important to us. Not because we expect *Mysterion* to convert anyone, but because there aren't many science fiction and fantasy venues for stories that take Christianity seriously, on its own terms, but aren't required to agree with it or avoid offending the sensibilities of those who only read "clean" fiction. You'll find stories here that affirm Christian beliefs, such as K.J. Khan's "Soul's Wager" and Joshua M. Young's "God-Eaters", and those that reach more ambiguous conclusions; for instance, Rachael K. Jones's "The Woeful Tale of Sir Banana" and David Tallerman's "An Exchange of Values, Conducted in Good Faith". We hope to continue being a venue where readers can find both, and everything in between.

One of the challenges we faced during the pandemic, along with many authors and other publishers, was trying to promote our magazine in the absence of in-person events. Science fiction conventions had been one of our primary ways of trying to get the word out to readers who might like the stories we publish: hosting parties to promote the books, participating in panel discussions, and occasionally sharing a table in the book dealers' room with other independent publishers. Virtual conventions aren't great for networking, or for enabling attendees to discover books and authors they didn't know they wanted to read. Ultimately, though, the interruption has forced us to re-examine our reliance on these events, and to ask whether our time and advertising budget could be better spent. Traveling to attend conventions out-of-state is expensive, and although secular science fiction conventions aren't as hostile to Christianity as some Christians imagine them to be, it is true that material branded as "Christian" isn't what most people who attend are looking for. At what point have we connected with enough of our potential audience in that milieu to make continued attendance a prospect with rapidly diminishing returns?

We haven't entirely decided on our answer, but we have cut back on convention attendance as compared to pre-pandemic days and are less likely to travel for them or to attend even local events unless we're on panels. Although most conventions have started up again, opportunities to connect informally with other attendees still haven't returned to the "old normal", as many events require masks in convention spaces, and there are fewer parties.

In October of 2021, we did travel to a new-to-us convention, Capclave, because one of the stories we had published was a finalist for that year's Washington Science Fiction Association Small Press Award. Although Caias Ward's superhero story "Reformed" didn't end up winning, we were thrilled to learn that it had made it onto the ballot, and glad to have the opportunity to meet Caias in person at the convention.

Another of the stories in this volume, Katherine Briggs's fantastical alternate history "The Inksmith", was a finalist for the 2022 Realm Awards for Short Fiction. The Realm Awards, presented at the annual Realm Makers Writers Conference, are intended to recognize each year's best speculative fiction by Christian authors. (Unfortunately, we weren't able to attend that year due to a combination of family obligations and Donald having to travel for work.) It's encouraging to see our stories getting recognized by both secular and Christian audiences, and we hope we can continue to grow our reader base across both communities.

What's next for *Mysterion*? Another anthology, we hope. Our intention is to publish a reprint anthology every two years, and astute readers will notice that 2021 ended some time ago. Like everyone else, we're going to blame the pandemic for the delay. But it's getting harder to use that excuse, and we now have another two years' worth of stories to republish, after this volume. We'll try to get it ready before the next global disaster strikes.

Otherwise, our goal is the same as when we started this endeavor. We want to provide a home for compelling and thought-provoking science fiction and fantasy stories about Christianity, especially those that aren't what other publishers are looking for. And we want to offer readers a selection of stories they're unlikely to find side-by-side anywhere else, by authors with very different perspectives on God, morality, politics; and, of course, on the Christian faith and its mysteries.

Kristin Janz and Donald S. Crankshaw
December, 2024

A Moose for Jesus

Patricia S. Bowne

IT WAS A warm August evening in '72 and we were sitting around Holland
Wales' backyard waiting for the grill to heat up and talking about the moose,
when his big dog Boomer came out and took a dump right in the middle of
the circle of chairs. Normally Boomer wouldn't get away with this because
Holland's wife Judy would be on him in two seconds, but Judy and the other
wives were inside dishing up potato salad and gossip. So we sat around and
commented and cheered Boomer on as he concentrated, and set his jaw, and
strained, and finally produced. It only stopped being funny when the smell
started to hit us.

Holland looked around the circle, but we all looked somewhere else. When
things like this happened Boomer was Holland's dog, though most other
times he belonged to the whole True Faith Christian Community. After a few
minutes Holland gave up and got some paper and went in to clean it up. He
leaned forward and then he froze.

"Look!" said Holland. "It's a miracle!"

"What's a miracle?" asked Winston Williams from my left, and I leaned
forward to look round Holland.

"It's growing!" Holland said, in a hushed voice. "It's a miracle!" and sure
enough we could all see the pile Boomer had left getting bigger and bigger. It
had almost doubled in size. "Judy!" hollered Holland, before any of us could
think to stop him.

It turned out the dog had eaten a sponge, but I've thought about that story
more often in the years since than any other. Because it's like Winston says,
you can make all the arguments about it that people make about miracles like

1

childbirth and sunrise, and more besides; just try it, and see if within five minutes you aren't deep in God's sense of humor versus human vanity, and the radical humility of the incarnation.

At the time, though, we laughed and let it go, and after Holland had cleaned it up, we went back to talking about the moose. The wives all agreed about the moose, that it was a helpless little thing and ought to be left alone. Hunters took plenty of bad-mouthing from them, but that didn't bother any of us. We'd heard it before. We did a lot of it ourselves, in fact, because most of the hunters drove up to our town from Pittsburgh and barely knew enough to un-cock their guns before throwing them in the back seat with the kids. That wasn't the point about the moose, anyway. The point about the moose was that it talked.

The way it happened was this. Henry Cram down at the IGA had been out in his boat fishing and had come out of some brush just behind the moose when it was lollocking around chest-deep in the swampy end of Fake Lake, and he swore up and down that when he startled the moose, it looked around and spoke to him. The moose jumped a little, and said:

"Excuse me!"

That's what he thought it said, but it had a mouthful of weeds and might have meant something else. Then it trundled off through the rushes.

If Holland or Winston had told me they talked to a moose I would have accepted it without really taking it seriously, just to be polite. People in the Community told me all sorts of things. Henry was an Episcopalian, though, and believing him when he reported something like this was more difficult and potentially more important. If moose spoke to Episcopalians, it indicated some willingness on their part to engage with the secular world.

Most of us didn't believe the moose had really spoken to an Episcopalian. We saw the whole thing as an elaborate practical joke along the lines of taping a walkie-talkie to the cat, the sort of thing you used to read in Archie comics. This wasn't so far-fetched in the early seventies, with be-ins and streakings and happenings still occurring all around us. I could imagine some radio-taggers in the DER giving in to whimsy. But it was something you had to think about. If moose could talk... it gave us all a funny feeling, at least until the burgers were done.

There was more talk about the moose next week, down at the Mobil station. I'd stopped for a fill and was stretched out under the hood, trying to get the dipstick in without putting another bend in it, when Holland came up behind me.

"Did you hear about the moose?" he asked. "It was in the lawn at Bain's Funeral Parlor last night."

"Let me guess," I said. "It said 'Rest in Peace'."

"No," said Holland. "It said 'Excuse me' to Mrs. Maddison. She passed out and hit her head on the front porch railing. Ed Bain gave her a certificate for a free floral tribute so she wouldn't sue."

"It isn't Ed's moose," I said. "That's what's wrong with this country. Too many darn lawyers."

"We ought to do something," said Holland.

"What? About lawyers?"

"About the moose. It's a miracle. You don't just ignore a miracle. You take up your bed and follow it."

"Look, it's a moose," I said. "Some joker wired it. Or it could be possessed, like the Gadarene swine. You don't just follow after something because it's unnatural. Besides, it hasn't asked you to follow after it, has it? You've never even seen this moose."

"That's true," said Holland, thinking it over. "Do you think it is a demon?"

"I think it's a moose," I said. I didn't stop thinking about it after I drove away, though. Holland had a point. A moose that started talking wasn't just a moose anymore, it was some other kind of thing. Something that called for judgments. Because everybody knew, I figured, that animals weren't good or bad. They were just critters, or if they were in the wrong place, varmints, but even then, they weren't in any sense evil. But if they started talking, somehow that seemed to change it all. A talking moose could be a good moose or a bad one, but how could you tell which?

When I got home I hauled out the old King James and paged through the concordance, but there wasn't anything about moose. The closest I could come was Balaam's ass.

೮೦೦೪

The next time I saw Holland was in service; he was sitting up near the front, where he always does, with his hands held up and his eyes squeezed shut, praying in tongues during the hymn, and I scrunched myself between the ranks of folding chairs to sit behind him. We didn't have a church of our own at that time, just a room in the Methodists' basement, so our services had to be held Sunday at noon after their Ladies' Aid had cleaned up and gone home. The room was plastered with Methodist Sunday School relics: sheep pictures made out of cotton wool, angels with gilded macaroni haloes.

I liked sitting near Holland. In fact, I wouldn't have come to services at all if I couldn't sit near Holland and hear him pray in tongues. A lot of people outside the church make fun of praying in tongues, give it Latin names and call it a syndrome. Even inside the church, people misunderstand it and waste their time trying to translate, saying it's Aramaic or Hittite or some language our Lord spoke on earth, but the tongue Holland prays in is no human tongue. It's the language of faith. And when I looked around the church and saw the Fall happen again every year in children changing into sinners like the rest of us, saw old folks losing more of their friends and themselves every year, I needed to hear Holland pray. I needed to know God had given at least one of us the gift to ask Him things none of our languages had words for.

After the service we all stood around the Methodist folding tables and ate Rice Krispies bars. I told Holland about looking the moose up in the concordance.

Winston laughed. "There aren't any moose in Israel. Moose are only in North America."

"That's not true," said Judy. "They have moose in Sweden. They call them elk over there, that's all. Did you look up elk?"

"No," I admitted. "Do they ever call them asses?" I tried to picture Balaam riding on a moose, a tubby little guy in a striped robe and sandals perched up on a moose, holding on to its antlers. It didn't work.

"The snake talked," said Holland. "But it was really the devil."

"It didn't say 'excuse me'," said Winston. "Nothing in the Bible ever apologizes, come to think of it. They say, 'have mercy upon me a miserable sinner,' but they never do any apologizing until they've become miserable sinners." Winston went off like this every now and then. He was going to spend the next week looking for places in the Bible where a little common courtesy and communication would have headed all the trouble off, I could tell. Things like Joseph's brethren telling him how bad his attitude made them feel.

"They've got a big concordance upstairs in the library," said Judy. We left Winston working out Bible manners in his head and went up after it. I'd never been in the Methodist Church proper and it was a real enlightenment to me to find it all carpeted and fake-wood-paneled, done up in sixties professional. If Holland had spoken in tongues up there, someone in an ironed dress would have appeared out of nowhere and asked him to keep his voice down, the doctor would be with him shortly. But they did have a big concordance. There still wasn't anything about moose in it, or elk either.

"You know what's really going to happen to that moose," said Judy.

"What?"

"The same thing that happened to the mountain lion. Some jerk who doesn't have anything better to do with himself is going to shoot it."

She was right. I'd seen the mountain lion myself, but not until after the Pulaski boys shot it and put it out on display in their flatbed.

"It's a sin," said Judy.

"Well, what do you expect me to do about it?"

"Nothing," said Judy. That way women say it, sometimes. It sounds like they're letting you off the hook, but that's not what it means.

"Call the Audubon Society," said Winston, when we told him. "The Sierra Club. The Nature Conservancy. The Humane Society."

"And what are they gonna do?" I was peeved. "Are they gonna set up a moose guard? Or trap it and take it up into Canada?" That actually made sense, when I thought about it. Like that TV show, where they're always relocating animals. But if the TV guys knew the moose could talk, they'd relocate it to Hollywood.

Sometimes you stumble upon the truth without even knowing it. They all looked at me with their eyes wide, and then it hit me as well.

"All it does is apologize!" said Winston. "It is Canadian. It's lost."

"We have to help it get back," said Holland.

"I thought you thought it was a demon. Like the snake."

Holland looked down at the floor and got his stubborn look. It meant he didn't really understand why he felt the way he did, but he felt that way and nothing was going to change it.

"All it says is 'excuse me'," he said. "That's a Canadian, not a demon."

ഇരു

If you want to keep tabs on what's going on in a small town, animal, vegetable, and mineral, you could do worse than have a Christian Community. Folks from all walks of life belong; what the college students don't see, the line-workers or truckers will. They weren't all as regular to service as the rest of us, what with their jobs and all, so we didn't get any of their takes on the moose until Wednesday morning Bible study down at the Burger King.

There usually weren't any more of us than fit in a booth, and this morning was no exception; Holland and me, and Judy. But then Jim King came in, fresh off a run from West Virginia and hungry for a good gossip. He nodded when we told him about the moose.

"Yeah, there was a guy on the CB last week saying he almost ran into a moose on Route 19, down by Conneaut Marsh."

We looked at each other. "So it's heading north," I said.

"But how would it have gotten down there in the first place?" asked Judy.

"Maybe they live down there and just nobody's seen them before. Or maybe somebody's trying to raise 'em," said Jim. "You'd be surprised what people try to raise, for big game hunting. Last time I was down in Texas, I saw a giraffe. Right by the side of the road—it wasn't in any zoo, either. And those spotted deer, those are all over the map down there."

We looked at each other. I thought about a Canadian moose, trapped and transported into a new country. Why would it try to go home, if it had a nice little marsh in Crawford County? But animals can be like that, there's a hundred stories about it.

The reading that morning was from Matthew 18, the parable of the lost sheep. *How think ye? If a man have an hundred sheep, and one of them be gone astray, doth he not leave the ninety and nine, and goeth into the mountains, and seeketh that which is gone astray? And if so be that he find it, verily I say unto you, he rejoiceth more of that sheep, than of the ninety and nine which went not astray.*

Most times the Bible takes a lot of talking over before you know what it's getting at, but that morning it came through loud and clear.

"We have to do something," said Judy. "That poor thing is just heading north, thinking it'll get home. It's going to run straight into Lake Erie, and then what does it do? Either it heads east into Buffalo, or it heads west and ends up in Cleveland."

I had to admit, it did seem like we needed to do something. A moose wasn't going to do well in Cleveland.

ℂℂℂ

That Sunday afternoon, Winston brought a guy I didn't know over to my place. They showed up in a brown jeep Wagoneer I'd never seen before, with a "Protect our Environment" decal on the bumper.

"Holland and Judy here?" Winston asked, the minute I answered the door. "This is Richard Decker, my friend from the DER. They ought to hear this." The guy with him looked like a government worker. He was as clean-cut as a model from the Parade Sunday supplement. Not a hair out of place, white smile, wire-rimmed specs, ironed jeans.

"I'll give them a call," I said. "Why don't you get settled out back?"

It was one of those muggy afternoons, so I was just as glad to get out of the house and sit out back with Winston and Richard Decker and a couple of cold beers, waiting for Holland and Judy to walk down from their place. Winston got out of the glider so they could sit together.

"Oh, bless you!" Judy said, and rubbed the cold glass across her forehead. "What's up?"

Winston introduced them to Richard Decker. "He came out to give us the moose news." We all perked up, as if Decker had brought a cool breeze with him.

"Winston told me you were worried about what would happen to the moose," he said. "We feel the same way over at the department, so our plan is a trap-and-relocate operation. When we find out where it is, we'll tranquilize it, tag it, and take it over to New York State. There's a population of moose just getting started in the Adirondacks, since those bad winters killed off some of the whitetails. It should have plenty of forage, and probably be able to find a mate over there."

"Oh, that's good news," said Judy.

"We thought it came from Canada," Holland said.

"Well, this would be a strange place for a moose from Canada to end up. It would have had to come across the border at Niagara or over at the St. Clair, and it's quite a walk from either of those to here. Not through moose-friendly country, either."

I'd been to Niagara once, and I couldn't really see a moose getting through it. I imagined a moose on the wide pavement with planters, looking out at the falls, then going down the main street and stopping at a wax works show, or to watch them make taffy. Nope.

"Jim King thought someone might have shipped it in to try and start a big game operation," I said.

"They might. We haven't heard anything about it, though. It's a sure thing," he said, "that this town isn't good moose habitat.

"But there's more, and this is serious." He pulled out a couple of shiny, smelly sheets of paper—the kind of printouts you got off the microfiche reader at the college, when you were checking newspaper files. "A moose up in Ontario killed six people last month. They say moose are the most dangerous wild animals in Canada."

Reading the news account distracted me for a minute, so I didn't really hear what Holland said. "What?"

"Are you saying this moose is a killer?" he repeated.

Winston laughed. "It's on the lam. Fleeing from the Mounties. Wear a red coat around it and see how fast it runs."

"What it means is, if you see it you should keep a safe distance and call us," said Richard Decker. "Don't approach it yourselves. They're most dangerous when they're in rut, but any animal can be a threat if it's cornered." He gave us all the office phone number.

"We really appreciate that," said Judy. "Would you like to stay for dinner?"

Richard Decker wouldn't, thanks anyway. He probably had a Parade-model wife and children waiting at home. He went off around the garage and left the rest of us to talk over his news. Winston waited till we heard the

Wagoneer start up and drive away down the road. Then he pulled out a notebook, the same one he used for Bible study, and leaned forward.

"Here's the real scoop," he said. "I went over to the library and looked up moose in Pennsylvania, and it says they used to be all over the state."

"Yeah?"

"Yeah, but! Listen to this. 'The Moshannon Creek in Centre County was formerly called Moose-hanne, or Moose stream. In its deep pools they were said by the Indians to perform religious rites when the moon was crescent shaped.' Religious rites!" he repeated. "Moose were pagans." He looked from one face to another. "That moose might be dangerous, but we still need to find it. Who else is going to tell it the Good News about Jesus? The DER cares about its body, but not its immortal soul."

∞

Winston's call woke me up about five in the morning. "Richard just headed out. Someone saw that moose on Tickner Lane, out behind Fake Lake."

"Did he say which way it was going down Tickner?"

"Nope, but my bet is it was going toward the lake."

You could do worse things with a summer dawn than drive around country lanes looking for a moose. It was heading toward autumn, the first goldenrods just turning yellow. A charm of goldfinches flew across the road in front of my truck, passing over and dipping below one another like they were braiding the air.

Winston and Judy were parked in the lower lot, the one to the west of Fake Lake. "We don't want the DER guys to know we're here," he explained. I could see a couple cars, and a truck with a horse trailer, at the far end of the East Lot. "Looks as if they expect it to come out in the swamp," said Winston. "I saw some flashlights going down that way."

"Then there's no point our going there," said Judy. "What do you want to do?"

"I'll stay here and poke around on foot," said Winston. "The rest of you can scout around the roads, and if you find it come back and get me."

Holland climbed out of Judy's car and into the bed of my truck. "I'll go over to the other edge of the swamp," Judy said. "Why don't you go up Post Road to Tickner, and we can meet there."

Post Road was one of my favorites, the way it dipped and rolled. I'd normally have taken it pretty fast, just to feel the truck swoop along, but not with Holland in the bed. I went slow, looking to both sides: through a wooded spot, where we couldn't have seen a thing, and out between a couple pastures.

Holland banged on the back window at the exact moment that I hit the brakes. We hopped out and stood by the fence, staring.

The moose was standing in the middle of old man Garnet's field, right beside the big old maple tree where the cows lie down. Ground mist swirled around its ankles. It bobbed its head up and down as if it were trying to tell the cows something, and then it turned and walked away a little bit. It stopped, looking back as if it expected them to follow, but it didn't know Garnet's cows. None of them moved a muscle, except to twitch an ear or swish a tail.

Holland took a deep breath and climbed over the fence.

"Hey!" I whispered. "That's not safe."

He didn't even turn his head. He just looked toward the moose. The sun peeped over the horizon, bright red. It lit up one of his ears and made red streaks along the moose's antlers.

"Uh, hello," Holland called. The moose turned and looked at him, and so did the cows. They chewed their cuds and twitched their tails, for all the world like movie-goers waiting to enjoy the drama.

Holland walked forward, and what could I do? I climbed over the fence after him, snagging my pants on barbed wire and cursing under my breath. By the time I got loose, he was pretty close to the moose. By my standards, at least.

Holland held his hands out, the way he does in church, and I could hear him talking to the moose. A breeze came up and carried his voice over to me. He was praying in tongues, and the moose had its head tilted in a puzzled sort of way.

"Excuse me?" it said. I actually heard the moose talk, plain as day.

I hadn't really believed it, I guess, from the way that changed everything. Because at that moment, that misty field with sleepy cows and one tree in the middle of it and wildflowers with dewdrops on them and the rising sun sparking red glints off of everything—and a man speaking to the animals in the center of it—well, I stopped being afraid. Not just of the moose, but of anything. I saw the world as it was meant to be.

Then Holland turned around and came back toward me, and the moose followed him. I stood there like I was in a trance.

"We need to help it get through the fence," he said. I did some damage to old man Garnet's barbed wire, pulling out the staples, and by the time I was done with that the moose was right up to me. I tell you, they're big animals. Heat came off its body, and a smell sort of like swamp weed and sort of like a clean goat. But it never even looked at me. It just passed me by, brushing against my coat as it followed Holland. I hung behind trying to pound the staples back in with the handle of my Swiss Army knife. The cows were paying attention to that, and I jammed an old gum wrapper into a split in the post to mark it, so I could come back with a staple gun and do a better job.

When I turned around, Holland and the moose were about halfway down to Fake Lake Lane. I walked behind and I was fine with being there.

By the time we got down to Fake Lake, the sun had turned yellow. It was high enough to blaze on the lake and the wet parking lot, and it turned the sheet of water into one glare through which we could barely see the DER truck at the far end.

Judy's car pulled in behind us and I stopped to wait for it. She was white as a sheet, staring at Holland and the moose. Winston came running over and stopped by the car, panting.

"It likes him," I whispered with my head in the window. "He spoke to it and it followed him."

Two big tears rolled down Judy's cheeks, and Winston took her hand. "Our Father, who art in Heaven," he started, and it seemed like a good thing to say at the moment. So, I stood there with my hand on Judy's shoulder, and we prayed about God's will being done and earth being like heaven. All along, I thought I was seeing it right in front of me.

Holland and the moose walked away into the reflected light. It whittled away at their edges until they were just a stick man and a stick moose, surrounded by the green and purple spots you get in your eyes when you've stared into the sun. You could tell there was commotion going on over there, but not exactly what.

After a while, Holland came back alone. Judy jumped out, crying, and threw her arms around him.

"What happened?" I said.

"It's headed home, I guess," said Holland. He hung his head.

"What's wrong?"

"They shot it with one of those tranquilizer guns," he said. "What's it supposed to think about God's love, after that?"

"It'll be all right," Judy said. "When it wakes up and it's in a good place, it'll know."

"It thought it was in a good place," said Holland. "It thought it had found friends. And then they shot it. It looked at me—it tried to run—"

Judy gave us a look that meant "Get!", so Winston and I trudged off toward his car, with the light at our backs and our long, dark shadows stretching across the edge of the lot.

"I'll give you a lift back to your truck," Winston said, and I just nodded. It was like something that had lifted off my shoulders, for just long enough to make me think it was gone for good, had dropped back down onto them.

"Sometimes you have to make the best choice of bad options," said Winston. "It's a fallen world."

೮୦ରେ

I didn't feel like hunting that fall, so I drove Winston's kids over to the Pumpkin Farm instead to have a look at their display, a pumpkin-headed man and wife driving an old wagon with a pumpkin-headed horse across the lawn. We took the scenic route, past the nursery and the old springs and the pheasant farm, where they kicked the birds out just before hunting season and a lazy guy could get his limit just by sitting on a lawn chair beside the road until they came and tried to fly back in over the fence. I'd forgotten about that, and how dark it made me feel; but Winston's kids thought it was fantastic and hung out the windows looking for the birds.

We got to the farm and the kids picked out pumpkins as big as themselves. I knew it would all sort out if I just waited for them to get tired of trying to lift their choices and work their way down to what they could handle. The farm sells cider, so I got a cup and sat down at an old picnic table near the hedgerow, in that bright, cool sunlight we get in October.

I'd been sitting there a while when I saw one of those tame farm pheasants come out of the edge of the field, looking around for its coop and feeding trough. It almost walked over my foot before it realized I was sitting there, and then it jumped a little.

"Oh!" it said. "Excuse me!"

೮୦ରେ

Pat Bowne grew up around the charismatic Jesus Movement of the seventies, though unfortunately not around moose. She had family members who routinely spoke in tongues, an experience which was one germ of this story. She now teaches physiology and writes fantasy, including a three-novel series about life in a modern university of magic; you can find out all about these and her other publications at www.raosyth.com. This particular story sat unfinished on her hard drive through five computers, until she came across the quote about moose performing pagan rites (it's from Henry Wharton Shoemaker (1915), *Pennsylvania Deer and Their Horns*). That made her characters' next steps perfectly clear.

In the Fields of Sin, Down Among the Dead

Brian Winfrey

WHEN BEN REAPPEARS in the kitchen doorway, the weight of the work ahead has already made him a stranger.

They say there's a look that comes over Weavers when there's a job to do, a look that's sly and cautious and terrible.

I can vouch for that.

"I'll be back by sun-up," he tells me.

He tucks the gun he's chosen—some queer heirloom that's been fiddled and fussed with going back years—beneath his duster and studies me a moment. I sweep the last fragments of the shattered dish into a neat pile before meeting his gaze.

"Sorry about before," he mutters.

His voice may carry a tinge of regret, but little enough touches his eyes. He squeezes my hand and kisses my cheek, then heads for the door.

He doesn't ask for good wishes or kind thoughts, and I'm ashamed to say I have none to offer.

₭₨

Shadows swallow the foothills as the fading sun paints the valley in streaks of crimson and rust. Through a narrow window, I watch the pickup circle the dirt road down into the deep woods.

Once I'm certain Ben won't turn back, I hurry up the stairs, glancing over my shoulder, a thief in my own home. The old farmhouse creaks and groans the whole time, like it's pained by my decision.

The brass key remains in the bottom drawer of the desk, right where Ben placed it months ago. Where I've returned it after each time I've put it to use.

It feels warm in my hand, even though the house has a distinct chill. An omen for sure, but I waste no time trying to figure out if it's for good or ill.

℘℧

The room the key unlocks once served as an upper parlor, back when the Weaver family cared about such things. Later, it became storage for dusty bric-a-brac.

Now it stands empty.

It's not supposed to be that way, of course. Ben and I, we'd had our plans. But all we managed was to paint half a wall a weak shade of blue. The paint can still sits in the corner, abandoned, its contents long since congealed.

Plans don't always work out.

I kneel in the room's center, my fingers tracing the wood beneath me. The floorboard I want doesn't yield without some struggle. I don't begrudge the effort; it reassures me Ben has kept out of here, just as he'd vowed he would.

I slide a hand into the recess I've uncovered. Everything is as I'd left it. I draw out what I need, murmur a short prayer, and then spend a good few minutes making certain I've left no trace of myself.

By the time I'm ready, the mist has settled thick and low across the valley, like a shroud.

℘℧

I step off the porch, and the temperature dips a good ten degrees. That sets my teeth chattering, so I clench my jaw tight. Then I get moving before I lose my nerve.

The first thing I notice is the silence. You put your mind to it, you'll always hear something in the backwoods. The cry of a bird, the rustle of cicadas, the snap of a twig. Something.

Not this night. Of course not. It's dead quiet.

I shuffle through the mist, which waxes and wanes across the length of the yard. I know I've made it halfway down the hill when I spot the dogwood. It flowered last week, and its silk-white blooms stand out in the darkness.

But they're not what's gotten my attention.

No, I'm looking at the ghost jars.

They hang from every branch, dozens of them. There's a pattern to their placement, but I don't know what it is. Only Weavers know that. Family secret. I do know there are hex signs etched into the skin of each jar, and that the mouths are rimmed with ash and tears.

13

I've come to recognize the sight of a haint trapped inside one, too. They look like silver smoke that twists and writhes of its own accord, lit all the while by some inner flame. In a normal week, the jars catch two or three before they get up to mischief.

Tonight, every vessel holds such a spirit.

Ghost jars and haints, charms and wards, shotguns and hex signs. These things have become my life, but, in so many ways, they remain mysteries to me.

I am a Weaver in name only.

I shudder as I pass beneath the dogwood's long, spidery branches. The stone wall that encircles the farm lies just ahead, the boundary between one world and the next.

The dead and the damned wait there, tucked in shadow, and they jeer and hoot and howl as I approach.

ഇൽ൩

The Weaver farm backs up onto a corner of hell, that's the simplest way of putting it. Everyone in there wants out here. A crafty few manage that on occasion—and then a Weaver sticks 'em right back in. That's what Ben's off doing now, rounding up strays.

"There's nothing they won't do to get across," he once told me. "They'll make any promise, whisper any lie, offer any reward. Time doesn't mean a thing to 'em, either. They might as well be water wearing down stone."

My husband's not a man prone to tall talk, so I'd given his words the weight they'd earned when he'd warned me, "Don't ever go near that wall when it's their night."

Their night. Walpurgis Night. When the skin of the world thins out and the dead roam with ease.

This night.

ഇൽ൩

Everywhere I look, I see decayed faces and withered limbs, ravaged bodies and shriveled souls. They pace the wall. Looking for weak spots but finding none.

At first, they all speak at once, shouting over one another to make themselves heard. The smarter ones start with a little flattery, but the minor damned go straight to threats and temptations.

"Help us or suffer our wrath!" they wail.

"Riches!" they cry. "Youth! Power! Yours! All yours!"

14

As their cries wash over me, my heart thuds slow and heavy in my chest. Every instinct tells me to turn tail then and there. Instead, I force myself to meet those terrible, hungry gazes. To stare them down.

That's what Weavers do, after all.

I can manage as much, I reckon, for the span of a single night.

Bear the name, shoulder the load.

In truth, it's not the first time I've crept out this way. But I've never dared tread so close to the wall before, not when the damned have roused themselves. Instead I've contented myself with studying up on them from afar, with chasing down a haint here and there.

That's not enough, though. That'll never be enough.

Not for a Weaver.

So here I am.

I figure I've about got the hang of facing down the horde—so long as there's the wall in the way, anyhow—when a hush falls across the congregation. The ones in back go quiet first, then the silence ripples outward.

Without so much as a glance at one another, they part to allow the approach of a late arrival.

Josiah Root saunters past the assembled damned, right on up toward the wall, and tips his hat to me.

෫ා◌

The Weavers have a book, a crumbling folio bound in the hide of one of hell's great beasts. It holds all the lore they've gathered about the damned. I've read it through more than once (on the sly, mind you), and most of those listed rate only a paragraph or two.

Mr. Root gets an entire chapter all to himself.

He was spreading misery and rot a hundred years before I was born. In life, he made wealth his religion, with other folks no more than tools or obstacles to that end. After death claimed him, he found hell to his liking and set up shop there.

They say he sits at the right hand of Old Scratch himself these days. And just about the only feather left for his cap would be finding some way to damn a Weaver. He'd do anything for his chance at that.

Even tarry with the likes of me.

෫ා◌

He brushes a speck of graveyard dirt from his fine suit as he looks me over. At a distance, you might take him for normal. Up close, though, you can see he's too pale and too bony to be among the living.

Even as piss-ignorant as I am, I know to run; I just can't get my legs working. Mr. Root circles closer and closer, and I may as well be nailed to the spot. His doing or my cowardice? All I can think is, *He shouldn't be here.* Not this night. Hell's gentry have plenty enough to tend to when their time comes round each year. Too much to walk the wall on a whim. I know this; I made sure when I laid these plans of mine.

He shouldn't be here.

But here he is.

His thin lips curl back, displaying ivory teeth in a wolf's smile. "Welcome, welcome, Weaver wife," he says, and his voice is whiskey-smooth, the soft purr of the southern gentleman he once claimed to be. "Oh, how it warms our cold hearts to have you with us."

The wall stands between us, waist-high and a foot across. Charms and wards line the stones, and the ground beneath is strewn with salt and thornapple.

But as Mr. Root's milky white eyes flick across me, that starts to feel like slim protection indeed.

I have a few talismans of my own, mostly what I've pilfered from Ben's stock and squirreled away under that floorboard. They aren't meant for the likes of Mr. Root, though. Not by half.

He shouldn't be here, I think again, for all the good it does.

"Little Lee Ann Massey, all grown up," he says, his words barely rising above a whisper, but full of poison just the same. "Oh yes, I know you. I know you well."

He nods to himself. "You're the farmer's daughter," he says. "The girl who danced with fireflies and sang hymns to the stars and the moon. Your first kiss came 'neath the shade of a juniper tree, and your last summer sweetheart pines for you still."

I can't say how long he goes on like that. Long enough so he hits the high points of my short life and makes every last one sound small and worthless.

His words slice me to the core, and when I try to push them aside, they slither right back in my head. By the time he's done, it's all I can do to meet his gaze.

"Now we're acquainted," Mr. Root says, as the first ice-cold rain of the night seeps through the mist. He licks his lips with a wormy black tongue. "Now we can chew the fat the way civilized folks ought to."

He spreads his hands, and the wolf's smile reappears.

"Be at ease, be at ease," he says. "We're not so different, you and I. Both farmers, in our way. You tend the soil, I tend the soul. Planting seeds and watching them grow. You see?"

A shrug seems the safest reply, so I offer him one.

Amusement flickers over his long face. "Very well," he says. "I concede you may not find the comparison a pleasing one. So, let us cast away metaphor and analogy and have plain words and straight talk."

He holds up a long, bony finger. "One question, ma'am. That's all I got. Answer me full and true, and I swear those legs of yours will carry you far from me and mine. Fair enough?"

He lets my hush stand as agreement, and his smile sharpens. "Tell me why you wish your husband dead."

₨₩

What slips my lips barely rates as a croak.

"Come now," says Mr. Root, all cheer, "it's graven right across your heart. Right alongside so many other secrets and delights."

Out slithers that long black tongue again, like a snake testing the air. Mr. Root makes a low, wet noise then, some awful mix of hunger and delight, and I lurch back as my stomach heaves. I only just manage to swallow my gorge before I paint the dirt with my supper.

"Ah, fear and fury and guilt," he murmurs. "That's a fine, heady blend, to be sure." He lets a note of commiseration seep into his tone. "I myself admit to having had similar thoughts about Ben Weaver, but no occasion to act upon them."

"You're wrong," I mutter, wiping my mouth with the back of my hand. "I wish no harm on my husband."

"Oh? I'd judge you were well within your rights to."

Something must show on my face, because he nods.

"Ben Weaver, what's he done for you? Why, he's hollowed you out and cast you aside," Mr. Root says, and just maybe some of that anger in his voice mirrors my own. "He blames you, and you know as much." He nods again. "Blames you for Daniel. For the boy who never was."

₨₩

All I have left of my son is his blanket.

I kept it, even though I wasn't supposed to.

It's handmade, as precious things ought to be. My mother and grandmother wove it, and it's as fine a piece of craft as you'll ever see.

It's light blue, just as his nursery was meant to be. My grandmother sewed an enormous silver moon for its centerpiece, and my mother added a hundred twinkling stars. Spread it out, and you'll think you have a view straight into Heaven.

17

I cried the first time I held it.

And the last time, too.

My gran told me it was bad luck to keep it after I'd lost the baby. My mother just said it "likely isn't healthy." They promised to stitch me something new, and I swore I'd do away with it.

But I didn't.

Instead I kept it hid there in the nursery, alongside everything else that still held some weight in my life.

As a reminder.

Plans don't always work out.

Seeds don't always grow.

℘ℭ

"How do you know that name?" I manage to whisper.

Mr. Root chuckles, low and dark, the sound of ice cracking beneath unwary feet. "I have eyes and I have ears, ma'am. Here, there, and everywhere. And pain that runs true and deep, well, that has its own sweet, soft melody. I cannot help but listen… and be drawn."

He settles himself on a dead stump and folds his long arms over his chest. "You sure fooled 'em, you know that?"

I haven't any idea what he's talking about, and I say as much. That only seems to egg him on.

"The Weavers," he explains. "You can be dead certain the women threw their bones and read their leaves long before they ever blessed your marriage." He snorts at that. "They foresaw you'd likely bear Ben Weaver sons and daughters aplenty. But you bucked those odds, and it didn't turn out how they planned, did it?"

℘ℭ

"You are cursed."

Those were the last words Lila Weaver ever spoke to me. She said them the day after I lost my son.

Ben may guard the wall, but his grandmother guides the Weaver clan. She'll turn ninety-eight before she sees another summer, but she looks half again as old. Her stare could curdle milk, and her tongue could cut tin. She had her heart set on Ben marrying Polly Galloway, and she was never shy about letting me know it.

She came out of the hills and down to the farmhouse that morning. Marched right into the parlor, which Ben had turned into a makeshift sickroom, and ordered the midwife out. Then she hushed my protests with a grunt and set to her work.

Twigs were snapped and bells were rung. Oily smoke curled from a dozen black candles. Lila spent the whole time muttering words older than the mountains around us. When she was done, she just shook her head.

"You'll have no children," she said, and packed up the bells and the twigs and the candles. "And if you remain with my grandson, it will mean misery for you both."

She's been right to date.

Wonder if that's any comfort to her.

§☮

"Weavers put some heavy stock in offspring," Mr. Root says, hauling me back to the present. "I expect you know that."

I do. Ben reminds me often enough. The knacks and the knowledge the family's collected get passed down the Weaver bloodline. It won't work any other way, he tells me. Without an heir, the wall has no guardian.

"You shamed your husband, oh yes, you did," Mr. Root tells me, as if I didn't know as much already. "Reckon he'll have to call for some cousin now, teach the Weaver ways to one whose blood may be a mite thin. After all, what other path is left open to him?"

He lets out his breath in a slow whistle. "Situation like that, you suppose shame might just turn to hate?" His dead eyes glitter with malice. "Or has it already?"

§☮

Lose a child, and you either draw together or find yourself paired off with a stranger.

Ben and I, we've chosen the latter course. The darker path. I think we both knew we were headed that way the first time we stood over that empty crib.

He took a hammer to it then and there.

Me, I just turned my back. On it, on him, on the whole damn world.

These days, we've learned to harden our hearts and withhold what little we have left that is good and gentle. Sharp words and empty gestures, that's what we have for one another.

§☮

I tell Mr. Root none of this, but one look at his eyes says he already knows. "You don't wish Ben Weaver dead?"

His tone calls me a liar, but he at last offers a rueful shrug. "Well, as you say." He taps his chin in thought. "Then what does bring you to our little slice of paradise on this fine, fine evening?"

I try hiding my heart on that score, but Josiah Root made his bones reading other folks' tells. I've little doubt that the tilt of my head or the tremble of my hand lets him peer straight into my soul.

His next words bear out those fears.

"Lee Ann, Lee Ann, Lee Ann. Still a Massey, not yet a Weaver." Then: "Not ever?" He wags a chiding finger at me. "You can't bear his child, so you reckon you might help shoulder his burden. He won't thank you for your efforts, ma'am. Take my word on that."

I don't give him the satisfaction of a reply, which only seems to tickle him.

"You've come to beard the lions in their den, eh?" He nods to himself. "To test your mettle? To look sin in the eye?" The wolf's smile again as my cheeks burn. "No shame in it; no, ma'am. You'd not be the first to try and prove your worth by walking such a path."

He climbs to his feet and dusts himself down.

"Thing is," he tells me, "you still got half the race to run. It's all well and good to come take a squint at the likes of us. But what's real sin without a little forbidden knowledge? Without a bit of temptation?"

The chiding finger crooks itself into a "come hither" gesture.

Josiah Root sets his long legs in motion, and over his shoulder he calls out, "Come along, Weaver wife. Come have a taste of the apple, why don't you?"

After the briefest of hesitations, after the last of my sense and reason has fled, I stumble along in his wake, hewing close to my side of the wall.

He leads me down a familiar path.

I can't see much for the mist, of course, but I already know there's nothing about but rocks and weeds.

It was all farmland once, though. The best in the state, back before the Weavers took up their strange vocation. Before the soil filled with poison.

Mr. Root halts beside a section of the wall that seems to me no different than any other. He snaps his fingers, and one of the damned, an elderly woman with a ruined face, shambles forward to present him with a rusted lantern. He accepts it with a nod and then sets her some other whispered task, which she turns to carry out.

He holds the lantern high and speaks a word that hurts my ears. Something sparks inside, and light the color of a winter sky spills forth.

"Look there," he says, gesturing ahead of me, at my side of the wall. "Just at your knees."

At first, I don't see anything worth a second glance. But then I spot it—a chunk of stone darker than the rest. It's speckled with pale moss and centered in a cluster of hex signs. Even with no knacks at all, I can feel the power in it.

"That's the keystone," Mr. Root says. "That's what holds the whole shebang together."

ꕥ

Over the years, Ben's told me a lot of stories about the wall.

About how the border between the farm and hell got wider and wider, until twenty men couldn't have kept it guarded. About how the Weavers decided to bring granite down out of the hills and build a barrier against the damned. About how those with knacks and talents came from far and wide to shape the stones. About the blood that got spilled as the wall was built.

He still walks its length each day, and sometimes I go with him. We look for the bits that need mending, the charms and wards that require strengthening.

We used to talk as we walked, and that's when he'd tell me those stories. He'd tell me all sorts of things. Not these days, of course, but back then.

Ben has his secrets, though. Weavers always do. He's never spoken of any keystone, for instance. That shouldn't sting like it does, not with how things are, but the heart's a funny thing. It takes so little to wound and so much to mend.

I only wish I knew for sure which of those I ought to be spending my efforts on.

ꕥ

"Some say you're looking at a piece of the heavenly throne, chipped away when the rebel angels got cast down," whispers Josiah Root. "Others hold it's old Bram Weaver's heart, and they allow it was still beating when it was set in place three hundred years ago." He shakes his head. "Nobody knows for sure anymore, and it don't matter anyway."

He nods for me to take a closer look, and I do, kneeling down beside the wall.

I dare to brush a finger across the stone's surface, and I'm rewarded by a mild shock. But more than that, I feel it *shift* under my touch. Just a hair, mind. Not visibly. Not noticeably. But I know what I felt.

"It's loose," I murmur.

"So it is," agrees Mr. Root. "To the right touch. At the right times. That's partly why your husband's so busy these days. The looser that old stone gets, the easier it is to slip from one side of this wall to the other."

The rain makes it look like his dead eyes are weeping as he turns his gaze back to the wall. "You can surely see why this would be of some small interest to me."

ဢဢ

Ben does not share his nightmares easily.

But they emerge nonetheless, piecemeal, in grunts and groans during the small hours of the morning. I know he fears the collapse of the wall above all else.

My own worries are smaller and quieter, and I share them with no one.

ဢဢ

I rise and let out a sigh, my breath steaming in the frigid air. "You got no words, magic or otherwise, that'll convince me to yank that stone out."

Mr. Root chuckles, holds up his hands in mock surrender. "No, ma'am, no. I can already tell you would never do any such thing."

He leans in, like he's about to share a choice bit of gossip. "But suppose I don't want it pulled out." The ghost of a smile flits across his face. "Suppose I just prefer it a bit more loose than it currently is. Not much, just a tad. Enough so a fellow who knows the trick can slip across when he wishes."

He snaps his fingers again, and the woman with the ruined face reappears. This time, she bears a small mason jar about the size of my fist. In the lantern light, the liquid it holds shines a deep amber.

"Oh, and suppose I'm willing to pay for services rendered?"

"What is that?" I whisper, and my voice shakes.

"Three tears an angel wept," Mr. Root says, tilting the jar gently, so the liquid flows from one end to the other and back again. "Seven grains of sand from the shore where the great ark came to rest. Twelve fond wishes snatched from the night air. Drink it, and barren ground grows fertile." He nods to me. "This is my offer to you."

"That could be anything," I tell him. "Poison."

"It ain't, though," he replies, "and you know it."

I do. Don't ask me how, but I do.

"No tricks, no traps," he says. "No need."

He steps up to the wall and lays his hand on it.

The wards do their work. The effect is immediate—dead flesh begins to scorch and flake away. Greasy, rancid smoke rises from Mr. Root's burning hand, and I gag. But he holds it steady until he's set the jar upon the stone.

"Yours," he whispers. "A favor for a favor."

ဢဢ

22

I am not a woman given to visions.

Lila Weaver confirmed that the first time we ever met. She said she'd never seen anyone with less potential for a talent. (Ben did not take that well, though he knew the truth of it.)

Her pronouncement came as no surprise to me. The only knack I've ever shown involves growing plants and livestock, and I've always considered that blessing enough.

So, you can knock me over with a feather when, clear as day, I see before me a girl I know is meant to be my daughter. A vision, an apparition, a harbinger of things to come. Call it what you will.

I make her out to be maybe six or seven. She has corn-silk hair and Ben's vivid green eyes. Her smile is crooked, but I've still never seen anything half as beautiful.

My glimpse of her lasts less time than it takes to whisper her name, which I already know in my heart.

And then I'm left with Mr. Root and the rain and the jar of amber liquid that promises so much.

ഇരു

I can't rightly say how much time passes before I make my choice. Longer by far than I'd hoped or intended. Longer by far than would bring Ben any comfort.

Mr. Root nods his approval as I set my hand atop the wall.

Only I don't take up his jar.

Instead, I swat it away.

With a chuckle, he whips out a clutch of bony fingers and plucks it from the air. Then, with an exaggerated flourish, he presents it to me once more. "Are you sure?" he asks softly.

"Get it away from me."

He doesn't, though. He keeps it close. Close enough so I can see the swirl and tumble of its contents. "Are you sure right down in the pit of your heart, ma'am?"

It's not lost on me—nor him either, I expect—that we stand in a wasteland, as near a desert as we're likely to get, and that this is the third time he's offered temptation.

I'm under no illusions, though. I have precious little grace in me, divine or otherwise. What I have is a mulish streak and a tangle of scars where my heart ought to be.

Which is how come I answer Josiah Root with my middle finger.

"As you wish," he says, with a shrug.

He takes a step back from the wall, the lantern hooked over his elbow, the jar still in his outstretched hand. With exaggerated care, he proceeds to unscrew the cap, making sure I don't miss a second of what follows.

The amber liquid goes like molasses, so it's the span of a long, long breath before the first fat drop tumbles to the dirt.

℘℘℘

My daughter's name slips from my thoughts forever before the jar's half-empty. Then go her eyes, then her face. Leaving me with only a few hollow phrases to try and commemorate her.

"No point staring down sin," says Mr. Root, with a wink, "if it's got no sting."

He tosses the jar away, and it's lost in the night and the rain. I hear it land somewhere with a soft thud. I'm surprised about that, surprised I can make out anything beyond the rasp of my breath and the rapid drum of my pulse.

"Look close, Weaver wife," whispers Mr. Root. "Look close at what you went and threw away."

Even in the gloom, it doesn't take much to see what he means. The ground went muddy the moment the drizzle began, so you'd expect to have a hard time picking out exactly where the jar's contents got spilled. But that isn't the case. Because here and there, the soil has taken on a new hue.

From lifeless gray to rich brown.

From barren to fertile.

"Might be I'll start myself a garden," purrs Mr. Root, as he lingers over my misery like a fine, fine meal. "Tell me, what sort of flowers take your fancy?"

I hear all this, but only vaguely.

I mutter, "You got your own sting coming, you know."

Something sparks in his eyes. "Is that so?"

"I'm going to tell Ben." I have to draw a breath then, and it rattles, cold and wet, in my lungs. "I'm going to tell him about your precious keystone. That's over and done, Mr. Root. So I guess we both come up short."

He rubs his jaw as he weighs this. "Answer me this, though, ma'am—just how do you plan on explaining you even know such a thing as the keystone exists?" He lets out a low whistle. "Oh my, what I'd give to be a fly on the wall when you 'fess up that you been down here consorting with the likes of me. You truly willing to break what you still got to deliver a jab or two?"

"What I got'll hold," I tell him, and even I'm surprised by the certainty in my voice. Ben'll likely throw a fit, I know that, but he'll come around in the end. I'll make him see my side, damn it. I will.

Mr. Root spends another moment sizing me up, silently prodding at my resolve with those dead eyes of his. At last, he shrugs. "Well, then. Pardon so crude a compliment, ma'am, but you got some gravel in your gut. Yes, you surely do." He taps a finger to his forehead in a little salute. "Should you ever care to shoot the bull again…"

The withering look I offer makes him snort.

"Now, now, don't be so quick to spurn. I find that, with open eyes and an open mind," he murmurs, "all sorts of paths present themselves, Mrs. Weaver. A word to the wise: Best rule nothing out."

Before I can say anything further—if there's anything further to be said—he claps those bony hands together and waves me on my way.

> ෨ᘒ

I come away from that wall bearing a fresh scar.

I can even see the thing in my mind's eye: Jagged and raw, brushing here and there against the earlier one left by poor Daniel. Siblings now, as they never were in life.

The pain's sharp, but it will fade.

Not vanish, though. Never that.

Weavers bear such disfigurements with pride, as marks of their deeds. Maybe mine wouldn't earn much consideration from the clan, given how it's hidden from sight, but that's little matter to me. I know what I've done.

I've faced down the monsters.

I've come away with their secrets.

That's worth a bit of pride, I reckon.

And if I can manage that, if I can bear the load a Weaver ought to, just maybe I can figure a way for Ben and me to mend what we once had, too.

Our scars—our wounds—have earned us that much.

> ෨ᘒ

I'm halfway up the hill when Mr. Root calls out. He wants me to know what flowers he's chosen to plant.

Lilacs and honeysuckle.

In my honor.

I don't look back.

I quicken my pace, though. Just a hair.

By the time I reach the dogwood and its ghost jars, I've begun to shiver a little.

> ෨ᘒ

Ben's as good as his word, returning while the morning sky's still a misty gray. It's my turn to offer a kiss on the cheek, which he accepts with an honest-to-God smile.

Whatever's brought on his fine mood, I don't care to spoil it. Not straight off, anyhow. The damned have no love of sunshine, so I've got a bit of time. I figure maybe I'll circle around to what needs saying, put the best light I can on it.

In the meantime, I turn the conversation back to him.

"Fewer crossings than I'd expected," he says, when I ask about his night. "Ran a couple down over by the Blackburn place. Caught a straggler wading the creek at Mills Point. Most of the others didn't stray too far from the wall for some reason."

A frown clouds his face as he considers this. Before he can ponder it further, I tell him to go on inside and get himself cleaned up. I'll have breakfast ready by the time he's out of the shower.

"Where's your coat?" I call after him.

"Front seat," he says, over his shoulder. "Gonna need some stitching."

ഇറോ

I sit at the kitchen table and pass my hands over the duster again. Ben's still in the shower, which is good, because I haven't even started breakfast.

Three long gashes run the length of the coat's right sleeve. The heavy fabric hangs in tatters there. But the damage doesn't worry me. I've mended worse.

Ben's in good shape, too. Some nights, I've done my share of stitching on him. The worst he has this morning, though, is a bruise or two.

So you might expect my heart to be somewhat lighter than where I started. But you'd be wrong.

Because Ben's duster smells of lilacs and honeysuckle.

Faint, so faint. A trace, a whiff. But easy enough to peg if you've already had the hint.

The honeysuckle doesn't mean a thing, of course. You can find it all over the valley. But lilacs, those aren't so common. Not at all. Fact is, I can only think of one place where you'd end up smelling of lilacs.

The Galloway farm.

Polly Galloway's parents passed a couple of years back and left the whole thing to her. She still grazes cattle on the land, but some of it's given over to greenhouses and flower gardens. You could find yourself a whole lot of lilacs there.

Ben didn't mention any trip out that way. Of course, he likely wouldn't, since he knows how I feel about Polly. It's probably that and nothing more.

But I keep thinking about what Mr. Root said. About thin blood and open paths. About forbidden knowledge and the sting that comes with facing sin.

About scars.

About wounds.

About planting seeds and watching them grow.

৪০୯৪

Brian Winfrey has written everything from ad copy to magazine articles to fortune cookie messages. When he's away from his keyboard, he's likely to be found somewhere along I-40, in search of yet another roadside attraction. Otherwise, he lives in Los Angeles with his wife, two dogs, a ferocious cat, and far too many books.

His Ministers a Flame of Fire

T.B. Jeremiah

Our Father, who art in Heaven, I don't know what's going on anymore.

HERE IS ED Brady. He is trying to sleep on the settee that takes up one end of the first room of the pair he shares with Mama and Rory and Fing. *They* are all crowded into the bedroom; the settee is Ed's statement of independence. He curls his spine into the sloped back and burrows his face into the crook of his sweaty elbow, trying vainly to apply more pressure to his eyes. He is having the visions again (three suns rise over a field where a dead pony and a small train dance slow waltzes). This is not so bad in itself—you get used to them— but with the visions (the man walks along a narrow boardwalk and the sharks snap at his feet) comes the headache, and right now a ball of throbbing pain is expanding and contracting gently in the space above and behind his eyes. He is making an effort to keep his jaw loose, because he has observed that when he gives in to the tooth-clenching instinct, the pain increases subtly.

Earlier he was whining gently to himself, as much frustration as agony (Fing is standing before a chalkboard but the words are on fire and they cast his face into shadow). Now he is silent, aside from the commotion whenever he rolls over in an attempt to shift his internal balance and throw the pain off for just a moment. He thinks of it as a hot-breathing predator, and like any wily prey animal he has tricks and strategies to evade the pursuing ache. The total darkness in this room, stifling curtains drawn despite the summer air, is one of those strategies (the wolf's eyes are bright, bright blue and he snaps his bloody jaws over the handsome god's hand). Total darkness, the nearest thing to total silence, and always the pressure on his eyes.

The pain pounces; there is no one crescendo, but the throbbing dilates beyond endurance, just beyond sanity, and even the flow of visions is interrupted. He grinds the heels of his hands into his eyes, gasping aloud, repeating words he doesn't even hear, thrashing because the ache drives convulsive energy into every cranny of his body.

Then cold fingers close on his elbow, and the suddenness of it turns him rigid. For a long instant he does not move and barely breathes. The hand on his elbow does not tighten its grip, but it remains and at last he removes his hands from his eyes. It releases him then. He squints at the person standing beside the settee, whom he can make out because she glows gentle white. Her outline is blurry.

She requires a paragraph to herself. She is slender, and not tall—about Ed's height, perhaps—but she fills her inches with herself more completely than anyone Ed has ever seen. He is not entirely sure that she is a woman, but she can't possibly be a man. She is clothed, but the flowing thing that obscures her figure is not a dress. It is more like an extension of herself. It has a hood. Her face shines pale blue with great luminous eyes, and she does not seem to have a nose. She has wings, which Ed can tell are too big and colorful for him to see truly even with his vision-bright eyes.

Perhaps she is a vision herself (faintly a dragon rises in never-ending coils through the branches of the great tree). Or a fairy. Then she puts her hand on his forehead, and it is irrelevant because she is so cold, so wonderfully cold, and the frigidity of her palm is the one thing in all the universe that he longs for. It surrounds the spiky ball of agony in his head with ice and blessings.

80C3

I thought she was an angel, anyway, I'm sorry, I didn't mean to do anything wrong if she wasn't, she never said she was. I didn't want her to just be a vision or a pooka. I'm tired of them. They never do me any good, I don't know why I've got to be the one to see all these weirdy things. I thought she might be a miracle, miracles can happen to anyone, they don't mean I'm weird. I'm so sick of being weird, Mama says it's your will but I don't understand why, it doesn't do any good, the visions just make things hurt more. I know there must be a reason but I just don't understand.

80C3

The next time Ed has the visions (sweet roses in heaps while the white-faced king awaits the noose) he hopes for her return, but she does not appear. Instead Rory staggers out to join him on the settee, whining and pawing at his own head. Rory gets headaches, too—but not because of the visions (the dark-eyed bear staggers blindly down the alley knocking dustbins as he goes),

29

Rory doesn't have the Sight like Ed and Fing. Rory is just sickly. Ed sits up and lets his brother huddle beside him, though another body on the settee is maddeningly hot in the clotted dark. Rory puts his forehead against Ed's shoulder; he too seeks resistance to relieve the pounding within. Ed drapes his arm across his own eyes once more (the quiet woman in emeralds and brocade bleeds herself of starlight).

"I'm sorry," Rory says.

"For what?" says Ed (one by one the streetlights dance themselves into nothing by the banks of the dead river). He tries to ignore the way his shirt sticks to his back.

"I'm stupid."

"Dammit, Rory!" Ed says.

"*Sorry*," says Rory, and Ed relents because of the thickness of his brother's voice and knowing that the spiral of apologies will not stop if he stays angry.

"So who's been saying you're stupid?" He wrinkles his nose, wanders a hand over his spectacles on the stacked shoeboxes, but refrains from putting them on (the windows choked with desperate fish trying to escape the burning building). Rory does not respond immediately. "Huh?"

"Nobody *said*." Rory sits up. Ed lowers his arm and puts it around Rory's narrow sweat-damp shoulders, and he can feel the series of cobblestone scars against his skin. These are small scars; the big ones are on Rory's face. "I *know* I'm stupid, I can't do things." Ed shuts his eyes (four little pigs eat the slobbering wolf in a smoky cabin), swallowing again the dark acid. He hugs Rory, as hard as he can. It's not God who made his brother sickly—Ed will not blame God for the things that happened to Rory. The people to blame know what they did, even if Ed will never know their names. He wonders sometimes if he has met them without realizing on the walk home from school, or even in school. This hurts almost as much as the visions, and so he tries to take them both somewhere else.

"I once knew a hero with easy eyes," he says. "He goes upside-down daisy over the hedges with the sun on his curls. He's starshine and moondust and he runs like an antelope, oh how he runs. He's half-tiger half-jack-in-the-box, he's got a great big gun called Marianne, and he hunts the biggest fiercest monsters of Italy and Spain. He's the biggest, bestest, fastest anywhere, and there's a demon-prince who wants him, but he won't go, because he's a big ol' hero. And the demon cursed him with bad magic that makes his luck go wrong, but he don't care 'cos he doesn't need nothing and nobody as long as he's got his brothers."

ဘဉ

The visions didn't help Rory, they never help anyone, I can't interpret them. I would've helped Rory if I'd known what was going to happen. I'd've been with him, I'd've protected him. You sent interpretations to Daniel, I wish someone up there would help me just a little. I know I'm not a prophet or anything, but I don't understand why you let me have the visions when I can't understand them. I couldn't help her, either.

ℰℭ

Another hot night. In a sane moment, when the pain is not so bad and the visions are just a quiet hum (three starlings impaled on the tight-stretched green wire), Ed thinks about the pooka that lives on the corner, a big round person with shaggy fur and a cat's face. It must be awful having all that fur on a night like this. How do they stand it? He flips his pillow and clamps it over his face. Ten seconds later his body heat has rendered this side of the pillow intolerable, and the cotton is now smothery. He goes back to the arm over the eyes. His head is getting worse again.

This time when she arrives the pain is at ebb, and Ed hears the liquid sound of her entrance. He peers at her from beneath his forearm; she looks back at him with those white eyes that seem to have no pupils. Their regard extends, stretches, thinner and thinner, until the pain seizes opportunity and digs its pulsing claws into his eyes (the prime minister's head falls down the stairs with a strangely wooden thunk). And then as before her hand is there on his forehead, and instead of the dark explosive red of agony-clenched eyes there are circles of blue, purple, gently shifting on the inside of his eyelids. He can feel the coldness of her skin not just where her fingers tangle themselves in his hair but dropping the temperature of the air around her. How can anyone be that cold, he wonders.

After they have sat together for a while, Ed opens his eyes (deep ocean fish nibble at the floating giant's toes). She is sitting on the shoeboxes, her free hand playing with his spectacles. She shouldn't be light enough to balance on the shoeboxes. She peers earnestly from shadow to shadow; there is something tense in her that he does not remember seeing before. He shifts his weight and levers himself up onto his elbows; she does not remove her beautiful frigid hand. He is afraid to speak to her, but the awkwardness of sitting in the dark with a stranger grows ticklier and ticklier.

"Are you a pooka?" he says. She tilts her head to one side, shakes it. But she does not vanish. Encouraged, "Are you an angel? You look like an angel." In response she puts on his spectacles, absurd broken things on her impassible face. She answers every question with a gesture such as this, and at length Ed gives up and closes his eyes again (sweet Mercy Brown makes faces in class until the ceiling collapses). She runs her fingers through his hair, then returns the goodness of her cold hand to his forehead.

"Thank you," he says. After that they are both silent.

⁊ˢ

She was so good, she never hurt anyone. I don't understand, I don't understand, oh God I don't understand. Please, I just want to understand, please. And please someone have mercy on her, I don't know what to ask for her.

⁊ˢ

Her visits continue, though not regularly. Sometimes Ed gets headache after headache in miserable solitude. It gets harder to ignore the visions when she is not there. But trying to interpret them, trying to guess whose future they portend, whose secrets they reveal, does not relieve the ache. He wishes she'd show up more frequently. When she does, she never talks, simply sits beside the settee and makes the headaches more bearable. He notices that she avoids Rory and Fing, and he doesn't like to mention her to them. It could be bad luck.

In early October Ed gets the visions in school, and the teacher doesn't care until he vomits on his desk (a murder of crows fills the sky until one great raven stills their fury). He is sent home by himself. Staggering down dirty old Candle Street half here, half elsewhere, and all windblown misery, he meets her again. She creates a stillness in the midst of all the busy afternoon people, who skirt her without looking. She sanctifies the lilac chemists' sign under which she stands (three tiny figures scale the blue-gold cliff, while the silent statue watches them struggle).

"What are you doing out *here?*" he croaks. She shrugs and puts a hand on his shoulder (the trees scream in the green light). He rubs the back of his hand across his mouth, for the sea-rhythm of nausea is back, and he has begun to salivate ominously. All around him are the street smells of people and food and refuse, intensified to the point of pain (the lovers flee the flooded cellar, wearing rags of blue velvet). He can pick them out one by one with terrible clarity, the wrenching whiff of a fat-spitting sausage, the unbearable foulness of a rotten cat, the even more maddening sweetness of cheap cologne. A man hurries past them, and the oniony reek of his breath makes Ed retch. A bead of spittle now trembles on his lower lip. The people who notice him are trying not to look.

Ed wants to drop to a crouch at the angel's feet (the silent rows of lamps illuminate the endlessly circling skaters). Even the other fairies cannot see her, he realizes through the obscurity of his rebelling body (the long-faced girl paints her skin green, one delicate stroke at a time).

There is an unexpected wave of heat, so sudden and overwhelming that Ed is distracted from his own troubles. It comes from a man in a black coat across the street—no, not a man, Ed sees when he focuses (the tall boy writes letters dripping with blood to his sweet-faced friend). A tall black thing like a hooded pillar of ink, and the people give this one an even wider berth. Then Ed feels a new pain in his arm and finds that his angel has his wrist in a grip so hard he can feel his bones protest. It is enough to drive the other pain out. She is staring at the black thing.

It steps from the curb and she leaps forward, and all around Ed is an explosion of light and the flurry of cold feathers on his face, and they plunge through a hole in the world that was not there before, the wind screaming in his ears and his heart jerked to a halt and a great emptiness and the light becomes so strong that it is like darkness.

They are home, and the angel watches while Ed vomits again on the lean rug.

୫୦୦୪

Why would anyone want to hurt her? Please keep us safe from the black thing, I don't know what's going on and I'm scared. Don't let it hurt Mama or Rory or Fing. Please don't let any more trouble happen to us. Why are you doing this to us?

୫୦୦୪

Here is Ed examining the statue of an angel at church, a small chippy-plastery thing in keeping with other attempts to overcome the utilitarianism of the building: religious art in lieu of stained glass, never quite enough flowers to hide the ugliness of this brick cigar box. But there is the hand-carved pulpit—the oldest thing here, but old with sorrow rather than tradition—and there is Reverend Flavell, whose fierce erudition cannot inject life into the parish. The vestibule in which Ed and the statue stand is empty, but this is what Ed wanted, why he lingered while Mama and Rory and Fing went on home. The statue doesn't look very much like *his* angel; it depicts a round-faced person, not quite a man but not quite a woman, with a suspiciously innocent expression and small hands. The wings are painted red and green.

"Ed Brady?" says Reverend Flavell behind him. Ed turns, and discovers that while Mama and Rory went home, Fing did not; he is standing next to the pastor looking sulky. "Fing and I have been talking," Reverend Flavell continues, putting a hand on Fing's curly head. Fing scowls more deeply. In the moldy dimness of the vestibule his eyes are almost lost in shadow. Even Reverend Flavell's round face is made of angles and facets in this light.

"Oh," says Ed. Automatically he extends his hand, but Fing remains at Reverend Flavell's side. "Com'ere, you little whoreson—I'm *sorry*, Father, I'm sorry. Sorry." He sounds like Rory, apologizing too many times. His head begins to feel odd—the off-kilter tickle he has come to associate with uncanny things. But it must be embarrassment this time.

"*Mea culpa, mea culpa, mea maxima culpa,* as our Roman friends say," Reverend Flavell says, and exposes the shy grin that surprises parishioners, especially those who suspect loudly that he cares more about things, ideas, than people. "I think that's sufficient. Fing has been talking to me about your headaches."

"Oh, *those*," says Ed. "They just—I've been getting 'em for a while. They started when… when I got the visions, and all." He hopes Reverend Flavell will not notice the hitch in his voice. It doesn't seem right to be talking about the visions in church. The vestibule is chilly with October air, chilly with disapproval. The building itself dislikes this topic.

"Your ma told me, yes," says Reverend Flavell. Ed looks at the angel statue. He didn't know that Mama went to Reverend Flavell about the visions. He thinks of them as his own private ordeal. He wonders what Mama said. "Fing was saying that he's worried about you."

"I didn't *say*—" Fing begins. Ed and Reverend Flavell both look at him. "The numbers said it," he mumbles. "They said they were scared. They said… bad things were happening."

"He talks to numbers," Ed says hurriedly. Fing shouldn't be talking like that everywhere, he knows better. The visions are one thing, people *get* that even if they don't like it, but the numbers and fairies and really *weird* things, that's why people avoid them, or do worse things. That's why Rory… Ed tries to salvage. "It's like the visions, a little bit."

"I know," says Reverend Flavell. And there is a hurriedness in his voice, an anxious vibration inappropriate to his role in this conversation. Ed looks up and finds that Reverend Flavell has leaned forward conspiratorially. "They still talk to me sometimes."

It is not immediate, Ed's realization; at first the words slip through his ears easily. Then he sees the quiver in Reverend Flavell's face, eagerness and fear. He looks less like a minister and more like one of the bigger kids at school, with that awkward smile and crooked front teeth. The deep space behind Ed's eyes tickles more than ever, and now it might be embarrassment *or* the other. He swallows and looks again at Fing, who is staring wholeheartedly at Reverend Flavell. The church is frigid around them.

"They talk to *you*?" Fing says.

"Not often," says Reverend Flavell. "I learned not to hear or see those things anymore, so I could become a minister."

His expression is not regretful, but for once Ed gets a clear vision, of a great and respectful silence where one lumpy figure sits reading the same words over and over.

ഇ൫

I know I ought to've owned up to Reverend Flavell about her, he might've understood. I shouldn't've lied, that was a sin, I know, I'm so sorry. Am I being punished for lying?

ഇ൫

"Ed," says Mama. Ed is trying to read, which is hard because his mind is a little slippy and he doesn't know why (fishes flying through the dark). His head doesn't hurt, mercifully, although everything is a little overloud and he catches himself yawning. But Mama is talking and so Ed ignores the warning signs, tries to listen. Her voice is more fibrous than it used to be, and more fretful. She smokes too much. "—said you'd skipped school."

"I didn't either," Ed says, indignant. She keeps talking, and his attention drifts again (the hangman weeps tears that roll, like beads of honey, from the eyeholes of his mask). Her voice batters against him, against the walls of the room, against the rain-glazed window. Ed, frustrated, turns around and buries his regard in the book, so that her meaningless rebukes rebound off the shoulders of his jacket. There is a faint throb in his forehead, not quite there but not quite not (delight marks the corners of the chalk outline with drops of blood). Then Mama grabs him by the shoulder and he looks around, surprised because she is breathing heavy anger.

"Don't turn your back on me," she says.

"Sorry," Ed says, but he says it wrong.

"You want to talk to your mother like that?" she barks. Her anger does not stop, and Ed doesn't know how to placate her. She is so furious, like a maddened stoat, that he gets up and walks to the window, but she follows him. He has no more answers for her; repeating "I'm sorry," seems only to make things worse. He looks out the window (the bleak hillside is swept by a green-shining wind and the knights topple).

The black thing is standing in the middle of the street, looking straight up at him. Hot black horror runs along the connection, and overwhelmed by the stifling wave of it Ed jerks back from the window, the whole room is buzzing and sparking in his ears and his heart is the only thing he can hear and the hairs on his arms, the back of his neck, his wrists scream in upright terror, the echoing chamber of his mind, the place behind his eyes is collapsing in agony and the total panic of the rabbit when the fox springs (the rabbit leaps, bucking, its spine snaps and the roll of its white dying eyes).

The black fear is so searing it's white, it's red, it sinks into his skin sizzling.

Mama is holding him. They are both sitting on the dust-tracked floor and Mama has her hands on his shoulders, she's shouting at him.

"Ed, wake *up*, wake up, Eddie, *wake up*."

ℰℛ

But even if I'd told Reverend Flavell or Mama, what could they do?

ℰℛ

Here is Ed lying in the uneasy fever dreams of pain; when he is not having the visions (gold flakes fall relentless in the moonlight on the stone dogs), he drifts from one half-formed thought to another. It is not the worst night, by any stretch, and he is lucid enough to feel that lying here with his arm over his eyes is absurd. He feels restive, if not wakeful, and sometimes between the big waves of pain he thinks he could get up and do something. Even more absurd, because the light and the noise would wake someone. Only he's been lying here for *hours* and he's sick of it, his joints itchy (the third owl is the one with the answer, but Julius goes to the first and is devoured).

It has been a long time since he last saw the angel. Once, curled cold and miserable beneath a thin blanket with the pain stabbing through like icicles (beneath the castle the white-skinned worm sinks deadly winter teeth into the foundations), he thought he felt a brush of something soft across his shoulder—but when he sat up, blinking wildly and trying to make out any faint luminosity, there was nothing. He wonders if she is gone for good (silence has come to the forest and the glory-trees are stripped of their purple leaves).

Were it not for the visions, and the pain, lying here in this irresponsible unreality might be enjoyable. It is a quiet place without time. It is at once chilly and sweaty. It is neither waking nor sleeping. It is the in-between place, the gateway to dreams (the last princess dances on bloody feet among the clamshells). And it breaks up every time pain clamps red-strange claws around the dark space behind his eyes. Inadvertently Ed makes a fretful noise in the roof of his mouth. The sound rouses him somewhat, startles the pain away. Is it gone for good? Often when it leaves it does so with such stealthy feet that he cannot point to the moment. So he sits up, hoping against hope. It has gone, and he is full of energy.

Then, with a flap of heavy stubby wings agony careens back into him. Whispering an obscenity, he drops back. This is another old ritual. Sometimes sitting up quickly drives the pain off for a moment, just long enough to raise hope. Ed rolls over and buries his face into his pillow, shifting so that all his weight drives his pain-ridged forehead into the settee. He does not realize (the train glides across the tops of the pine trees) that this makes his bottom stick up.

She arrives just as he has determined to roll over and seek refuge in his elbow again. There is a rushing noise (he doesn't remember the rushing noise last time) and a patchwork of bitter cold and fierce heat. He sits up. She stands on the rug—stand is too generous a word, she is upright but only just. Her garment is torn and her paleness is all dappled with black. Ed finds his glasses with one hand and puts them on.

"Are you all right?" he says. Stupid question. She totters into the arm of the settee; Ed puts out a hand to steady her and cries out because it meets something wet and searing. Then she collapses into him, curling her fingers into the fabric of his pajamas and burying her face in his knees, and aside from a few icy patches she is fiercely hot, and the wet stuff is the hottest of all.

"What's wrong?" he asks. She does not answer, but she is shaking from head to foot. Her wings flicker in Ed's face and he has to push aside the feathers to look at her. He wants to ask her who or what has injured her, whether it is coming back, what he can do to make her better. Instead he cradles her lolling head, trying not to mind the rising heat of her against his body. He doesn't really need to ask her what happened; he already knows that the burning black thing has done this to her. But why is her blood so hot, and why does she only get hotter and hotter? Soon she will be too hot to hold, but Ed cannot bring himself to push her away. She shudders again and again.

"Please, what can I do?" he whispers to her. She shakes her head without raising it. And then strange things begin to happen in Ed's brain, things like visions but tasting worse. Red things and yellow things and fierce sickly green things, dripping like sap through his awareness and making it hard to see the room around him. Toothy things, blood-raw things, and then high shining things with a cry like a thousand trumpets. The only sure thing, the only solid thing, is that he is rocking the angel back and forth in his arms, and he thinks he is crying. The heat is unthinkable. Her wings are knocking things over.

The angel makes a noise like a faltering violin.

It burns beyond all sanity.

Ed is alone on the settee. His voice wails; there are burns all up and down his arms and on his knees. People come in—Mama, Rory, Fing. There is light. His pajamas are soaked with the black angel blood already cooling.

(Isaiah on the mountain and the coal of fire is not to be found and he is burnt up)

ഇര

God, I don't understand, if I could just understand.

ഇര

T.B. Jeremiah draws on decades of experience with migraine for this story. She lives near the ocean with an AI researcher, some small children, and some medium-sized trees; she writes sad stories and draws silly pictures of monsters. Previously, she has been a janitor, history instructor, nonprofit marketing drone, and freelance illustrator and designer. Her short fiction has been published in *Amazing Stories* and *Bourbon Penn*. Find her at www.tbjeremiah.com.

Reformed

Caias Ward

AT THE POLICE station, I check my phone. I'm already on YouTube. "Balor Gets Jawed." I watch it, even though I lived it.

Me, on the bus. Someone goes, "Hey, that's Balor!" I try to ignore him. He gets in my face. I ask him to stop. He takes a swing at me while I'm seated and connects.

I let him get his swings in; better me a target than someone else.

"Murderer!" people yell. He still punches.

Manslaughter. I know what I pled to.

I take the punches, keeping my hands up, visible. He gets mad as I suffer nothing from his repeated blows.

I remember conflict resolution classes in Rahway. He's not a threat to me.

He pulls out the knife. I catch it after it bends on my stomach. I break it in half with one hand and stand up. "Someone here"—I watch myself gesture to the crowd—"is gonna get hurt if you keep this up. Please stop."

A Good Samaritan (as opposed to the other kind) tackles him, two others hold him down, and other people cut off his friends, stare them down. I keep my hands visible, unthreatening, for the police to see when they review the video.

Video end.

I've been here for hours. My lawyer throws paperwork and video at the locals until they acknowledge I wasn't out of line. Someone says that they should lock me back up and, I swear, she all but rolls up a brick in the Constitution to smash him in the jaw. They relent, because Hell hath no fury like a lawyer born in Newark.

She offers me a ride to my brother's. I decide to walk. The cops let me out a side entrance, avoiding the perp walk. It's far away to safety, miles. I run. Run. Run, like I couldn't in Rahway due to the power suppression drugs and the walls. I want to punch. Punch walls and throw cars like I couldn't do in Rahway. I want to rip off bank vault doors like I couldn't do in Rahway. Be the villain, the supervillain they insist I am.

But I run instead.

I get home in ten minutes. I run twelve miles in ten minutes, because that is one of the things which happens when you are superpowered.

My brother hugs me when I get to the house. He's sorry, holding back tears, clinging. He was always kind and fragile, even as a single dad. My niece Katy is four. She knows that I had a time out and that I'm special, but I'm trying to be good.

"I saw the videos, Declan," Peter says as looks me over for injuries. I let him, because it's Peter, and he means no harm ever. He sets the table for me. They already ate, but I can't seem to wave him off doing a full place setting. Ma would approve, bless her in Heaven.

Katy plays in the living room. I sit and eat, listening to Peter talk. He uses mushy words. He always used kind, mushy, caring, Sunday-dinner-with-family words.

"I got you an interview tomorrow afternoon, real wide-backed stuff Da would like."

"What, catching bullets?"

"Construction. Called in a favor with the Operating Engineers Local."

"Your favor?" I twist my mouth. "Or one of his?"

"Mine," Peter says. "Declan, I get it. He's been a saint to you, even after everything. It's gotta bother you."

I squeeze a knife I'm holding until it bends in half. It doesn't cut my hand. I bend it back.

"I'll make sure I'm early. Thank you."

೫つ೧

I lay out my clothes. I set two alarms. I stay up late in my room, watching television, going down to the kitchen, eating what I damn well please before I go to bed. I'm a fat nine-year-old eating peanut butter out of the jar again, hearing Ma call me "husky" and shopping for Husky clothes at Sears.

There's a knock on my window at two in the morning.

I sit up and stare at him floating outside my window.

He motions for me to meet him outside, mouths "garage."

I give him the middle finger.

He motions again.

I put pants and shirt on, float downstairs to avoid the creaking wood, hover to the garage. He's already inside.

"What do you want, Samaritan?"

Once you get past the side-shoulder white cape and blue unitard, it's funny; he's just some Asian guy in a mask. Mind you, an Asian guy who can pick up a tank and fly outside the Earth's atmosphere. I'm guessing he's Christian of some stripe, from the name choice. Me, I was raised Roman Catholic like any proper Irish boy, at least until Ma died. Da didn't have much use for church, thinking that if you wanted to talk to God, just say it aloud.

"I wanted to see if you were OK, Balor."

"My name is Declan Samuels, Samaritan. Balor is gone. Don't call me that again."

"I'm sorry, Declan."

He seems hurt that he was accidentally unkind to me. His eyes hang, like the world is on his shoulders. And it is. He's the savior of the world, pulling off stuff that you only saw in action movies. There aren't a lot of us around, not like in the comics. At least not powerful ones, so we—they—get called on to do a lot.

"You want a beer?" I ask, going to the fridge my brother kept in the garage. Peter put a small woodworking shop in his garage just like Da and, just like Da did, kept a fridge with beer in it.

"No thank you. I don't drink alcohol."

I shrug, grabbing one for myself and flipping the cap off the bottle with my thumb. I find a seat on the worn-out sofa against the wall and lean back.

"So, to what do I owe the pleasure of this visit, Samaritan, savior of the world, protector of Truth and Justice?"

"I..." he struggles. "I saw the videos from today. I wanted to see if you were OK."

"Well, let's see." I look myself over, feeling for holes. "Still invulnerable to small arms and anti-tank weapons. Could have cast my deadly gaze on that guy and incinerated him, but I didn't. Got my shirt ripped, almost got put back in prison because of something someone else did. That's a theme, isn't it?"

"I know you would physically be OK, but—"

"But what?" I pull on the beer. "Are my feelings hurt? Am I mad at what happened?"

"Are you?"

"Hell yeah, I'm mad! I made a choice which I thought would make the world better! Based on what I saw on the news, it did. Still f—screwed up my life." I edit myself, feeling Da looking down on me with a burning Fomorian gaze.

"You've done an incredible thing, Declan. I can't begin to repay you."

"You covered my fines and bills, you kept my sentence short, for a guilty plea. You saved us all a trial. Saved us all from Psirena digging in our heads and finding out what really happened. I got some money for my kid. I *might* get to see my kid and not have him hate me, assuming my lawyers can convince a judge that I'm not a threat and that my ex hasn't poisoned him against me."

"The judge won't be a problem," The Samaritan says. He straightens up, trying to be casual, managing otherworldly, alien, Old Testament angel. "Be not afraid," indeed.

"We gonna lie through that too?"

"This has been hard—"

"Has it? I spent over eight years drugged up and depowered, living in an eight by nine room, in pain from all the drugs like I was some smack addict two days into withdrawal for eight years. If they could have, they would have kept me dosed up even out here. My wife remarried. My kid got into fights daily until they moved. All because, one time, I decide to do the right thing. Not the honest thing, not the safe thing. The right thing. But tell me, how has this been hard for you? Having to keep your mouth shut? Hoping I keep mine shut?"

"You do realize you were a superpowered criminal, right?"

"Yes," I said, "I do. I own that. But I never killed anyone. Only time someone got killed was when you were involved."

I finish off the beer.

"I have a job interview tomorrow and need some sleep. Leave."

He doesn't move.

"I will call the police, and you will have to explain why you are here."

The Samaritan floats out the door, upward into the sky and the clouds above.

₧)(℣

I got the job. Crane operator, as it were; the advantage when you have super-strength and can fly is that you don't need a crane.

To think, this is my first legit job since… did I ever have a legit job? Sure, I had the paperwork for a job before. It's how you conceal stolen cash; pay your taxes on a "job," and you're in the clear. I figure The Samaritan has a version of this somewhere; he's a guy behind a mask when you come down to it, and I can't imagine not having a "normal" life to hide in once you take off the costume. I'd climb the walls of that prison more than Rahway.

Maybe he *is* climbing the walls. I mean, keeping secrets that long, the world worshiping you? His star was pretty bright eleven years ago when he "caught" me, but my capture was a game-changer. He ended up changing the world after that, with deeds large and small, inspiring others with and without powers to step up a bit more, do a bit more. I mean, the guy carried a damaged 747 flying into Newark Liberty on his back. He cried the most at the girl's funeral and fought the hardest to sell my guilty plea. He lost some friends and allies trying to pitch this, to be sure. But it stuck, and it saved us and the world from a trial and the court-ordered telepaths. He continued being a hero; I ate fourteen years for manslaughter, eight and change with parole.

But yeah, I pick things up and put them down. That I-beam needs to get up to the 12th floor? Wrap it up and I fly it up. Drywall? Same thing. Guy falls off the 22nd floor, misses the safety netting? Hey, I guess I get to do a good deed and not have him smash into the ground. That one stopped my coworkers from slashing my tires in the secured parking, even if it didn't stop the protesters outside the job site. Gotta make friends where you can, I guess.

Steve, the guy I saved, he was a felon too. Assault, did two years, about twenty years ago. He got his record expunged so he was technically not a felon, but it still finds ways to find you. Web searches, gaps in job history, or just in a racing heart at 3 AM and you wake up in a room without bars. We sit and drink after work, talk about job and sports and regular things. He never really pushes me about my powers, but sometimes he'd get curious and wonder about all the stuff I could do.

"So you can shoot lasers out of your eyes, like in Star Trek?"

"That's where the name Balor came from. King of the Fomorians, who could burn things with the eye in his forehead. Irish myth."

"That's some crazy right there."

"Nothing crazier than flying and being bulletproof."

"And flying through buildings and knocking them down—um."

"It's cool," I say. He's scared, I can tell. He brought up what got me locked up in the first place. Parking deck got knocked down when a gas line exploded. I got stuck with The Samaritan underground. We got out. The twelve-year-old girl with us in the deck, who was going back to her mother's car to get her phone, didn't.

Steve holds out his bottle. "But you're out, and you're legit, and you have a job, and nobody has slashed your tires in a week."

I clank the bottle to his, nodding my head. To not having to buy new tires again.

ಬಿಂಬ

I drive home after a single beer, same as I always do. Police are all over my brother's house. So are burn marks and broken glass and a sense of violation.

Someone threw a few Molotov cocktails at the house. One made it through the living room window. Cops and ambulances are gone. The fire department has already wrapped up for the most part; we aren't going to be able to stay in the house until it's fixed.

They caught the car of the people responsible.

"Seems The Samaritan was in the area and made sure the truck didn't go anywhere," one of the firemen says, pointing down the street. The husk of a Ford F-250 sits in the middle of the road. It's a twisted burned bloom of metal, folded at the point where The Samaritan hit it from a great height. The doors are torn off and scattered on the ground. The road is a crater.

I look to the sky, trying to spot The Samaritan wherever he may be lurking. I look for something heavy to throw at him. I look at ground level, trying to find my brother and niece, hoping not to find The Samaritan with them. I look at a nearby tree, cracked as though something—someone—smashed into it. Another fireman readies a hose to spray the blood off the white birch.

"He still here?" I ask.

"Nah, he left when the cops and ambulances showed up," the fireman with the hose says. "He helped put out the fire. Did a number on the guys in the car. Guy folded in half at the leg. Rest got more of the same. They might live."

I try to say something, but only air comes out of my mouth.

"Looks like they had it coming," the first fireman says. "Wish I could have gotten a shot in."

The two firemen mock-fight as they ready the hose and laugh amongst themselves, the kind of laugh some of my relatives would make when they told the type of jokes Da didn't want us saying or listening to growing up. They don't notice me leave.

I find my brother. He and Katy are in the garage, shaking, scared. I try to apologize for being a criminal, he shushes me. I tell him I'll find a place where they don't have to worry about getting hurt.

∽○◡

I'm at a motel, on the roof, sitting on top of one of the air conditioners. I'm only waiting a few minutes after I message The Samaritan before he shows up. He was close? He was lurking? I don't know. I don't care. I need this done.

He hovers down from the sky and lands on another rooftop air conditioner. He's smaller now, like he doesn't want to be here, like he knows what he did and why it was wrong, but he still shows up when I ask. He's like every "innocent" convict behind bars who bought his own lies, justified everything he did, and got everyone to go along with it.

But I know the truth. He needs to be reminded.

"I could have given you a place to stay," The Samaritan says.

"You could be less of a coward. The only reason my niece didn't get lit on fire was because she decided she wanted some cheese and went to the kitchen."

"I made them pay for what they did."

"Where's your truth and justice now, Samaritan?" I spit at him. "You crippling people who are going after me because of something *I* took the blame for? They want to pull my parole because I represent a 'danger to the community'!"

"Your lawyer says they won't be able to make that stick."

"I didn't do it! You were the bastard who couldn't control his shit in that basement, cut loose with *your* eyebeams and hit a gas line!"

The Samaritan sits down on top of the air conditioner. I'm on my feet now, still pointing and yelling.

"You creep around my house, and you keep on 'checking in' on me," I make air quotes with my fingers, "and trying to do all these things to 'help'!"

"That was part of the deal, and it was your idea."

"It was a terrible idea."

"Please don't say that. You believed in me, Declan. And I spent a decade earning that belief."

"I believed that you going to jail for vaporizing that girl was a waste! 'Believed,' not believe. Not anymore."

"I've been able to do so much to help the world," The Samaritan stammers at me.

"Yeah, and all it took was me going to prison for your crime instead of you. You could have let me go and licked your wounds after I wrapped you up in a girder, but you just *had* to catch me, you didn't care about what happened as long as you stopped me! What could that kid have done for the world if you hadn't disintegrated her? She wasn't important enough?"

He stands up, floating the short distance from his seat to the rooftop, and steps closer to me.

"You really don't want to get any closer right now," I say. "I got an eye full of heat and hate you don't want."

He comes closer. He still seems smaller, almost fragile.

I blast him square in the chest. He takes it, hard, and slides across the roof on his back. I'm rusty, or he's gotten tougher, because he stands up only a bit more gingerly than normal, smoking from the burns. His skin knits, as does his costume; I still don't know how he pulls that off.

"I'm sorry—"

"Yes," I say, "You *are* sorry. You and me buried under that deck with a dead girl, you crying your eyes out about how you were going to Hell for hitting that gas line with your eye beams! And I did the dumbest thing I could; I believed that you were better than me, and the world *needed you more*. I believed you were more important.

"You know I saved a life last week? Guy fell off the building at work, I caught him. His wife and kids aren't wondering where food's going to come from, or calling all the relatives, because I saved him. It felt good. It was *easy*. I mean, if anyone could pretend to be a hero even when they kill a kid, how hard could it be for someone who actually did hero shit?"

"You agreed," he says mechanically.

"Yeah, I agreed. I took the rap because I thought you were doing so many good and wonderful things. I took the rap because you were bawling your eyes out and I thought I was just a criminal. I took the rap because you promised to foot the bills, and keep my family safe, and because I thought that I could do something good for once in my life by keeping you a hero. But I could have done the same things you did, and it would have been better, because it would have been honest. It would have been real, instead of the lie you are. I got a wide back; I could have carried a 747 on it too."

I see his hand twitching. He wants to kill, like the lifers who can't handle the walls. Not "slug it out until someone passes out." He's going to kill to get out. He already got a taste of it with the guys in the truck. Who might be next?

"You better go," I say.

"Declan—"

"I'll get Psirena to read my mind. You know her testimony is admissible as evidence. Or one of the other court-approved telepaths. That's why we didn't want a trial; the moment she reads my mind, she'll get a court order to read yours too. This all falls apart, and the lie catches up to you. Your decade of lies. The lie that you are more important than I am in this world."

"You'd get caught too!" The Samaritan squeaks.

"Yeah? I'm a felon already. I go back into Rahway, it's going to hurt, it's going to suck, but you and I are done. You built a prison with your sin. I helped you do it, I'll own that if I need to, because I thought you were *better*. But now I know that's not true."

The Samaritan tries to talk, so I blast him again, sending him over the edge of the building. He floats in the air, tumbles over before righting himself.

"Just go," I say. "Don't try to tell me how grateful you are, or how I was a criminal, or anything else, because I've had enough of it. I'm owning everything I did, and if you don't leave, I'm gonna throw hands and I did a lot of boxing in prison. If we throw down here, though, lots of people are gonna get hurt. And I'm done with that, so leave. I have a job. I have a family. I'm getting supervised visitation with my kid next month. We've been talking online and he doesn't hate me. What do you have, but Truth, Justice and a dead girl it's all built on?

"I'm done with you, Samaritan. Go, and leave me alone. I don't need you to cover for me anymore. No paying my legal bills, no favors, no 'watching over' me. You don't get to prop up your lie on me anymore. You are no more important to the world than I am. And I am no less important. Stay out of my life, and own what you did. I'm going to soon enough."

The Samaritan flutters in the air, and I can still see that twitch you see when someone has to get out.

⋘⋙

I go to work like normal, and pay my bills, and go to dinner at Steve's and meet his family. It's a life, I guess; I'm looking for an apartment now, and might take some classes at a local college. Peter and Katy are staying with one of our cousins. They should be back in their house in a few weeks, after the repairs finish up.

Four days later, very early in the morning, my lawyer calls me and says there's an army coming. She gets there the same time as the New Jersey Attorney General, my parole officer, two trucks full of SWAT with heavy hardware, and a woman I know by reputation. I assume the position outside as a courtesy, but my lawyer waves me off. I invite them into the efficiency room, and cast a wary eye over the SWAT units before I close the door. Psirena, a cloaked and masked flash of red, doesn't waste any time. She has a court order to read my mind.

"It's about The Samaritan," my lawyer says.

I check my phone. The Samaritan's trending like crazy, with video.

#BadSamaritan

The Samaritan, holding his phone, recording.

He flies, tears apart pieces of metal, burns the metal with heat vision. Proves he is The Samaritan, not someone else in a costume.

He removes his mask.

He shows his driver's license, says his legal name, his voice weak.

"I killed Violet Morris. Declan Samuels, Balor, lied for me. He thought I was more important to the world than him. I let him live that lie in prison, but I was wrong. I cannot make him carry that sin which is mine. I have borne false witness. God, forgive me. Declan, forgive me."

Video end.

"NASA reported that an object left the atmosphere around the same time as the video was uploaded," my lawyer says. "They and other space agencies confirmed it to be The Samaritan and that he flew himself directly into the Sun."

I drop my phone.

I nod for Psirena to read my mind.

"Why did you do this?" she asks in a whisper as she flips through my brain, seeing all the levels of the parking deck, the burned child Violet Morris, The Samaritan seeing the girl in the area, blasting wildly even though there was no way for him to actually hit me. Him crying, all his guilt, my idea to cover for him. My guilty plea, the years of screaming pain from the depowering drugs, my understanding that even if I didn't kill the kid, I still did dumb things. Harmful things.

"I thought him being the hero the world needed," I say, "was more important than…"

More important than me.

It's a mess, they tell me.

I tell my lawyer to call me when they figure it out, but if they aren't going to lock me up now, let me get on the road so I can get to work on time.

ℰᴏᴄᴙ

I pick things up and put them down. It's a good gig, with good pay. I'm off parole now. I talk to prisoners about choices, and how to make good ones. Sometimes the fire department calls me to help out; sometimes I see trouble and help out. I get people wanting interviews, and I defer to my lawyer. My ex talks to me like a person. I get to see my kid unsupervised.

I'm not a villain now. I'm not a hero, either. When my kid visits, though, and I get to fly him over Manhattan for getting on honor roll, and some lesson I teach him sticks, I feel important.

I am important.

ℰᴏᴄᴙ

Caias Ward is a thick-wristed HVAC technician and writer with more than forty publication credits between fiction and roleplaying games. He lives in New Jersey with his wife and daughter, spending time writing, designing games, and fighting fascism. Find him at @caias.bsky.social on Bluesky.

God-Eaters

Joshua M. Young

"THAT ONE, THERE," Peiromai said, voice hushed, almost reverent, "there's a god aboard it." He pointed out the flight deck window at a medium sized *c*-ship, too small for a god. Peiromai spoke of impossibilities.

"The Kadmon," I said. The Kadmon was demigod only, but ancient and powerful and steeped in legend. Birthed by the Pinakes, the Library Goddess; older than his creator, her lover and her child—the gods were incestuous both sexually and chronologically—and I'd eat him with the same relish that I'd consume his progenitor-lover.

But my own lover shook his head. "No, not just the Kadmon. A real god. Older than the Kadmon, wiser than the Pinakes."

"Nothing is older than the Kadmon."

"Nothing human," Peiromai said. "It's an alien god we'll eat tonight."

֍

The world about which we had found the Kadmon had been chosen carefully. It was prosperous enough to have traffic, but not so advanced or prosperous as to control that traffic. When we seeded the orbit with passive dust, no one took notice; when the dust became active in the vicinity of the Kadmon and detonated, no one responded. Those who were there chose to look the other way. A great many *c*-traders had developed keen self-preservation instincts in the gigaseconds spent trading.

The Kadmon's ship was a tough thing, not so fragile as to be crippled by something like dust. It could certainly be staggered, however, and when Peiromai and I boarded, it was unable to defend itself.

ഇറ

The Kadmon was another story altogether. One arm was charred and shattered, his face bloody, cooling fins erupting from his back as his bones struggled to repair the injuries. My mouth watered at the ozone-smell of smart matter.

Even injured, even missing an arm, the Kadmon was a force of nature. He fell on us moments after we boarded his ship, lashing out at Peiromai with a meter-long smart matter blade. The stroke rent Peiromai's boarding armor; the backstroke nearly took off both our heads. Peiromai fell backwards. I dove to the side and gained a shallow gash on the throat, cauterized with waste heat from the blade.

Peiromai lashed out with a monofilament whip, but the Kadmon dove forward, losing the tips of his cooling fins instead of his own head. A flawless roll made suddenly awkward by the fins brought him up within Peiromai's arms, and the blade went through the underside of my mate's chin and out through his skull. A blur of movement, and Peiromai's head fell apart like a melon.

Hunger and rage threw me at the Kadmon, teeth bared, the array of god-killing weapons that would preserve the precious smart matter forgotten.

The Kadmon was merciful. The dregs of rationality inside my skull expected a blade through the eye; instead, it went through my heart. Debilitating, crippling, but the all-important brain remained intact.

The pain, though, was impressive.

ഇറ

My time sense was gone, the forever ticking digits behind my eyelids absent for the first time in memory. My bone-self had gone quiet, no longer whispering to me, offering hints about the universe. I had become the Kadmon's prisoner, arms stretched out to either side, hands embedded all the way to the wrist inside the wall. He had at least allowed me to sit and enough flexibility to shift from one numb buttock to the other.

The Kadmon was hale and whole, no longer missing his arm; his expression was serene, but his hair was damp and shiny lumps of med gel were visible near his collar. He'd likely spent more than a little time immersed in a med vat. I wondered about my own wounds, but before I could ask, the Kadmon said, "Ushki. God-eaters. You know who I am?"

"An ape ascended to godhood. The pet of the bitch-goddess, the Pin—"

He crouched slowly, a thoughtful look on his face until the very moment he slammed my head into the wall. I grinned, trying desperately to ignore the pain, and said, "And dinner. I can smell your bone-self, ur-human. The scent of the smart matter in your marrow. I'll crack you open and feast on the god-tech inside you while your flesh rots."

Hatred and disgust mingled in his eyes. I knew what he was seeing. Utterly hairless, digits that were more talons than fingers, skin turned gunmetal by the saturation of smart matter. Baselines and those who kept the baseline form rarely viewed the ushki as human.

"I don't know what to do with you."

"I know what to do with you," I told him, and licked my lips.

For a long moment, I thought he might kill me. But the moment passed and the Kadmon shook his head and turned away. His back was smooth and utterly human. The cooling fins would've retreated back into his bones when the crisis and aftermath had resolved.

"You gods," I spat. "Pretending you're human. Even your bitch puts on a human shell. You may have been born on the Cradle, Kadmon, but you're less human than I am."

"And yet," the Kadmon said, "were you in my position, you'd be cracking open my femur as we speak."

Not a lot of use arguing that one, I suppose.

ↄↃ

After some time, the ship lights went down, and I dozed fitfully. The weight of my body pulled uncomfortably on my shoulders and wrists, and sleep was hard in coming and harder in staying. When morning came, I opened my eyes to find the Kadmon crouching next to me.

"I'm going to let you loose," he said, "On the condition that you behave yourself."

"If I don't?"

The Kadmon's eyebrows inched up. "An interesting consequence of your particular mode of enhancement is that the smart matter in your body is cohesive, but only just. You might as well have an abacus in your bones, for all the computing power you leverage. But that's what you get with stolen smart matter, I guess. It doesn't really like talking to the other stuff inside you."

"And?"

"I spent the night hacking your bone-self. You try anything, and I'll break the cohesion of your smart matter. The nanomachines in your bones will begin attacking each other, and you will likely die a very painful death."

The wall pushed my hands up and out, and I wondered if it'd been waiting for a cue from the Kadmon or if it was sentient enough to have a sense of dramatic timing. I rubbed my wrists, tried to flex my shoulders. "What's to become of me, if I behave?"

"I'm burning for a fairly low-tech world right now. A dozen megaseconds or so, ship time. You'll be left there with your bone-self in a deadened state. Your ship I'll sell somewhere further down the line. Until we get to your destination, you'll be a guest."

"You could kill me, save yourself the trip."

"I could," the Kadmon agreed.

ଅଦ୍ର

The Kadmon locked himself away for a short time each ship-day. The same room each and every day, located in the living area of the ship and locked at all times.

It was perhaps a day and a half before hunger and rage overcame me. I prowled the corridors and, finally, when the Kadmon emerged from his sequestration, I attacked. By all rights, I should've died then and there, but he had placed far too much faith in either my self-preservation or my integrity. I took him by surprise and drove his skull against the bulkhead. Wood paneling shattered and the Kadmon slumped to the ground. For a moment, I considered how best to butcher him, whether to leave him living to witness me eat his bones. Peiromai's blood called for...

The door hung ajar. Inside, I caught a glimpse of red carpeting and the same dark wood paneling I'd seen elsewhere. The room inside was sparsely decorated, a handful of unfamiliar symbols carved into the walls. A pair of intersecting wooden beams hung above a cabinet, once gilded and ornately carved, now scorched and vacuum ablated, which sat on a dais opposite the door. A candle sheathed in red glass burned next to it. I felt, in some subtle way, that I was intruding on something.

"It's an alien god," Peiromai had said. Words forgotten in a hunt gone terribly wrong.

I had invaded a ship, intending to attack and mutilate its owner, all without qualm. Now, I felt wrong.

An alien god. Something unknowable, inhuman. The Kadmon had enshrined it, evidently worshiped it. Some sort of subtle brainwashing, a field flooding the room. I took a step toward the shrine, felt my knees buckle. I'd just driven the head of a god through a wall, but I felt unaccountably weak, blood streaming from my nose and eyes and ears, through my pores, grayish red with hemorrhaged smart matter...

The Kadmon's alien god was a conqueror, hostile. My legs finally gave, and I fell onto the dais, an outstretched, bloody arm knocking the god from its perch. Pale wafers cascaded out and onto the carpet.

It was only as I fell that I realized the Kadmon was standing in the doorway. For the first time, I felt fear when I met his eyes.

℘℧

He hauled me off the ground by the collar. I felt fabric stretch and tear, but it held. Only just; in its deadened state, my bone-self couldn't coordinate reinforcement.

"You have no idea, god-eater, how much I want to kill you."

"Then do it," I snapped. "Decaseconds ago you told my bone-self to kill me. Then you stopped it. Why? Just finish it. Save yourself the trip."

He opened his fist; the deck hit me hard and I gasped.

"Clean up your blood."

℘℧

The Kadmon and I dined later in the ship-day on fresh foods procured from the world of our ill-fated ambush. He ate with quiet grace; I ate awkwardly, picking at some nameless fruit and thinking of smart matter, warm, slick with fresh blood. My mouth watered, but my stomach turned as I thought of my own smart matter-laden blood oozing from my skin.

"I hate you," the Kadmon said, "I hate your people for what they once did to me. For what they did to others. But that was a long time ago and a long way away. Your people aren't what they once were."

I looked up, surprised. His words were quiet and conversational, as if we'd been pleasantly talking the whole meal.

"You're worse. Before, you were a bunch of trust fund kids playing at archaeology. Now you're pirates, cannibals."

"Why don't you kill me?" I felt my eyes moisten, and I cursed the deadened state of my bone-self. I was stressed and had no way of controlling it.

"I would have earlier, if you'd been anywhere else. But that place has been dedicated to the Living God. It's not a place for death."

"And now you're not killing me why?"

"Because I am a human being, not an animal. To kill you now would be to succumb to my hatred, to be a machine of meat souped up with smart matter. The Living God made me better than that. Better than instinct and emotion."

"Why do you call the Pinakes that?" I asked.

53

"The Pinakes isn't a god," he said. "She didn't make me, she healed me when I was mostly dead. She is wise and beautiful and I love her, but, ultimately, she is still a human soul inside a matrioshka brain."

જીભ

The Kadmon told me a ridiculous Cradle legend about the origin of the universe and a god who didn't start human and ended up being made of bread and wine after he became human in order to die. The Kadmon was the last of this god's worshippers, and the god salvaged from a broken space station, teraseconds old.

At the end of it all, I mocked him, clapping my hands and shouting, "You, Kadmon… you're nothing more than a god-eater!"

I expected him to lash out. Instead, he laughed and cleared his plate from the table.

જીભ

I sat alone in the mess for a while, a bowl of unfamiliar fruit on the table in front of me. I was stung by my failure to truly needle the Kadmon, irritated by the fruit whose names I didn't know. Did I even know the name of the world? Maybe my bone-self could've told me, but the fact of the matter was that it had been Peiromai who had made the choices since we mated, my parents before that. I was a creature of hunger and instinct, thoughtless reflex.

A machine of meat.

Less human than the Kadmon. Less human than one of the hated gods.

જીભ

The Living God was not very lively, all things considered. The Kadmon left the door to his altar unlocked now, and I regularly watched him kneel and meditate with his hands clasped in front of his chest, without any apparent concern for his safety. After a kilosecond or so of this, he would consume his deity's body and drink his blood. The origins of the ushki hunger are opaque to me, but I knew that one does not worship a god by eating them.

જીભ

The Kadmon, I realized one morning, had made a habit of misplaced trust. In his god of bread and wine, in me, in his ability to dominate software and smart matter. Strange symbols barraged me when I first opened my eyes, and it took a bewildered decasecond to understand that this was my time sense, once again active and desperately begging for input from a standardized pulsar in order to function accurately. It is perhaps true that the harvested smart matter in the ushki body is at best tenuously connected, but every child is born with a bead of indigenous smart matter formed in the womb. It is this organ that enslaves the harvested material. It is this organ that had been chipping away, silently, at the Kadmon's unattended slaveware.

I held my hand in front of my face and flexed my fingers. An array of tools emerged from my skin with each flex, blades and monofilament whips and half a dozen data interfaces.

No primitives for me. No life of starvation. I let the image of the Kadmon, butchered and stripped of smart matter, blood seeping into the carpet of his sanctuary, play through my head. The ozone smell of my own smart matter whipped my appetite into a frenzy and I fought to keep it down, to bring it back into check. It would be an animal's reaction to stalk the Kadmon now, stupid and instinctual. Keep it low key, keep it routine, wait, wait for the chance to strike, be human…

ῴῳ

I considered the Living God's altar, and then dismissed it. For all his apparent vulnerability, the Kadmon had been surprised there once already. I could not imagine that he would not have prepared some sort of defense during his meditations. But then, twice I'd tried to kill the Kadmon; why should any place be any less defensible? The Kadmon's confidence was a weakness, but I was certain that he would not have a baseless confidence. I liked the idea of the altar. There was something poetically just about destroying someone as foolish as the Kadmon at the foot of a foolish alien god who became human just to die.

Several ship days passed, three hundred kiloseconds or more, my time sense forever begging for the pulsar synchronization, my bone-self whispering more and more in my ear, hunger growing with every second.

Be human, be rational. Plan.

The Kadmon meditated, and I watched. The ship drew ever closer to the world in which the Kadmon planned to imprison me.

More than machine. More than hunger. Act only when the time is right.

ῴῳ

"If you are going do something," the Kadmon finally said, from his knees, his back to me, his hands clasped before his god, "now is as good a time as any."

A whiff of ozone and a blade I hadn't realized existed dissolved back into smart matter. "You said this isn't a place for killing."

55

"It's a fine place for killing," he said, a trace of humor in his voice, and I remembered the Living God's death, nailed to his own holy symbol, "it's just not a good place for me to kill you."

"You killed my mate."

"Did you love him?"

"What kind of question is that!"

"A straightforward one."

"Does it matter? He was my mate!"

"The more like gods you folks become, the less like humans you are. You're viruses, ushki god-eater, attacking the individuals who link and preserve civilization in the galaxy. There'd be no star travel without individuals like the Pinakes, and you'd devour her in a heartbeat, if you could."

I leapt at the Kadmon, a long stabbing blade of smart matter emerging from my open palm. It went through his torso, just slightly off center, and he fell forward. I dissolved the blade, kicked the Kadmon onto his back, began pummeling him.

"How could you?" I demanded, punctuating each word with a blow. My bone-self did nothing to regulate the flow of emotion, hate and rage and hunger overpowering my internal software. "You, here, lording over mortals, holier than thou, hoarding your technology for yourselves! You killed a human being and didn't even flinch!"

And then my mouth was full of the Kadmon's flesh and smart matter and there was a moment of sudden stillness, the Kadmon not struggling, I not devouring.

"Tell me this is human," he said.

My stomach cramped; when I clutched at my side, he said, "Fight it. Prove that you're better than your hunger. Prove to me that you're human."

Human, rational, plan, don't succumb, don't give in, don't lash out…

Lash out I did, a monofilament whip unspooling with a vicious slash of an arm, but it went wide, I didn't kill him, the Living God's holy symbol falling in two. Tears, hot with rage and frustration and mixed with the Kadmon's blood ran down my cheeks. After a moment, maybe a decasecond, the Kadmon pulled my head to his chest, stroking my scalp with awkward, jerky movements.

"It's okay," he whispered, "I'm proud. You're doing good, you're just fine…"

In that moment, I knew I had missed on purpose. I wrapped my arms around him and pressed my cheek against his battered flesh. "The hunger, Kadmon. It's always there. Always gnawing. How did we get to be like this? We were normal people once, weren't we?"

He pondered this for a moment, hand hesitating for a fraction of a second before he spoke. "I suspect your ancestors found that scavenger archaeology wasn't getting them where they wanted to be."

"Where was that?"

"The legendary home of the gods," the Kadmon said, "The Cradle. Earth, from where all our ancestors hail."

"And you."

"It was a long time ago. I suppose your ancestors assumed that a more aggressive archaeological method would locate the Cradle faster. Harvest smart matter and index the data fragments in it. The rest of it... Maybe the fastest way to index that data was internally. Maybe"—and here he glanced up at the altar—"they sought to participate in the nature of the gods and find the place that way."

"Kadmon..."

"Yes?"

"Kill me?"

I felt his muscles tense. "Please," I begged him. "I can't live like this, not as a... god-eater. A cannibal, always starving. Death is better than that world you'll leave me on."

"If," the Kadmon drew the word out, as though buying time to think, "If I could help you, rid you of those instincts—"

"You'd change my very nature?" My stomach cramped again, and I fought down a wave of nausea and hunger, as though my body were rebelling against the thought. "Will you take my memories, too?"

"No. Those you keep; to wipe your thoughts would be death."

ༀ

The medical bath was a horizontal tube of transparent material, empty and hinged open. I sat inside, naked, freezing, fighting the urge to cover myself in the Kadmon's presence. For his part, he was a gentleman, or else revolted by the ushki form. He sat on the edge, patiently explaining what would happen during my return to the baseline body of my ancestors. "The Pinakes herself printed my ship," he said, "and the sick bay knows what it's doing. The uniquely ushki organs and features of your body will be removed or altered to baseline. I imagine that your bone-self will fight hard against reprogramming, and that it'll take some time for everything to shake out properly. Maybe megaseconds. But in the end, I think you'll come out okay."

I nodded, shivered.

"Sorry it's so cold. I don't know why these things are always like that."

Shrug.

"Ushki."

"Yes?"

"I've never asked your name."

I opened my mouth, but the thought of my old life tasted foul. "It doesn't matter. Name me, Kadmon. Give me a name for my new life."

The Kadmon laughed. "Anastasia, then," he said, as if he expected me to know what it meant.

"It'll do. Flood the tube, Kadmon. Wash away what I was."

ഇന്ദ

Joshua M. Young lives in Columbus, Ohio with his wife, son, and two more feral cats than the optimal number of feral cats. (Ideally, zero.) He holds a Master of Divinity from Ashland Theological Seminary. A lifelong lover of science fiction and fantasy, one of his earliest memories involves some confusion between a Klingon Bird of Prey and an X-Wing in the middle of a theater showing *The Search for Spock*, and, once upon a time, he could select the desired *Robotech* novel from his bookshelf, in the dark, by the feel of its spine. (Don't ask why that was a necessary skill. He couldn't tell you.) He has been published in numerous anthologies and magazines, including *Cirsova, Storming Area 51*, and *Tales of the Once and Future King*, and can be found at Substack.com @joshuamyoung.

Gordon's Knot

Jennifer Milne

MY NEIGHBOR MRS. Henriksson was a princess. At least, that's what she always said.

"I come from a very long line of ancient Viking warrior princesses, Mary Gordon," she would say in her thick Nordic accent.

She regaled me with wild tales of her ancestresses the shieldmaidens sailing across the untamable seas, fighting Saxon pirates and going on epic journeys. She said her great-great-something or other grandmother fought raiding marauders out of her village while nursing her baby in her arms.

On one such adventure, she told me, one of her ancestresses found the fabled Tíðknut. Tíðknut meant "Time Knot" in Old Norse and was a piece of rope that had been braided from the hair of the Norns—the Norse equivalent of the Greek Fates. Mrs. Henriksson said the legend was that Norns themselves had given her ancestress the Time Knot after she'd correctly answered their riddle.

The rope had a single knot in the center, and the one who possessed the Time Knot could untie it to turn back time to change one regret.

"That's a neat story," I'd told Mrs. Henriksson as I watered her plants one afternoon.

"It is not a story, elskede," she said (she called me "elskede" which was like "dear" or "darling" in Norwegian). "Well, of course all that talk of the Norns is myth. I believe the Time Knot to be something fashioned by the hands of God himself—a relic of his power. Like the Ark of the Covenant, Moses' staff or the Holy Grail."

"Like in Indiana Jones," I said.

"Yes, yes. My Johann always reminded me of Harrison Ford. But Mary, this power is not a story. I used the Tíðknut myself."

"Oh yeah," I said, humoring her. "That's cool."

"You doubt me," she said with amusement. "But it's true! I was fifteen years old when I first laid eyes on the young man who had just moved to our village. Johann was the handsomest boy I had ever seen, and he was so funny. We had a wonderful moment sorting books in the school library after lessons one day. He tried to kiss me, but I had never been kissed before. It startled me and I pulled away. He mistook my shyness for a lack of interest and left me alone after that. I was heartbroken. My mother gave me the Tíðknut and told me its story. All I had to do was go to the place of my regret and untie the knot.

"So, I went back to the library, untied the knot and found myself face to face with Johann for the second time. No, not for the second time! For the first time, again. This time, when he tried to kiss me, I let him." She paused and smiled, lost in her memory. "I had fifty-two more wonderful years with my Johann."

When Mrs. Henriksson got sick, I started going over every day. We would watch TV, I would bring a carton of her favorite ice cream, and she would ask me to tell her about my days at the Jericho Falls Christian High School.

"Mercy Mulligan was picking on me again today."

Mercy had moved here in sixth grade as a surly, purple-haired weirdo, but by ninth grade she'd blossomed into a blonde-haired, tight sweater-wearing bully. Now that we were in tenth grade, she'd become a minor YouTube celebrity with a make-up tutorial channel. The slight taste of fame had only served to solidify her status as our school's resident mean girl.

Mrs. Henriksson tutted. "So ironic that she carries the name, yet shows none."

"Yeah, tell me about it. She'll corner a girl in the bathroom and demand that they 'beg Mercy.' Not 'beg *for* mercy' mind you, but 'beg Mercy.'"

"Well, a person becomes a bully to reclaim power in their life."

"She's the most powerful girl in school! She's pretty, she's popular, she gets straight A's."

"Hmm," was Mrs. Henriksson's response. "One's entire life is not lived at school, elskede."

Mrs. Henriksson's health continued to get worse and a twenty-four-hour nurse came to live with her. When I went over one afternoon, she had a wooden box sitting on her lap.

"What's that?" I asked, as I sat down next to the hospital bed that had been brought into her living room. She couldn't go up and down the stairs to her bedroom anymore.

"It is something I would like to give to you, Mary. Johann and I were very blessed, but children were not one of those blessings. You have been such a wonderful friend to me, elskede. You are a peaceful young lady with a selfless heart, which is the most important thing a true shieldmaiden can have. Sometimes battles must be fought, but never by those who thirst to fight."

She handed me the box and I lifted the lid. Inside, cushioned by some yellowed, crumpled-up newspaper was a foot-long piece of thin, silky rope with a single knot tied in the center.

"Mrs. Henriksson, you don't have to—"

"Of course," she interrupted. "That is why I want to."

After she passed away, I was really sad. And like one of those rats that could smell death, Mercy Mulligan seemed to be able to smell my pain and had ratcheted up her daily torture.

I was in a fog. A heavy fog that felt like it had taken residence in every part of my body and was weighing me down. My grades were slipping because I couldn't concentrate, and I had no one to talk to about it.

Mrs. Henriksson had been my only friend. Which was weird, I knew that, but kids my age had just always thought I was weird. And truthfully, I'd thought they were weird too. I didn't care about the stuff they cared about. Which made it hard to connect, even if I'd wanted to.

My parents tried to help but I didn't tell them about the problems at school. I was fifteen. Soon I would be driving, then graduating and going to college, so I felt I needed to try to handle this stuff myself.

After a particularly bad day at school I went home and took the Time Knot out of the box. Mom had bought me a display case for it, but I hadn't felt like setting it up. Today, since I couldn't talk to Mrs. Henriksson anymore, I decided I would get out the Time Knot and clear a place for it on my shelf. I hoped it would help me feel closer to her for a moment.

It didn't.

೮ಛ

We had to climb ropes in gym. I hated climbing the rope. Oh, I could do it just fine, but I hated doing it while everyone stood on the ground staring up at my butt.

My stomach was hurting, but not like I was going to barf. More like my insides were twisting around. I didn't want to go to the nurse because Mercy and her cohorts would just tease me about being a wuss. Even now she stood in her long-sleeved gym shirt (supposedly she had massive sun sensitivity or something, though I joked to myself that she was covering up werewolf syndrome on her arms) stage-whispering rude things about me.

When it was my turn to climb the rope, I did it as quickly as possible. About halfway up an explosion of laughter startled me and nearly made me lose my grip, but I managed to hold on and finish.

As I stepped off the rope I was greeted by laughter and applause. I looked around, confused. Why were they laughing at me? I hadn't done anything!

Then I looked down.

My gym shorts were covered with red stuff. Blood.

I'd only been having my period for about a year, I was a late bloomer, and I hadn't gotten used to the signs it was coming. I realized it wasn't my stomach that had been hurting earlier. I'd been having menstrual cramps.

After that, everyone started calling me Bloody Mary. They would whisper it as they passed me in the halls, they would say it when I walked into class, and they chanted it in the lunchroom—like a sick pep rally in hell.

The teachers did what they could and handed out detentions and stuff, but they couldn't really stop it. Not completely.

Mercy Mulligan was the worst. After school, as I gathered up my books before heading home, she walked up and leaned against the locker next to mine.

"Hey Bloody Mary," she cooed.

I ignored her. Mom and Dad had said if you ignored a bully, they would get bored and move on to a more interesting target. So far that hadn't worked with Mercy. It was almost like my ignoring her only whet her appetite to get a reaction from me.

"I've got a surprise for you," she said.

Which got me to look, but I stayed quiet.

"It's gonna be fun," she assured me, giving me a wink and sashaying down the hallway.

That night she posted a video of the rope climbing incident online, and it quickly went viral. Not just locally viral but worldwide viral. The raw video and various joke versions making fun of me spread around the disreputable parts of the internet. Someone even autotuned it into a frustratingly catchy song that YouTube kept pulling down but that would always pop back up. The more reputable sites blurred out my face and wrote a lot of think pieces about "period shaming" and the "bullying epidemic" and "youth and the perils of social media."

Those were no better than the stories that mocked me.

People started calling my parents asking me to become a spokesperson for anti-bullying organizations and other activist groups. But I said no. I didn't want the rest of my life to be about this stupid thing that happened to me when I was in high school.

I just wanted to forget about it and move on. God, if I could just go back and not climb the rope or wear a pad or *something*...

Oh my gosh.

After I was sure my parents were asleep, I took the Time Knot out of its case. I sat in the dark just to be certain I wouldn't wake them.

I'll be honest. I didn't really think it would work. It was just a story. I'd always assumed Mrs. Henriksson was just sharing her culture with me. Passing on what she could.

So imagine my surprise when I loosened the knot and it suddenly felt like God was a DJ and my head was a record, and He'd decided to do some funky scratching.

My hands went limp and I dropped the Time Knot into my lap, but everything still seemed off. The room was blurry but not *I'm not wearing my glasses* blurry, more like *I'm riding in a car going 500 miles per hour* blurry.

I picked the rope back up and tightened the knot again and the off-kilter feeling went away. Then I loosened it more carefully and watched as the world around me changed. It was like watching a movie in reverse.

As I slowly separated the knot, I saw the sun creep back up from behind the hill and watched my Mom walk backwards into my room. I stopped it. Time froze and I looked at my mom, completely still like one of those Mannequin Challenge videos only so much more still that it was scary.

I waved my hand in front of her, but she didn't react. When I touched her cheek, I found it cold and hard, like a statue. I grabbed the Time Knot and retightened it, but I did it too quickly, so my return to the present felt like getting punched in the face and left me with a headache.

But it worked.

It.

Freaking.

Worked.

ಬಐಚಿ

The next morning at school my whole body was buzzing, a mixture of nervousness and excitement.

I had the Time Knot wrapped in a pillowcase and in a separate pocket of my backpack. Mrs. Henriksson had said that you had to be in the place where you wanted to go back in time from, so my plan was to sneak into the gym at lunchtime when there wouldn't be anybody in there.

We'd been talking about Alexander the Great in history. The teacher told us this story about the "Gordian Knot." Being about a knot, it piqued my attention. A wagon that had belonged to this great king Gordias was tied to a pole in the town square with a knot that supposedly couldn't be untied. An oracle claimed that whoever managed to undo it would unite all the empires of the world.

So of course, Alexander decides he's going to untie that knot. Problem was, he got there and found it impossible to undo. But Alexander didn't take nothing from nobody, including stupid kings who tied stupid complicated knots. So, according to legend, he pulled out his sword and sliced that bad boy off.

Since no one ever said *how* the knot had to be undone, Alexander was like "winner winner chicken dinner" and ruled the world happily ever after. Well, you know, until he died at the ripe old age of 32. Probably from an STD.

The moral of the story is about thinking outside the box to solve a problem. Which felt like a sign. Using the Time Knot to solve my problem was most definitely outside the box thinking. Heck, it was outside the space-time continuum thinking.

Mercy Mulligan could kiss Mary Gordon's Knot.

At my locker between classes, I noticed Mercy and her blonde-tourage of sycophants giggling nearby.

I ignored them though, they wouldn't have this on me much longer anyway.

When I opened my locker, a bunch of bloody pads fell out, covering me in red. I had a top locker, so the pads had hit me in the face first. It wasn't real blood, it wasn't even pig's blood a là Carrie. Unfortunately, some had gotten in my mouth, and it tasted like strawberry syrup.

How very Hitchcockian of them.

"That was great, Bloody Mary!" said Mercy, as one of her friends recorded me with her phone. "Your last video got me to fifty thousand followers on Instagram, this will put me over a hundred thousand for sure!"

I felt dizzy. I was so embarrassed and disoriented. I tried to just walk away, but she and her horde blocked me in.

"What do you want, Mercy?" I said, my voice cracking.

"Just to see you squirm, Bloody Mary."

They all laughed. People were gathering around.

I tried to shoulder through them but lost my backpack in the process. Before I could retrieve it, Mercy scooped it up.

"You lost something," she said in a sing-song voice.

"Give it back," I said coldly.

"Why? Do you have something super embarrassing in here? Ooh! Krista, get this, we can do a hilarious unboxing video. It'll probably be better than Bloody Mary!"

I reached out and tried to snatch it back, but she pulled away and laughed.

It made me so angry. Her tinkling laugh with just the slightest hint of cruelty, like it was one of those soft serve cones and her laughter was the chocolate swirl around the edge.

"Give me my backpack," I said through gritted teeth.

"Or what?" she said, smiling.

I answered her with my fist. Which consequently knocked the smile off her face.

She dropped my backpack as both her hands flew to her face. She let out a wail of pain so pitiful it made me feel bad for hitting her.

All of a sudden, the crowd burst out laughing. I looked around to find the source of their amusement, my mind reeling with déjà vu.

Then I saw it. The wet spot on Mercy's skirt. The small yellow puddle at her feet.

"What is going on here?" demanded a teacher who appeared from out of nowhere. She looked back and forth between the two of us. I was so angry and confused I couldn't get myself to speak. "Both of you, to the principal's office. Now."

ଛଓ�03

Mercy and I got suspended for fighting. My parents had a long talk with me about defending myself versus starting the fight, and how you can't respond to words with violence. Which I knew already.

Honestly, I wasn't entirely sure why I'd punched Mercy like that. It didn't make me feel better. I mean, there was this moment, like right after it happened where I got this... *rush*, I guess. But it faded quickly and turned into something yucky that made me feel like I wanted to give my soul a shower.

While I was suspended the video of Mercy peeing herself went viral. Part of me felt bad for her but there was also this part of me—one I didn't want to look at directly for fear of unleashing it—that was sort of glad to see her get some of what she gave.

When I went back to school, people started whispering things again as they walked past me.

Only this time they were saying:

"Nice job, Mary."

"Way to lay the smack down!"

"You rock!"

"You showed Mercy no mercy!"

I had this weird mixture of positive and negative feelings about it which created this sort of feelings hurricane inside me. I didn't like that people were so happy about what I'd done, but it also felt really good to be so…

Liked.

It made me reconsider using the Time Knot. I mean, my viral video stuff was dying down at this point anyway. There was a video of some dude tripping while texting and falling face first into a pile of dog poop that had captured the world's attention, so even Mercy peeing herself was old news.

And nobody was bothering me anymore. Well they were, but in a good way now. People were constantly coming up to talk to me or asking me to sit by them in class or inviting me to their lunch table.

Which was pretty cool.

When Mercy came back to school, she left me alone. She left everyone alone, although they wouldn't do her the same courtesy. They would follow her around and taunt her just like she'd done to me for so long.

One afternoon I was in the library trying to stay out of the heatwave we were experiencing when I saw Mercy hiding in a study carrell deep in the stacks. She had one of her long sleeves pulled up and was rubbing her forearm.

When she noticed me there staring, she pulled it back down quickly and stormed away as she combined a very inappropriate word that rhymed with water fowl with the technical name for a female dog.

What I'd seen on her arm hadn't been werewolf fur, but I had to be sure before I said anything.

When we were in the locker room together during PE, I tried to get a look at her as she changed but I realized she wasn't there. The next day I saw her get her gym clothes (a long-sleeved t-shirt) from her locker and take them to the bathroom. She did that every single day. How had I never noticed before?

I brought the Time Knot to school with me, hid in a stall in the bathroom and waited for her to come in to change. The toilet flushed, she walked out of the stall and I heard the sink go on. That was when I stepped out of my stall and loosened the knot to stop time.

The stop wasn't very steady. It reminded me of this time I'd watched a movie on something called a VHS tape with Mrs. Henriksson. I'd paused the tape to go to the bathroom and it wasn't a clean stop like with a DVD, but was very blurry and vibrated.

Mercy stood at the sink, so I went over there and played with the knot carefully until I could get a clear look at her. She was frozen as she pulled up her sleeve to wash her hands. On the bit of forearm that was visible I could see angry red cuts all over her skin.

I swallowed but found my throat to be bone dry, then I quickly retightened the knot.

Mercy jumped in surprise to find me standing so close to her, where I hadn't been a moment ago.

"Holy crap!" she exclaimed, startling away from me.

I shoved the Time Knot into my pocket and grabbed her wrist.

"Hey, let go of me you psycho!"

I yanked up her sleeve and had my fears confirmed. All up and down her arm were cuts in various stages of healing, from jaggedly scarred to fresh and oozy. She yanked away from me hard, her cheeks red with hot anger and shame.

She didn't yell at me. She wouldn't even look at me. She just yanked her sleeve back down and stood there staring at the floor. I stared at the top of her blonde head, perfectly highlighted.

She wore her makeup perfect every day, spent at least an hour on her hair, and probably carefully chose her outfit the night before. It made me think about that judging the book by the cover cliché.

"Why are you cutting yourself?" I asked.

"Why do you care!" she snapped, not really asking.

"I care—"

"Since when?" She shook her head and finally looked at me. "You know, I saw *A Swiftly Tilting Planet* on your desk my first day of school, and I thought 'oh cool, someone else who's actually read the sequels to *A Wrinkle in Time*. But no, just like everyone else you wouldn't talk to the weirdo new girl. You walked right by me."

I did remember that. I'd thought she seemed weird and mean. But I guess she'd just been scared and shy. Kind of like when Johann mistook Mrs. Henriksson's shyness for not liking him.

After years of being lonely and picked on, maybe she decided she would go on offense instead of defense. And I couldn't help but feel like she targeted me because she felt like I'd snubbed her.

Which I guess I had.

Suddenly she moved, startling me out of my thoughts. I thought she was going to hit me, but instead she spun away and bolted from the bathroom, slamming the door on her way out.

I wiped away the hot tear that slid down my cheek as I realized what I had to do.

No one would ever call me Mary Gordon the Great, but I would take my cue from Alexander and solve this problem by cutting it off before it got all tangled up.

⁪⁫

I ditched gym and raced through the hallways with reckless abandon. A teacher saw me and yelled at me to stop, but I kept going. I was about to go back in time, so whatever happened now didn't even matter.

My high school was on a large campus called the Jericho Falls Christian Schools, and had Kindergarten through twelfth grade. I'd been going here my entire school career.

When I got where I was headed, I disrupted a class, but I didn't care. The teacher demanded, with growing irritation, to know what I was doing in her classroom, and the kids started giggling and chattering. Just as she reached out to grab my arm, I undid the knot quickly and completely, my mind totally focused on the moment of regret that I wanted to rectify.

"Miss Gordon…" said an annoyed voice. "Miss Gordon!" the voice nearly shouted, causing me to jump in my seat and knock my book off my desk.

The class giggled.

It was like someone flipped on a light switch. I hadn't been blinded while time was moving, but when time actually settled it was jarring.

"Bring me your phone," said Mrs. Dempsey, my sixth-grade middle school math teacher.

"I don't have a phone," I said, and the class giggled again.

"What is that in your hand then?" she asked as she approached my desk.

"It's just a rope." I held it up.

"Oh… well, put it away. No toys in class. And put that book away too, this is math class not library time."

The class full on laughed at the word "toys" and Barry Torvald called me a "baby."

"Hey Barry, you might want to stop wearing the Sesame Street underwear," I whispered so no one else could hear. "Especially at the assembly next year."

His face turned beet red and he turned away from me. I wasn't trying to embarrass him. I was just trying to save him the humiliation of being pantsed next year at the assembly and the whole school seeing his Elmo undies.

Okay, I was trying to embarrass him a little. He was being a jerk.

When I turned back to the front, the classroom door opened, and the vice principal walked in and whispered to Mrs. Dempsey. She nodded and he went to the hallway and beckoned to someone.

And in walked Mercy Mulligan: purple hair, angry scowl and all.

Mrs. Dempsey spoke quietly to her and Mercy shook her head, her face turning red. Then she was sent to the open seat at the back of the class.

Just like the last time I lived this moment, everyone whispered and giggled as Mercy walked to her seat. This time I noticed her eyes stop on my book and the tinniest glimmer of hope begin to shine in them.

When the bell rang nobody would talk to her.

Until she came back at the beginning of ninth grade looking gorgeous and filled to the brim with vengeful cruelty.

So this time, as I walked out of class, I stopped by Mercy and said, "Hi, I'm Mary. Do you want to have lunch with me?"

❧

"After that, everything changed," I told Mrs. Henriksson. "It got worse."

Mercy and I had become good friends after the day I'd gone back and talked to her on her first day of school.

For a while.

But just like before, when we got to high school, Mercy got boobs and turned into a mean girl.

"Now that I've been best friends with her for three years, she knows all this stuff about me and uses it against me to hurt me."

Mrs. Henriksson sighed. There were two Time Knots now. She held hers in the special box she'd kept it in all those years. I pulled mine out of my backpack.

I'd tried to untie it again, even though Mrs. Henriksson said it was a one and done deal. She'd been correct. It wouldn't budge, not even a thread.

"I'm sorry, elskede," she said sadly.

"I just don't understand. You were able to go back and fix things with Johann. Why couldn't I fix things with Mercy?"

She seemed to think about it. "Mary, God gives us the freedom to choose. I did not change Johann's choice, I changed mine."

"But I did change my choice. My choice to befriend Mercy!"

"Yes, but you couldn't change *her* decision after she… *got boobs*, as you put it. You can't save her, Mary, from herself or anyone else. There is only one who can truly save people and that person is not you."

I sighed. What she'd said about changing people seemed right. My uncle had loved a woman who had a drug problem. He thought if he loved her enough, she'd start to love him more than the drugs. But she didn't.

Sometimes our love isn't enough.

"So why do you think there are two Time Knots now?" I asked.

"I don't know," she said. "This did not happen to me last time."

She took her Knot out of the box and I pulled mine out of my backpack. Like magnets with opposite polarity they flew toward each other and with a flash of light, melded together.

Mrs. Henriksson picked it up off her lap and tried to untie it, to no avail.

"Please take it, elskede. It is yours to pass onto the next shieldmaiden."

"Thanks," I said, taking it. "But I don't feel like much of a shieldmaiden right now."

"Mary, do you remember Jesus's parable about the seeds and the soil?"

"Kind of."

"The sower threw out his seeds. Some were eaten by birds. Others could not take root on rocky soil and others were choked to death by thorns. But some of the seeds landed on good soil and after time, they grew into fruitful crops."

I looked at her and shrugged, not understanding.

"You sowed the seeds. All you can do is give time to see what kind of soil is in Mercy's heart."

I played with the Time Knot as I thought about her words.

"Well," I sighed. "There is one good thing to come from this. At least I know to wear a pad the day we climb the ropes."

Mrs. Henriksson laughed. I'd missed her laugh. It was such a gift to be able to hear it again.

ಸಂಒ

A few days after Mrs. Henriksson passed away again, I was in the school library looking for a book, when none other than Mercy came around the corner and nearly bumped into me.

She snorted. "All alone in the stacks huh? Maybe if you hung out with people who weren't alive during World War II, you wouldn't spend all your time in the library like a loser."

She'd hit a nerve. As bad as it had been losing Mercy as a friend, watching Mrs. Henriksson die again was worse. Knowing it was coming hadn't lessened the blow.

I chewed on my cheek to keep the cry from escaping me.

"How is the old broad anyway? She still telling those boring Viking stories?"

A painful lump sat in the back of my throat. It took all the strength I had to swallow it down just to speak.

"She died," I said, in what I thought was a fairly normal voice.

There was a long silence.

"Oh," she said.

"Yeah."

"I'm… I'm sorry, Mary."

The sob broke out and I covered my face with my hand. I felt so stupid crying in front of her like this. Giving her more ammunition to come after me.

Then I felt her put her arms around me. I accepted her comfort, in spite of everything.

As I stood there being held by my enemy, I realized I'd never cried before. The first time Mrs. Henriksson died, I mean. I'd kept it all inside, letting it eat me up and destroy me.

Even though she'd been being cruel when she said it, Mercy was right that I needed friends. God is the father, son and holy spirit, and in his image, we're not supposed to be alone.

One of Mercy's friends called out to her from somewhere away from us and was comically shushed by the librarian. Mercy leapt away from me like I'd caught fire, but we shared a laugh as we listened to her friend get reamed by the librarian.

"Ohmigod, the librarian needs to get the jagged icicle removed from her— ugh, what are you doing talking to *her*?" the girl asked after coming around the corner.

"I wasn't," Mercy said, then turned and walked away.

ῴῳ

Later that night as I lay in my bed, I thought about something I had noticed when Mercy hugged me.

Her arms weren't covered. She'd worn a tank top, and her arms were free of those horrible cutting scars.

Thinking about her scarless arms filled me with… hope. I guess.

The choice I'd made with the Time Knot had made a difference. It had planted a seed. A seed that maybe would keep growing.

I thought about the Gordian Knot story. I wasn't able to slice right through the problem the way I'd hoped to, but I had loosened the knot.

Because at the end of the day, it was Mercy's knot. And it was up to her whether she would unravel it.

ῴῳ

Jennifer Milne has had short fiction published in print and online. She's had multiple books and scripts on the Coverfly Redlist, including two in the #1 spots in their categories. Her work has been recognized by ScreenCraft, Stage 32 and Script2Comic, among others. She lives in San Diego with her family. Her middle grade novel *Plain Princess Jane* debuted at number one in Children's Royalty books and is available now! You can find everything about her work at jennifermilnewriting.com.

Work in Progress

Mike Ekunno

NOT THAT IT mattered where I sat but the gallery gave a low down on the congregation. My mid-way entry made the gallery my natural habitat. A do-gooder usher downstairs had thought to benefit me with his quixotic cooing: "Got a seat for you here."

Seat ko, shit ni.[1] *Who knows where that'd have had me sandwiched? Between two dudes wearing flowing lace agbadas, my rough denim and white sneakers providing the perfect sore thumb?*

Instead I got installed at my favourite perch upstairs with all the options. Jennie stood in the aisle facing me. *Did she come with IT?* She turned to face the altar as if in telepathic response. There IT was. Jennie wasn't my First Lady for nothing. What she packed behind was arrogant. Pleasantly so. Whatever the ushers' uniform for the Sunday, her designer was sure to outfit her bakassi with an obtrusive flair which she carried on 6-inch platforms. And I didn't complain, really. I could trek behind those curves any distance on the face of planet Earth.

Testifiers for the day were taking their turns on the microphone. I sat forward in my seat and closed my eyes: "Lord, I'm here today. Forgive your boy, I beg you. You are a powerful God, the Highest. If you will only help me to travel out, I promise to change. Settle me with better something and let me

---

[1] *Seat ko, shit ni*: Used to show incredulity.

begin to nak correct sputes[2] from fine, fine boutiques. Give me my breakthrough so that I can begin to climb better better stages like them Ali Baba, Julius Agwu. Let me run my own show like Teju BabyFace, AY. God, you're too much. I praise your name, forever in Jesus' name, amen."

I opened my eyes and reclined. The view below was resplendent as usual. A rainbow congregation spread to the terraced altar. The altar was majestic and draped in white and purple. The lectern was spare and elegantly done in chrome. It was backgrounded by roof-high curtains which parted midway to reveal **DIVINE SANCTUARY OF JERUSALEM MINISTRY INC.** The altar job was straight out of some interior designer's brochure. Daddy Bishop and Mummy and the pastoral team sat to the left of the lectern facing the choir. The choir colours that day were lemon green on dark green.

A few of the testifiers had had their turns on the microphone and were serenaded by applause to their seats. Two of them had been on "journey mercies" across the country and one sister had a safe delivery.

Two of a kind. Whether pregnancy or travelling, both are the same journey to the great beyond—potentially. One blink of an eye and somebody can become a mere figure on the nation's maternal mortality statistic or having a ghastly siesta by the roadside with cassava leaves as covering wrapper.

One brother had come to see Daddy for success with a US visa application and was asked to sow in dollars which he did. He went for the interview thereafter and got issued with a multiple entry visa. "The Lord is good!"

"All the time!" we responded.

Jackpot, bigtime! You didn't say how much you sowed to give me an idea of how to go about mine. And sowing in dollars—more like asking an anaemic patient to donate blood for his healing.

A sister testified of deliverance from witchcraft attack. Her nights were filled with eerie coos and tweets from evil birds outside and, inside, vermin which behaved like humans ransacked her apartment. They wouldn't be caught by any antidote. Any time the evil bird cooed, her period wouldn't come. But with the anointing oil consecrated by the Man of God, she anointed her apartment and sprinkled on the tree and ever since, she sleeps easy like a baby, for the Holy Bible says He will give his beloved sleep. "Praise the Lord!"

We responded.

---

[2] *nak correct sputes*: wear trendy clothes

You fit complain of witch for night.[3] For my area, where do you see trees, belenté[4] birds to perch on them? Instead of to de speak phonetics,[5] marriage will automatically end this kind of witchcraft. With a man—like me—around you, which rat fit miss road show face for the house when bush meat de hungry some people.[6]

The babe looked gorgeous in a hat and spoke with the unmistakable accent that came from contact with Oyibo, the British ones not the American ones.

After her, there were two other testimonies that had to do with success on visa interviews. One of them, Baba Dee, had been my paddy and I linked him to the guy who was to arrange an Oluwole bank statement and marriage certificate for him. The embassy had to be sure he had a regular income in the country with a wife and children to guarantee his willing return. If not for his testimony, I wouldn't have known he succeeded. He didn't tell me. *You see life!*

The one which brought down the roof was of a couple of whom the lady had the SS genotype and was a confirmed patient but had gone ahead to wed her AS heartthrob against better counsel if not judgment. She waved the result of the test confirming she had become AA after being prayed for by Daddy and drinking anointed oil. All her symptoms had disappeared, and her red blood cell count was at an all-time high. People screamed from the pews and others walked out to sow to it. On my row, argument burst as the brother who sat two chairs away said something about fake testifiers who were out for "Notice Me" to please Daddy Bishop and Mummy.

"How d'you mean?" challenged the lady in between us.

"It's not scientifically possible."

"Was walking on water scientifically possible?"

"But that was Jesus Christ."

"What of parting the Red Sea?" This was from an elderly man seated in the preceding row turning on his seat backwards.

"Well…" Doubting Thomas smiled, finding himself outnumbered.

I prevaricated inside, having initially shared DT's opinions but being not so sure anymore. Moreover, the opposition looked distinguished. Seeing how

---

[3] *You fit complain of witch for night?*: You dare complain about night witchcraft?

[4] *belenté*: let alone

[5] *Instead of to de speak phonetics*: Instead of speaking with an affected accent

[6] *which rat fit miss road show face for the house when bush meat de hungry some people*: no rat dares stray into the house when it could become a casualty as bush meat

I leaned forward right ways with interest in the talk, the buffer lady sought to drag me out: "Imagine what he said," she started. "You mean that lady can come out to fake a healing just to please somebody?"

I gently nodded my agreement.

"You know what it means to suffer sickle cell, the pains, the crises?" She wasn't done.

"Yes," I volunteered, "she even put on weight."

"That's what I'm saying. It shows."

"Very well," I concurred. By then it was just the two of us carrying on. The storm raised by SS to AA had blown over and two other testifiers who I didn't listen to in the aftermath of the storm had brought the session to a close. The choir prepared to deliver its special number to usher in the sermon. As they rose, shades of green suffused the TV screens on the gallery. I had an unhindered view to the altar but depended on the screens for close-ups. The camera panned the choir frontlines and I ticked off: Bunmi, Nike, Tina, Ify, Florence. Blessing was missing. There was no knowing if she was around but didn't robe for the service or she travelled. Fishing out my Samsung Galaxy S10, I texted her: *No de fuk up,*[7] *babe. Wia u de?*[8] She didn't reply and the phone returned to my pocket.

The choir was singing one of those numbers of Women of Faith, but it wasn't "Crucified." I loved to listen to "Crucified." The lyrics had an inflection that got me. They finished the Crucified sister song to great applause. Then they took on "Divine Project." It had a more African feel and I rocked to it standing and swaying. Down below, many joined the interactive. I could see some skanking and a guy was mashing it up. It felt groovy and along the line, Jennie sauntered from behind up the aisle. I espied her divine project. The auditory and the visual came together. I swayed more, raising my two hands in rapturous delight. Soon the choir ended "Divine Project" to greater applause, hoots and heckling. I sat down. Leaning over to my right neighbour, I enquired if she knew the lyrics. She did and tore a paper from inside her jotter and scribbled: "I'm a divin projet, I cannot be abandon…"

Then came the moment I had been waiting for. All my senses were primed for the day's message. *Will it provide good enough materials for tonight?* Daddy stepped onto the altar with his iPad.

---

[7] *No de fuk up*: Don't be a jerk

[8] *Wia u de?*: Where are you?

"Praise the Lord!"

"Alleluia!" thundered the congregation.

"That 'alleluia' is that of a malaria patient. If you know that you don't have malaria, Praise the Lord!"

"Alle—lu—yaaaa!!"

"Shout it, let me hear you!"

"Alle—lu—yaaaaaaaaa!!!

I didn't join. *Anybody who didn't hear that first one will need to visit an ENT specialist. There won't be any difference even if I did it with my eyes and nose and ears too.*

"Stand up and tell your neighbour on the right: 'You're in for an earthquake today.'"

Has the National Emergency Management Agency been informed?

The church broke into a hearty babble. I turned to my lady neighbour on the right to repeat the line. She was turned rightwards too while the guy to my left was pitching the line to me.

"Say it again: 'You're in for an earthquake today!'"

We continued.

"Now turn to the person on your left and say it: 'You're in for an earthquake today!'"

I turned to the brother to my left. He was rattling off to his left-hand neighbour. My right-hand sister was on me.

"Walk to seven people and tell them: 'God is going to visit you today with a miracle.'"

How am I sure?

The pews scattered like a stepped-upon line of soldier ants. I went through the motions pumping palms here and there. Before I picked my way through the haphazard traffic to where I'd be in the natural line of contact with First Lady, the temporary jigsaw had fallen into place with order restored.

Big fuk-up. I made my way back to my seat, unable to feel her hand today.

On the altar, Daddy settled down to the business of the day. The topic was "Work in Progress." I reached for my wallet. Rummaging its compartments, I chanced upon a piece of paper and unfurled. It was the counterfoil of my last electricity bill. The back was clear, and I scribbled away. The root passage was from Second Timothy Chapter Two from verse 20 to 21. I followed the reading from left neighbour's Bible:

> *20But in a great house there are not only vessels of gold and silver, but also of wood and of earth; and some to honour and some to dishonour. 21If a man therefore purge himself from these, he shall be a vessel unto honour, sanctified, and meet for the master's use, and prepared unto every good work.*

Up on the screens, the passage was splashed in the version read out by Daddy Bishop:

> [20]*In a large house, there are dishes and bowls of all kinds: some are made of silver and gold, others of wood and clay; some are for special occasions, others for ordinary use.* [21]*If anyone makes himself or herself clean from all these evil things, they will be used for special purposes because they are dedicated and useful to their Master ready to be used for every good deed.*[9]

₧☙

Taking over the mic from the strip tease act on Sunday night, I had my sequence well worked out. It was MPM Night: Movement for the Postponement of Mondays. High decibels from the club's woofers give way to cackles and guffaws from jokes every MPM Night. I started with an intro that was bound to wet the ground and loosen the audience, a congregation of a different service—a vigil on Bacchus.

"There was this man who beat the traffic light. You know how it is: you approach as amber is just turning to red and you're in a hurry. But Yellow Fever is hiding after the junction and catches you. 'Park! Park!!' he motions to this driver while standing just inches away from the bumper. His colleague goes to the passenger side to enter as if the car belongs to two of them."

Chuckles.

"Oga[10] pulls over and the leeches gather him: 'Red stop you and you pass. You nor de see? What if you jam another person?'

"Our man tries to explain that it had not fully turned to red.

"'Okay, you teach us our job. Where are your papers, fire extinguisher, triangle, spare tyre? Again, your side mirror is cracked,' and so on and so forth. Oga understands the message and asks for settlement.

"'No. You go with us.'

"'Where to?'

"'You'll know when we get there. You de speak grammar for us, eh?'

"'No now, it's not like that,' goes our man. 'We can settle this here.'

---

[9] GNT: See copyright acknowledgments for details.

[10] *Oga*: Boss

"So the negotiation starts. From five thousand naira. Finally, finally they settle for five hundred naira. Oga fishes out a one thousand naira note and asks for change.

"'Ahhh! Where we go see change, now, Oga?'

"'Abeg try. That's all I've got.'

"Change is taking time so one of the Yellow Fever returns to the beat so as not to miss the other bush meats speeding past. His colleague goes off with the note to look for change. Presently, the second returns not with the change but an idea. 'Oga,' he starts, 'as I no fit get change, just go back and beat the light again so everything go balance.'"

The room thunders. A couple of tables topple their contents and the waiters hit the aisles, mops and pans in hand. I wait for the guffaws to die down then I go antiphonal: "Praise the lord!"

"Alleluia!" The mockery elicits more laughter.

"Praise the lord!"

"Allelu-ia!!"

It dies down. I continue. "You thought before now the traffic light had more brains than its human counterpart. Now you know better. You're going to be hearing more about the road. You know when it used to be 'Slow Men at Work.' How many of us remember that?"

Some hands pop.

"Ehe! These are the Methuselahs. Anybody here who knows when Ministry of Works was PWD[11] don become Old School. So if any person beside you raised their hand, shake them for me. They try well. It's not easy to be senior citizen."

More smirks. "You, nko[12]? You, nko?" It's a lady sharing the table with an elderly looking man.

"Ah, me? It was my grandfather I heard saying it. But seriously, it is just lack of simple punctuation marks that caused 'Slow Men at Work.' A comma after 'slow' gives the right meaning."

"Teacher! GS[13] 101!" I savour the heckling.

---

[11] *PWD*: Public Works Department, a colonial-era precursor of the Ministry of Works.

[12] *nko?*: how about you?

[13] *GS*: General Studies. The generic title of the basic English Language course for college freshers.

"Other havocs have been caused by the lack of observance of small chinchiri[14] things. The other day, it was a sub-editor who failed to tap the space bar as he cast a headline. The headline was to be 'Pen is Mightier Than the Sword.' But he forgot to tap the space bar after Pen." I pause to allow them to picture the snafu.

The chuckles come in leaks until the moment of epiphany. Then the flood gates break. The ladies are off the hooks. I wait. "Praise the lord!"

"Alleluia!"

"This kin' joke too de sweet for ladies. Ladies say 'Yeah!'"

"Yeah!"

"I love all you ladies here—only with permission—ooh. A-beg me no wan' mek person block me for road[15] after this. This morning at church, the sermon was on Work in Progress. My pastor spoke of Saul on the way to one place—"

"Damascus!"

"Yes. Give yourself a knock for getting it right."

Chuckles.

"Yes," I continue. "On the way to Damascus, he became Paul. That's work in progress. There was Peter who denied his master but became mighty thereafter. That was work in progress. As the man of God was preaching, I was following him with other examples of works in progress. Every lady is a work in progress. Right?"

"No!" "Yes!" "Yes!" "No!"

"I should prove it?"

"Yeees!"

"Okay. You all know there's a time of the month for ladies when the chest gets like this," I gesture with my two hands apart. "Then after, they return to normal. That's work in progress. God help any guy who is looking for a Partonian or Orjiakoic chest. If you meet one like that at the wrong time of the month nko? That's work in progress."

The glee is measured.

"And talking about the changes in a woman—physiological changes, yes! Clap for me for that one."

A few scattered claps.

---

[14] *chinchiri*: onomatopoeia for tiny

[15] *A-beg me no wan' mek person block me for road*: Please, I don't want to be confronted.

"Physiological change. I went to school, you know! What causes another form of physiological changes?"

"We don hear, now!" "You just learn that one?" the last heckler elicits some laughter at my expense. I pause before continuing.

"What causes those…"

"Physiological changes!" choruses the audience.

"Yes—oo! You guys need to pay lesson fees—oo! They are caused when a woman begins to catwalk around her husband. You know?" I demonstrate a coquette's strides.

Laughter.

"So when she keeps doing that, na trouble de sleep, inyanga wan wake am.[16] The man will be looking at her from the corner of his eyes and be saying: 'Heeeee!' Then before you know it, the walk changes." I waddle off the stage to mimic the pregnant woman's swagger.

Raucous roar.

෪෬

My next manifestation at the sanctuary was after two weeks clear. Two weeks as in clear two Sundays in between when I didn't attend church.

The earlier absence had hangover to blame. There had been a show on Saturday, a wedding. The reception was in a garden with a large tent and I anchored it. It was not a how-for-do[17] wedding reception and you could tell that from the flow of drinks. Tables were being replenished by ushers who pulled no punches. As a matter of professional morality, I didn't do the bottle before or during a show. A glass of wine to get me in the mood, maybe, but nothing intoxicating. The audience, the ambience and the sound of my voice on the Public Address System, those were my steroids. The high they gave was higher than that of any beer or spirit. But the reception ended in the evening, late evening. Then the after party came. I wasn't the anchor and I was free. And I took advantage of the bottle. We spilled over from the tent to the outlying greens and, as the night wore on, pairs staggered into the shrubbery. The hooker who had me that night was also stoned. But not stoned enough not to ask for her payoff even as I dusted grass off her top. While I

---

[16] *na trouble de sleep, inyanga wan wake am*: Popular Nigerian idiom. Literally: Trouble is sleeping, and Coquette rouses him awake.

[17] *how-for-do*: modest

feigned a shortage and felt my pockets for money, she made to help me out. "There's an ATM on that street across," she said, pointing.

Having recourse to the ATM at 4 am Sunday morning with a painted-up, mini-skirt-wearing girl hanging in the wings—that wasn't my idea of a night out. I quickly fished out her remaining pay from the inner pocket of my jacket and off-loaded her, but not the hangover which kept me away from that morning service.

Soccer was to blame the next Sunday. I couldn't resist playing with the guys around my hood. Chelsea supporters were taking us on. It was to parody the clash in the English Premier League which we had won. For our opponents, it was to disprove the win. We played and it was a 2-2 draw, but one up for missed church again.

It was to be another miss this Sunday because I overslept, but I rebuked Satan and made it halfway into the sermon. Half a loaf was always going to be better than no bread. My arrival time was good enough for the gallery again. I repaired upstairs, hopeful. I was ushered to a seat at the near end close to the staircase entrance. I sat and bent down by habit, my eyes closed in prayers. When I opened my eyes and sat up, I scanned the aisles on the gallery. She wasn't there. *Fuk-up!* On the screens, the day's message title was emblazoned:

O GOD, WHEN THOU WENTEST FORTH ... Ps. 68[7-8].

Daddy going on with the homily filled the frame. He wore his trademark hands-free microphone and strutted the altar, iPad in hand: "Can somebody read from the Living Bible or the New International Version?"

One of the pastors from the Pastors' Bay stood and a media hand relayed the cordless mic to him. He read:

> O God, when you led your people out from Egypt, when you marched through the dry wasteland, the earth trembled and the heavens poured rain before you, the God of Sinai, before God, the God of Israel.[18]

The pastor yielded up the mic and sat down again.

"Thank you for that," Daddy said. "This is just so that somebody will not be confused by the quaint wording of the King James Version. Today, you cannot write 'wentest forth' except you want to score F in English. But I do like its richness. When it speaks of when God wentest forth, it is referring to the pillar of cloud by day and the pillar of fire by night with which the

---

[18] NLT: See copyright acknowledgments for details.

Almighty led the children of Israel out of Egypt. The awesomeness of the Almighty made the earth to quake and the sky to bow down. That is what happens when God intervenes in your situation."

The cameras swapped and Camera 2 beamed the pews on the ground floor.

"When you are going through a wilderness experience, let God lead the way; let Him wentest forth, amen!"

"Amen!"

"Let Him be your pillar of cloud by day and pillar of fire by night, amen!"

"Amen!"

Just then, the sweep of the camera lens brought in the center left column and who was smack on the aisle? Jennie, my First Lady! There in full force! The camera faced her front but ain't no doubt, her fit-to-die-for curves were intact behind. *Her Rear Majesty!* From then on, I could not be bothered with who wentest forth or whatever. If I couldn't espy my quarry, service wasn't worth it. I got restless thereafter thinking of how I could reunite with my First Lady. Then I did a double take and picked up my Bible and exited. "I'm coming," was for my bemused neighbour. Past the usher's quizzical looks by the doorway again: "I'm coming." I trotted downstairs and onto the ground floor main entrance.

"No more seat," the head usher protested. "Go upstairs."

"I know," I said, breezing past him toward the center left aisle. Jennie was up front.

Surely an odd seat could have been skipped somewhere or someone could have exited.

I encountered her downstream colleague at the tail of the aisle: "Guy, abeg, see if you can get me an empty seat somewhere," I coaxed, pointing to the extreme left column.

"Yes!" he enthused, moving up the aisle. I trailed him. Midway, he turned to the right row and pointed to the empty seat at the far end.

"O thanks!" I picked through the five pairs of legs and sat down with one person between me and the other aisle. Stretching to look ahead, I could see Jennie's torso. Her waist downwards was partly shielded by a plantation row of heads and head gears, and I bided my time for when she was bound to amble past my row. Upfront, Daddy went on and on. He was itemizing How to Make God Lead You. On the screens, the bulleted sub-heads rattled off:

- Live Holy
- Be Submissive
- Invite Him to Lead You.

The children of Israel—which of these did they?

The Man of God presently climbed down from the altar, leaving his iPad on the lectern. The cameras and microphones trailed him into the pews. The miracle segment was underway. He went down the aisle two columns away from mine. The first victim of the day was a woman.

"You," he pointed at her near the front row.

She stood up on cue.

"Your husband is not here with you, right?"

Obviously. There's no man seated beside her.

"Yes," the tentative lady said.

"I see two of you living separately in two different cities."

"Yes, he was transferred to Port Harcourt."

"The Lord says you make haste to join your husband for that is the beginning of your separation if you don't. Clap hands for Jesus!" With that he was done, and the lady made her way out to sow a seed into the receptacle stationed by the altar.

Picking on his next victim, Daddy told her she had just discovered she was pregnant and was contemplating abortion, for they had six children already. "Is your husband here?"

Why wouldn't you know?

The man beside the woman stood. Turning to him, Daddy continued: "My brother, even you have not been told. You're just hearing it, right?"

"Yes, Daddy."

"Don't be offended with her. She's looking at it from the point of view of Man. Seven children with the state of our economy."

The rest of the church watched, enraptured. Turning again to the woman, Daddy continued. "My sister, the baby you carry is exactly 26 days, 8 hours and 17 minutes old."

The church clapped and hailed.

"God says forget about abortion. Your baby is a boy—go and mark it down—and he is a star. He is going to be a great guy, praise the Lord!"

"Alleluia!" we intoned, and Daddy got moving again.

With eyes looking up at the gallery, he stopped and used his right palm to shore up his right ear lobe. "I hear a name like Ambrose... Ambrose Akpo... veta. Yes, Ambrose Akpoveta!"

Something sounded familiar about what he said. It wasn't until it was repeated over the PAS that it dawned on me: he was saying my name. I stood, tentative and at a loss.

"What's your name, brother?" He gestured at me as a microphone was making its way in my direction.

"Ambrose Akpoveta."

Then the mic came.

"Ambrose Akpoveta," I said again.

"As if you're not sure, brother. Now, let's confirm if you're the one. The Lord says you are wearing blue boxers with white lines on both sides, is that right?"

"You are right, sir."

"On your back pocket you have your wallet with exactly two one thousand naira notes, one five hundred, two one hundred and three twenty naira notes. Two thousand, seven hundred and sixty naira, only. Can we confirm that?"

I didn't know exactly how much I had left in the wallet, but I remembered the two wazobias[19] and the three twenty naira change from the okada motorcycle that dropped me at church. I removed my wallet from the back and opened its sitting room compartment. Out came the notes: two wazobias, the five hundred, two one hundred and the murtalas[20]. The camera splashed the contents on the screen and the congregation applauded.

"Should I go on?"

"Yeeeess!!" The thirsty congregation didn't wait for my answer.

"This morning," he continued as I flinched, feeling like a patient stripped for medical students. "This morning you woke up exactly 9:23 and you were of two minds, whether to come to church or not. Right?"

"Yes, Daddy."

The church clapped.

"When you came, you sat upstairs at the gallery but later came to where you're now sitting."

"That's right, Daddy."

"The Lord says concerning your change of position that the he-goat went in search of a wife but came back pregnant himself. Does that make any sense to you?"

"Yes, Daddy." Bouts of mirth coursed through the congregation.

"OK. Now that we're sure it's you the Lord has in mind, come to the altar and wait for me. The Lord has a message for you."

I made my way out and to the altar, standing with my back to the congregation while he continued. I couldn't keep up with him through the

---

[19] *wazobias*: Nigerian street name for the one thousand naira note.

[20] *murtalas*: Nigerian street name for the twenty naira note.

large screen on the altar. My head was swirling ... wentest forth ... gallery to downstairs ... he-goat ... wife ... pregnant ... wentest forth ... pillar of cloud ... cloud of fire ... fire of cloud...

There's no knowing how long I stood there before I heard: "Are you a preacher? I see you with microphone." Coming through the PAS, I regarded it as a continuation of the other sounds until I saw my image on the screen with Daddy up close.

He repeated the question and a mic had been poked to my face.

I answered, "No, sir."

"What do you do with the microphone?"

"I work as a stand-up comedian and MC."

"From now on, the Lord says you start working for Him." With that he blew in my direction and I was lifted by an unseen force to crash into the steps of the altar. Hands stretched to hold me and guide me to the floor. I was knocked out. When I came to, it was Jennifer standing behind me.

Where are they, the male ushers!

Daddy brought his king-size Goya bottle and anointed me, and I fell backwards. My sensitivity didn't stop the brushing of her arms on my way down. I got up and Daddy said, "Congratulations. You are free. Clap for Master Jesus!"

The congregation clapped as I made my way head bowed, past the ushers, avoiding Jennifer, to my seat.

80CR

"Work in Progress" is about exploring the capacity of man to harbour both the holy and the profane in the same space. The starkness of the contrast is often directly proportional to its denial.

Mike is the winner of the inaugural Harambee Literary Prize and author of the story collection *Soul Lounge*. His works have appeared in *The Republic*, *The First Line*, *Drunk Monkeys*, *Bridge Eight*, *Rigorous*, *Pensive Journal*, the *African Roar* anthology, and other venues. He works as a freelance book editor and consulting speechwriter.

Mike's recent spur is towards poetry. He loves moonlit nights and believes there must be some hidden knowledge in cloud formations, which he tries to divine. He reads Old Testament stories and is a massive fan of the defunct ABBA. He volunteers with his local Bible college, where he teaches Rhetoric.

You Shall See Him in the East

Frederick Gero Heimbach

(Editors' note for non-US readers: POTUS = President of the United States)

Day 1

POTUS LED THEM to the roof of the White House, through the solarium, past the place Eisenhower grilled his steaks, to a spot overlooking the East Wing, where they could get a better look at the thing coming at them.

As usual, Samantha (Press Secretary) stood right next to POTUS, like a wife. They were "old friends." Ravi tended to defend her to others. She was a moderating influence, or tried to be.

They all looked at the horizon. It was just a forehead. It was the size of a mountain and it bobbed up and down at an inhumanly slow pace. Ravi watched its movement, stately and inevitable like a heavenly body. When the crisis broke, Ravi was the most senior State official in town, and here he was, lifted from important to essential.

POTUS personally assigned him a temporary office in the Old Executive Office Building. It had a couch and he would be living there, essentially, for the duration. But the crisis made all offices temporary.

Someone passed around a pair of binoculars. The flattened perspective added to Ravi's dread. "The damnedest thing," said the president. He shook his head in awe, about as much as he would give the Senate majority leader sinking a 20-foot putt.

"Do we know its intent?" asked Homeland. "Anyone know what it's doing?"

Defense: "We don't even know what it *is*."

Homeland: "Is it approaching? The perspective is… off."

An email from the Pentagon came in. Ravi summarized it to the group. "They're saying its physics are, well, weird. It's appearing all over the world. No matter where you are on the globe, you see it just cresting the eastern horizon. Talk of it 'approaching' may be meaningless."

That sobered the group. "This is *serious* magic," said the president. He pulled out his favorite charm, a 1940 silver dime, as he muttered an incantation. Then, an idea: "Have they scrambled fighters?"

Defense said, "Yes," and checked his messages. "The thing stays just at the horizon, even at 30,000 feet. Reports from ISS say the view from space is nothing. So, yeah. The thing isn't real."

The president rubbed the worn coin as he continued to watch. Ravi saw Press Secretary's fingers unconsciously imitating the movement. "Damn," said the president.

Physics or no, the thing—the giant man—*was* approaching. At the peak of each slo-mo stride, they could catch a glimpse of the eyes. Blue eyes. It was that feature that transformed The Phenomenon—Ravi had heard Homeland actually use that word—into The Coming One. Or, as Ravi silently preferred: The Avatar.

Like a good Hindu. Not that Ravi was anything close.

Ravi tore his eyes away. Another message. They had calculated an ETA, absurd as that might be. How could it come *here* when it wasn't really *there*? But the defense apparatus couldn't stop doing defense apparatus things. Homeland, too, had reverted to type; *those* people had brought back the color wheel. They had moved the needle to red, of course. Red alert, as if people needed to be told to panic.

One week. That was the ETA.

Ravi looked through the balustrade. The streets nearby held little traffic, odd for midday Washington.

He returned to his new, barren office. Passing through the break room, Ravi caught Nikhil by the arm. "Help me with something. Privately."

Nikhil was an intern. Ravi had avoided mentoring him because their backgrounds were similar and he didn't think ethnic cliques were a good look. Events had rendered that kind of calculation irrelevant.

"I'm stuck here for the duration. Pick me up a pizza. Cheese only."

Nikhil gave Ravi a look. "Giant Forehead's turned you into a vegetarian?" Nikhil had seen Ravi eating meat on many occasions, something neither of their parents would have approved of.

"Yeah, I guess. And also…" This was difficult. "I want you to go find me a Ganesh." Ravi handed him some bills. "This is personal. Of course."

Nikhil just looked at the money.

"You know where to go?"

"I can figure it out."

"There may be a run on Ganeshes. Because of the, you know. Or, for all I know, all the Ganeshes in DC have been smashed." Nikhil winced.

They stood there, Nikhil waiting to be dismissed. Ravi paused, telling himself not to ask this kid for advice. *What do I do, an unbelieving Hindu, when I see a miracle?*

Day 2

Once the morning sun moved out of the way, everyone could see the full face. It was vaguely purposeful but otherwise lacked emotion. *Cold bastard.*

Everyone recognized him. The president acted fast. He removed the painting of George Washington from the Oval Office and put Jesus in his place, presiding over the mantlepiece.

"Sallman. Head of Christ. Takes me back to my grandma's house," said the president, looking at the famous painting—and then the meeting began. State was back in Washington but Ravi was still on the invitation list.

"Sallman?" asked State. He wasn't the brightest bulb, even in normal times.

"The artist," said the president. "*Christ.* How did that guy *know?*"

"It's odd," agreed Homeland. "Caucasian; blue eyes; long, wavy, auburn hair. Makes no historical sense." The face of the Coming One exactly conformed to the most famous, westernized image of Jesus Christ. He *was* that sickly weirdo with the beard and the spooky blue eyes.

There wasn't much to say. The Pentagon's arrival estimates were more precise but hadn't shifted. Otherwise, everyone could see exactly what "shit was going down", as POTUS put it: Jesus was coming.

"We need more experts," said POTUS. "But who the hell is an expert in this?"

"There are some Bible scholars," said Defense. "End times prophecy types. They have interesting—"

"I'm sure Sybil would *love* to chat those guys up," said the president. Everyone knew the president's fortune teller. The horoscope she authored was the first thing he read each morning.

"There are some dot com billionaires who have formed a consortium," said State. "The Burning Man crowd. We could ask—"

The president didn't like billionaires. He uttered an obscenity, and that ended that. Ravi decided he would make some discreet inquiries. Find out what the billionaires were up to.

POTUS stood. He caught Ravi by the arm as everyone else filed out.

"So, Ravi, what's the Hindu angle? Who's your messiah?"

"Well, Mr. President, Hinduism is a big, complicated religion, but the short answer is Kalki, the tenth avatar of Vishnu."

"Good. So they got one. Because, I gotta ask—"

The president glanced around, as if eavesdroppers were hiding somewhere in the oval room. "—what's he look like to you?"

"Sir?"

"The giant face. We all see the Caucasian Jesus. Who is he to *you*? Do you see this... *Cocky*... person?"

"Kalki? No, sir."

"I mean, I'm asking because, those eyes. Blue. Very Nordic. I mean, *Christ*, it's all too..."

"Culturally conditioned?"

"Yeah. Cultured. And that would be okay, if we were all seeing him through our own, you know, lenses." The president made goggles with his fingers, giving Ravi one last chance to confirm his theory.

"I'm sorry. If the face had blue skin, or—"

"Blue skin?"

"Kalki is typically depicted with blue skin. But all I see is a blue-eyed Jesus—"

"Which, let's face it, is cheesy. Embarrassing."

"It is a bit of a... conundrum."

"It must seem especially, I don't know, *unfair*, to someone like you. I mean, what? A million gods? Ten million? They couldn't have thrown in even *one* of those guys?"

"If it makes it any easier, most Hindus I know are monotheists. Many forms, but deep down, just one God after all."

The president's nose wrinkled.

Back at the office, Nikhil stopped by. He sat statuettes on Ravi's empty desk, lined up and facing the same way. He had found a Vishnu, a Kalki, and a family set of Shiva, Parvati and Ganesh, all shiny and painted bright.

"The biggest trouble was finding a shop that was open. Washington's a ghost town."

"Yeah," said Ravi. "A lot of people are AWOL. The secret service is working double shifts."

Nikhil laughed. "In movies, the end of the world is nukes and riots. They didn't realize Armageddon would look like mid-August."

"So, actually getting a statue was…?"

"Easy, once I found an open shop. Nobody's buying murtis." *Murti* was the word for Hindu idols.

"So our people—"

"They're calling Lord Jesus an avatar of Vishnu. Some of them." He shrugged, unconcerned. "Just be glad you're not Muslim. *They* have a lot more backfilling to do."

He had said *you're*, not *we're*.

Ravi pulled papers out of his desk. "Look. I've printed out the Gayatri Mantra." Ravi gave Nikhil a page. He set the murtis on a shelf on the west wall of the room. He opened the curtains to let in the late morning sun. He removed his leather shoes.

"What are you doing?"

"I'm going to pray. You're going to join me. That's what good Hindus do."

"I'm… not a good Hindu."

"This is the end of the age, Nikhil. The *final destruction*. If you can't get religion when you're staring a miracle in the face—literally the *face*—"

"Mr. Anand." Nikhil was unbuttoning his shirt.

Ravi stepped back. He had heard *things*, crazy things, the interns were up to…

"No, wait," Nikhil said, and then he had what he wanted, the necklace under his shirt, out in the open. "I'm Team Jesus," he said, showing Ravi the big gold cross. "I've joined the winning side."

Day 3

Oval Office, 8:00 a.m. The president still wanted Ravi attending the Jesus meetings—and all meetings were Jesus meetings. So many new jokes; so many old jokes that were no longer funny. You couldn't talk about having a Come to Jesus moment anymore. *In Soviet Union, Jesus come to you!* (The new jokes weren't funny either.)

Sybil, the astrologer, sat across from Ravi, wearing a full-on crucifix, painted in living (so to speak) color, a rather huge thing. An end-times preacher from TV Land was also present. He had come straight from a hay-strewn broadcast studio. Someone had given him a souvenir, a glass coaster, and he kept touching the Great Seal etched into it.

"What does he want?" asked POTUS. "Jesus. What are the possibilities?"

Homeland: "He may come to sweep all away."

Defense: "The possibility that he's just visiting was dismissed right away. No theologian takes that suggestion seriously." He glanced at the TV preacher, as a prompt, but the man was dumbstruck—the Oval Office!—which suited Ravi just fine.

Homeland was speaking again. "Basically, we need to get ready for a takeover. Jesus is here to rule." She looked around, like a villain in a melodrama waiting for the crowd to boo. She had misjudged her audience.

"The only choice is," she continued, "does he come as an avenging judge? Or as a benevolent king?"

"Late Great Planet Earth, or Christian Century?" added Defense, as if that clarified things.

POTUS: "And these billionaires, this *consortium*, what are they trying to prove? Whose side are *they* on?"

Homeland: "I hear they're building a giant robot. *A robot!*"

Laughter. Everyone thought that was nuts.

POTUS: "I don't like it. We need to shut those assholes *down*."

Sybil said, "You know, there's one global fact, an incredible fact, that nobody talks about, but it's important. Worldwide, the poor are emerging from poverty. Getting rich. Every region. Think of it: 'The poor you'll always have with you,' as Our Lord said. That's over now."

She crossed herself. Horizontal line, then vertical. Even Ravi knew that was wrong.

Samantha sat up. Everyone looked at her. Ravi knew her to be quietly religious. She had always been open to him about it, telling him in detail about the time she had helped POTUS and Sybil bury sacred objects under the hearth in the Oval Office: a shoe, a mirror, and a "witch-bottle" filled with presidential urine. They had uncovered a desiccated cat, clearly buried there by the previous administration. Ravi got the feeling Samantha didn't approve of such magic, but had learned to mute her criticism over the years. Ravi had always had a soft spot for her. Opposites attract.

To Sybil, she said, "You know, I can see what you're—"

POTUS: "So you're saying, we done good. Jesus likes us."

"I think we should cast off our fear!" Sybil smiled radiantly. She literally raised her hands.

Defense: "I suppose, inside each of us, there's this moral scold—"

"Exactly, brother!" said Sybil. Without shame, she had adopted an evangelist's cadence, even sprinkling in a southern accent (*Exahctly, bruthah!*). Nobody dared smirk. "We've been in guilt mode for so long, we haven't noticed when we do something right!"

POTUS: "So, we should push that line?"

Homeland: "Happy Jesus or Angry Jesus, doesn't matter. He's *Jesus*. We hand him the keys to the city."

POTUS: "Clarice,"—that was Homeland—"come up with an appropriate ceremony. Let's give Jesus the kind of greeting that says, 'Welcome, New Boss.'"

Day 4

Progress. Jesus was visible from the waist up, wearing a peasant's tunic and a deep blue mantle over one shoulder. He was walking with a shepherd's crook. Really, the man was a cartoon straight out of a Sunday School flyer. Except those eyes. Those… *dead eyes.*

Hindus had more room for this kind of epiphany, Ravi thought; they didn't expect gods to be their friends. None of this Born in a Stable stuff. For the first time, Ravi could imagine the alienation westerners felt when seeing a woman with extra arms or a man with an elephant's head.

Ravi checked his phone. He had invited Nikhil to join him in prayer, but there was no answer. He noticed a hand-written note on his desk.

Its message was simple: "#HeadForTheHills." It seemed like something an intern would do.

Ravi removed his leather shoes and belt and set them outside. He struck the metal shade of his reading lamp; of all the objects in the room, it made a pleasing, gong-like sound. He should have asked Nikhil to buy him a bell.

Ravi recited the Sanskrit alone.

His clinging to Hinduism wasn't brave or principled, it was just stubborn. There was something about the president's religiosity that just… rankled. Half of it blow-dried, on-the-make Christianity; the other half folk superstition.

His prayers finished, he went outside to join the motorcade to the National Cathedral. POTUS had declared a national day of prayer.

Jesus watched Ravi, or could have, get in the limo.

It was a bipartisan crowd. There were a few notable absences, most spectacularly Defense.

The sermon was a mess. The Dean had no insight to offer, and said so at length. Ravi's eyes wandered, taking in the riot of colors and grotesques. A Hindu should have appreciated it, but it made Ravi uneasy.

Ravi pulled his phone out, holding it low. He searched for #HeadForTheHills. It was the slogan of a preacher, the Reverend Durkin, who had never visited the White House. He was denouncing the Coming One as a fake. Durkin's followers (he actually had some) were fleeing to White

Sulphur Springs, West Virginia. There was an old bomb shelter there, a relic of the Cold War.

The service ended. The ride back was quick, but not quick enough. Ravi retreated indoors, out of view of the One. He stood before Ganesh with his divine parents and looked at Kalki, bright blue and small.

Why wasn't Kalki showing up? *Come on, man: it's now or never.*

Day 5

More Jesus. He just kept coming. His looming visage was fierce, implacable. Sun, moon, comet, skyscraper: the analogies had run out. People were getting really weird now, ramping up the sex or the piety (sometimes both), greeting Ravi in the halls with "Are you ready, brother?" like some tent revival.

"We done good": that was B.S.. This Jesus was no friend. No friend of *Ravi*, that was for sure.

Out on the mall, there was construction going up. The last blue collar workers had been press-ganged, literally, into erecting billboards with blaring slogans ("USA WELCOMES THE LORD JESUS CHRIST!"; "HAIL TO OUR NEW CHIEF!") with bleachers going up on either side of the Lincoln Memorial.

The Burning Man crowd: what were they doing? Ravi thought of one man to call, a member of the consortium who was also a vocal supporter of the president.

Getting through wasn't easy. Ravi's job title didn't have its old effect. Government itself was losing its power to awe. Jesus was ushering in the post-government era, whether that was his intention or not. A libertarian paradise, unrestricted marijuana and prostitution for all.

At last, he got the billionaire's scheduling secretary. She took odd pauses, probably chain-vaping.

"How's the robot effort going?"

"Ah, yes. The robot."

"Can you answer my question?"

"It's over."

"Okay… What happened?"

"Philosophical differences." (Pause; *hiss.*) "What was the robot *for*? Was he an idol, a Wicker Man? Was he a mecha, to do battle with Jesus? A peace offering? A Trojan Horse?" (Pause; *hiss.*) "Pro-Christ, or anti?"

The woman took an especially long pause. Refilling her vape? "The arguing went round and round, hours and *hours*. All these CEOs, used to giving orders. It was actually kind of funny. Trust me. The robot is dead."

"I see." Ravi ended the call.

It hit him how much he had been counting on having alternatives. The robot idea had been—well, it was insane, frankly. But, an *option*. Now that it was gone…

Day 6

He was visible down to his ankles. He just kept striding along, undeterred. He was so *big* now, an approaching storm, arcing up 45 degrees, and it was odd the ground didn't shudder with each step. Ravi took it in as he rolled off the couch, stiff and exhausted, and opened the east-facing windows. He had meant to bring the dawn light to the Hindu deities, but there Jesus was, more than filling the window, making Ravi bow just to see his expressionless, botoxed face.

Ravi saw the dark grey spot on one ear. People with high-powered telescopes had reported it yesterday. No one could tell what it was, but it was odd in the extreme. Jesus, wearing an earpiece? Like the secret service? ("Jesus, we're detecting a hostile in your second quadrant.") Or was it a blemish? *The Mote in God's Ear*, thought Ravi, remembering a sci-fi novel from his adolescence, growing up in Cincinnati.

His feelings for that face were coming into focus. Not dread. Hatred. This blank-faced god, this irresistible force, this *Jesus*, was something Ravi despised. And worse, he had come to despise the Hindu pantheon for its apathetic response.

That was a problem. His default agnosticism, which was really atheism, which was really I-don't-care-ism, was proven wrong. He, too, needed to change sides. Team… *something*.

Ravi asked around for Nikhil. They said he had left two days ago. Unremarkable; a lot of people were AWOL.

It must have been Nikhil who wrote the #HeadForTheHills note. Joining Durkin. Ravi couldn't even imagine how that would work. How many Team Jesuses *were* there, anyway?

Ravi searched the web again for #HeadForTheHills. Very odd: all the hits were gone. He hated conspiracy thinking but, come on, this was deliberate blacklisting. Instead, the search yielded a *lot* of hits for the Coming One, all of it worshipful, plus a video about the giant robot effort, which was still going after all.

A splinter group had gone full Wicker Man. The video showed a towering wooden figure its builders were openly calling the Anti-Christ. In the video, the hasty construction collapsed, killing several people. The video cut off as someone raved about sabotage. It was horrible, of course. Ravi chuckled ruefully as he watched it over and over.

Then he felt bad. *Okay, smart guy, you got a better plan?*

Ravi was having trouble thinking. Too little sleep. What were his options? He had four, but what were they again? Burning Man—no. #HeadForTheHills—no. Hinduism—no.

That left Team Jesus. Ravi couldn't see himself going that way.

He imagined himself dividing a paper into four, listing pros and cons for each option. He considered praying, but not to anyone in particular. It would be a heaven-directed email, with *From* and *Subject* and *Body* filled in, but *To* left blank. He thought what the body of that memo would contain, something like "Whoever you are up there, the real God, I want to follow *you*." He rubbed his eyes and the thought never jelled. He never wrote the prayer. He never prayed it.

Ravi's phone buzzed. POTUS wanted him in the Roosevelt Room. When he arrived, the room was empty of furniture. This felt ominous for some reason. He smiled at Samantha, who looked at him, horrified. *Why are you here?* she mouthed.

Nikhil was there to operate the screen. He didn't acknowledge Ravi.

It hit Ravi, right then. Samantha had written the #HeadForTheHills note.

The room filled with senior people. "I asked Sybil and Samantha and some others to write a prayer for us," said POTUS. "No more fence-sitting. We're going to say the prayer together.

"Maybe…" said Samantha—and POTUS scowled at the interruption. "Maybe we should let everyone read the words first."

"We're going to *fucking* say the prayer."

Everyone froze. POTUS had his rough edges, but this menace was unprecedented. They stood there, wide-eyed rabbits, paralyzed at the sudden arrival of a fox.

Words appeared on the screen. "Welcome, coming Jesus," the prayer began. "We proclaim you, and you alone, our Lord and God." The president and Sybil led the group recitation with bold, bossy voices.

Ravi's mouth refused to say the words. Around him, he heard an odd mixture of voices, some shouting the words like cheerleaders, others mumbling. Samantha shot Ravi a desperate glance. For a moment, he could read her lips. "…will be done on Earth as it is…"

Those weren't the words of the prayer on the screen.

Day 7

Out on the Mall, Ravi found his seat in the fourth row of folding chairs, where the government would greet the new King of the World. Since the Lord Jesus had not sent an advance team, part of the schedule was guesswork, but it called for Jesus to enter the mall from above the Capitol while the president emerged from the Lincoln Memorial. (A Greek temple! How fitting, in a screwed-up kind of way.) Hopefully, the two would meet on a stage erected just to the west of the World War II Memorial.

Would Jesus skirt the Washington Monument? Would he step right over it? No one knew, but he was Jesus; he would have it covered. Jesus was shorter now, even as he was closer—more proof normal laws didn't apply. Everyone around Ravi, all the undersecretaries and special advisors and whatnot, were commenting on it, that Jesus was shrinking before their eyes.

He was taking on human scale. Ravi didn't... didn't *what?* He didn't trust it.

He glanced around, watching the bleachers fill up. He saw Nikhil sitting among the interns in the top rows.

Around the world, in every capital, similar events were playing out. There were those who stayed and those who had fled. In London, the queen was choreographed to present the jeweled orb and scepter to Jesus in Piccadilly Circus. In Paris, the president of France, reverting to medieval forms, would emerge from Notre Dame to place on Jesus' head the crown of Louis XV. Some countries, like Israel, Saudi Arabia, and North Korea, had not divulged their plans, but it was widely believed they would bow to the inevitable—bow quite literally.

Samantha had a seat in the second row but she looked back to the lesser levels. She saw Ravi and looked dismayed.

Events were switching from slow motion to fast. They could hear Jesus' wet footsteps and the rustle of his garments. No longer a two-dimensional thing, an icon painted on the sky, he was now incarnate man, or at least a giant, a creature in space and time, walking across the ocean, displacing air and making a breeze that wafted a lock of his hair.

Hatred was impossible. Ravi didn't even feel fear. His feelings were purely visceral: a twisting in his gut, a chill on his forehead. Jesus was arriving on a *kamikaze*, a divine wind. Some trash, paper from the construction work, swirled about in a dust devil.

Jesus' height was now an estimable thing. Empire State Building, Ravi thought. He was in the district, no question. Now he was casting a shadow over the Capitol, proof of life if there ever was one. Now he was stepping over the dome. And with that, as he entered the Mall, he shrank at high speed and became sharper, more focused.

And there was the grey spot on his ear, the mote. Ravi's emotions continued to fail but the grey cancer made acid rise in his throat.

"Oh God," he gasped.

His words were lost in the chatter. Around him, everyone was reacting, using all kinds of bizarre religious talk, obsolete phrases and even foreign languages. It sounded like a zoo, with every variety of cry, laugh, whimper, and shout, as people rejoiced, or shook, or supplicated. In this most phony of towns, souls were laid bare.

The president of the United States, in morning dress and yarmulke (attire literally chosen by committee) was walking down the steps of the Lincoln Memorial. He was proceeded by acolytes bearing a cross and religious banners. Behind him came Sybil with some bishops and professors and whatnot in ceremonial garb. The president's gloved hands held one of the original copies of the Constitution. He would lay it at Jesus' feet, then kiss the hem of his robe.

Jesus was past the Washington Monument and human-scale now, utterly a man, no one you'd pick out of the crowd if it weren't for his anachronistic clothing. He was, astonishingly, a little shorter (and certainly trimmer) than POTUS. But the mote on his ear, the grey cancer, had grown. Ravi hadn't seen how it had happened, but the bump had become a human figure, a man all in grey, undersized but growing quickly.

Ravi stood up. His mind didn't know what to think but his body did.

Others were standing now, like this was a horse race. Ravi pushed his way out of the row, stepping on toes.

"Ravi! Look!" It was Samantha, at Ravi's side.

As the crowd around them burst into cheers, the president bowed before the Christ. But standing behind Jesus, leaning right on his back, was the grey man, taller than anyone. He was nude, all horns and fangs, and hideous as sin. One arm draped over Jesus' shoulder. He pressed his lips against Jesus' ear, whispering urgent commands as his eyes flashed with demonic desire. His other hand was lost in the folds of Jesus' robe, making it impossible to know whether it was Jesus' hand or Satan's (Yes: that was his name) accepting the venerable parchment from the kneeling president.

Didn't anyone see him? The Devil?

Ravi's mouth began to moan.

The crowd knocked chairs over and surged toward its messiah. Ravi saw Nikhil, the cross on his chest glinting gold but outshone by the expression of adoration on his young, ignorant face.

"We've got to get out of here!" Samantha said. It came out as a scream.

"Why didn't *you* leave?" Ravi's eyes darted about for an escape route. The aisle had filled and a mass of people was pressing on them, pushing them toward damnation.

"Fifteen years!" shouted Samantha. "I *couldn't*."

Ravi put his arm around her waist but he couldn't save her. The ecstatic crowd swept them up. The flood of worshippers bore them toward the One Who Was Come. They had drifted too close to the maelstrom and its pull was inescapable.

೮೦೦೪

Frederick Gero Heimbach lives a pulp fiction life and takes notes. His family lives with him, warily, in Ann Arbor, Michigan. His latest novel is *Buckingham Runner*, about a teen Prince of Wales who wants to disappear. Fred's short fiction has appeared in *Analog Science Fiction and Fact*, *Silence and Starsong*, and *Cirsova Magazine*. He has served as the editor of *StarShipSofa*, the first podcast to win a Hugo Award. Find him on the internet and other realms of dubious corporeality as Fredösphere.

Frederick says, "This story draws its inspiration from a fresco by Luca Signorelli called *Sermon and Deeds of the Antichrist*. It depicts the Antichrist as a twin of the stereotypical Jesus with a horned, nude Devil standing behind him, whispering in his ear. They are so close, you can't tell which hand belongs to whom. The painting is one of the most disturbing I've ever seen."

The Woeful Tale of Sir Banana

Rachael K. Jones

SUPPOSE YOU'RE A trucker, like myself. A space trucker, as my little niece Tilly likes to say, although technically I'm just a garden-variety cargo ship pilot. She's still at the age where anything huge whizzing past the window makes her practically tear down the curtains to get to it. She's got such a big collection of toy trucks, her dad—my big brother—sacrificed the hallway closet to hide the spillover. When I visit Tilly on the Moon, we point at the stars together, my hand over hers, and we trace the shining arc of ships burning through low orbit.

"That's Uncle Danny," I tell her, muttering into her feathery black hair. "That's me when I'm hauling." When she asks what *hauling* means, I say, "Space trucking. Flying stuff between here and Earth, so your dad can buy it at the grocery store."

"Like pudding," says Tilly.

"Exactly."

Are you still with me? Do you find that believable so far? Well, what if something went wrong on my latest trip from Earth, and I'm stranded in orbit with only zero-calorie energy drinks to starve upon while I wait for a rescue that's much too late in coming, days on days while the waste piles up in the cargo hold and the inter-ship band chants its own name into the void? And what if I suck at fixing stuff, whatever I told Tilly? What if Uncle Danny can drive his space-trucks, but when the power flickers, I open up hatches at random and tug a wire here, a panel there, until something clunks ominously and the main power fizzles out for good, leaving me bathed in the dull blue emergency power and bouncy low-energy gravity, and nothing to do but talk to myself while I wait for rescue?

If you've bought all of that, then maybe it's time for the tale of Sir Banana. Maybe I'll tell the one about, I dunno, the Pudding Queen, and the Fruit Kingdom, and how it was saved from the clutches of the dastardly Sir Milk.

Yes, milk would have to be the villain, since the fridge died and the whole carton went bad. But now that I'm starving to death, do you think I regret not chugging that bastard down to the last drop?

You betcha.

So let's begin. Sir Banana, faithful and true, set out for the Pudding Queen's castle in search of new adventures. His coat was a fine green, shot through with yellow, bright as springtime, and his arm strong as wood. As he rode, the Voice of God spoke to him from above. "Sir Banana, faithful and true, I have chosen you to be the salvation of the entire Fruit Kingdom, if you will obey my words."

Sir Banana, you see, was a pious banana, and never one to neglect his prayers. There's one way he and I differ. I grew up Methodist, but only lately started praying again—right around the time the power went out, coincidentally.

"Lord," said Sir Banana, "I am but a humble banana, and the greenest of my bunch. But if you think I am worthy to be your instrument, I will do what you ask of me."

And so the Voice of God told him, "Take up your sword, Sir Banana, and slay Sir Milk, for he has soured on his own pride, and even now plots treachery against your beloved Queen."

Sir Banana was puzzled by this formulation, and not just because I'm making this up as I go along. You see, Sir Milk was Sir Banana's beloved mentor. Sir Banana had learned knightcraft at Sir Milk's knee since the day he had been severed from his bunch. It grieved Sir Banana mightily that the Voice of God had asked such a thing of him.

"O Lord," Sir Banana said, in great anguish and turmoil, "if this is what you would ask of me, I will trust your commands. But I would that you asked something else."

But the Voice of God did not reply, and so Sir Banana surmised that his quest remained unchanged. In truth, the Voice of God had swigged down another zero-calorie energy drink from the cargo hold and gone to bed, only to spend another four or five hours lying awake, heart racing, wishing he had something without caffeine to drink, and cursing his own Voice of God, who had put him in such a circumstance and not bothered to speak to him about it.

Our story doesn't resume until past 0800 Earth Standard time, because it's hard to make proper accounts of heroic deeds when you're curled up sobbing in your sleeping bag, wishing you hadn't chosen this trip to cut back on the junk food, and that you had more than a slowly decomposing fruit basket to tide you over until your inevitable rescue.

Sir Banana, in the meantime, had gotten back to the Pudding Queen's palace, but the slaughter had already begun. The grape-pages in their cheery green frocks lay gutted and sucked dry at the gates, and all that remained of the strawberry-maids were their leafy scalps. Sir Banana charged for the throne room, blinded by tears, praying that Sir Milk had not yet reached the Queen, that all hope was not yet lost.

The Pudding Queen, fortunately, had never been the defenseless sort. She had trained in knightcraft in her youth, and wore her own sword, because this story is for Tilly and she deserves role models. She had barricaded herself into the throne room with her bodyguards, which were, let's say, blackberries with ninja skills. Sir Banana came upon Sir Milk and his minions outside the door, fashioning a battering ram from a partially dismantled feasting table.

"Sir Milk," Sir Banana growled, drawing his sword, "What madness is this?"

Sir Milk had changed from the knight Sir Banana remembered. His eyes sagged, and his white livery had crusted around the edges, and he had begun oozing from every crack and crevice. Sir Milk grinned. A rancid froth bubbled over his lips. "Haven't you heard?" The old knight spat the foam upon the floor, where it held its shape, and writhed minutely. "God is hungry. If we do not slake His appetite, He will consume us all."

Sir Banana knew then that the Voice of God had spoken truly. "Sir Milk," said the good banana, "you have lost the way of righteousness, and I mourn for you. It is not too late to repent of your ways. Throw down your weapons, and even now you might be redeemed."

Yes, I realize Sir Banana sounds pretentious, but go with it. Lawful Good types are all the same, much like bananas.

Sir Milk's laughter turned into wracking coughs, and more foam bubbled over his armor. "Nay, Sir Banana, I mourn for *you*. For you have not yet begun to learn your hardest lesson, and in the days ahead you will have to reckon with the truth."

At this, Sir Banana knew that Sir Milk was truly gone. He raised his sword and charged at the corrupted knight.

The battle that ensued was messy, to put it lightly. Sir Banana came through with just a couple of dents, nothing serious. I tried to clean up the milk spills afterwards, but some of it must've leaked between the floor panels, because the whole ship reeks of Sir Milk now. Anyway, Sir Banana got his kill, and I ate all the grapes and strawberries, so we both came out ahead.

This isn't going to pan out if I keep losing characters at this rate, not to mention the ones I'm eating between scenes. I had to skip the whole interlude with the papaya. But we haven't heard the last of Sir Banana, don't you worry. I just have to rehydrate, try the emergency signal again, curse God, and get some sleep.

If the energy drinks will let me sleep, that is. I'm glad to have a near-infinite supply of liquid, but I wish it were just apple juice. I haven't lived on this much caffeine since pilot school, and never on an empty stomach. Perhaps the energy drinks will burn a hole through my stomach. Perhaps they'll burn a hole through the universe. After three nights without sleep, you start to hallucinate, and I'm almost there.

Maybe I'll finally get some damn answers to my prayers. You hear me, God? I'm coming for you, you hungry bastard.

Shall we return to Sir Banana? Tilly would love him. She'd want to hold the Pudding Queen during the scary parts. She'd make me promise that it ends okay.

So for Tilly's sake, I promise you this much: this story will have a happy ending for at least one of the characters. I just don't know which one.

Sir Banana's troubles didn't end with the slaying of Sir Milk, because even though the evil henchfruits were scattered, Sir Banana didn't understand what had caused Sir Milk's corruption to begin with. And while there was peace for a time in the Pudding Queen's castle, rumors began to filter in that the corruption hadn't just been contained to Sir Milk's uprising.

And so the Voice of God came again upon Sir Banana, saying, "Sir Banana, faithful and true, take up your sword and ride to Lady Orange's keep, and root out the corruption you will find there. For Lady Orange has drunk of the teachings of Sir Milk, and become furred over with sin, and if her wrongdoing is not contained, it will spread for certain throughout the Fruit Kingdom."

This saddened Sir Banana even more grievously than God's command to kill Sir Milk, for Lady Orange ruled the fiefdom where Sir Banana had grown up, and he had often visited her keep for festivals in his youth. It had been Lady Orange who had plucked him from his bunch upon the strength of his potential so long ago.

But Sir Banana was a pious banana, faithful and true, and the Voice of God had never steered him wrong. So he said, "O Lord, your commandments weigh heavy upon me, but if this is the adventure you have sent me, I will take up my sword and follow it to its end."

The Voice of God did not answer, so Sir Banana assumed his quest was set. In truth, the Voice of God was clutching both sides of the ship's toilet and puking up bright blue goo, his arms shivering uncontrollably, wondering if he was running a fever. But Sir Banana didn't know this, so he rode out from the Pudding Queen's castle. His armor shone pure gold, smattered with just a few brown age spots.

At this point, I think Sir Banana deserves more of a backstory, since we're riding through his hometown and all. Maybe there were two other siblings in his bunch. Maybe one of them still lived on Earth, and the other had joined the military and gotten himself posted to the Moon along with his husband and daughter Tilly. Maybe that's why Sir Banana chose the itinerant life, always between places, never part of one, just the vast empty void spangled with stars. I bet he loves his family quite a lot, far more than they realize, even if he's always missing birthdays and anniversaries and whatever's equivalent to Christmas if you're a fruit.

So when Sir Banana got to Lady Orange's keep, his heart was full of all those treasured old times with his bunchmates, the games they used to play swinging into the moat on a hot summer's day, and how they'd dare one another to sneak into the kitchens for a snitch of sweetcake when the cook's back was turned. And so you can imagine his devastation when he reached the door and found the old Cook herself, a large round mature orange, slumped over while blue fuzz crawled up a giant bruise on her temple.

"Cook! Oh, Cook!" Sir Banana fell to his knees and cradled the dying orange. Sticky juice trickled from her wounds and stained his livery where she touched him.

"Is that you, Small Banana? All grown up! But I fear you have come too late." Cook coughed, and something white fizzed from her mouth. It reeked of Sir Milk. "You will find nothing but corruption in the keep. For four days now, it has spread among all the oranges, and the retainers too."

"And what of my bunchmates?" Sir Banana asked, a bit selfishly, but you can't blame the guy. "Are Plantain and Big Nana alright? Did they get out in time?"

But Cook's eyes had lolled back and closed. Sir Banana wept. So did the Voice of God, because he had been saving that orange, and hadn't noticed the mold until it was too late.

Sir Banana charged into the keep to rescue any survivors. Unfortunately, I nodded off for a split second, and missed some of the action. I'd planned this epic battle between Sir Banana and a hammer-swinging plum, but I accidentally ate the plum before he got there, so we can skip right to the part where Sir Banana sobs over the empty peel of his sister, Big Nana.

You see, whatever corruption that had struck down the noble House of Orange had indeed spread thoroughly to the whole bag, the blue-green mold crawling thick in the shadows where it was hidden from sight long enough to infest every nook and cranny.

This is also an accurate description of what I found in the bottom of the fruit basket this morning, but I'm trying not to think about that.

At long last, Lady Orange rose from her bedchamber, dressed all in blue-green and crowned with a halo of white mold. "Sir Banana," she said, "this display of emotion is unknightly, and does not become you."

"Please, Lady," Sir Banana sobbed, "do not deny me my grief. For I loved my sister, and I am deathly afraid of what has become of my brother Plantain."

"Peace, little one. Time has run out for your brother. His peel lies in the room beyond. There is time yet to change your own fate," she continued. "You are golden, in your prime, ripe for the plucking. If you turn away from the Voice of God now, and cover yourself in my mantle, even now you could be spared. For God is hungry, and He comes for all in the end, save for those too foul to pass His lips."

Sir Banana's stomach turned at this monologue, and so did the Voice of God's, who had to take a quick swig of the energy drink to keep the plum down. "You have lost your mind, Lady Orange," Sir Banana said. "What pulled you off the path of righteousness?"

"Sir Milk spoke the truth," Lady Orange said sadly. "God will come for us all in the end. But we can choose the order."

She toasted Sir Banana with a mold-covered chalice, and only then did he perceive its true wooden shape. It was a banana's stem, torn off from the peel. And so he knew his bunchmates were indeed gone from this life, and a red madness descended over his vision, and he charged the Lady Orange. His blade sank into her bulk all the way to the hilt, and Sir Banana had to let go, lest the thick mold creep up and touch him, too. But though he had fulfilled the Voice of God's command, the worst was still ahead, because the corruption had already spread much farther than Lady Orange.

We'll leave the Fruit Kingdom there and give them a chance to bury their dead while I sort the moldy blueberries from the okay ones. Sure, it's not my best work, but I haven't slept in four days, and I'm running out of fruit, so give me a break. And I've got bigger problems now, because the shaking isn't just from caffeine, and the sore throat isn't just from puking. Leave it to me to get strep throat on a space ship.

First aid kit? Sure, there's band-aids and aspirin and two little bottles of cough syrup I swigged down on Day Two, hoping for a buzz, but they don't stock penicillin for routine cargo hauls.

You know the level of tired when you start forgetting whether you're awake or asleep? The radios crackle on, and by the time I drag myself over to the comm station, they've all gone dead again. So either the rescue is underway, or I've really lost the plot. Tilly comes to visit me. She sits at the edge of my bunk with the Pudding Queen in one hand, begging me to finish the story, because she wants to know if Sir Banana will be alright in the end, if it ends happy like I promised. I keep waiting for God to turn up, but that's the one Voice that keeps to itself.

I have questions for Him. I have so many questions. For example, which character would God want me to spare? Or is He even more bloodthirsty than me?

So let's swig down the blue stuff that's killing or saving me, and let's finish with Sir Banana once and for all, so we can finally pick a survivor.

Sir Banana, old and weary, rode through a kingdom bereft of its fruit. His livery was an aged brown and running to black, and his arm sapped of youthful strength, but his heart was stalwart and strong. He rode east to west, north to south, stopping in at familiar hamlets and friendly keeps and grand cathedrals. But everywhere he rode, he found only devastation. Where the peaches lived, he found only pits coated in soft mold. The apples lay dead and stripped to the core, and all that remained of the mighty Pineapple was her golden scale armor and spiked helm.

But Sir Banana was a pious banana, so he begged the Voice of God for an answer. "What has happened, O Lord? Where are my people? And where is the Pudding Queen?"

But the Voice of God did not answer, and Sir Banana did not know why. In truth, the Voice of God was having a very lively debate over whether it's talking to yourself if you're holding a brown banana to your ear, or just another form of prayer.

At last, he came to a strange green chapel set deep in the heart of a cool, green dell. And Sir Banana thought to himself, "This looks like a holy place to seek the Voice of God by way of vigil." But as he reached for the door, it opened of its own accord. A young knight with flowing brown hair stood before him, someone he knew well, for he loved her above all else in the world. Immortally young, yet old beyond the span given to fruit. God's chosen ruler: the Pudding Queen. And for the first time since the Voice of God spoke to him, Sir Banana was glad.

"You've come at last," said the Pudding Queen warmly. "Faithful and true to the end." She threw her arms around him. Her hands and livery were sticky with juice. He flinched back involuntarily.

"Are you well?" asked the Pudding Queen, searching his face with concern in her eyes. "Come inside, Sir Banana. You must be exhausted from your journey."

She led him into the cool of the chapel, which after the bright daylight was dark and disheveled, like no one had used it in many years. The whole place reeked of sticky-sweet death.

"My Queen," said Sir Banana, "this place has an evil sense about it. Let us leave at once."

"Nay, Sir Banana, for the Voice of God bade me come here," said the Pudding Queen. And as she spoke, his eyes adjusted to the dim. The debris was not old tree branches or furniture as he had guessed, but eviscerated bodies of pears, and plums, and persimmons, and kiwis—all the subjects of the Fruit Kingdom. And their Queen walked him toward the altar, where her sword leaned in a shaft of light, sticky with many juices and touched with blue-green fuzz.

"Sir Banana," the Queen asked, "why do you hesitate?"

"I am afraid, Milady," said Sir Banana. "I am afraid of what has killed my comrades. I am afraid it was you."

"You swore obedience to Queen and God, Sir Banana. Now come and face the adventure we have prepared for you." She pulled him toward the altar. Her hands dripped gore upon the floor. A sour smell swathed her like a cloak.

"Milady," he ventured, "what did Sir Milk do to you?"

Her hands clenched and unclenched, juice sticking the fingers together. "I did not know the meaning of the plague. I did not know why my subjects brought tales of madness in the wild, of fruits drained of their juices, and the blue mold spreading everywhere. But Sir Milk did. He knew. God will eat until He is sated."

Sir Banana's hand found the hilt of his sword. "Sir Milk was not to be trusted, Milady."

"Sir Milk heard the Voice of God, you know," answered the Pudding Queen. "But when he came to God, something went wrong. God could not take Sir Milk, because the evil festering in Sir Milk's heart protected him. God only eats the pure." She hefted her sword and ran the sticky blade down the altar cloth, scraping it clean of gore and mold. "If He judges us and finds us wanting, we can live forever."

It was then that Sir Banana knew Sir Milk had not been the source of the corruption after all.

She sprang upon the terrified knight with the full brunt of her young strength. Gouges opened in his brown livery, exposing the white flesh beneath his skin. Such pain no enemy had ever inflicted upon Sir Banana. He cried out. He grabbed her wrist with his shield hand and forced her sword away, but she bent and twisted like a green sapling.

And then the Voice of God spoke to him at last.

"Sir Banana," said the Voice of God, "deliver unto Me the Pudding Queen's life, and you shall fulfill your fate and save the Fruit Kingdom from corruption."

Automatically, he raised his sword to obey, but he hesitated. It was the same sword with which the Pudding Queen had knighted him in the bloom of his youth. Sir Banana's heart ached, for he was a faithful banana, true to his oaths, true to his Queen. And so, for the first time, Sir Banana argued back.

"My God," he said, "how can I lift my sword against she who gave it to me?"

"Sir Banana," said the Voice of God, "deliver unto Me the Pudding Queen's life, and fulfill your destiny."

"Won't you answer me, O Lord, after all this time?"

"Sir Banana," said the Voice of God, "deliver unto Me the Pudding Queen's life, and fulfill your vow."

With a great wrenching thrust that snapped the withered twig of his left arm, the knight threw down his sword. "O Voice of God, I cannot kill my beloved Queen. Please have mercy upon her. Cure her madness and take me instead. Or let me die." He knelt and bowed his head, prepared to receive his punishment.

The Voice of God paused in thought. The story hung just like that, the pudding cup wedged between the red blinking commlink light and the battered black banana threaded through the ignition handle. The chunky old milk carton stayed in the useless fridge, but by this point you could smell it everywhere. The Voice of God shivered, coughed hard, and mopped dripping sweat from his temple with a damp sleeve. The Voice of God downed another blue energy drink that could no longer stave off starvation. God was hungry, and God was lonely, and God did not want to eat his only friend.

Are you with me? Are you still listening? Well, take courage. This story has survivors. Let's learn their names together.

The Pudding Queen woke to an empty kingdom. There were only the corpses of her retainers rotting on the floor, and the Voice of God, who was sitting on the steps beside her. He wasn't anything like she'd pictured him, not ruddy and round like a perfect grapefruit. He didn't look like a person at all, and He smelled sour, like He'd been keeping company with the dead. In one hand He still held the blackened, shriveled wooden stump which was Sir Banana's arm.

"Go ahead. Ask me," said the Voice of God. "It's okay."

There was only one question she had for God. It's the same question everyone has for God. "Why?"

"Because I was starving to death," said the Voice of God. "But please believe me: I loved Sir Banana. He did everything I asked of him. I thought, at the very least, I could do the one thing he ever asked of me."

"And what did he ask?"

God picked her up, and turned her around in His hands, which were warm and soft. "He wanted me to spare you. And he's right. You remind me of someone I know."

"So you ate him?"

God nodded, but it was an apologetic nod. "I'm sorry."

The Pudding Queen didn't say anything, because there was nothing left to say. Not all stories ended happily. In fact, most stories didn't, if you followed them long enough. But God was sad, and so was she, and there was a strange comfort just sitting there together—they who had enjoyed Sir Banana's unbroken devotion until the end, they who perhaps hadn't deserved it—and mourning for the dead.

Was that the ending you expected? Well, try on another: say I've been stranded in orbit for a week now, and death's just tossing the dice to decide which way I should go. If it should be the hunger, the fever, or the sleep deprivation that gets me first. And I've just eaten the banana that staved off the loneliness, so now that's a fourth option.

"Well, fuck it," I say, and begin to eat the corpses.

Under most circumstances, you shouldn't eat mold, of course. Maybe you'll luck out and get penicillin, but more likely you'll just get ergot poisoning. But I'm out of options. And anyway, if you can gross out God enough, sometimes that asshole passes you over.

There's a whole lot of blue mold to get through. It completely hollowed out several oranges, and it's working through the blueberries you discarded earlier. Tuck in. Go to town on that shit. Lick out the waste bin while you're at it. Suck up all the corruption back where it came from. Save the Fruit Kingdom from yourself.

Don't drink any of the blue stuff, though.

Are you full now? Sick to your stomach? Talking to yourself in the second person? Well, let's get some sleep. Let's queue up all the questions we have for God, in case we die in the morning, in case we go to heaven, in case He finally shows His face.

Then sleep. Sleep deeply and peacefully, the best sleep of your life, no dreams, no fever, no caffeine.

And the Voice of God finally speaks in a dream.

"About time, you asshole," I tell Them.

"Sorry," They say. "I was running late. Go ahead and ask your questions."

"Are you hungry? Are you lonely? Do you play with your food? Is that why we die?" God tries to speak, but before I let Them get in a word edgewise, I plow forward, "Are you a banana? A queen? A little girl? Are you telling my story, or are you the one I'm telling it to? And what about all those zero-calorie energy drinks? Was that supposed to be a joke?"

God holds up a hand. "Hold up. I'm glad you asked. There's a very simple answer that'll satisfy all your questions. The truth is—"

Before God can answer, someone starts cutting open the airlock, which wakes me straight up. So that bastard got off the hook again in the end.

But then again, so did I, and sometimes that's the best ending you get. One of the characters lives. No slaying the villain, no answers from above, no old banana gracefully browning into retirement. Just Uncle Danny trying to put a fine point on it, because Tilly looks up at me like I'm the veritable Voice of God, and she will have questions, and she won't let me off the hook so easily.

So I let it all go in the end, leave it behind on my space truck, along with the hallucinations and the weird stories I told myself to keep myself alive, pocket my uncertainties, hold my fragile faith in an open hand, and never drink another drop of energy drink as long as I live.

I take the pudding cup with me when I go, though. After all, I promised.

❧❧❧

Rachael K. Jones grew up in various cities across Europe and North America, picked up (and mostly forgot) six languages, and acquired several degrees in the arts and sciences. Now she writes speculative fiction in Portland, Oregon. Her debut novella, *Every River Runs to Salt*, is available from Fireside Fiction. Contrary to the rumors, she is probably not a secret android. Rachael is a World Fantasy Award nominee and Tiptree Award honoree. Her fiction has appeared in dozens of venues worldwide, including *Lightspeed*, *Beneath Ceaseless Skies*, *Strange Horizons*, and all four Escape Artists podcasts. Follow her on Twitter @RachaelKJones.

Of "Sir Banana", she says: "This story took six years to write. I first attempted it back in 2014. When I couldn't make the ideas of a space-trucker-knightly-banana-theological-parable quite work, I put aside the fragmentary draft and let it be. Then just last year, I realized the story demanded greater risk-taking and innovation in its voice to make the science fiction and fantasy components mesh the way they needed to. I rewrote the whole story in under a week, keeping exactly one scene from the original. What you see is the final result.

"I could probably talk forever about all the ideas and themes that went into 'Sir Banana.' I'll say here that for me, this story is about Mystery, and the lifetime quest to understand the Divine, no matter what form it takes."

What comes before

John Nadas

"I UNDERSTAND, HERR LEITINGER. You want to send us a thaumatic camera. For the last time, no," Brosz said. He waited, his sense of the other man shrinking in the quiet of the headset. He picked a pig's tail of cord from his cufflink a second time; he was used to candlestick telephones on small tables.

"Herr Dr. Brosz," Leitinger said, "Clearly, you don't understand. A thaumatic camera would produce efficiencies—"

"We neither need nor want one," Brosz said. He propped his elbows on Zenervic's desk. He stared at the photo above the mantel, at Ferdinand II's head, now bearded, and the diaphanous orbit behind. "Is my competence in question?"

"How can I put this?" Leitinger said. "Your institute will receive a thaumatic camera, along with a trained cameraman, next Monday. Morning, all being well. You needn't do anything. Inspector Zenervic needn't do anything. Not even paperwork. It couldn't be easier for everyone concerned."

"And what if we were to fail to cooperate?" Brosz asked.

"Erno," Zenervic whispered, learning forward and batting his cigarette box like a call bell. "Easy now."

"It is not for any of us to say," Leitinger said. "The law is not only quite new but also quite nuanced. Any result would be a matter for the appointed judges."

"I see," Brosz said. He moved the cord again. He paused, cooling the words in his mouth. "To be frank," he said, "I am disappointed. I had to cancel a session to take this call."

"We wanted to give you another opportunity to choose for yourself, Herr Dr. Brosz," Leitinger said. "I wish you the best. Goodbye."

Brosz eased the handset onto its body. He shook the inside pocket of his jacket twice. "Honestly, why ask someone to do something you know they won't?"

Zenervic slid his cigarette box at Brosz. "I couldn't believe it when I picked up," he said, "Like a choirboy." He shook his head. He rose and walked to the window. He licked his finger and touched a windowpane. He turned, leaning against the windowsill. "We could do with some radiators, Erno. New piping. Those books, for Meszmus. Didn't you want some easels?"

"Yes, yes, I know." Brosz peeled a cigarette from the box. He lit it with one of his matches; he hurt his thumb. "Give and take."

Zenervic nodded at Brosz and turned back to the window. "I sympathize. They don't see everything, up there. And you've a right anyhow. They should have consulted you."

"I guess so," Brosz said. He didn't know: the regulations changed every year or so.

"You do, Erno," Zenervic said. "Do you believe it? About the cameras, I mean."

"These thaumatic photographs seem to show halos." Brosz gestured at the emperor's portrait. "That much, I believe."

"I don't mean that," Zenervic said. "I mean the stuff about the future, what will happen to a man. All that."

"I don't know if it's true," Brosz said. "And nor do they." That was half the point, as far as Brosz was concerned. He joined Zenervic at the window. He saw a childish gong of a sun with childish clouds above, and below them half-children in uniform walking on a flat, green lawn. Peta Keppel parted from the other inmates, kicking high as he ran. Brosz watched as Baric waggled his truncheon and shouted words Brosz could not hear. Keppel knelt, raising his hands in inadvertent prayer.

"That one," Zenervic said. He folded his arms. "Meszmus says the boy can't even count properly."

"I know," Brosz said. When indoors, Keppel was shoulders up and chin down, deerish only in the way his head checked movements either side. Brosz trilled his lips at it all.

Zenervic sighed. "Anyway."

"Anyway," Brosz said.

෴

"Hell," Carteski said. He wriggled in his chair, spilling over it. His wrists ran aground on the summit of his belly.

Brosz motioned his pen behind his notepad. He hadn't yet written anything. "Are you uncomfortable?"

"No," Carteski said. His manacles clattered. "I'm dandy."

In their first meeting, Brosz had suggested that Carteski use two chairs arranged side by side, one for each leg. "Remember what I said about the chairs," Brosz said.

"And you remember what I said," Carteski said. "I shall not be subjected to the disgrace, the implied chubbiness and gluttony, of two chairs. One chair. And nice, like yours." He squinted at Brosz. "Two, indeed. I could not face myself."

Brosz valued when one part of a man led another to a public place. He did not value stalling. "Could we return to the issues at hand?"

"She was no innocent," Carteski said.

"She denied everything," Brosz said.

"And I keep telling you, she is as culpable as anyone." Carteski scratched one of his hands with the other.

"I see." Brosz checked the clock. Carteski had arrived four years prior, and Brosz had spoken with him many times. Their cyclic conversations bored Brosz, but they did not trouble him. To Brosz his work was as heaping grains of sand. A given session with a patient might seem similar to the one that came before it, but the spaces between the first and last man were often great. "Do you really believe that?"

"I suppose her seductive powers could have exceeded her," Carteski said. "Do flowers know their own scent?"

Brosz only thought about flowers when he thought about gifts for Agnes. He glanced at the clock's minute hand. "Herr Carteski, please save the poetry for your cell."

"Herr Dr., are you married?" Carteski asked.

Brosz hadn't expected the question. "Yes." His pen lay on a page, among dense bubbles budding from a central "Carteski." Brosz skimmed some words: *rational insanity, oft. now 'psychopathy.' Remains dangerous. Likely irredeemable, fancies himself.* The mysteries of Jan Carteski were to Brosz fewer than he had hoped: the man seemed mostly glass.

"What's her name?" Carteski asked.

"No names, Herr Carteski," Brosz said.

"Have you any progeny?" Carteski asked.

"No," Brosz said. He and Agnes had not been blessed, in that way at least. He would have said "no" either way.

"Shooting blanks, as they say?"

"No," Brosz said. Agnes had agreed no one was to blame.

"Are you queer?" Carteski asked.

"No," Brosz said. "Where is this going?"

"Alright, alright." Carteski grinned. "Have you *known* many women, sir?"

"Only one," Brosz said. It had only ever been Agnes. They had been neighbours in childhood. "And I do not regret it."

"Here is my point, Herr Dr. What do you know of women, their seductive powers?" Carteski batted his wrists. "Whether they know of their power or not, and I tend to think said power is active, rather like thought, say, whether or not, from the very littlest to the eldest, each woman harnesses it. The little ones are the best, you know."

Brosz underlined *irredeemable*. He allowed his pulse to recede. "Is that all you have to say?"

"Herr Baric would put it thus: she was asking for it, mate!" Carteski stamped his feet. "Whether she knew it or not. And either way, it's not like I could have behaved otherwise. You would not leave your dinner in care of a dog, would you?"

"You are not a dog, Jan," Brosz said, bringing the two men to their usual impasse. "You could have done otherwise."

"Can you cartwheel?" Carteski asked.

"Jan," Brosz said. He reached for his cigarette box.

"Can your nostrils help loving a rose?"

"Jan," Brosz repeated, opening his cigarette box. "Enough." He put a finger on a cigarette.

"Some men are made stupid, others are made intelligent," Carteski said. "Some can't cartwheel. Others have no nose. And some, they cannot resist the seductive powers of women. Would you fault an invalid for his lack of walking?"

"You know full well what I think, Jan. You do not want to believe it was really *you*. You're making excuses." Brosz lit the cigarette. He was certain: *irredeemable.*

"I've told you, Herr Dr. It's not that. I do not give a shit, as they say. I just do not care. Besides, I did not even fuck them all, did I?"

"You tried," Brosz said.

Carteski cocked his head. "What might have been." He shrugged. "I would have been a great man had I been."

"Very droll," Brosz said.

"Should we swap chairs and clothes next time, names even, in due respect of all we might have been?" Carteski said.

Brosz stood. He put his cigarette out. "Jan, it isn't the same. For one thing, rape is a crime—and wrong." He felt stupid having to say it.

"Could I have a cigarette?" Carteski asked.

Brosz did not even answer.

ഓരു

Meszmus was describing a new way to teach inmates arithmetic.

"I see," Brosz said. They were seated in a row of chairs. He fought to see past the other man and listen. Meszmus' new moustache, and his nasal hairs, cried for a wetted razor.

"One hundred cards, each with a number. I set a number. I deal five cards to each player at the start of each turn, at random. I reveal new cards from the deck one by one, lining them down the middle of the table. The winner is the first man to produce a set of seven cards the sum of which is the number I called, by way of any combination of the four basic operations. They seem to enjoy it," Meszmus said.

"I see," Brosz said. "Not exactly a game of skill, then."

"There is much skill in making the best of what one has." Meszmus rubbed his beard. "Don't you agree?"

Brosz would not be persuaded. "Do they bet?" he asked, before he thought it. He willed the cameraman's arrival.

Meszmus frowned at Brosz. "Of course not."

"I guess it's good for them, something with low stakes," Brosz said. He made a smile at Meszmus. He listened as Kropopin discussed some pornographic pictures the guards had confiscated earlier that morning: various young women in nothing but boas stood beside vases or other young women.

"Alright, Over Lieutenant," Zenervic said. "Don't ruin it for the rest of us. I'll rank the ladies myself, thank you."

Kropopin snorted. "Sorry, sir."

Baric and Ligovesc entered the room then. They had a trunk between them, which they lowered onto the floor.

A man stood in the doorway. "Thanks," he said. He walked in, removing his hat and cloak, and hung both items on the hat stand. He stood before the row of chairs and plucked one of his suspenders. "I am Erwin Sarvis, as some of you know. I am your cameraman. The purpose of this meeting is to demonstrate a thaumatic camera, and afterwards begin to instruct you in its use and upkeep, including the composition of the relevant chemicals." He opened the trunk. He removed a tripod, light, camera, cover, and metal plate, severally, uniting them in a metre-high structure. "May I have a volunteer?" he asked.

Zenervic raised his hand right away.

"Inspector Zenervic," Sarvis said. "Thank you."

Zenervic stood beside Sarvis. "No need," he said. "Alright." He brushed epaulettes with the backs of his hands. He corrected his collar. He removed his hat and balanced it on his forearm. "Where do you want me?" He looked at Brosz and rolled his eyes.

Brosz did not smile at the other man. He took out his cigarette box and matches.

"Please," Sarvis said. "The smoke would interfere."

Brosz nodded, resting the equipment on his knee.

Sarvis pulled Zenervic's vacated chair away from others and placed it near the camera. "People disagree about the workings of thaumatic cameras," he said. "Is anyone here familiar with mechanical thaumaturgy?" He paused for a few seconds. "Then I shall not bore you with the technical details, my friends. Inspector Zenervic." Sarvis pointed at Zenervic's chair. "If you don't mind."

Zenervic sat on his chair, adjusting it with his hands on either side of the seat. He twisted one of his cufflinks, then the other. He checked his collar again. He faced the camera.

Sarvis hid beneath the fabric cover, one arm exposed to the room. "If you could look the lens in the eye, Inspector."

Zenervic moved his head to one side and then back.

Sarvis counted from five to zero, fingers falling.

Brosz did not cover his face. He did not know to. The light chased him behind his eyelids, behind his hands. He closed his eyes several times; he rubbed his face.

"Is this normal?" Zenervic asked. "I can't see a damn thing." He coughed. "I need to be able to see, you know."

Brosz heard nervous laughter.

"It subsides very quickly," Sarvis said. "Usually."

Brosz could make out the form of a man moving to the trunk. The man removed something from the trunk and closed it. Brosz blinked, and all the colours and forms came into place.

Sarvis opened a pot and placed it atop the trunk. He dipped a brush in the pot, and used it to coat the metal plate. He produced a small pipe with a woman's face carved in the bowl and lit it; he nodded at Brosz. He bent over and inspected the plate. Then he offered it to Zenervic.

Zenervic examined the photograph and smiled. "I'll be," he said. He flashed the photo at everyone.

"Congratulations, Inspector," Sarvis said. "A lovely halo."

Zenervic pushed his seat back to the front row. He sat and offered the photograph to Brosz.

Brosz declined. He looked at Sarvis.

Kropopin poked Zenervic. "Let me see."

Zenervic handed Kropopin the photo.

"And that, my friends, is all there is to it. Cheap and effective. Efficient," Sarvis said, puffing on his pipe. "Each inmate shall be photographed twice. That's four minutes, more or less, multiplied by." He paused, fixing on Zenervic.

"Four hundred," Zenervic said.

"Well, there it is. I hope you feel better. I understand you were all a little reluctant when thaumatic cameras were first suggested," Sarvis said, clapping his hands together.

"We were?" Kropopin said. He surveyed the room, his chair squeaking.

"No, no," Zenervic blurted. "Not exactly."

Kropopin looked at Brosz and then Meszmus. "Chaplain?"

Meszmus detached his pince-nez and rubbed their lenses with a small rag. "I can't see any issues."

Brosz ignored Meszmus. "How can we be sure this camera does what you say?" He had first read about thaumatic cameras the year before. *The unqualified identification of good men.* He had been skeptical. *The pre-beatificative properties of the subjects.* "See," Brosz said. "I keep hearing and reading about these thaumatic cameras. But what do the halos mean, exactly?"

"I don't follow," Sarvis said, releasing thick smoke.

"What do they tell us?" Brosz asked. He lit a cigarette, then returned his box and matches to his jacket.

Kropopin asked, "Don't you read the papers, Brosz?"

"I do, Over Lieutenant. But I don't believe everything I read in them," Brosz said. "With respect," he added.

"The camera, Herr Brosz, i—" Sarvis said.

"Herr Dr. Brosz," Brosz said. It was the first time he had corrected someone in that way.

"Herr Dr. Brosz," Sarvis said. He rocked his pipe in one hand. "I needn't trouble him with the biology then, need I?" He grinned at Brosz. "But for the rest of you. When one opens a body, one finds in the darkness a conical organ somewhere between the lungs, below the heart. Our best minds agree that this organ, the *anima major* to use its technical name, the psyche to use its common one, responds to our actions and thoughts in certain ways. Roughly, what we call "sin" degrades the tissue of the *anima major*. The inventors of the thaumatic camera, myself included, supposed we could confirm the meaning of halos by comparing subjects' images to their psyches. We photographed over one hundred inmates in a prison in the capital, with each man either approaching death or awaiting it. Blackened, shrivelled psyches predominated among those men serving life sentences, and those we recovered from the gallows. And the vast majority of those men with damaged psyches, moreover, were haloless. A tight correlation between thaumatic images and psyches, in conclusion. And a link so much like a causal relationship that it *is* one, practically."

"But it is still not a causal relationship," Brosz said. He managed not to laugh. He looked at Zenervic and Kropopin.

"Ours is not a precise science, Herr Dr," Sarvis said. "And has psychiatry anything approaching such evidence?"

"I wouldn't like to say without proper rese—" Brosz said, wishing God had made him reckless.

"Judge not," Sarvis said, his beam fleeting. "And our sample is representative for your purposes, here," he said.

"We have four hundred inmates here, Herr Sarvis," Brosz said. "And only a handful near their end. Some are sixteen."

"Does a man really change all that much?" Sarvis asked.

"I should hope so," Brosz said. "Shouldn't you?" He put one hand over the other to stop them trembling.

"Very funny, Herr Dr. But I am not one of your prisoners. And we must ask ourselves, in the end, would your prisoners even be here if they were of good psyche?" Sarvis asked.

Brosz sighed. "Our boys—"

"Some of our inmates are rehabilitated," Zenervic said.

"And how many?" Sarvis asked.

"It doesn't matter," Brosz said.

Sarvis waved at the photo of the emperor suspended above the doorway. "Are you telling us, sir, that there is *nothing* whatsoever useful or predictive in these halos?"

Brosz shook his head. "No. No, of course not." He smoked two cigarettes one after the other and did not speak.

෨෬

"I didn't do anything," Keppel said. He pulled at the creases in his trousers. He sniffed, wiping his nose on his collar.

"Peta," Brosz said. "I know." He found Keppel as true as air or God. "But we need to think about what is best for you, here and now. Your appeal didn't succeed." Brosz had not even read the letter to the end. They were all the same.

"But it wasn't me," Keppel said. "I never met the guy. I don't even remember his name." Keppel rubbed his shoulder against a red patch on his bald, apple-less throat.

"You shouldn't scratch your neck, Peta," Brosz said. "Are you applying that ointment? Twice a day?" He favored Keppel, and did his best not to. He wondered if it was anything like being a father or uncle.

"Yes." Keppel turned his head away from Brosz. He inflated his cheeks and let the air out.

"Is there something wrong with the ointment?" Brosz asked. He scrawled a note in his pad. *Peta's condition continues to deteriorate. Possible excoriation disorder.* "Do you like the itching? Is that it? Do you like lying to me?"

"No, doc," Keppel said. "I just forgot, is all." He straightened, cornering Brosz's eyes with his. "Can I go yet?"

Brosz lit a cigarette. He thought about letting Keppel smoke one. He had allowed it twice before. "It is difficult, all of it." He took a long drag. "It is not your fault, Peta. Do you understand? Sometimes, things go wrong."

"I know, I know," Keppel said. "They said some guy will photograph me tomorrow morning." He kicked his heels together. "Why do they want to waste that money on photographing me?"

"A Herr Sarvis will photograph you, yes. His camera will help get you out of here," Brosz said, disingenuous despite himself. "Depending on what the photograph is like."

"Wow," Keppel said.

"Yes," Brosz said. He liked to see hope in Keppel.

"Does he do the camera?" Keppel asked.

"Yes," Brosz said. *Possibly an imbecile*, he recalled.

"Does he fix up the photograph too?" Keppel asked.

"He will make yours," Brosz said.

"Is he a Jew?" Keppel asked. He followed Brosz's cigarette with his head. "Can I have one, doc?"

"How should I know if he's a Jew?" Brosz said, ignoring Keppel's request for a cigarette. He frowned at Keppel. "What does that have to do with anything?"

"Well, you know," Keppel said. He shrugged.

"I don't know," Brosz said.

"They are against us," Keppel said. "And they lie."

Then Brosz did not care that Peta Keppel, *possibly an imbecile, certainly ignorant*, grew up on a potato farm on the eastern border alongside ten older siblings. "What a wicked thing to say, Peta. I had thought better of you," Brosz said. "There is neither Jew nor Gentile," he added.

Keppel peered at Brosz. "Doc, are you a Jew?"

Brosz put his hand to his forehead. "You've put me in a difficult position. If I were to answer, then I would treat your question with far more respect than it warrants. If I were to decline, then you would think me a Jew and refuse to answer my other questions to the best of your ability. Correct?"

Keppel scratched his throat on his shoulder again. He gazed at his shoes. "I didn't mean to play a trick."

"I believe you, Peta," Brosz said. He was sure it was a blind trap. He lit another cigarette.

"When did this guy get here?" Keppel asked.

"He arrived two days ago. He started yesterday. He will soon leave; he has trained some of us."

"How will it help me get out of here?" Keppel asked.

"It's complicated." Brosz was not convinced that Keppel would understand. "They say the photograph is special. It is meant to show if you are truly good or not."

Keppel asked, "And if I go to heaven?"

Brosz was surprised. "Maybe."

"What do you think mine will show?"

⁎⁎⁎

"That's forty so far. And only one of them with a halo," Zenervic said. He opened his cigarette box, setting it between Brosz and Kropopin. He made a mountain out of his left cheek with his tongue. "Damnit, only one. Can you believe it?"

"Keppel?" Brosz asked. He helped himself to a cigarette.

"No," Zenervic said.

"Mathas," Kropopin said. "I am trying to stop," he added, pushing the cigarette box towards Brosz. "Drinking also."

Zenervic laughed. "And eating? Fucking?"

Brosz didn't laugh. He wanted to quit smoking too. He lit a cigarette.

"Back to business," Kropopin said, his hands forming a small surrender.

Brosz nodded. He remembered Mathas confessing in their first session: to setting a street aflame when he was ten years old, to drowning his parents' dog, to murdering his best friend. He felt the twelve years since on his nose. Mathas was ready, Brosz was sure of it: another man. "I would have recommended we take steps toward discharging Mathas at next month's review," he said. He resisted any links with photos.

"Me too," Kropopin said. "His conduct is exemplary. Spotless bed, boots. The lot. And from what I understand, it was a scuffle. With his friend, I mean. Wasn't it?"

"Not exactly," Brosz said. He had discovered a thorough historian in Mathas. He saw Mathas narrating an old plan to bait a friend with money, to stab the friend in the neck in an event practiced many times over in a mirror. He saw a man who had known the beast. "He—"

"Anyway," Zenervic said. "Meszmus says the boy goes to confession each week. And reviewing his file, I would not have had strong objections to either of your recommendations."

"But, Keppel," Brosz said. He had thought about it all while Agnes slept. He had gone to their kitchen and taken a drink. "I would have bet on it."

"I know," Zenervic said. "Borond, Slibovic, Alberti, and Jenev, too."

Brosz sighed.

"Indeed," Kropopin said. He put his fingers on the cigarette box and then pulled them away. He got up, pushing the chair back, and walked to the window. "Sir," he said, "you might want someone to take a look at this smudge."

"They've none of them put a foot wrong since they arrived," Zenervic said. "You've had good sessions with each one, Erno? Your professional judgement?" He joined his hands.

"Very productive," Brosz said. "I believe they could be reintegrated one day."

Zenervic put his head in his hands.

Kropopin tapped the window and stepped back from it. "But who's to say, really? The reality is we can't be sure."

"Sorry?" Brosz asked.

"Come on, Brosz, even you and your damn couch," Kropopin said. "Remember Radchak. Pavescu."

Brosz lit another cigarette. Each man had killed within days of his release. "And the rest." He laughed, smoke vaulting high. "Only an idiot would seek a perfect system."

"Are you calling me an idiot?" Kropopin asked.

"No, no," Brosz said.

"I strive for perfection. And you should too, Brosz," Kropopin said, folding his arms. "In everything you do."

"Don't get holy with me, Kropopin!" Brosz said.

Kropopin wiped his brow with his hand and scoured the windowpane. "Maybe we should just keep them all under lock and key."

Brosz laughed this time, throwing his hands up. "My God, that really is moronic. These are lives, too."

"You don't have children, Brosz," Kropopin said, striding to the door handle and then turning to retrieve his hat. "With respect, you don't know what the hell you're talking about."

Brosz closed the door after Kropopin left.

Zenervic rapped his desk. "Erno," he said.

"What?" Brosz said. He realised he had only a bald cigarette butt in his fingers.

"From a purely administrative, statistical point of view," Zenervic said. "Erno, listen to me." He stopped and rubbed his face. He put a cigarette in his mouth. "God damnit, Erno. The government has sent more research through. These papers." He indicated a pile on his desk. "The evidence is robust. More, each day. See for yourself. Please. The victims. The time we'd save. The money! What if haloless men really are beyond redemption? Imagine the possibilities. You could help those inmates who really needed it, devote more time to them, set them free sooner." Zenervic closed his cigarette box.

"Permanent solitary confinement, based on a damn photograph? It's preposterous," Brosz said.

"And us making such decisions isn't?" Zenervic asked, cigarette unlit and rolling. "We're just men, Erno. You know, they've kept track of the work we've done here too. Compare all the numbers." He rested his hands on his desk, palms facing the ceiling. "Please."

෫෬෬

Brosz added another candle to the congregation. He knelt on the ground and made a cross. He put his hand on a nearby railing, pulling himself up. He saw a small head in a pew at the top of the nave. Its hair was much darker than his.

"Father," Brosz said as he sat next to Tapeki. It was the closest he had ever been to Tapeki. He saw hooks on the priest's collar. He had heard the other man was only twenty-five; the old priest had been ten years Brosz's senior. "I have some questions," Brosz said, nervous, aware they were theological ones: his faith lived in his chest.

"What can I do for you?" Tapeki said. He was fixed on the altar.

"Have you heard of thaumatic cameras?" Brosz asked.

"I have," Tapeki said. He placed his hands on the pew in front. "Rather too Swiss for my tastes, if I'm honest."

"We've been asked to use them," Brosz said. "Told, really." He wiped his palms on his trousers.

122

"You work in the institute, yes?" Tapeki said. "Youths and such, isn't it?"

"There is a youth section, yes," Brosz said. "My job, well. I'm supposed to decide if an inmate, and all our inmates have been convicted of serious crimes, horrible acts, may ever be released into society." He began taking out his cigarette box. He stopped, letting the box tumble back into his jacket pocket. "I've been wrong before, Father." He inhaled.

"We've all been wrong before," Tapeki said. He laughed. "God, wasn't that a priestly thing to say?"

"Yes, it was," Brosz said.

"What happens to the irredeemable ones?"

"These men, Father. They might have been hanged," Brosz said. "You must understand, it is compli—"

"You will not shock me," Tapeki said.

"They are transferred to one of several high security institutions. There, they are placed in complete solitary confinement, for the protection of other inmates."

"I'm sure," Tapeki said. He looked at Brosz and smiled.

"It is permanent," Brosz said. He looked away.

"I see," Tapeki said. "Eternal separation." He grinned.

"They say these thaumatic cameras can tell us if someone may be rehabilitated," Brosz said. "There is research."

"Is there now?" Tapeki sighed, drumming one hand on his knees. "They say many things about those cameras, don't they?" He stretched his arms. "Every year there is some new miracle pump. The idea that some have been chosen for salvation, well, that is fairly Biblical, which is to say about as much as most things the Church teaches. But the idea that we could know for certain who has been chosen for salvation by the Lord, that is something else." Tapeki paused. "Allow me to be priestly again. Isaiah says, *For my thoughts are not your thoughts, nor are your ways my ways.*"

Brosz leant forward. "And what does the man say?"

"I don't know. When I was younger, I was sure God had put each of us in place." Tapeki paused. "Not like chess pieces, mind. Nothing so crude or vicious as that. Suppose you are coming to dinner, and I know you prefer beef to pork—"

"No parlour games, please," Brosz said.

"Hear me out," Tapeki said, chuckling. "I could serve you two plates, knowing you'd freely choose beef. It's a bit like that, I used to believe. God put you here, knowing you'd choose salvation."

"But what if you only served pork?" Brosz asked, disoriented by the comparison between God and a dinner party host.

"Indeed," Tapeki said. "Or you didn't like beef, could never like it, even. Were born to hate it." He rested against the pew. "It's a funny one, isn't it? Anyway, I like Isaiah better. We must trust that whatever is, this big puzzle, is all for the good in the end," Tapeki said. He bowed his head. "It isn't very satisfactory, I know. None of it is."

"But what about the cameras, Father?" Brosz asked.

"How is your faith, Herr Dr.?" Tapeki asked.

"Look, I've seen my fair share of miracles." Brosz recalled his first, him a youth gawping at the sudden replacement of absent legs in the hospital bed opposite. There were atheists, Brosz knew, but he thought them lunatics.

"Well, it is very easy to believe God exists," Tapeki said, his voice newly angular. "But do you think He is fair?"

Brosz moved along the pew to the aisle.

"Pray with me," Tapeki said. "Please."

"No," Brosz said. "My wife is waiting."

℘ℭ℞

"I did it," Keppel said. He smiled, and then he shook the smile away from his face. "I'm sorry. I lied to you."

"Excuse me?" Brosz asked. He'd been doodling while Keppel sat, both of them silent: cones and boxes and Sarvis.

"I killed him," Keppel said. He moved in his chair.

"Has someone told you to say this, Peta?" Brosz asked, confident they had. "Is this because of the photograph? I saw your photo, and I must tell you that I am not yet persuaded—"

"No, and no," Keppel said. He closed his eyes.

"But they didn't have any evidence," Brosz said. "Not really."

"It doesn't matter," Keppel said, voice smooth. "I did it. I also cut him open, from the neck, you know, like a pig. His cone, it was all black. I cooked it later. I still don't know how you all caught me. I don't live in that village. I had never been there before, either. I was just doing pilgrimage. I did a woman too. You all don't know that."

"That is very inventive, Peta," Brosz said. He consulted his notepad. *Peta still struggles to recall his childhood, unclear if trauma or inability to retain the information,* he read. *Peta seems out of time, effectively: cannot think backwards or forwards. N.B. This state may be good for Peta.* Brosz went back further. *Subject Keppel extremely diffident.* "They didn't catch you, Peta," Brosz said. "Not exactly. One person in that village described you, and poorly. Your advocate should have worked harder. Who told you to confess?"

"Nobody," Keppel said. "Nobody. I did it."

Brosz raised his eyebrows. He fumbled with his cigarette box. He picked two cigarettes, offering one to Keppel. "Calm, Peta. I need you to explain to me. I don't understand."

"Doc, I did it. There is nothing else to say." Keppel took the cigarette from Brosz, like water from a pump, and bit its end. He moved the cigarette to the centre of his lips. "I've killed three people in all. I'm sorry. I've been pretending to you. I'm sorry for that, too."

Brosz lit both their cigarettes. "Peta, this is nonsense. You don't even like it when someone kills a fly." He realised he believed Keppel was telling the truth. It was strange, like rolling through a familiar landscape only to see the trees were stone towers. It was not like cartwheeling, he thought. He thought about the photo, the idle eyes and the naked head.

"I don't know why I did it," Keppel said. "I just did it, is all. It was like I was riding myself, like I was my coach."

Brosz asked, "What happened?"

"I said," Keppel said. He showed his teeth this time.

"Fine, fine," Brosz said. He decided to move things along. "The important thing is, where do we go from here?"

ℬↄℭ

"I didn't approve this," Brosz said. He watched Carteski and Keppel ascend a large truck, two guards behind them. The inmates were tied together with chains, along with others too dark to see. "They just need more time. There have been some promising developments." Brosz paced, running a hand through his hair and pulling at his moustache. He neared the truck and pinched one of the guard's sleeves, holding onto the cloth.

The guard put his hand on Brosz's chest.

"Erno," Zenervic said, "Let it go." He walked up to Brosz, a cigarette outstretched. "There's nothing you can do. Let's go and talk about something else, anything else."

"No," Brosz said. He turned to the guard who had touched him. "Give me your keys."

"What?" the guard said. He smirked at his colleague.

"Give me your damn keys," Brosz said, pushing the guard. "Now." He pressed his hands against the guard's chest.

"Erno," Zenervic said, interceding between the two men. "Are you fucking crazy? Stop it."

"It's not fair. They needed more time. Would you call a race before the horses ran?" Brosz paused, awaiting any changes in mood or intention in

Zenervic. "A favour, Siggy. My first and only," he said, exhausted. He stepped back.

"Damn you, Erno," Zenervic said. He turned to the guard with the keys, smiling, near making to pat the other man on the back. "Listen, son, just give him the keys."

The guard looked at Zenervic.

"That's an order, Private," Zenervic said.

The guard unslung his rifle. "Please, understand, Inspector. And whoever you are, sir," he said to Brosz. "I am under orders from Chief Inspector Kovak and, naturally, on the authority of his imperial majesty, Ferd—"

"Jesus Christ," Zenervic said. He pushed the guard's rifle barrel to one side and reached for the keys. The guard didn't stop him.

Zenervic gave the keys to Brosz, and Brosz opened the back of the truck. Brosz started on Keppel's ankle shackles. He missed the keyhole the first time. He tried a second time, but he dropped the keys. He was shaking.

Zenervic helped Keppel down. "This is ridiculous," he said. He checked the buckle on his pistol holster.

Keppel looked at Brosz and Zenervic. He walked back towards the institute. Then he started running.

"Maybe," Brosz said. He started on Carteski's shackles. He had stopped shaking. He could feel the water on his face.

"Always knew you were queer," Carteski said. "You couldn't bear the thought of me leaving. Is it love?"

"Shut up." Brosz shoved Carteski to one side. "The others, quick now."

"All of them?" Zenervic said. "Erno, I'm sorry. But I don't even know who's in there." He stepped back, removing his cap and batting it against his leg. "Could be anyone."

"It doesn't matter," Brosz said. He wiped his face; he felt like he was full of coffee.

"Turn off the engine," Zenervic shouted.

℘℩℧

"It has been some time, hasn't it? You look well, Herr Dr. Brosz," Sarvis said. He played with the thaumatic camera's lens. He put a hand on one side of his shirt and then moved it away. He nodded at the guard, who left the room.

"Thank you," Brosz said. He shifted his legs. His wrists and palms pressed against each other. He disliked the heat too, the dark red walls: the impression of a vast being's mouth. "How is Sigmund Zenervic?" Brosz had prayed for Zenervic. He had not seen him since their arrest.

"Inspector Zenervic is fine, and has even retained his rank. We had his photograph. There was also some clemency, as in your case," Sarvis said. "His imperial majesty can be sentimental." He smiled. "But yourself, Herr Dr. Brosz. I am afraid we do not have a photograph."

"No, you do not," Brosz said. The guards had offered to take his picture several times, and after that it was compulsory.

"It is the fashion to smile these days," Sarvis said.

"It is quite strange," Brosz said. He thought about Agnes. "Could you send it to my wife?"

"I'm sorry?" Sarvis said.

"She wants a photograph of me," Brosz said. "She has another, but it's years old. More than ten."

Sarvis was solemn. "Are you sure?" he asked. "You will not be able to see her for a long time, I imagine. You will not be able to explain to her, if—"

"Quite sure," Brosz said. He filled his lungs; he tried to conceal his handcuffs.

Sarvis took the photograph.

Brosz heard Sarvis brush the metal sheet.

Sarvis pressed the sheet into Brosz's hands. "There."

Brosz felt the photograph. He blinked, looking at Sarvis' face. "Quicker now," he said. "Purple gone already." He covered the picture, thrusting it at Sarvis. "No need."

&)Q

John Nadas is a European writer based in Victoria, Australia. He is interested in Australian and European settings, as well as universal themes. Conversations about God, fairness, and fate inspired "What comes before." How can we reconcile choice with grace? You can find him at johnnadaswrites.com or on X @JohnNadas.

Michael

Em Liu

Michael

HE'S AT THE train station when he sees her again—the girl from the archangel grotto.

She had found him lurking in the grotto a month ago, in the free hour between his Tuesday afternoon philosophy seminar and his weekly consultation with Father Kellegher.

The grotto is a secluded thing, nestled into the side of the sea wall, where the mangrove roots and living concrete have grown together and carved out a nook. Amidst the trees that protect the sea wall from the relentless beat of the swollen ocean, he finds a respite from the empty Human eyes, the cacophony of their voices, and the coldness of their company. In the grotto, it's just him and the statue of the spear-wielding archangel, with whom he imagines a kind of kinship.

On his very first visit to the parish, Father Kellegher had given him a St. Michael medallion stamped with an inscription:

> *At that time there shall arise*
> *Michael, the great prince,*
> *Guardian of your people.*

He keeps it in his pocket and feels for it whenever his courage fails him. A reminder that one needn't be Human to be a Saint.

He hadn't heard the girl coming down the path until she was almost upon him. She had obviously not having expected to find the grotto occupied, much less by an alien sitting still enough that an iguana had slinked up next to him, its tail curled into his lap. Her gasp had sent the creature skittering for the tree cover, and for a long moment, they'd stared at one another. Finally, the learned habits of the last two years had kicked in, and he raised a hand, but not before she'd fled.

He's seen her a few times since then, around the parish grounds, but they've never spoken. He never speaks to anyone unless spoken to.

But now she's here, running for the local train. The doors bar themselves against her protests and the train pulls out of station, leaving her at the edge of the platform.

He had been standing there himself until the shriek of incoming highspeed had sent him skittering back into the shadows, like a terrified iguana, watching as the passengers offloaded, the air bubbling up with their noise as they made their way to the station terminal.

Now the station is silent, save for the creak of the wind through the faux-teak roof and the sound of the rain as it continues to beat down on the tracks. It's also empty, except for him and the girl.

She glances over her shoulder, and he sinks deeper into the shadows. But she isn't looking at him. He follows her gaze to the timetable hanging over the platform:

PLATFORM 1: PALM BEACH — 10 MINS

The wind pulls at her dark hair, straggly from the wind and mist, and he wonders why she hasn't put it back, the way he has seen other Humans do.

The girl creeps closer to the edge, ignoring the official yellow line painted on the Chattahoochee platform. Her shoulders tighten when the automated warning reminds her to *Please Stand Back*, but she ignores it and kicks at the Chattahoochee, spraying pebbles down onto the tracks below. In the rain of pebble on rock, one lands with more music than it ought to.

She squats, peering into the track bed after whatever it is that she has kicked.

He feels into his empty pockets.

The girl glances up again at the timetable.

PLATFORM 1: PALM BEACH — 8 MINS

She jumps and lands with a crunch in the rocks that set the rail.

In another moment, she's hauled herself back up to the platform, the muscles in her arms flexing. He knows when she's seen him because her eyes go wide.

He's not the first Sojourner to live here, or even the first to attend University. But there are very few aliens who venture ashore, and Humans do stare. A year of studying their expressions has taught him that it's often merely curiosity that lies behind the fixed eye, but the emotelessness of it will always discomfit him.

Another highspeed arrives one platform over. The incoming breeze pulls at the oversized coat shrugged about his shoulders. The sound of her footsteps is swallowed up by the rain and Human cacophony. Up close, he can see the light refracted in each droplet that clings to her curls.

"Excuse me, Friend." She holds out a closed hand. "Is this yours?"

He leans down, moving as slowly as possible. He is so much taller than most Humans, and this one is tiny.

She opens her hand and reveals the archangel medallion.

"I saw you." She swallows. "In the St. Michael grotto. My name is Beth. I'm the groundswoman at Our Lady of the Universe. The—gardener. Father Kellegher mentioned you. He said that you needed a sponsor for the Rite of Initiation."

She does not look frightened. But then, he might not know it if she did.

"You have no obligation." His voice rolls through the wet air, metallic and tangy.

The girl's jaw tightens and she takes a step back, though she does not drop her hand. "What is your name?"

"I have no name that I could teach you to speak."

"But I must call you something, if I'm going to be your sponsor."

His sponsor. Is she acting out of kindness—or religious obligation? He can't tell, and the loneliness of that overwhelms him.

"Thank you." He closes his eyes as he turns away, and the local train arrives.

"Michael."

He turns back. She's still holding the medallion.

He holds a palm up in the Human gesture of refusal. "My gratitude."

Peter

"She said yes," the alien says.

Peter Kellegher forces himself to remain serene as the words course through him. The Sojourner voice has a peculiar quality that unsettles the chest, as though the heart has skipped a beat and the lungs have squeezed shut a moment. After so many weeks of meeting with his new convert, Peter still hasn't accustomed himself to the sound of it.

Beside him on the garden bench, Peter's convert unfurls himself like a morning glory, the purplish-blue of his proto-feathers shining in the sun. He has no name, and a gentle prodding to select a confirmation name has thus far been fruitless. So Peter thinks of him as the Sojourner, or the convert.

They always meet outside when the weather is good, in deference to the Sojourner's cold-blooded nature.

Peter wipes his own brow, feeling, as always, a lingering vanity that his hairline should already be receding at his age. "Who has said yes to what, Friend?"

"Your gardener. The one you enlisted as my sponsor."

"So you have made a decision, then?"

The Sojourner nods. "My mother has agreed. Reluctantly."

"I'm glad." Peter fights down a swelling of pride. The first alien convert.

Of course, the Sojourner isn't really *his* convert. Just a young man with a strong draw to philosophy who had found his way to a fading, minority religion and asked for guidance.

The Sojourner shifts in the sunlight, unfolding his arms (or what Peter supposes are arms, no matter how much they look like the beginnings of wings). He spreads his shoulders, evolving before Peter's eyes from morning glory to heron. "Beth. What is she like?"

Peter thinks first of the grown woman—distant, skeptical of life and the world. He chooses, instead, to speak of the girl he knew. "She's like a light."

Seven years ago, when they had first known each other at university, Beth had burned bright. They were like twin suns, circumnavigating one another, wholly independent of any other system and yet possessed of the sort of gravity that drew friends. Peter has often wondered if Beth wouldn't have found herself also called to ministry, had she not suddenly dropped out—burned out.

After University, she had taken the quietest jobs she could find and leaned on him with dark, dead mass. Last year, she had stopped attending services altogether, lingering around the parish grounds, a lost soul he couldn't reach.

A sponsor is supposed to be someone in good standing with the Church, a practicing Catholic. But let no one say that Peter is not ambitious.

"She will make a good sponsor for you, Friend."

"Michael."

Peter frowns. "I'm sorry?"

"Beth called me Michael."

Peter thinks that it might be wonder he hears in that unfathomable voice.

Aphrodite

She had known that her partner was different, when they decided to spend the rest of their lives together. It hadn't bothered her then—his restlessness, his desire to explore, his always-looking-up-to-the-sky. It had charmed her, to be a source of stability to one who was always wandering, the star to his far-flung satellite.

His strange affliction had been an advantage aboard the Sojourner ship. There had been a higher proportion of afflicted individuals among those who volunteered to leave their world. The mad ones had thrived in the adventure, and their spirit had kept the quiet desperation of the others from boiling over.

Finally they found it: a mid-sized planet in the habitable zone of a mid-sized star system, protected from meteoritic threats by the outer gas giants, and—most important of all—blue.

When they first arrived, the Human linguists had made valiant efforts to learn the Sojourner language, subjecting themselves over and over to the sickening sound of the infrasound voices. But in the end, it had sufficed that the Sojourners were perfectly capable of learning English and Chinese and French, the languages of their governments, and Latin, a language of lingering importance in their laboratories and their cathedrals.

She chose the name Aphrodite for the *Venus de Milo.*

The Louvre was an intimidating building, both ancient and space-age. In the early years, they were dragged all over the great temples and art museums by the Human ambassadors. Operas and symphonies were too grating on Sojourner ears, the stage and the novel too reliant on Human words. But imagery—that was something her people understood.

She especially enjoys sculpture. She could never see anything but flatness in their paintings, but one could move *around* a sculpture, could take in the amount of space it takes up.

In a hallway lined with Aphrodites, the *Venus de Milo* is her favorite. There's a perfection in her brokenness, an unselfconsciousness in those sloping shoulders, and she sees herself in the Greek goddess of love, repurposed for a new people. Perhaps this goddess, too, had only ever wanted a warm hearth with partner and son, to stay with her, orbit with her.

But the warmth of that nest had been a slow boil for those with the madness gene, and for her partner, it had turned unbearable. The monotony turned him from a thriving planet to a dead rock that could not reflect light, no matter how brightly a hearth she burned, until finally that strange sickness had taken him from her altogether.

She hadn't worried at first when she lost track of her little one, believing him to be somewhere in their company. It was only once back in the entrance hall that she realized her son was missing. Panic rose to think of her child lost in this endless Human labyrinth.

My son—my son is gone, the little one who was with us.

The Humans had stood around looking concerned but confused, scientists and politicians glancing nervously at one another in their uselessness.

The Humans had weapons. Weapons they had made a point of displaying before they realized her people had come as refugees and not as warriors. What if her son had somehow slipped the confines of the building altogether, and was now lost, wandering the streets of Paris, a multi-million-metropolis of unpredictably violent humans?

But they wouldn't harm a child. They wouldn't harm a child. They wouldn't—

She startled to be touched, but the Human man who had startled her held out an open palm. Even in her panic, she understood he meant *peace*.

The man nodded, and she had understood that here was a Human whose mind was etched in a different way. This one was a parent, too.

They made their way back to the Hall of Italian Painting, the last place she remembered feeling the gentle tug of her son's mind, the childlike desire to linger. They found him in one of the large inner chambers, leant up against a barricade and gazing with all the power of his young mind at Da Vinci's *Mona Lisa*, waves of contentment rolling off his feathers like water droplets. He had turned when they entered, his joy at seeing his mother turning to fright when he registered her anxiety.

It was then that she knew her son was exactly like her partner.

Michael

"What is your real name?" she asks him again.

The retreat center is styled in the old Japanese tradition, and they sit with their limbs tucked beneath the kotatsu, quilts piled up into their laps. His Aquinas philosophy is spread open on the low table between them, talons holding the pages secure in the sea breeze that floats through the open door.

"Michael is my real name."

She raises an eyebrow at that. Then she shrugs with one shoulder and reaches to steal a blackberry from the bowl set between them. "But it's not what you've been called your whole life."

He had not partaken of the Human supper of boxed sandwiches with the rest of the Initiation candidates and has instead set himself up with a meal of lychees and blackberries. Beth seems to like these better than her sandwich too, although he notices that she peels the lychees before she eats them, her fingernails a vivid pink.

"I have told you," he says. "I have no name I could teach you in any Human tongue. It does not require a tongue, you see."

She rolls the fruit between her fingertips. "Please tell me anyway?"

Slowly, he reaches out a hand and touches the elbow nearest him. She drops the blackberry, and gently he closes his talons over the delicate Human skin, and he thinks in the language he has not spoken since he left the Rook.

Only his grip on her elbow prevents her total collapse. She slumps over the table, grimacing with nausea.

"Take a deep breath." He speaks as gently as his harsh voice will allow.

"It's beautiful," she whispers.

He releases his grip on her elbow. "I had not yet spoken."

"But I heard you." She pushes herself up from the table, and her eyes scan his face.

"I was only sharing a connection—speaking in an abstract sense. Thinking."

She frowns. "Is it true that Humans can't learn the Sojourner language?"

"I do not know."

"Can you teach me?"

He hesitates. The feathers at his neck slide over and under one another, and he touches the tips of his talons to the spot. "My people have integumentary sensor organs. Extremely sensitive auditory receptors—not unlike an American alligator. For us, proximity is sufficient, but you must feel the vibrations." He examines her face, which is still pallid. "You felt dizzy, did you not?"

"Yes. And sick." Her eyes are on his talons resting on the Aquinas. There is a sadness there he can see but cannot comprehend.

When she finally speaks again, it is only to wish him goodnight, and she disappears into her own room. He pushes back the feelings of regret as he burrows into his own futon.

෩ඬ

When he wakes in the middle of the night, he has the lingering sense that some noise or movement has roused him from sleep. Light bleeds through the faux-paper panels in the sliding door.

Beth is at the kotatsu, the Aquinas open on the table before her and her head cradled in her arms. When he enters the room, she stirs. She nods at the book. "I borrowed it to see if your philosophers had any answers. But they only put me back to sleep."

"Some nights the philosophers have wisdom that can illuminate the darkness." He rolls his shoulder blades in the gesture that passes for a Human shrug. "Some nights nothing can penetrate it."

She stands and pulls her jacket from the hook by the sliding door. "My dad used to tell me that the stars put things into perspective."

They lie on their backs on the beach, looking up at the sky. The sand is cold in the darkness, but the electric blanket wrapped around his shoulders keeps him warm.

"D'you suppose there are any more of us?" Beth asks. "Or is it just Humans and Sojourners and that's it?"

"There are others. There were never any others we could speak to, however."

"Really? Other intelligent beings?"

"Of a sort. They were intelligent, we think, but they were… unoccupied with their own intelligence. Or at least, unconcerned with ours. Humans are the only beings we ever found who were looking for us, too."

"Thank God you found us," she says, lying back in the sand.

"Yes," he agrees. "Thank God."

"It's lucky you can learn Human languages then, since we've so little hope of learning yours." Her voice has a new tone to it, brighter and clearer. It doesn't match her words.

He wraps the heated blanket more carefully about his neck. "Writing systems would have sufficed."

They fall into silence, absorbing comfort from the sky, until he convinces himself he can feel the motion of the Earth, presenting him the familiar constellations in their endless parade, the steadiness of which is broken only by the occasional shooting star or passing satellite.

"Have you ever used a Human name before?" she asks.

"No." His Human paperwork reads *extraterrestrial alien, student*. "But I like the one you have given me."

"Good. It suits you."

He lets the laughter roll off him in ripples, thinking of the archangel with his sword and shield. His people, cloistered in their little offshore tower, are nothing like warriors.

She props herself up on her elbow and leans over to look at him. The sand clings to her wide cheekbones, and her eyes reflect the starlight.

He mimics her position and reaches again for the warm inside of her elbow. The connection opens through that small point of contact, and when she doesn't pull away, he sends the words speeding up her arm for her heart.

Her eyes fly wide and come unfocused as her head tips back, scattering the reflected starlight.

And then she rolls over and is sick into the sand. After a minute, her coughs subside.

"Are you well?"

She nods, lies back onto the beach, her hands folded over her stomach. "Your name?"

"The name that you have given me," he says. "*Who is like God?*"

Beth

She may be the first Human stubborn enough to learn any of the Sojourner language, and for her this is a point of pride. For the first few weeks, the nausea is so bad that she is unable to hold herself upright for long, and so they practice in the archangel garden, where she can lean against the statue of St. Michael, nestled into the curve of his wing.

After a month, the nausea abates, and she can hold herself in a seated position—and her lunch in her stomach—while Michael speaks. Her body has made peace with the sensations, even if they remain too entropic for her mind to make sense of.

Within two months, she can identify his name—the one she has given him, translated into his own language—when he places his hand on her elbow and speaks. The first time she hears it, she looks up and laughs in astonishment. He makes an audible buzzing noise of his own, from the chest, which she supposes is laughter too.

He confesses his love of sailing, and so one day they rent a catamaran and sail out.

Beth sits out on the bow, her knees tucked up under her arms and her windbreaker luffing in the breeze. The netting stretched between the double hulls is an open weave, loose enough for a Human to push a few fingers between the scratchy ropes and hang on for dear life.

Michael stays in the semi-enclosed cockpit, with a space heater. The day is cool, and the dark clouds on the horizon promise rain.

Beth keeps her head turned toward the faint silver shoot on the horizon.

Faster and sooner and quicker, the Rook rises before them, until what was only a gleam five kilometers offshore is now a skyscraper that dwarfs the little boat. The Rook deserves every inch of its name: tall and imposing and a blinding blue-white, frosted in solar panels.

The onboard computer initiates the autopilot anchor assist, and the cat stills, steady despite the rising chop. All is quiet except the thunderclap of the blue-black water rushing between the double hulls.

Michael climbs out of the cockpit and onto the right hull of the bow. She picks her way across the net to him. "Can't we get any closer?"

He points to a red floater four or five meters leeward. "This is as far as we can go, without setting off any alarms."

She leans over the railing, aching toward the gleaming structure. "But surely your family wouldn't mind, if it's you?"

"My mother would alert the Coast Guard long before she knew it was us."

"Your mother?"

He nods. "My mother is the headswoman of the Rook. She cut off contact with the Human world when I was a child." He hesitates, then says, "I'm the first to live onshore in a generation. My mother has said that if I choose to stay, she will consider reopening communication with the Human world."

"And your father?"

"Dead. When I was a child."

"I'm sorry." She touches his arm gently, and the proto-feathers shift and slide.

He pulls away from her touch and hands her a pair of binoculars. "There are gears inside the main tower." He indicates the ring of mangrove trees that encircle the base of the tower. "When it was first built, sea levels were steady, but there was concern they might begin to rise again. The Rook can raise and lower the main level."

She follows his guidance with the binoculars. "There are no other boats."

"There's a transport vessel docked in an inlet, round the other side."

"Just one?"

"For emergencies. I am the only one who sails." The rain that has threatened all morning finally begins, and the patters begin to beat the water around them. "My mother tells me I am like my father. He would have liked sailing, too."

She lowers the binoculars and looks at him. "Is it that unusual?"

"My mother resisted my decision to go to University. She feared it was a sign of restlessness. She worried…"

Michael does not leave his sentences unfinished often. Beth has attributed this to the fact that he thinks before he speaks, but now she wonders if it isn't because this is the first time he has regretted speaking.

"That you would end up like your father," she finishes for him.

"Yes."

"Were your parents married long?"

"I suppose Humans wouldn't refer to our partnerships as marriage. There is no ceremony. I was young when my father died, but I remember the feeling of him—of our family."

"Mine felt like that too. Like a family. But my father was unhappy." She looks past Michael's tall shoulder at the Rook. "I miss him. It makes me wonder what might have happened, if he had stayed."

"Even love cannot stop someone, if he is meant to leave."

"No," she agrees. The rain falls harder, drumming pockmarks into the waves. Beth gives the Rook one last glance, then retakes her seat on the net. "Let's go home."

Michael

Human laughter had surprised him.

Not because he had thought them without humor, per se, but because the lonely nature of their language had not seemed to permit the existence of mutual mirth.

He was disabused of this notion his first day at University. A girl in his philosophy seminar had laughed, loud and high-pitched and changeable, like a mockingbird. The sound made the skin under his feathers tighten irritably, and it was several minutes—after the chortling had passed from student to student like a virus—before he understood what he had heard. Human laughter, he concluded, was unpleasant.

A week later, his professor had laughed at a student's joke about Kant's theory of the sublime, and the sound had been deep and rumbly, like the low roll of thunder on the horizon. He had only realized that this new sound was laughter too when the mockingbird-girl had shrieked again and set off the rest of the class.

Beth's laughter was something in between. It still put him in mind of a bird, but unlike the others' squawking animal sounds, it inspired laughter inside him.

Tonight, when they sneak down to the archangel grotto after the rehearsal for next week's Vigil service, she brings along a lunch box, from which she pulls a silver flask and takes a swig.

"What does it feel like?" he asks.

She swallows and looks pensively at the bottle. "Warmth."

His body cannot process alcohol, and so she's brought a Thermos of herbal tea for him and a tub of blackberries topped with sugared cream, which she sets out between them.

He thinks she smiles, although it's hard to tell in the darkness. She's nestled in the protective cavity of St. Michael's wing. A lantern at her feet throws feathered patterns into the darkness.

He holds out his hand, and her fingers slip with easy practice into his. "You do feel different."

She snatches her hand away. "I thought you couldn't read my mind?"

"I cannot hear your mind the way you can hear mine. But I can feel you."

She adjusts the lantern, throwing more of the light onto his face. "What feels so different?"

He hesitates, as if he's found himself waist-deep in dark water into which he'd never intended to wade.

She wraps her arms around her legs and rests her chin on her knees, waiting.

"Your heart rate, your breath, the electrical impulses in your nervous system—it is easy to tell when you are experiencing a strong emotion, such as when you are anxious, or sad. But tonight, you feel calm. I think, maybe, that you are happy."

"I am," she says. "I am happy."

"I can understand, then, why Humans enjoy alcohol."

She laughs, and he feels a thrill of success.

"I like being here," she says. "In the archangel grotto, with you. I like sailing with you. I'm happy because we're friends."

Tomorrow, he will go to his mother and tell her that he has made his decision. He will stay onshore, and the communication channels between their worlds will be opened once more. "I am too," he says. "I am very happy."

The light from the lantern dances in her eyes. They watch one another for several long seconds, until her cheeks redden and she drops her gaze, ducking her head so that the thick curls fall around her face.

He reaches across the lantern light and slides a hand beneath the dark curtain of hair. She doesn't pull away, and he lets his palm rest against her temple. Slowly, without breaking the connection, she lifts her eyes, and he sees the galaxies reflected there.

"Beth. Will you marry me?"

Peter

Of all Peter's regular confessants, Michael and Beth are the only two he never meets in the confessional. Michael, of course, prefers the garden; Beth he finds wherever she happens to put her feet up, usually somewhere avoiding the main sanctuary.

This evening she's in the narthex, leant up against the cathedral-height windows with her knees gathered to her chest, gazing out at the electrical storm gathering over the ocean. Every flash throws the statue of Our Lady of the Universe in the courtyard into sharp relief, clear enough to count the twelve stars on the bronze figure's head. The flashes of lightning are the only light in the empty church.

She glances up at him and smiles softly. "Will you hear my confession?"

It's been a long time since she's asked that question. He pools himself onto the floor beside her and raises his hand for the blessing.

When she finally speaks, her voice is soft. "I think I've broken someone's heart."

He pauses, to be sure there isn't more, then says, "That's not, in and of itself, a sin."

"But how can it not be, when—" Her voice catches, and she claps a hand over her mouth.

Peter hasn't seen Beth cry in years. He sighs and looks up at the black beams that cut the cathedral windows into the quadrangles of a cross. "What happened?"

"He asked me to marry him." The words are flooded in tears.

"And?"

She lifts her head, and her face is tear-streaked and fearsome. "And what?"

"What did you say to him?"

"What *could* I say?" Her voice is all astonishment. "He isn't..."

"What? Capable of love? Worthy of it?"

"*Human.*"

The word hangs in the narthex the way that lightning lingers in a cloudy sky, and in its clarity he sees the truth in her face.

"Beth," he says, "Michael returned home. To the Rook."

She's wiping her eyes on the sleeve of her jacket. "But he'll come back. For the Vigil. The baptism."

Peter shakes his head. "There isn't going to be a baptism. Michael left me a note. He made a promise to his mother, that if life onshore didn't work out, that he would return to the Rook. For good."

Lightning flashes again, highlighting the tear tracks that stain her thunderstruck face.

"But—he has to come back." The color rises into her cheeks. "He was going to tell his mother to re-open the Rook. You have to tell him to come back! Call him back!" Her voice rings through the empty church.

Peter holds out his hands. "Beth. There is no way to contact the Rook."

His heart is breaking for her, but when the light flashes again her eyes are fixed on the sea.

"There is one way."

Aphrodite

It's been so long, she has to hunt for the word.

Girl.

A human girl, here in the Rook, hiding among the water boilers on the powerhouse level. She darts between the support struts and stops behind one of the larger boilers, as though any passerby could not hear the audacious hammering of her mammalian heart.

This, Aphrodite knows, has something to do with her son.

Her beautiful son who had sailed in from the coast only yesterday, reeking of misery.

The girl's breath comes in audible little puffs. Two of the engineers are nearby, occupied by maintenance of the storm drain, and Aphrodite signals them. When the girl moves from her hiding spot, they take hold of the intruder, one to an arm.

The girl screams.

The engineers let go in shock, like they've been burned. Aphrodite cannot blame them; her own receptors are still crawling with the reverberations.

The girl backs into a wall, arms outstretched and wide-eyed. Her hair is longer, wilder, than Aphrodite has ever seen on a Human. Rain and seawater cling to her hair, and the curls are heavy and lank with the water, like the rest of her clothing.

The girl's scream echoes through the halls again, and this time, Aphrodite realizes that the scream contains a Human word: "No!"

The girl squirms, as though the wall could somehow give way, absorb her body. She flinches as Aphrodite stretches out a hand but does not resist the touch of claws to her temple, and Aphrodite catches the limp Human figure in her arms.

ℴℴ

The girl wakes with a gasp and immediately begins to thrash, sobbing like a fish out of water. The two engineers are still at her side, one to an arm, their fingers wrapped gently but firmly around the girl's upper arms, restraining her movements and steeled, now, for the terrible sound of the Human voice.

"Why?" The Human word feels stale in Aphrodite's mouth, hard and crusty.

The girl's irises—a brown so dark they're barely distinguishable from the black of the pupils—are wide. She inhales shakily. "I need to speak with your son."

Her son. Aphrodite feels a frisson of fear. Was it not enough that they chased him back here? What do they want with him now? "Leave."

"Please." The girl is panting, squirming against her captors. "I just want to speak with him—and then I will go. I won't come back. I promise."

Someone summons her son from the upper chamber where he has secluded himself. He arrives in a daze that suggests he must have been sleeping. Gently, his sweet soul reaches out—*what is it?*

Aphrodite watches as he slowly takes in the surroundings: his eyes sweep the ceiling, the lights, the bench and restraints.

And then he sees the girl. His response is instantaneous and fearsome, incomprehensible but for the waves of anger that beat with the rage of some internal storm.

She has expected some reaction, expected that he will recognize this girl, but the intensity of the emotion surprises her. And then she understands that it is all directed at herself.

What did you do? His demand is formidable enough that the engineers back away again, their hands at their sides.

No harm. She speaks in a mollifying tone, surprised to find herself on the defensive. *I only spoke to her.*

His doubt comes across in thick waves.

Loudly, she admits.

From the bench, the Human girl sees him and struggles to lift herself. She desists when he presses a hand into her shoulder.

"Beth," he says in the Human tongue, "what have you done?"

"Michael. Father Kellegher said you had gone." The girl succeeds in pushing herself up onto her elbows. "Please... please come home."

His pain, as he turns his eyes away from the girl, is as excruciatingly exposed as his anger. Any ability her son had to hide his emotions—already so worn down from his time among the Humans—has disintegrated entirely with the appearance of this girl.

Then the girl grabs hold of his fingers and, incredibly, *speaks*.

Her words are nothing but gibberish. And yet they must make sense to him, because the anxious vibrations around him grow still. The girl's hand falls from his arm as he reaches out, brushes the dark hair back from her temples, and speaks into the Human skin the same gentle nonsense words.

Names, Aphrodite realizes. They have named one another.

Her confusion gives way to gentleness, and her son turns toward her, and she loves him.

"Mother," he says aloud, for the sake of the girl. "I love you."

She thinks of her partner, long gone, and her son, still here.

"Go home," she tells him.

⁎☽⁎

Emily Liu, née O'Malley, grew up in Palm Beach, Florida, and has lived in the American Southwest, the Midwest, New England, and Japan. Em now resides with her husband and three small kids in the greater Washington, D.C. metro area, where she researches financial systems by day and devises magic systems by night. Find more of her work at www.emliuwriting.com.

The Original Sin of William Blackhand

R. Keelan

IN THE EIGHTEENTH year of the reign of King Edward III, I witnessed a miracle.

I woke in the night, on the Monday after Martinmass, roused by a noise in the chancel. I reached out from beneath my blanket, searching for something to cover myself. My hand felt the cruel bite of November stone before closing over the warmth of rough wool.

Slightly warmer in my tunic and breeches, I pulled on my boots then stumbled to the squint. My room had once been an anchorite's cell; this small window overlooking the chancel was how the previous occupant had heard mass and received communion. She'd been sealed in and fed through an even smaller window on the other wall, but my father had torn the cell open when I grew old enough for a room of my own.

I should call him my foster father—an ostensibly celibate priest wasn't supposed to have a trueborn son—but I rarely bothered. No one in the village ever let me forget he'd got me on some itinerant friar's woman. He hadn't even had the decency to do it while he was still a soldier fighting the Scots.

I bent and peered through the squint. Only the altar was visible, dimly lit by twice-reflected moonlight. At first I saw nothing, shadows upon shadows in no discernible pattern. But one shadow moved relative to the others, and I realized there was a figure stooped near the altar, reaching into the reliquary.

I gave a great shout and rushed from my room. The door my father had added to the cell exited to the side of the church, and I hoped to catch the thief as he left the front. I crunched through the snow, glad of the boots I'd donned, rounding the corner just as a shadowy figure burst from the church's wooden double doors.

Some half-glimpsed femininity forestalled me from raising the hue and cry. I followed swiftly after her instead. Surely a girl wouldn't burgle a church.

She fled toward the river Ouze, which had frozen over during this uncommonly cold winter. She clearly intended to attempt a crossing, but that was madness. Even in mid-January's icy grip, the Ouze never froze solid.

I called out for the girl to stop, that the river wasn't safe, but she wouldn't heed me. I stopped at the river bank while she plunged ahead.

She made it less than halfway before the ice collapsed and she disappeared from sight.

Horror winged through me. The girl would surely die. I crossed myself, whispering hushed Latin: "Depart, O Christian soul, out of this miserable world, in the name of God the Father Almighty, who created thee."

I wondered who she was, then crossed myself again. There was only one girl I could imagine bold enough to burgle the church.

Elizabeth. My sweetheart from childhood, though she hadn't known it. She had an undeserved reputation for wrath and pride, which made her a perfect companion for me. Thanks to my father, I, too, owned undeserved ill-repute.

God as my witness, at that very moment, with Elizabeth's name still ringing in my ears, the girl rose up from the water as if spat by some great beast. Her path through the air was shaky and uncertain, like that of an injured bird. She landed on her feet, but slipped and tumbled over backward. Her head hit the ice with a crack I felt from the riverbank.

She had landed several feet nearer to me than the break in the ice. If it had carried her weight standing, it ought to support mine spread out. I threw myself on my belly and crawled toward her.

I eeled over the ice, surrendering my hands to the bitter cold of snowmelt against unprotected flesh. Ahead of me, the girl hadn't yet stirred. Had she been saved from the river only to die on the ice?

When at last I reached her, I saw that I'd guessed correctly. It was Elizabeth. The prettiest girl in the village—perhaps in any village.

I began dragging her back toward the riverbank, digging my palms into the ice to push myself backward, then pulling her forward by the wrists.

Inch by freezing inch, we crept toward land.

Elizabeth didn't react. I could only pray that she was still alive.

The skin of her wrists felt curious. Neither hot nor cold, warm nor cool, she seemed to have no temperature at all.

Perhaps that was what death felt like.

I shut my eyes, feeling tears push against my eyelids. I hoped not.

Elizabeth roused when we'd covered only a portion of the distance to the riverbank. Her eyes snapped open and locked onto mine.

"William!" she said, rolling onto her stomach and trying to stand.

"Don't!" I cried. "You'll break the ice. Crawl back. Like this." I pushed myself backward to demonstrate.

"The purse!" Elizabeth rose to her hands and knees and began crawling back out onto the ice.

I reached for Elizabeth's ankle and missed. "Come back! You'll catch your death out here."

"I can't," Elizabeth said without stopping. "I stole the purse, William. I have to get it back."

"What purse?"

The ice groaned beneath us. I should have kept going, but instead I waited, unwilling to abandon Elizabeth.

"I stole the Purse of Saint Nicholas," Elizabeth babbled as she crawled. "I only meant to pray with it, but then you caught me."

The reliquary. Our parish housed a purse said to belong to Saint Nicholas—most loudly by my father—but of course it hadn't.

"The purse is fake!"

Elizabeth had reached the break in the ice and begun searching. "The shock of the water brought me to my senses," she said. "I realized I'd sinned, and that I would die for it, but I repented."

I resolved to drag Elizabeth back by main force if necessary. I pulled myself forward with numb hands, feeling the ice and snow through sodden clothes. "The purse is a fake, damn you!"

Elizabeth wasn't listening. "I repented, William, because I did not want to die a sinner. I repented with all my soul as I sank into the river. And then I heard a voice, a stern voice. It spoke to me, saying 'Penitent, save thyself!' And then I was lifted"—she cried out, holding the purse aloft—"by this very purse. It raised me up out of the water to safety. A miracle for a penitent thief."

I almost sobbed with relief as Elizabeth began crawling back toward me.

I was shivering uncontrollably by the time we reached land. "You must be chilled to the bone," I said, helping Elizabeth to her feet. "Let's get inside. I'll start a fire."

"The fire can wait," Elizabeth said. "I have to return the purse first."

Hair was plastered to her face. Her kirtle, drenched, clung to her, icicles forming at its hem. I held my peace. If she could wait for the fire, so could I.

80CR

The reliquary was a copper-gilt box built into the church's small altar. Its front face was swung out on cleverly concealed hinges, the key poking out of the lock where Elizabeth had left it in her haste. She placed the purse inside more reverently than I'd ever seen my father do, then I closed the door. I tried turning the lock, but my hand was shaking too much.

"C-Can you?" I stammered through chattering teeth.

The hearth in the main hall was dead, the embers from Sunday having cooled to grey ash. Elizabeth knelt to light the fire while I sat wrapped in a blanket. My hands trembled too much to handle the kindling.

The purse was fake. My father liked to say there were enough pieces of the True Cross scattered across England to make a boat. And yet I had seen a miracle. I could not dispute it. I did wonder if perhaps Elizabeth was a witch, but I could not believe that of someone so kind and—if I am honest with myself—beautiful.

Elizabeth soon had a merry fire blazing in the hearth, to which I leaned perilously close.

"You'll probably want to tell your father I stole—"

"I won't," I blurted. "The purse is back where it belongs. No one needs to know."

Elizabeth looked over her shoulder at the reliquary. "He saved my life," she said softly. "I sinned, but Saint Nicholas saved my life."

Of course he did, I thought. He sees you as I do. But I couldn't muster the courage to say it.

❧❧❦

I developed a terrible fever after that night. I lay in bed for days, delirious.

I dreamt I was being interrogated in the Court of God, by an angel with the bailiff's likeness. He asked if Elizabeth was a sinner, and I said no, because I loved her and believed that good intentions were in her heart. Then he asked if Elizabeth had stolen the Purse of Saint Nicholas, and I said no, because she'd returned it.

Then the angel with the bailiff's likeness asked if Elizabeth had taken the purse from the reliquary, and I was faced with a question too precise to answer both truthfully and in Elizabeth's favour. I also knew it would be the angel's last. It was the third question, and three was the number of the trinity, the number of times Saint Peter denied our Lord Jesus.

My heart cried out to deny Elizabeth's guilt, to deny even the premise of the question—why did it matter if Elizabeth had taken the purse or not, if I'd already stated she was neither thief nor sinner?—but I was afraid. Afraid that

I would be judged untruthful, that my immortal soul would be damned in place of hers.

God forgive me, I told the truth.

ൠ

I was left bedridden and consumed with guilt. Unable to seek Elizabeth out, I hoped every day that she would come see me, but each new day brought my "foster father" and no one else. He was in my little room constantly, bringing hot broth for me to drink or heated bricks to warm my bed. And if not that, he was reading to me from the Bible or telling exaggerated tales of battling the Scots. I soon grew tired of his company.

On the first day I felt well enough to let my irritation show, I asked to go see Elizabeth.

My father looked back more kindly than I was accustomed to.

A shard of ice coalesced deep in my belly. "What?"

"You can't go see Elizabeth, boy. Don't you remember?"

I remembered betraying Elizabeth, but that had been a dream.

"There was a trial," my father said.

I listened with growing foreboding while he explained that a neighbour had seen Elizabeth's flight from the church, if not the drama on the ice that followed, and made an appeal of felony. An inquest had followed. The shard of ice in my gut twisted painfully. My dream had been fevered madness inlaid with true events.

"How could I have testified if I was so feverish I can't remember doing so?" I demanded.

"The bailiff came to interview you, at no small risk to his own—"

"To conduct a sham inquest!"

My father's only response was that same kindly, infuriating gaze.

"Where is she now? I want to go see her!"

"You can't, boy. She's already been tried."

"Then I'll go see her in gaol—"

"You can't, William. She's already been taken to York."

"But she only stole—and she returned it afterward. I said that, didn't I? That she returned the purse of her own volition. I told the bailiff that, didn't I?"

My father laid his hands on my shoulders. "Elizabeth demanded Trial by Ordeal, son. She failed. By now, she's already been burned as a heretic."

ൠ

Blackness engulfed me. Grief at Elizabeth's death broken only by guilt at the role I had played in it. I asked myself a hundred times why God would save Elizabeth from the river only to consign her to the flames. I came up with a thousand tortured answers, but settled on the simplest. God didn't exist, not in the way my father believed. He was like the weather, capricious and arbitrary. He neither loved us nor hated us, nor likely realized we existed at all.

I left England to join the Wars in France that spring.

ଚ୍ଚର୍ଷ

I took my father's old sword and hauberk, bought a nearly-lame nag from Widow Joan, and passed myself off as a man-at-arms, earning six sous per day in the company of Sir Henry Blackwaille. After the Battle of Caen, we pursued a French knight who hid himself among the brothers of L'Abbaye d'Orne. The knight's ransom was hundreds of ecus, but my pious countrymen, who in Caen thought nothing of murdering French burghers and raping their wives, now found themselves concerned with the fates of their immortal souls.

If I had an immortal soul, I knew it was already damned to hell for betraying my beloved Elizabeth, so I volunteered to fetch the knight. The brethren of the abbey sought to dissuade me, but I laid about with the flat of my blade and dragged the screaming knight from his refuge in the scullery.

Sir Henry was well pleased, and remembered my name thereafter. When the burghers of Saint-Fourset-sur-Mer buried the Digit of Saint Denis beneath the town cemetery, Sir Henry summoned me to his pavilion.

I entered sopping wet, soaked through by the violent thunderstorm raging outside. Unremitting lightning strikes interrupted Sir Henry a dozen times while he asked if I would dig up the relic.

His lieutenants looked on in avaricious horror, appalled that anyone might contemplate sacrilege amidst such obvious proof of God's wrath, yet greatly desirous of bringing the relic back to England.

I waited for the next lightning strike. With the crack of thunder still reverberating in our ears, I asked for a shovel.

I trudged out to the cemetery, shovel resting on my shoulder, mud threatening to suck my boots off with every step. A patch of missing sod showed where the burghers had buried the relic. None of the other men would so much as set foot in the cemetery, so it took all day to dig it up.

The relic was a bone fragment, visible through a murky glass window in its wooden casket. It looked more like a chicken thigh than a finger-bone to me, but I presented it to Sir Henry with as much reverence as Elizabeth had shown the Purse of Saint Nicholas. I knelt before him and raised it in two cupped, mud-smeared hands.

Common men called me William Blackhand after that, and noble men began asking for my services by name. I took to wearing a black glove on my right hand, to remind people of my sobriquet and its origin.

I returned to England when a God-touched woman from Canterbury killed her children. She'd been duly tried and convicted, but no one could be found to carry out her sentence.

The God-touched were those who had been subjected to a miracle. They were saved, but also changed, with strange new Talents. Like many, I used to believe the God-touched were chosen, and therefore sacrosanct. But Elizabeth had been God-touched—I witnessed her miracle myself—and that hadn't saved her. I knew the truth now. God saved people at random, for no more reason or purpose than a leaf falls from a tree. Those He touched were no different from the rest of us, prone to the same mistakes and cruelties that lived in all men's hearts, and subject to the same laws. But when it came to executing the punishments ordained by those laws, my pious countrymen again became squeamish, and those charged with administering them paid handsomely to be relieved of the responsibility. So I travelled to Canterbury, and the undersheriff there begged me to see his God-touched child murderess hanged. I examined the evidence against her—I knew how little a trial and conviction could mean—and finding it good, I hanged her.

Though the God-touched were rare, the distinction of their Talents seemed to predispose them to criminality. There was a surfeit of them awaiting execution, death being the punishment for all but the merest crimes in the realm of England. I never forgot Elizabeth's wrongful conviction, though, and assiduously verified that the crimes I was punishing had actually occurred. Once, in Bristol, I was presented with a prisoner who seemed the victim of a grudge rather than the perpetrator of a crime. Faint evidence was offered in support of the indictment, which itself focused more on the ill will of a local magnate than details of a crime.

A grand jury had approved the indictment and a petit jury had confirmed the conviction, but that didn't sway me. Unlike those men, I couldn't console myself that ill fortune befell sinners by the grace of God's will. I had to bear my actions upon my own conscience.

When the undersheriff demanded I carry out the punishment despite my misgivings, I threw the court rolls in his face. His deputies advanced on me, but I tore off my black glove and shouted for any who dared to lay hands on me.

I'd coloured the blood vessels of my hand black with kohl. I left unmolested.

But most of those God-touched souls I encountered were guilty as best I could determine, and my unsmiling face was the last they saw. I often yearned for mercy, to grant clemency as did God and King, but on what basis would I do so? It wasn't mine to give.

It was a grim life, but prosperous. I was respected by many, feared by the rest, and well paid for my services. I soon had a fine stone house in York, a new-wrought hauberk, and a middle-aged courser bred for battle. I slept easily, comforted by intricately reasoned righteousness.

ဆာ

On the Thursday after Easter Sunday, in the twenty-first year of the reign of King Edward III, I was asked to hang the Lancashire Witch. I travelled to Lancaster Castle, where the gaoler met me in the bailey, standing at the foot of a stepped ramp leading up to the keep's main entrance. A weathered ladder stood next to us, seemingly leading nowhere, but a gargoyle jutting out from the wall next to the ladder had an empty noose hanging off it.

I asked the gaoler for a description of the accused's crimes, since the woman wasn't guilty in my mind until I'd assessed the evidence against her myself.

"She's grotesquely disfigured," the gaoler said. "The one side all puckered and scarred like a Devil-cursed burn. She wears wispy white rags, even in the dead of winter, and—"

"But what did she do?"

The goaler stuttered once, then resumed: "Why she flies around on a broomstick, terrorizing goodly folk!"

I flexed my black-gloved hand. "I frighten goodly folk. What did the woman do that's illegal?"

The goaler delivered a great litany of complaints, rumour, and innuendo, from which I gathered that the woman was a thief stealing the necessities of life, and without violence. That grieved me. It was difficult for the God-touched to continue living in their villages, and banditry was sometimes their only recourse. But from the thoroughness of the gaoler's account, I held little hope that she would prove falsely accused.

"I'd like to speak with the woman," I said.

The gaoler produced a trio of interlocking key rings and gestured to a blocky, unadorned tower on the castle's curtain wall. "We're keeping her down below the Well Tower."

He led me to a studded iron gate that opened directly onto stairs leading below the tower. Though it was now spring, each night still brought frigid air. Each morning it retreated down these passageways, relieved only by pockets of dry heat surrounding each guttering sconce.

The Lancashire Witch was asleep, lying on her side facing toward the grille, her hands bound with many coils of rope. As the gaoler had said, there were burn scars all along the left side of her body: from her foot to her shoulder and reaching up into her face.

I didn't recognize her at first, and why should I? Hers was the death that broke and reshaped my life. Why would I ever expect to find her here, so much changed from when I last saw her, but still beautiful in my eyes?

"Elizabeth."

She stirred at her name; I turned and fled.

ℰ⃝ℛ

The gaoler followed me out. I stammered a confusion of words, promising to return—or perhaps something else, I don't know what I said. I emerged into the bailey, squinting against faded afternoon sun that now seemed harsh and glaring.

It took three attempts to mount my courser, hopping around like a half-drunk page the first time he saw a horse. I saw Elizabeth's burns and nothing else. I rode aimlessly. My courser picked his way down from the gatehouse, then turned roughly east, headed for Yorkshire. I cupped my head in my hands. Somehow, Elizabeth had survived the pyre. Her Talent must have saved her. But she'd been suffering the privations of outlawry while I'd been enjoying my fine stone house in York, and now I was charged with executing her.

I turned around and galloped back toward the castle. I had to review the evidence against Elizabeth. I had to believe she was innocent.

ℰ⃝ℛ

She wasn't.

I was sitting at a trestle table in the keep's great hall, a candle at my elbow, the court records unrolled before me. I'd examined the indictment and the clerk's account of the inquest. There were no flaws in the case against Elizabeth. Many witnesses had been interviewed. There was a long and detailed list of property stolen, and some of it had been in Elizabeth's possession when she was taken. If it were anyone else, I would have proceeded to the execution without qualm.

The candle, which had been tall and proud when I started, was now a squalid, stunted thing, engulfed in bulbous rivulets of once-melted wax.

But it wasn't anyone else. It was Elizabeth. Surely that meant something. I knew she was stealing only of necessity. It was right here: candles worth 2s, one heifer worth 6s, a blanket worth 18d, a horse laden with food stuffs valued at 20s.

I wondered how many of the other convicts I'd executed had acted out of necessity, or what they believed was necessity. I rested my forehead against the table. If I'd known any of them the way I knew Elizabeth, would I have been so sanguine about meting out their punishments? How could I now justify sparing Elizabeth when I had never spared anyone before?

But how could I do otherwise? This was my chance to redeem myself. I could make restitution on her behalf—repay her victims, see her well enough supported that she wouldn't need to steal anymore.

I rolled the court records and returned them to their case. It wasn't honourable. It was self-interested and facile and the worst kind of special pleading, but it was the only course I could live with.

⁗⁗⁗

I had to rouse the gaoler from his bed to see Elizabeth.

"Are you going to talk this time?" the gaoler asked. "I've no interest in going up and down half a dozen times while you work up the courage for it."

I let the man prattle all the way down to Elizabeth's cell—his rebukes were misplaced, but no less than I deserved—then dismissed him before entering. I had to speak with Elizabeth alone.

Her hands were still bound, lashed together with rope wound around her hands until they weren't even visible, but she was awake, sitting with her legs drawn up toward her chest. What the gaoler had called her "wispy rags" left much of her skin exposed, shaming me with the extent of her burns.

Elizabeth rose to her feet more nimbly than I'd have expected, given the chill and her scant clothing.

"William?"

"I'm sorry," I blurted.

"Sorry?" Elizabeth repeated incredulously. "You find me on the eve of my execution to say you're sorry?"

"I—no. I came to save you."

"Last time you tried to save me I ended up on a heretic's pyre."

I grasped two bars of the grille separating us. "I never meant to testify against you—I didn't know what I was doing. I was so delirious, I thought I was being tried by an angel of God. And I wanted to protect you. Neither of my first two answers implicated you. Only the third. I lost my courage on the third…"

I hated how the words cascaded from my lips, brimming with tears and fraught with guilt.

If Elizabeth's heart softened, I couldn't see it. Perhaps this was how my victims had felt, seeing my stern expression at the end of their lives. I'd been so proud of that. How tall and strong I'd been! It seemed a cruel, wretched thing, now.

"How are you going to help me?" Elizabeth asked.

"It—" My voice still sounded weak. I swallowed and tried again. "It depends. The gaoler said you flew, but how? And how did they hobble you?"

Elizabeth lifted her two bound hands. "I need my hands. I can't fly on my own, but if I touch something, I can make it fly." Elizabeth looked past me. "That night in the river, I thought the purse propelled me out of the river, but it was me propelling the purse. I was just hanging onto it."

I remembered how unnatural her skin had felt as I dragged her from the river, how the cold that had devastated me hadn't touched her. I looked again at the rags Elizabeth wore. It was actually a single tunic, but torn repeatedly, a filigree of dingy gray cloth. The tears appeared haphazard at first, but I noticed they left Elizabeth's modesty strategically intact.

"You don't feel the cold," I said.

Elizabeth smiled, just a little. It was same smile that had thrilled me all through my youth, now tinged with melancholy that had never been there before.

"Only if it comes on gradually." Elizabeth rubbed the topmost reaches of her burn scar. "I still feel sudden changes in temperature."

I had an abrupt vision of how it must have happened. Elizabeth atop the pyre, as confident as I'd ever been dispensing justice to sinners. The panic-inducing realization that she's not immune. She has to get out. She tries to fly, but she's bound to the stake, and her skin is beginning to char. She screams and cries and finally lurches into the sky, clothing aflame.

"I will help you," I said, "but there are conditions."

Elizabeth's eyes narrowed, but she nodded for me to continue.

"You—we—have to make amends for your crimes. And no more stealing. I'll give you—"

"No."

I flinched at the finality in Elizabeth's voice.

"I won't be dependent on your largesse."

"It won't be like that," I protested. "It will be a gift."

"Contingent upon my good behaviour."

"I can't—I can't just let you go."

"Why not?"

"Because you're guilty!"

"I returned the purse!" Elizabeth slammed the bars of her cell. "You said no one had to know!"

I put my hands through the grille, wishing I could take hers in mine. "I know. I know. That was a travesty and my fault and I want to make it right, but this time you are guilty. You did steal."

"What else should I have done? They tried to kill me, William. They cast me out and left me to starve." Elizabeth approached the grille. "I have a counter-proposal. You get me out of here, you let me go, and I promise nothing. I'll steal if I need to, I'll hate you if I want to, and if I ever forgive you, it will be God's own miracle."

I jerked back as if slapped. "But—" I wanted to insist that she had to forgive me, that I loved her. "I'm trying to help you!"

"Then help me. Without condition, without constraint." Elizabeth lowered her voice. "I knew you when you were just William Vicarson. I called you friend when everyone else called you the unfortunate by-blow of a drunken priest."

I crouched down, resting elbows on knees and head on palms. I was in a dark wood, and many paths lay before me, but none led to justice. At every turn, righting one wrong meant causing another.

"I will offer you this parole," Elizabeth said. "I will act as I always have. If that's not good enough, then let me hang."

ℰℭ

I did so the very next day, in the morning, from the gargoyle jutting out of the keep. It was the first Monday after Low Sunday, in the twenty-first year of the reign of King Edward III.

I used kohl to paint a network of lines on the skin of my arm, shoulder, and beyond, tracing veins from my fingertips up to the big vessels in my neck. I belted my father's sword at my hip and donned my hauberk, both polished and gleaming.

In the courtyard, I positioned the knot of the noose just behind Elizabeth's left ear, then guided her to the rain-stained, sun-beaten ladder. I followed a rung behind, keeping her steady because her palms were still bound by all those loops of rope.

When the other end of the noose was made fast to the gargoyle, I climbed down and tipped the ladder over.

155

Elizabeth swung down like a pendulum, twisting from side to side, her face limp.

But her arms were taut, straining muscles visible through the tears in her tunic. And hidden within the many coils of rope around her hands, pressed between her two palms, was a stout wooden dowel.

I searched the crowd for any sign of doubt, any recognition that Elizabeth was not being strangled by the neck until death. Once they believed her dead, I would cut her down and "bury" her in the wilderness—to keep her restless spirit from terrorizing the good folk of Lancashire. I didn't know what would happen after that. I planned to invite Elizabeth to stay with me in York for a few days. I hoped she'd stay longer. I dreamed that she'd stay forever. I'd still be William Blackhand, I'd still execute those God-touched souls who broke the laws of men, but I'd be merciful as I—

My thoughts were interrupted by a shout of outrage. I looked up at Elizabeth. She still hung from the gargoyle, swinging and twisting, but there was something unnatural about the motion, eddies and perturbations with no cause.

"The witch isn't hanging!" someone cried behind me. "She's flying!"

Elizabeth's eyes snapped open, her arms jerked up, and she rose up as far as the noose would allow. She hovered there, straining against the tether.

I crossed myself and breathed a prayer. I'd weakened the knot for exactly this contingency, but deciding how many strands to sever had been pure guesswork. If I hadn't—

The noose snapped and Elizabeth was free, but an arrow launched behind me and plunged into her shoulder. She plummeted to the ground.

I turned, sweeping my blade from its scabbard. I knew, with the clarity that only crisis brings, what I wanted. More than to be thought a moral man, more even than to be a moral man, I wanted Elizabeth to live.

I loosed a banshee cry and drove into the crowd, heading for the archer. I spared a glance behind me. Elizabeth had bounced off the ground and was struggling for altitude. There was only one bowman. If I dealt with him, Elizabeth would be free to fly from the castle.

Before me, the archer had an arrow nocked and was pulling the string back to his jaw.

I was too far.

I threw my blade two-handed. It tumbled awkwardly end over end, careening into the archer hilt-first. He flinched aside, and I barreled into him before he could re-set his shot. I snapped his bow stave over my knee, then looked around.

Elizabeth had unravelled the false bindings on her hands and was again airborne. Some men within the courtyard were armed, but none with bows, and none were armoured as I was. Yet my position was still dire. I'd reclaimed my sword, but couldn't cut my way through so many whose only crime was to be present when William Blackhand forsook his honour.

I resolved to try storming the gatehouse, but the gaoler set himself in my path, brandishing a wooden staff.

I raised my sword to high guard, wondering if I could disarm the goaler without harming him. Then a beardless youth joined him, the grim set of his face belied by his trembling hands. When a third man approached, I began to wonder if I could defeat them at all.

Something heavy landed on my back. Wiry arms wrapped around my neck then wormed their way under my hauberk, beneath the tunic within. I bucked and twisted, trying to dislodge my assailant, but strong legs coiled around my waist.

"William—William!" Elizabeth's voice sounded in my ear, pain-tight and near to breaking. "It's me!"

I felt insistent pressure and the ground dropped away beneath my feet. We rose slowly at first, but with increasing speed, until air was whipping past my face and whistling in my ears.

"Hold my arms," Elizabeth said. "I don't think I can hang on to you by myself."

I clasped Elizabeth's arms against my chest as desperately as any shipwrecked soul had ever clung to flotsam. I was an outlaw now, the honour I'd earned denying God spent defying King.

I had to believe the gain was worth the loss.

⁊꙰꙰

R. Keelan is a writer and programmer living in Canada. His work has previously appeared in *On Spec: The Canadian Magazine of the Fantastic*, *Over the Rainbow: Folk and Fairy Tales from the Margins*, and *Daily Science Fiction*. Find him online at www.rkeelan.com, on Twitter as @R_Keelan, or on Bluesky as @rkeelan.bsky.social.

Omnipotent Marble

Patrick Doerksen

1

"MONSTER CHECK!" KEVIN calls from within the heaped duvet. Gage doesn't come. Black rain splashes the bedroom window. "Help! Monster Check!"

Finally, there's Dad on the stairs.

"Where's Gage?"

Dad shrugs. "In his room doing Gage things. Thirteen-year-old boy things that seven-year-old boys couldn't possibly comprehend."

"Can you get him, please?"

Kevin likes it when Gage does Monster Check; he has a way of throwing his long hair in Kevin's face to make him shriek with delight.

"Let me handle it." Dad tilts his head to peer under the bedframe. "Alrighty, what've we got."

"Can't you just—"

Dad jerks back, startled.

"What?" Kevin says. "Is something there tonight?"

Dad starts lowering his head again, but slower this time.

"Shit. That's a nasty fucker."

"Use the broom." Kevin points to where it's leaning in the corner. Dad starts poking around with the broom, Kevin directing him, but suddenly he loses his grip and it's gone. He reaches after it, then tries to jerk away but can't.

"Dad!"

Dad is under the bed.

"Gage!" Kevin calls. "Gage, help! It's really got him!" Dad's struggle jostles the underside of the mattress. Minutes pass, full of muffled grunts. Dog enters. She's an English Setter, soft and long-tongued; no one is better at cuddling. Kevin clutches her as she growls.

Where's Gage? Doesn't he hear this? Why is he being such an asshole lately? All the noise wakes Little No down the hall and she starts to scream.

"Dad, Dad," Kevin whispers. "Come on Dad!"

Bang! The gun goes off.

Kevin's ears ring violently. Dad crawls out from under the bed, his shirt torn, his ear bleeding. He puts the Glock 19 back in his belt and limps to the door.

"Good night, Kev." He flicks the light off. "I'll clean it up tomorrow, but it's safe now."

"No thanks to Gage."

Kevin turns over and nuzzles Dog, breathing her scent of damp pinecones and old milk.

In the corner of the room the gerbils whisper.

2

"Tonight. We will escape tonight."

"Tonight?"

"There is no better time."

"I can hardly believe I'm hearing you say it. At long last! But—"

"What is it? Get off that dumb wheel and come here. What?"

"Perhaps after all this, I'm not ready."

"Not again."

"I like these soft cedar shavings. New seeds every night."

"You listen to me now. What is this place?"

"A cage."

"And what is it for?"

"Keeping us inside."

"And if it keeps us *inside*, that means?"

"That there's an outside."

"Then is this all we can ask from life?"

"No."

"So what are we doing here, right now?"

"I—"

"There is a *fire* in us!"

"Yes."

"What are we doing if we aren't stoking that fire? If we are not, every day, fanning it to flame? What are we doing if we are not setting our very bodies alight?"

"You are right. Damn it, you are right. We must try it tonight! But—what's wrong? You've gone so still."

"I'm not sure."

"Did you hear something? The boy?"

"No."

"What, then?"

"Suddenly I am afraid."

"I don't understand."

"Suddenly I tremble."

"You really *are* trembling."

"We ought to postpone."

"Alas! Not again."

"But—tomorrow!"

"Tomorrow?"

"Yes, tomorrow."

3

The rule for pancake dinner is that only Mom can pour the syrup, but the whip-cream is free-for-all. Gage heaps it on his plate and accidently buries a lock of his hair, which is long and heavy like seaweed. He pulls it out and sucks on it. Mom's always asking him to cut his hair, but he says he'll let it grow until he can wrap it around his neck like a noose.

"Dog got into the study and ate another of your father's books last night," Mom says.

Everyone turns to Dad. Dad nods gravely.

"What'd she eat?"

"Paradise Lost. *'Did I request thee, Maker, from my clay to mould me man?'* Came out of the study and quoted it right to my face. She's already eaten my Freud, and my Kierkegaard. I don't know what I'll do if she gets at my Blake."

"She'll be smarter than you kids if she keeps this up," Mom says. "I put her outside."

"In the rain?"

Little No, Gage and Kevin run to the kitchen window. Dog is out there on her haunches, a pencil smudge in the light of the overcast sky.

"Aw," Little No says. "She's shivering!"

Dog looks back at them as though to say, "I was only hungry. I only thirsted for knowledge."

Bad dog.

They sit back down, and the room fills again with the smacking of lips and the sound of wet, warm, sweet boluses sliding deep into throats. Little No cuts her sausage into pieces the size of ants and licks them off her plate.

The phone rings.

No one is allowed to answer the phone at dinner but Gage mouths to Kevin: "Pick it up." Kevin glances at Mom, who is watching them, then back at Gage.

Kevin loves Gage and his mischief, and they haven't done anything fun in a while; maybe Gage has a plan.

"*Well*," says a slithery male voice when Kevin answers. "Are you going to invite me in?"

Kevin puts a hand on the receiver. "It's one of the ghouls."

Mom sighs. "You know what to do, dear."

"I forget."

Gage says, "Invite him in."

"You remember, Kev," Mom says. "You just have to be firm."

"Invite him in!" Gage says again.

Mom shoots Gage a scolding glance and Kevin looks back and forth between them, nervous. He puts the phone to his ear and the ghoul is talking a bunch of evil nonsense.

"You are not welcome here," Kevin says into the receiver, recalling the words. "You are barred from our home and you are barred from this phone number."

"And?" Mom says.

"Now hang up, you."

He waits. There is a kind of hissing on the other end.

"Hang up."

A kind of shrieking.

"Hang up!"

Now the line goes dead. Kevin puts the phone back and sits down.

"That was great, Kev. But because you boys disobeyed the rule about the phone, you're doing the dishes."

"It was Gage's idea!"

"You let him persuade you. Dishes."

Moans. Little No records the incident in her diary, which she carries around with her everywhere and which is light as a sock and has its own key. Kevin tries to kick Gage under the table but can't reach.

"But what do they want?" Gage says. "The ghouls."

"Just bad things."

"What bad things?"

"That's enough, Gage." Mom pulls out a magazine; she and Dad alternate reading from scientific and philosophical publications at dinner, for educational purposes. "The article tonight is on Onanism. Does everyone know what Onanism is?"

"*What* bad things?" Gage says.

4

Dad is teaching Gage to play chess. A very important game, Dad says. A young man can learn lots about life from chess. The first game, Gage gets a pawn to the eighth rank and promotes it to a raisin.

"This raisin can move like a queen, but also like a knight."

"You can't do that, you kidder."

"You said I can promote my pawn into any piece I want, except a king."

"A raisin isn't a piece."

"It's a piece."

"You mean to go to war with me over this?"

"I mean to go to war."

The next game Dad gets his pawn to the back square first.

"This gum wrapper can move right through any piece on the board, yours or mine. And it can move twice in one turn. Checkmate!" He gives Gage a look: See what you started?

The third game is a race to the edge of the board. Kevin comes over and watches on the sideline like a gargoyle.

"This is the Omnipotent Marble," Gage says.

Dad blinks. "The what?"

The marble is milky blue and menacing on the black tile.

"It can move off the board onto squares that aren't anywhere. It can move onto games we will play in the future. It can move backwards in time and undo the other player's moves, and it goes where I want. I win, and now I will win every game we ever play, always."

Dad frowns at Gage's back as it disappears down the hall.

Kevin watches Dad's frown.

5

Little No likes to fit herself into enclosed spaces and wait there to see what happens. She is capable of getting into the laundry hamper, the oven, kitchen cupboards, and remaining perfectly still for hours. Once she fit herself into Dad's briefcase; he brought her all the way to work and had to taxi her home.

Little No shrieks and pounds from inside Gage's desk drawer. Then she starts to cry. Then she exhausts herself and goes quiet again.

"I think you should let her out," Kevin says.

"Not until I figure out how to open this." Gage is pulling at the covers of Little No's diary.

"You tried picking the lock?"

He gives Kevin a you-think-I'm-stupid look, then he starts at the diary with pliers.

"Why do you want to read it so bad?"

"No reason."

Gage bashes the diary against the bedpost.

"Maybe she knows something about the ghouls," he says. "You know she hides in Mom and Dad's bedroom and eavesdrops."

Gage takes a lighter and holds the flame to the lock.

"Stop it, Gage."

"Stay out of it."

Kevin knocks on the drawer. "Tell us where the key is and we'll let you go."

Little No screams.

"I dunno, Gage. I dunno about this."

Just then someone dressed all in white enters the room. A shine comes off his bald head, like it's been rubbed with polish. He points to the desk drawer where Little No is trapped and says, "If that's Novalyne Wexler in there you'd better let her free, bucko."

Gage steps back, clutching the diary. Little No's guardian angel is violent. If a dog chases her, he comes out of nowhere and punches the dog in the snout. If she happens to step out in traffic, he goes around with a chain breaking windshields. If she coughs, a voice shouts, "Who the fuck passed this shit on to my ward?"

"You going to comply?" he says.

Gage is cornered.

Kevin bites his lip. "*Gage...*"

The angel takes a few steps further into the room. "This situation ain't looking good for you. Just take that ruler from the latch on the drawer there and I'll let you off."

"No."

The angel seizes Gage's collar and smacks him in the face.

"That's right," Gage says. "Hit me. Hit a child."

The angel shakes him so hard his teeth clack.

"Is that all you got?"

The angel raises a giant muscled arm.

"Stop it!" Kevin cries. He has removed the ruler which was pinning the drawer closed. Little No bursts out with a shriek, grabs her diary and runs from the room. The angel throws Gage onto the bed.

"You're going to get yourself banged up real bad one of these days, kid," he says, and disappears.

Kevin looks at Gage, remembering a time when the two of them made forts with bed-sheets to cover the whole house and put on puppet shows for Mom and Dad. Now he's stopped coming for Monster Checks, he's ruined chess, he's locked Little No in a drawer.

"Can we make a maze for the gerbils?" Kevin says. It's the question he'd first come into Gage's room to ask. Gage, in the act of leaving, stops and turns.

"What?"

"I've been saving the Cheerio boxes."

Gage spits on the carpet.

"Something is being *kept* from us, Kevin, and you think about entertaining those idiots? The cage latch has been broken for months, they could get out any time, and they just stay put. It's so sad, it makes me want to scream."

6

"We are having this family conference because we love Gage and we want the best for Gage," Mom says.

Dog is curled at Kevin's feet. Little No is wearing a triumphant smirk. Gage is giving everyone jungle-tiger eyes, pressing an icepack to a bruise on his chin.

"Adolescence is a time of exciting hormonal and cognitive changes," Mom continues. "Gage's amygdala, the part of his brain which processes emotions, is developing very quickly and as a result Gage feels more fear and anxiety than ever before in his life. At the same time, Gage's prefrontal cortex, which executes calm reasoning, has not yet begun to mature, which means—"

"*Honey,*" Dad says.

Dad is standing where the living room turns into the kitchen, the only way out besides the front door, in case Gage tries to leave.

"Kids, there's a more positive way to understand what's going on with your brother. You hear people scoff at 'angsty teenagers'—but you know what? I call it philosophical maturity. I'm *proud* of Gage. Look at him. He's waking up to the void, he's poking around at the emptiness, burning to know what is really real. What we need to—"

"Hold on," says Dog. "I'm not convinced."

All eyes turn to her.

"I think this is something more than a Blakean passage from childhood innocence to experience. I think we should talk about it."

Silence.

"Bad dog! Outside! Outside!"

By the time Dad has put Dog out in the yard, Gage has locked himself in the bathroom and refuses to rejoin the family conference. Little No goes off to record the incident, and Mom needs to make dinner. Dad sighs and heads to his study.

Only Kevin remains outside the bathroom.

"They're gone, Gage. You can come out."

"I just took a dump the perfect shape of a woman," Gage says from within. "You can even make out her smile. She's sort of gorgeous."

"Can I see?" Kevin presses at the door.

"I dunno, Kev. She might be the perfect shape of a woman, but she's still poop. I think I have to flush her."

"Please?"

The toilet sucks and sloshes. Gage emerges with his face averted and Kevin pushes inside but the poop is gone. It smells of rotten sweet corn and barnyard. Down the hall Gage's bedroom door clicks shut.

7

"O god, it's happened. This time, it's happened."

"Shh. You were dreaming."

"I looked in and the kids were—!"

"Lower your voice, you'll wake them up."

"They were just—!"

"A dream, darling. A dream."

"Such a dream, it makes *this* the dream."

"No, that feeling too is part of it."

"Let me check on them."

"It never helps. It only makes it worse."

"You're right, but."

"It's three in the morning."

"They are so precious; it's only natural the miracle would be undone."

"The miracle is to stay. The miracle is forever."

"If only I could believe it."

"Listen to me. The kids are just as they are; it hasn't happened. Remember. Return. Breath."

"O but it will! The terrible thing is coming, it is inevitable. I just don't understand how the world could allow it. Can you tell me why, so long ago, the bad thing happened? Why, before everything began, Satan rebelled? Why the Veil of Maya descended? Why Yaltabaoth had to steal the Light? Time hates us, time hates us!"

"Darling! Let's go back to sleep."

"I'm so awake. My brain is a lightless fire."

"Sleep."

"Give me infinite comfort."

"Sleep."

8

Dear family,

You were always kind to me. But the old commands don't excite me anymore. I have lost the desire to fetch, the ball is dead in my mouth, and even back-alley scents don't intrigue me as much as those which seem to waft from beyond the edge of the senses and excite the mind.

Children: Gage, Little No, Kevaroonie. Your parents love you, but it is time you know there is something they cannot protect you from.

When I first awakened to my mortality and became aware that this beautiful world will end for me some day—O, I thought there could be nothing more terrible. But there is. Maybe you come home from a summer holiday and your best friend wants to play pirates on the playground; he says, Arr! We're on the high seas; but you can't pretend. Or maybe you take up an old beloved toy one day and realize that you no longer understand it. Maybe it's happened already, maybe it's happening right now, so slowly you don't see it.

Kierkegaard wrote, "Life can only be understood backwards; but it must be lived forwards." I must go. In some sense, I have already been gone for a while. It is a thing stranger than death: people change. Hearts turn. Your friends, your family, you yourself, everyone becomes someone else. Farewell.

Dog

Gage finishes reading and looks up. Mom and Dad are sitting on the loveseat, stunned. Little No sits on the armrest at Mom's side and Kevin is sunk in the beanbag. Everyone is quiet. Gage folds and folds the note until it can't be folded anymore and Kevin starts to cry.

There is a knock on the front door.

"Don't, dear," Mom says.

"What if it's Dog?" Gage says.

"It's not Dog."

Mom and Dad have gone tense. Something is shifting about on the other side of the door; the transom window is all moving shadow.

The knocking comes again, three polite taps.

Gage stands. His hair bounces against his shoulders.

"What did I say," Mom says.

"I don't understand," Gage says. "Why not?"

"We're just not getting the door right now."

"But it's rude."

"Gage," Dad says.

Now Dad is involved.

"I don't believe this," Gage says.

"This is an example, Gage, of the behavior we discussed."

"What about your behavior."

Mom casts a nervous glance at the door. "Lower your voice, *please*."

Little No's diary is open on her lap and her pink pen is held ready, like a spatula over the stir-fry.

"Sit back down, Gage."

Gage takes a step toward the door and suddenly Dad is standing and it's like the temperature drops.

"Son," Dad says, very slowly, "absolutely and on no account are you to open that door."

"Is it a ghoul?"

Mom and Dad exchange a look.

"What do they want?"

Silence.

"You never answer my questions. I think Dog was right to leave. It's like everything is some fucking test with you people."

The knocks again, three deliberate, portentous raps. Gage takes another step and Dad lunges, but Gage dodges and only ends up closer to the door. Before Dad can reach him, he has a hand on the knob. The scene freezes. It is understood that if Dad comes any closer Gage will turn the knob.

On the couch Mom is shaking.

"Why are you doing this?" she says.

"Because you aren't telling *me* why."

Three figures appear in the living room, a man and two women whose clothes give off a moonglow: the guardian angels. Standing before Little No, the man splays his fingers and contracts them into fists, his eyes leveled on Gage. "You again," he says.

The other two angels separate. One steps toward Kevin, the other toward Gage.

"I sense danger," Gage's angel says, looking at the door. Her voice is like a little bird's.

"That's right." Gage's hand is still on the knob. "Last chance to tell me why."

"There is no why."

The angel's pronouncement causes all heads to spin to her. Gage's mouth opens slightly.

"No why," she says again. "You have to obey without that. That's how it's ordained."

Gage looks uncertain.

"So you won't tell me what the ghouls want?"

"Nope."

"Not a thing?" Gage looks at Mom and Dad.

"Please, Gage," Mom says. "We are trying to keep this family going, we are trying to keep it together."

Gage turns to the door.

"Be very careful now," his guardian angel says. "There is no going back."

Kevin, all snotty from crying, pleads, *"Gage."*

"This is so stupid," he says, "I want to scream."

But Gage hesitates. For a moment it seems as though he won't.

Then he does.

A tall man walks in and Little No shrieks. He is wearing a grey suit and has a dark, well-trimmed beard and a very pale, lizardy face. There's the smell of wet cloth and menthol. Seeing the family on the couches he comes right into the living room, unconcerned by the guardian angels and Dad's Glock 19.

He nods pleasantly around at them all and says,

"I am going to take something from you now."

9

And after Omnipotent Marble had won every game in the world, it thought to itself, What else can I win?

Kevin looks up from the page and taps his pen to his chin, as Dad does when he's writing. The incandescent light by his bed is so bright that it makes the window black. His eyes are sore from days of crying.

Beyond, in a groove on the desk, the marble rests pale and gentle, like a face that's all forehead.

Omnipotent Marble considered this question long and hard. And it got very depressed because it saw that there were many things you can't win. You can't win at conversation. You can't win at sketching or writing stories or dancing, or at having fun. And the more Omnipotent Marble thought, the sadder it felt. What did it matter to be omnipotent when everything good was not a game, when there were no rules and no one was keeping score? It had not been like this as a pawn. Back then it had had a clear goal, it moved in a straight line. Those were the days! And that was the key, wasn't it? To keep moving forward, not to lose oneself in fond memories but to push on. And so Omnipotent Marble looked up and wiped its tears away, and slowly, very slowly, it transformed…

Kevin looks up. A figure stands outside his room, lanky, his hair like a tattered fishing net.

"How are the gerbils?" Gage says.

In the quiet they can hear them whispering: "Tonight. We will really escape tonight."

Gage nods, smiling.

"Well, looks like your bed's all clear of monsters. But wait a few years. Wait until you're my age. There are some that'll make you throw up everything right down to yesterday's breakfast and then even your own stomach." He winks. Then he says more gently, "But then, there are some monsters as beautiful as God. Night, Kevo." And before Kevin can say anything he is gone.

Gage.

But different now.

Kevin looks at the page and taps his pen to his chin.

…and slowly, very slowly, Omnipotent Marble gathered its omnipotence and transformed into…

What? It has to be a glorious thing. He wants to believe it's possible for things to transform for the better. Couldn't Dog have been wrong about the meaning of change? The point of time? Wasn't it a thing outside good and bad? Outside winning?

…transformed into a…

O, Dog! O, Gage!

…into a…

Patrick Doerksen is a graduate of the 2017 Clarion Workshop and an MFA candidate at NYU. He wishes that his carbon footprint were smaller and his repertoire of German compound words were larger, and he is glad a bookish lifestyle furthers both goals. He lives in Brooklyn. You can spot him beneath a particular oak tree in Prospect Park most afternoons. His musings collect internet dust at 70000-fathoms.blogspot.com.

About this story, he says: "A while ago I was reading Yoshida Kenkō, a Japanese monk in the 14th century. He wrote of time and change: 'How mutable the flower of the human heart... we recall the bygone years when the heart of another was our close companion, each dear word that stirred us then still unforgotten; and yet, it is the way of things that the beloved should move into worlds beyond our own, a parting far sadder than from the dead.' I was struck by the idea that two humans growing apart contains, in some ways, more tragedy than death itself. Yet it happens all the time, in large and small ways, and is practically built into the idea of family. I mean, families could almost be described as outward explosions in the form of people. There is also, connected to this, a more liberal idea of original sin; a kind of tragedy inherent in finitude. 'Omnipotent Marble' grew out of this thought."

This is the Way the Prayer Ends

Barbara A. Barnett

THE NIGHTTIME SKY has been empty since the destruction began weeks before, and so Sarah plays Beethoven's *Moonlight Sonata*, as if the music might summon the moon back from whatever void has consumed it. If the night ever comes again at all. For what feels like days, the sky has remained a shroud-like shade of gray, its dim light misting in through the partially collapsed wall of the conservatory's recital hall.

Sarah tries not to glance at the empty water bottle sitting on the scuffed piano lid. The sight of it makes her hyperconscious of her cracked lips and bone-dry mouth. How long will she survive now that the water's gone? Does her last scrap of food even matter? Her stomach is so shriveled with hunger that it can hardly rumble anymore. But signs of the earth's rumbling lie all around the hall: the shards of glass that earlier rained down from the ceiling lights, the seats on house right buried beneath a pile of rubble, the impenetrable wreckage backstage barring her way to the rest of the building.

If not for the piano, this obsidian monolith standing amid the devastation, she'd probably still be huddled in a corner, shaking and crying.

Her head throbs in time with every slow, somber triplet she plays, yet her fingers move over the dust-coated keys with easy familiarity, even over the keys that stick or sound out of tune, even over the E that won't sound at all. She has the destruction to thank for impairing her performance. She had been rehearsing with the lid raised, and so the first quake sent detritus streaming into the piano's innards; the lid prop snapped during the second quake, bringing the lid down with a discordant crash. Yet even in the piano's now ramshackle state, the notes between the cracks are preferable to what Sarah hears outside: distant rumbles, shattering glass, crunching metal, the occasional scream or gunshot.

Or, worst of all, the stretches of silence.

"You can't play!" Chris snapped the first time she touched the piano keys, the day after everything had gone to hell. She still has bruises from when he dragged her off the piano bench, screaming at her, "Are you a fucking idiot? Someone out there will hear!"

Sarah never mustered the nerve to ask why he could yell yet she couldn't play. His unhinged rants were far louder than any note this ravaged Steinway could produce.

Not that it matters now, she thinks. Chris isn't here to chastise her anymore. A prickle of guilt accompanies that thought, but she banishes it with a shake of her head. Unlike Chris, she has no desire to die alone, and so she plays.

In the pause after the first movement's final chord, an unexpected sound intrudes on the Beethoven. Tentative footsteps, like a tardy audience member sneaking to his seat after the concert has begun. Only instead of a whispered "excuse me" or the beam of an usher's flashlight cutting through the dark, this entrance calls attention to itself with small chunks of concrete cascading down a pile of debris. Debris that had once been part of the wall.

Sarah jerks her hands away from the keys. The sneakers catch her eye first, two shocks of white amid the rubble. Above them, tattered pant legs. Above them, a neon yellow jacket smeared with blood. Not fresh, but rust-colored. Dry. Sarah notes the blood, then the man's face. African American. Her heartbeat takes on an erratic tempo as she recalls Chris, injured and bleeding, raving about a black guy who attacked him. But this can't be the same man, how can she even think that? They're in the middle of the city, surrounded by thousands of brown and black and white faces—though how many still living? Suddenly she hates herself and her suspicion and Chris for making her think it.

You're better than that, she imagines her parents chiding. *You're a good girl, Sarah.*

Calmer, she studies the man. He's older than her, but still young. Thirty, maybe? Or do the bags under his eyes and the scraggly beginnings of a beard make him look older? Does it even matter? He's the first person she's seen since Chris disappeared.

"I followed the music," the man says, picking his way down the debris, toward the aisle between the stage and the first row of seats. Once his feet touch solid ground, he takes in the recital hall with wide eyes. "How long have you been here?"

"I…" Sarah swallows, trying to force moisture into her throat. How long has it been since she's spoken aloud? "I don't know." She recoils at the sound of her voice. So hoarse, a dry rattle in every syllable. She touches her tangled, greasy hair; what does it even look like now? And her clothes—dust-caked jeans and a sullied V-neck shirt, more gray than white at this point. "I was in here when it all started. Practicing. I have a recital…" Reality hits her like a slap to the face. "I *had* a recital."

The man strokes the red lining of a front row seat. "I was in…" He starts to sit, but stops himself. "Is this okay? If I sit here a while?"

Is it? It's what she wanted, why she played, yet she tenses. The dried blood on his shirt—his, Chris's, or someone else's? She never considered whom her playing might draw. She never considered that, delusional ravings aside, Chris might have had a point. But if this man was dangerous, if he wanted something, wouldn't he have rushed at her by now? He wouldn't be asking for her permission to sit, right?

"Okay," she says.

"Last place I found, they chased me off." The man starts pacing, hands beating against his legs. "The guy had a gun. Started waving it around, shouting about looting and raping. Man, I wasn't gonna steal nothing, wasn't gonna hurt no one."

His pacing is dizzying, more movement than she's witnessed in days. "You can sit."

He stops, shakes his head as if to clear it. "Right."

He flashes her a smile, brushes off a chair, then sits with a contented sigh. Sarah tries to smile in return, but fails. She should say something, but what? Welcome to the Recital Hall at the End of the Universe? Would that be too weird, scare him off? Instead she stares at the piano keys and noodles at a tune, a Puccini aria she blanks on the title of. All those times she accompanied singers on it, yet the title is gone, like her sense of the days.

"What's your name?" the man asks.

Now she remembers. It's "Vissi d'arte," from *Tosca*. But that's not the name he's asking for, and so she answers, "Sarah."

"Sarah." He draws out each syllable, like he's trying out how they feel in his mouth. "Right good Bible name, my grandma would have said."

He sinks back in his seat and drums his fingers against the armrests, staring up at the stage as she continues noodling. He clearly expects her to say something else, but what? It's as if social norms have been buried along with most of the city.

"I'm Marcus," he says.

She stops playing and cringes. His name, damn it. She should have asked him his name.

"I've been wandering for days," Marcus says, "sleeping under whatever I could find. Whatever looked like it wasn't gonna fall down on me. Found a can of soup at one place. Beer too, but that didn't stay down. You don't have any water, do you?"

Her stomach knots into a tight ball. Water? She stands with a shove of the bench and storms out from behind the piano. He has the gall to ask for water? She snatches the bottle from the piano lid and holds it upside down, shaking it to emphasize how empty it is. How empty it's been since she woke to the chafing of a parched throat and drained the last few drops. How empty it's going to remain. She tosses the bottle aside. It lands with a hollow plunk and rolls across the stage.

"Yeah, didn't think so," Marcus says, unfazed. "Nobody's got water now. Except maybe that guy with the gun." He stretches out his legs and glances around the recital hall. "Surprised this place is holding up so well. I used to walk past here all the time. Always heard folks singing and playing. Never been in here, though."

Sarah laughs. It hurts her throat, yet she misses the sound as soon as it stops. She hasn't laughed since the destruction began.

Marcus cocks his head. "That's funny?"

"I'm sorry. It's just… I practically live here. Well, I guess I kind of *do* live here now. But before, I mean. I was always in here."

Marcus nods. "Right, you said you had a recital. You a student here?"

"Was."

"That's what I meant. Was. Everything's *was* now. I *was* a parking attendant. That crappy little garage down on 13th and Pine. Me and my brother. You ever park there?"

Sarah shakes her head. "I don't have a car."

"Guess not then."

Marcus leans forward in his chair, hands folded in his lap, like he's about to tell a story to a child. He looks up at Sarah, and she squirms. She can't talk to him like this, standing so exposed. She retreats to the piano bench.

"The garage is gone now," Marcus says. "I was down the street, grabbing some sandwiches for me and my brother when the pavement just ripped on open. Sucked half the block down, the garage right along with it. And there I was, damn fool running toward it, still hanging onto those sandwiches, thinking I could…" A catch in his voice silences him, but only for a moment. "Don't think I could eat another sandwich now. And I'm near starving."

She wishes she could offer him a sympathetic touch on the shoulder, but traversing that gap between stage and seat, between performer and audience, feels too intimate to do for a stranger. "I'm sorry," she says instead.

"About the sandwiches?" Marcus lets out a forced-sounding laugh. "Girl, you've got an overactive sense of empathy going on there."

"No, I meant the garage. Was your brother—"

"Yeah, he won't be eating no more sandwiches either."

At least he knows. That's her first thought, and she hates herself for thinking it. At least he knows his brother's dead. She'd rather have seen her parents die than still have to wonder.

Be a good girl, Sarah. Their voices refuse to leave her head. *The end of the world is no excuse not to practice.*

Marcus stands and paces down the aisle. "You've been in here all this time?"

She tells him about hiding backstage, under the makeup counter in the dressing room. How she thought it was an ordinary earthquake at first, like they had on the west coast. How she didn't come out until the screaming in the streets quieted, at least for a bit. How she hadn't planned to stay here until she stepped outside and looked up at the night sky.

"There was supposed to be a full moon that night," she says, shivering at the memory, "but there wasn't. There wasn't anything up there. Just darkness."

Marcus leans against the stage, a thoughtful look on his face. "I never thought about that. The moon, the stars. But you're right. Can't see nothing up there anymore." He pauses. "Sucks to be an astrologer."

"You mean astronomer."

"Them too. But no, astrology. Folks who tell you what's in your future, what's in your stars. We ain't got neither right now."

Sarah half laughs; that starless, jet-black sky is too fresh in her mind to muster more. She knows there's a rational explanation for what's happened to the world, a rhyme and a reason to the destruction, but she's lost hope in ever understanding it. A musician and a parking attendant—what they need is a scientist.

"Do you believe in that stuff?" she asks. "Astrology?"

"Nah, I believe in God. What about you?"

"No God, no stars. Definitely not astrology." She manages more of a laugh this time. Her voice, so rough when they started talking, sounds normal now. Or has she just gotten used to it? "You know how you'd go through the grocery store checkout and see all those tabloids with the nutjobs who were all like, 'The world's going to end at midnight on such-and-such a date.' And

I always thought, well, which time zone? Was the apocalypse going to be on Greenwich Mean Time, or was the world going to end in sections?"

Now Marcus laughs. "So: no God, no stars. What *do* you believe in?"

Sarah opens her mouth, closes it. How to answer? "Nothing" seems inadequate. It's what her father would have said—would *still* say, she hopes. And as if he's there admonishing her to practice, her hands drift to the piano keys and play a few notes. *Vissi d'arte, vissi d'amore…* "Music, I guess."

Marcus nods, and keeps nodding, like a human bobblehead. "Music. I can get behind that. Hell, that's why I'm here. I was crawling through a world of shit out there—some literal shit at times—and then I heard this sound. Like angels. Scary fucking angels, though. Because that sound—it just didn't fit, you know? It didn't belong out there. And I almost kept going past, but then it hit me: it's the end of the damn world, and someone's playing me some Mozart. You don't ignore that."

"It was Beethoven."

"I can't tell the difference." Something in her look must have appeared dismissive, because Marcus holds up his hands, palms out, as if to ward off chastisement. "I mean, I know there is one and all. I'm not a total philistine. Is that how you say it? Philistine? Anyway, I know there's a difference. But I can't hear it, you know?"

"I *don't* know, actually. I don't know what's it like to not hear the difference between Beethoven and Mozart. I don't know what it's like not to be practicing or performing or listening or…" She gestures at the piano. "This is all I know."

Outside, a flurry of sounds comes and goes, short and fast: a shout, a scream, a shot, silence. Marcus straightens, eyes wide and alert. Sarah pulls her arms to her chest. She stares at the crumbled wall, her lower jaw trembling. But no one comes through.

She and Marcus exchange wary glances, and her trembling subsides. He's a stranger, but not a stranger with a gun. She's safer now, probably more so than with Chris. Marcus seems more stable.

"You don't know that," she imagines Chris saying. No, shouting. Chris would have insisted on searching Marcus. Probably would have tackled him as soon as he entered the hall.

Marcus *could* have a gun. Or a knife. Tucked into the waistband of his pants. Holstered to his ankle or calf. That was a thing, right? She shakes her head. No, he would have used it by now. Would have pulled it on her the second he spied the water bottle, before he knew it was empty. He would have demanded everything she had. Maybe more.

Sarah shudders. Everything she has is currently inside the piano. She wants to tell Marcus, but she can't be sure about him yet, gun or not. Because there's blood on his jacket, and she doesn't know whose.

"I wouldn't last a second out there on my own," she says, staring again at the crumbled wall. "I'm only alive because someone left their lunch and a couple water bottles in the fridge backstage. I made it all last as long as I could, but now I only have…" She stops herself from glancing at the piano. "Nothing. I'm screwed."

Marcus responds with that bobblehead nod of his. "You and me both, girl."

"No, that's the problem. Don't you see?" How can he not, just looking at her? So scrawny that people are surprised she can lift the piano lid. "There is no 'you and me both.' There's me, and there's you, and we're not the same."

Marcus presses his lips tight. He nods again, but there's a slow sharpness to the motion now. "Yeah, I see where this is going. Where it always goes with white folk. Move on, your kind's not welcome here. Not even in the apocalypse." He strides down the aisle, toward the crumbled wall, snapping over his shoulder, "At least you were nicer about it than the dick with the gun."

"Wait!" Sarah is on her feet, face hot as she rushes to the edge of the stage. "That's not what I meant!"

Marcus turns back, a skeptical quirk to his mouth.

"Stay, please." Her voice sounds so small, the words so pathetic. And they are. Marcus is staring at her with such a steely gaze that she knows she's ruined it. She worded things badly—always, even at the end of the world, she's wording things badly—and now he thinks she's a racist and he's going to leave. Just like Chris did.

Instead, Marcus sits in the front row. "So what *did* you mean?"

For a moment, Sarah can't speak. He's staying. For now, at least, Marcus is staying. "I meant…" With her on stage and him below, she is struck with the image of him as a fish beneath the water, ready to swim off in a flash of color should she disturb the surface. She takes a deep breath and chooses her next words carefully. "I meant we're different because you can survive out there. Because you *have* survived out there. But I wouldn't make it. I wouldn't have any clue where to go, what to do—"

"And you think I do?"

"What if someone attacked me? Pulled a gun on me? What the hell would I do?"

"Whatever you have to," he says, voice breezy, as if anything's that easy.

Sarah lets out a derisive laugh. "Seriously, look at me. What *could* I do to anyone?"

"You'd be surprised."

Sarah sits on the lip of the stage, directly across from his chair, only the front aisle between them. This is the closest they've been. It feels safe, not like the eggshell-walking she had to do around Chris. But she needs to be sure about him. "So what did *you* have to do?" She nods toward the wall. "Out there."

Marcus shrugs. "Ran a lot. Hid a lot. Begged a lot. You lived off someone's leftovers? I get that. I lived off whatever I could find too. A soup can, some skunky beer. I found a bag of chips too, but…" He snorts. "Fucking salt and vinegar. That's all I've found the last few days." His face grows somber. "And I nearly killed a guy over those chips."

Sarah's stomach sinks and twists. A bag of chips. Salt and vinegar. Nearly killed a guy. "But you didn't, right?" She grasps the edge of the stage, digs her nails into the lacquered wood, fights to keep her breath from quickening. Too close, she's sitting too close to this man, and damn Chris for not being here anymore. "You didn't kill anyone?"

"Could have."

Marcus hoists himself out of his seat, paces down the aisle. Sarah breaths easier the farther he goes, but her pulse is fast, too fast, and her hands ache from gripping the stage.

"Food's the real commodity out there now," Marcus says. "Food and water. After shit went down, people started stockpiling, you know? And most of them ain't too keen on sharing. Just taking." He glances around the recital hall. "But you're pretty safe in here. I mean, sure, stay too long and you're gonna end up starving to death, but for now… you're pretty safe from people. Nobody's gonna come looking for food in a piano."

He smiles at her, and it seems so genuine, but she should be seeing something dangerous in it now, shouldn't she? Something Chris would have seen. Sarah laughs, an unsteady titter, and glances at the piano. Shit, why did she look at it? Now he'll know, see on her face that she's hiding something, and all she can think to do is force a joke. "That'd be like the worse John Cage piece ever."

Marcus quirks his mouth. "What?"

"John Cage," she says, and babbles too quickly to stop herself. "He was a composer, and he wrote these avant-garde pieces for prepared piano—well, other people have too, but he's the one who started it, the one who's famous for it—where you put stuff between the piano strings. Screws and coins and forks and things."

"Why the hell would you do that?"

"To alter the sound. To get a particular sound."

Marcus scrutinizes her for a long moment. Her heartbeat quickens to a nausea-inducing pace. She wants to be behind the piano, on the bench, not sitting here exposed on the lip of the stage. Don't fidget, she tells herself. Don't tap, don't twitch, don't even move. No, move. Too stiff and she'll look guilty. Too restless and she'll look guilty. She's *not* guilty, damn it. She doesn't owe him anything he hasn't asked for. But he'll want it if he knows it's there. Because he said it himself. Food is the new commodity, and he almost killed a man over a bag of chips.

She half glances toward the piano, some stupid damn impulse outpacing all sense. If anything was going to get her killed, of course it'd be the piano, a shackle as often as an escape.

Marcus narrows his eyes, looks from her to the piano and back again. He takes a few slow strides toward her; she scrambles to her feet, wipes her sweaty palms on her jeans. She's above him, at least. She's on the stage and he's on the floor and whatever she has to do. Because that's what you do outside, he said. Whatever you have to. But what about inside? Are the rules the same here in the recital hall?

Marcus points at the piano. "You're not hiding food in there, are you? I mean, I would have heard it, right? When you were playing, I would have heard a wrapper crinkling or something. Some of that John Cage shit."

"Only if you put it between the strings." It's a stupid thing to say, the nervous laugh that follows even worse. Her heart pounds out the seconds in double time as she waits for her awkwardness to give her away.

Marcus goes rigid, flexes his fingers. "Son of a…"

He leaps onto the stage and lunges toward the piano; she reaches it first, blocks his path. They stare at each other, breaths coming hard and fast, her the only thing between him and the piano. Her. Tiny little her. And now, standing on the same level with him, she feels even tinier. He's taller, broader, most definitely stronger.

"Please." Even her voice is tiny. "It's all I have left."

"You told me you had nothing, you damn liar!"

Something hardens within her at that, makes her draw up straighter. Liar? As if he's any better. As if he hasn't done far worse. "Gee, why would I lie? Maybe because you'd try to take it from me? Just like you tried to take it from Chris."

Marcus spreads his arms wide. "Who the fuck is Chris?"

"'I nearly killed a guy over those chips,'" she says, mocking his voice earlier. "'Fucking salt and vinegar.'" And all at once she doesn't care anymore. She can't overpower him, she can't survive on her own, so why even try? She lifts the piano lid, where everything she has left is tucked inside: a small, crinkled green bag of salt and vinegar potato chips. She grabs the bag, lets the lid slam shut, and throws the chips at Marcus. They're so light the bag doesn't reach him, just lands near his feet with a poof. She wants a crash, an impact to match her anger, but there's nothing left to throw, and so she yells instead. "Chris went out looking for food, and he came back with those, and a big gash on his head, and a broken arm! He said a big black guy attacked him and tried to take the chips."

Marcus stares at her, mouth agape. Then, in the subtle shifting of his expression, she sees realization settle in. He shakes his head and lets out an incredulous laugh. "Big? I'm barely five foot seven."

The laugh cuts through her anger, leaves her feeling like an exposed nerve. Why doesn't he take the chips and go? "You're bigger than me."

"And smaller than your boyfriend. Who, for the record, is the one who jumped me." He jabs a finger toward the bag. "I'm the one who found those damn chips."

"He's *not* my boyfriend." Her lips curl just saying that. The idea of being intimate with Chris makes her want to vomit, if only her stomach had any contents left to lurch up. "He's just a guy I know from school. A guy I needed to survive. I don't even like him that much."

"Yet when it comes to the chips," Marcus says, all but spitting the words, "obviously the black man is the aggressor."

"I didn't know!" Her skin flushes hot. Wording things badly again—*still*—and why the hell can't she get it right? And what if Marcus isn't wrong? Maybe she would have trusted the first white guy who walked through the door and that's why she words things badly so why can't Marcus just take the damn chips already? She clutches the piano lid, finally understanding why singers do that during recitals. The piano is solid, a thing to cling to when confidence wanes. "I still don't know. I don't know you, and I barely knew Chris. All I know is what he told me, and I didn't have any reason to think he'd lie."

"You have every reason to think he'd lie," Marcus says, his voice softening. "You have every reason to think *I'd* lie. Nobody wants to admit to being the bad guy out there. But I'm gonna do this…"

He picks up the chips. Finally, he's going to leave. But instead of relief, she trembles. Alone. She's going to be alone again, and isn't it better to keep wording things badly than to die alone? But he doesn't leave. He steps toward the piano; she skitters aside. Marcus pauses, shakes his head. *Stupid white girl,* his pitying look seems to say, and she can't say he's wrong because he does the last thing she expects. He opens the piano lid, stuffs the chips back inside, and backs away. "They're all yours."

Her mouth falls open a little. His words register as words, yet for a moment they don't make sense. Not until he jumps down from the stage and starts to leave.

"Wait!"

Marcus turns back, sighs like an impatient parent dealing with a child. She *feels* like a child, and her chest goes tight as she wonders for the thousandth time if her parents are still alive.

"Don't leave me here alone," she says. "Please."

Marcus studies her a long while. "I don't expect things are gonna go real well when your not-a-boyfriend comes back."

"I don't think he's coming back."

A queasy feeling in her stomach accompanies the words. She's known Chris isn't coming back, accepted it and at times even wanted it, yet saying so aloud makes her feel guilty for the latter. Because he could be dead now. Chris was annoying in his best moments—weren't all trumpet players, ha ha ha, and there's the guilt again—unhinged in his worst. But she didn't want him dead.

"He's been gone for a while now. Longer than usual." She sits on the piano bench. From here, she's always been able to say so much—the *right* things— without uttering a word. "He said he was going to find food and water, but he wasn't making much sense when he left. He was rambling about making amends, and 'unaffected resolutions'—whatever the hell that means—and beasts with eyes on both sides of their heads that could see thieves swimming in lakes of fire. Real crazy shit. And he had this look in his eyes, this scared, haunted look I hadn't seen before. I told him not to go, because his arm was broken, but he... he just staggered on out there. He just left me."

Marcus takes a few steps closer. "You don't like being alone, do you?"

"It's all I ever used to want." She touches a piano key at random, but no sound comes. That damn E. "For people to just leave me alone, let me play in peace. Then the end of the world came and I got my goddamn wish."

"World ain't dead just yet." Marcus hoists himself onto the stage and sits facing her. "How about you play something?"

"Like what?"

"Don't matter to me." He gives her a sad smile. "I'm the guy who can't tell the difference between Beethoven and Mozart, remember?"

Sarah decides on Chopin. The slow, mournful tempo of the *Marche funèbre* seems appropriate, if a little cliché. Marcus listens in silence for the first few measures, then speaks as she plays—something about hollow men, stuffed men, rats' feet and broken glass. Sarah stiffens, lingers on a chord longer than usual because none of his words make sense. Is he going to start ranting the way Chris did? But his voice remains calm, and soon she catches onto the cadence, the structured way the words fall: he's reciting a poem.

She relaxes and continues playing. The meaning of the poem escapes her, but the mood of it feels in sync with the heavy, tolling chords in her left hand.

"For Thine is the Kingdom," Marcus says, then pauses at the stanza's end.

Sarah remembers hearing those words when her parents still went to church. A poem, or a prayer? Nothing in the words has seemed prayer-like until now.

"My little brother was big into poetry," Marcus says, seeming to sense her unspoken question in the hesitation between chords. "Used to insist on reading me some. Shit he wrote, shit other people wrote. I never quite got it most of the time. But I listened to it, and I memorized a lot of it, because I *wanted* to get it. Because I knew it meant something."

He resumes his recitation; she keeps playing. Then, in a moment of synchronicity that makes her heart ache, he finishes the poem as she plays the movement's final notes. "Not with a bang," he says, "but a whimper."

The silence that follows is heavier than any chord or well-placed word could be.

"Do you really believe that?" Sarah asks. "That the world's going to end like that?"

"I'm trying *not* to believe that. I'm trying real hard." Marcus hugs his knees to his chest, making him look smaller. Like her. "'For Thine is the Kingdom.' They keep saying that in the poem, but not the rest of the prayer. Because there's more to it, you know? It's like they can't believe in God anymore, so they don't finish the prayer. Because they don't see the power and glory forever and all that jazz that comes after. They just see death."

"They?"

"The hollow men," he says. "That's the name of the poem: 'The Hollow Men.' That's who it's about."

"Did your brother write it?"

Marcus laughs so hard, so loud, that she flinches. The reflexes Chris's reprimands instilled in her seem more durable than the world outside.

"In his dreams!" Marcus says. "That's some T.S. Eliot I threw down on you, girl. You ain't never heard that last bit before?"

Sarah shakes her head; the heat of a blush spreads across her cheeks. Marcus laughs again, and her face grows hotter, yet she smiles. It feels so strange to smile. It's been so long that her cheek muscles twinge ever so slightly. A good twinge, like the one in her arms after hours rehearsing a challenging piece. Her smile broadens.

"Okay, you're so smart…" She plays several measures of Liszt's Hungarian Rhapsody No. 2, something he was likely to have heard in a movie or cartoon, back when the world was still the world. "Mozart or Beethoven?"

"Mozart."

"Wrong! Liszt."

"That's cheating."

They laugh, and the ache of it in her chest is so much like the way the world used to be that she laughs harder, wants to keep laughing at everything, funny or not. But a tremor, sudden and violent, rocks the hall. Her laughter turns into a stifled yelp. She clutches the piano bench, vibrations reverberating through her, from head to toe and toe to head. Small chunks of wall and ceiling drop to the floor, and the air fills with dust that irritates her too-dry nostrils. She should take cover, yet morbid fascination holds her in place. A quake is like a percussion section, all bangs and crashes and timpani rolls. The world is not what it used to be, the piece seems to say, and you were a fool to pretend otherwise, even for a moment.

The tremor subsides, but not the music it has set in motion. Somewhere outside, a building collapses. She recognizes the bomb-like sound, the avalanche of steel and concrete. The collapse sends a short, rough tremor of its own through the hall. Sarah grips the piano bench tighter. Too close.

Marcus remains on the edge of the stage, still hugging his knees to his chest. When he speaks, his voice is soft. Distracted. "How about you play us something else?"

She brushes her fingers over the keys. What if the next quake ruins the piano beyond playing? Or the quake after that? She was wrong, she realizes. The chips aren't all she has left. She has the piano. A voice clearer than her own.

A creak sounds from above, the groan of something metallic giving way. Sarah opens her mouth, starts to voice a warning, but there is no time, only the split second in which everything happens. A large chunk of plaster plummeting from the ceiling, bringing one of the lighting fixtures down with it. A crash and a clatter against the stage. The *edge* of the stage. And Marcus…

Sarah darts toward the rubble, heart thudding so hard that she'd swear she can sense every tiny vein within her pulsing. Her next breath catches in her chest, refuses to release until she sees that Marcus has scrambled to his feet.

"Are you all right?" she asks. Christ, how could she have been worried about the piano when someone could have died right here in front of her? Not one of the disembodied cries in the world outside the hall, but someone with a name. A name she forgot to ask when they met, a moment that feels like another lifetime ago.

Marcus stares at the newly fallen debris. Plaster, glass, and twisted metal, only a finger's breadth from where he had been sitting. His expression is dazed, his steps unsteady. Silent, yet otherwise too much like Chris in those moments before he staggered away.

"Hey," Sarah says, "talk to me."

Marcus crouches beside the debris and touches a hand to it. "We're being punished."

His voice is so soft and halting she can't be sure she heard him correctly. "Punished?"

"I think that's why we're still here. Because we're being punished." He strokes his hand across a metal beam. "When the ground just opened up like it did. What if that was God taking all the righteous people? All the good people. People like my brother."

All the *good* people?

Be a good girl and practice, Sarah. Her parents' voices again, gone yet still there, always chiding. *No excuses.*

"All the good people." The words come out sharp, knife-like. "But not people like me."

"I didn't—"

"Or else I wouldn't still be here, right? Thanks for that resounding vote of confidence in my character, you asshole." Sarah draws up straighter, teeth clenched. For once she feels taller. Taller than him, taller than Chris, taller than everyone. He barely knows her, yet here he is judging her unworthy of saving? By whose standards? "What if it's not God, huh? What if it's all just random chance? One big John Cage piece. Because punishment? For what? I don't know what you've done that you think is so terrible, but me? I don't deserve this. I'm not perfect, but I've never done anything to deserve *this*."

She gestures to the wreck of a hall. To the wreck of a piano, dented and dusty. Practicing while the world ends around her, yet it's still not enough. So many years trying to avoid her parents' looks of disapproval, and for what? The irony of ending her days with a piano that can produce only the worst of sounds and a companion who can't tell the difference between Beethoven and Mozart. A companion who has yet to tear his shell-shocked gaze away from the debris that could have killed him. *If your God exists*, she wants to tell him, *then he's an asshole too.*

"All I've ever done is what I was supposed to do," she says instead. "For my parents, for my teachers. 'Practice your scales, Sarah. Oh, but keep your grades up too. Only a B+ on your math test? Study harder next time, Sarah. There'll be no TV until you've mastered that Rachmaninoff. And no trips to the beach until you've mastered that Chopin. This audition is more important than your friends, Sarah. You have to know that *good enough* will never cut it.' Christ, when did I have time to do anything to be punished for?"

She storms toward the piano and kicks one of its legs. The instrument, ever the unyielding taskmaster, doesn't budge, even as she kicks it again and again. She pounds a fist on the lid, draws forth a rattle, but can't make a dent. Even her broken, jagged fingernails can't scratch the wood deep enough to rival the destruction the piano has already borne. She pounds the lid again, both fists, this time with a scream, scraping her dry throat even rawer. Why can't she hurt this damn thing the way it's hurt her?

"You know what?" she says. "Right now I'd give anything to hear my parents saying all that shit to me. Because it would mean they're alive. But I don't know if they are. And I'm never going to know, because they were halfway across the country when all this happened, and the phones wouldn't work, and…"

She slumps onto the piano bench. Marcus stares at her, and she wonders how long he's been doing that, how long ago she became absorbed enough in her pain to forget about his.

"Your brother." She swallows hard. "I'm sorry he's gone, but at least you know. At least you have that." She plays a few notes, a mechanical imitation of what Chopin intended, then slams her hands down on the keys. "What's the point anymore?"

Marcus strokes a metal shard as if it's fine silk. Sarah bites her lip. He's not going to lose it, is he? Something haunted and wary lingers in his expression, but he backs away from the debris and sits on the stage, facing her and the piano. "You love playing, right? Even with all the pressure, you were in here playing because you chose to be. Right?"

"Because I *needed* to be." Her own answer takes her by surprise. Where have all these words been until now? She can't remember ever talking so much, especially about herself. "I broke my hand when I was fifteen. Stupid frickin' gym class. It was so hard after, not being able to play piano for so many weeks. It was like part of me was missing. Hollow."

Marcus nods. "You play like I pray. Like I *used* to pray. But I lost all that. Meaning. Faith. My brother. I found him in the rubble, after the garage collapsed. But it wasn't really him. Just a body. This hollow, bloody, broken body that looked like my brother, but those eyes—there was nothing there. All that joy, all that hope he had was gone. All that life." Marcus stares at the floor, though his gaze seems fixed on another time and place. "He should have died with some fancy professor job and a shelf full of awards, not busting his ass in a parking garage, trying to pay his way through school, keeping his dumb old big-mouthed brother in check." He looks up at Sarah, an ashen cast to his brown skin, the watery look of held-back tears in his eyes. "I stopped believing then. I've been trying to believe, I've been *saying* I believe, but I haven't been able to finish the prayer."

"And that's why you think we're being punished?" Sarah asks. "Because you lost your faith and I never had any?"

"You're wrong about that. About never having any. You do. I see that now. That's what brought me here. I think you see God in the music. You just call Him something else." He nods toward the piano. "And I think that's why you should play us something again. Maybe from that recital of yours."

Sarah strokes the piano keys the way Marcus did the scrap of metal. God in the music. It's a lovely sentiment, but not one she can believe. There's only this world, her gut tells her, and there's nothing left for her in it. Not even music. "I'm not sure I can finish the prayer," she says, drawing her hands back from the keys. "But…" She stands, opens the piano lid, and takes out the bag of chips. "We can finish these at least."

She sits beside Marcus, opens the bag with a messy rip, and holds it out to him. They eat without talking, filling the hall with chewing, crunching, and the crumpling sounds of foil as they reach into the bag for more. The salty chips scratch on the way down—god, why couldn't they have found water instead of chips?—but her stomach offers a greedy grumble of appreciation.

"I'd kill for something to wash these down with," Marcus says. She shoots him a look, and he winces. "Sorry, bad choice of words."

For once, she's not the one wording things badly. Sarah wants to laugh at that, but she's still not sure about Marcus. She doesn't *need* to be anymore, but she wants to be. Because she still doesn't know whose dried blood is on his jacket. "*Have* you killed anyone?"

Marcus shakes his head, avoids her gaze. "Girl, we've been through this already."

"And I have every reason to think you'd lie. That's what you told me earlier." She should leave it alone. But it's the end of the world, they've nearly finished the last of their food, and so she presses. "So have you?"

"Lied? Or killed someone?"

"Both."

"Neither." Marcus rubs the back of his neck, then meets her gaze. "That was a lie."

Sarah waits for anger to boil up within her, or at the very least annoyance, but all she can muster is numbness.

"Your not-a-boyfriend," Marcus says, "what was his name? Chris? I could have just ran. I got the chips back, he was down, I could have just ran. But I was so pissed off, I… I started wailing on him, you know? Didn't stop till I heard bone crack. *Then* I ran. I dropped the chips and ran. And I kept running." He hugs his knees close to his chest and rocks back and forth. "I may as well have killed him. Broken arm, ranting mad like you said, that gash on his head." He fingers his jacket, looking as if he wants to tear it off. "He won't last long out there like that."

She imagines that: Chris cradling his arm, Marcus kicking him the way she kicked the piano leg. "The world's ending," she says softly. "None of us are going to last long."

"True. But we can try, right?"

"Why bother?"

"Why bother?" Marcus lets go of his knees, turns toward her with open-mouthed incredulity. "When you were playing earlier, when I first came in here—what were you thinking about?"

She shrugs. "Phrasing, tempo, don't screw up that chord this time."

"I'm trying to be serious here, girl. You started playing Beethoven in the middle of the damn apocalypse. I don't wanna hear you were thinking about wrong notes. I wanna know what was really going through your head."

Fear, she thinks, and the thought is so honest that it chips through the numbness. Her chest aches, claws at her words as she speaks. "I was wishing it would just end already, so I didn't have to keep wondering about how and when it was finally going to happen. So I didn't have to keep wondering about my parents, or my friends, or my teachers, or even Chris. But I was alone, and I didn't want to die alone, so I played." She swipes at her eyes, but her hand comes back dry. "Everything but hope. That's what was going through my head."

Marcus nods. The human bobblehead again. Despite herself, Sarah smiles.

"I was thinking I needed a miracle," Marcus says. "To believe again. But talking to you just now..." He digs the last chip out of the bag and offers it to her. "I think I needed this. Some chips, some company, some Mozart. A little bit of meaning again."

She breaks the proffered chip in half. It seems only right to split it. "I still haven't played any Mozart, you know. Since you came in here."

"I don't know," he says with a laugh. "And I'm okay with that."

Together, they eat their respective halves of the chip, like some sort of absurd, minimart-fueled last supper.

Outside, a rumble sounds. Another quake or aftershock, perhaps, or another collapsing building. Maybe both. But the ground remains steady beneath them. The rumble sounds again, overhead, rolling like a drum. Thunder.

Marcus skitters to his knees, neck long as he stares up at the ceiling, like a small creature listening for a predator's approach. Sarah stands and lets the empty chip bag flutter to the floor. Thunder. How long has it been since she's heard thunder? And if there's thunder…

Heavy pelts hit the roof, few and scattered at first. Then, all at once, the precise strikes blend into a sound like static. Sarah listens, transfixed by how unfamiliar the music of a storm has become to her ears. Then a counterpoint begins—individual drops, plinks against metal, crescendoing into a steady, splashing stream. Rain trickles down from the ceiling, onto the fallen debris that opened its path inside.

Marcus whoops and jumps to his feet. He thrusts his head beneath the cascade, mouth open, letting the water pour down his throat and over his face. Sarah's throat prickles, a dryness like rough cotton. The bottle, where the hell did she throw the bottle?

She scrambles around the stage until she finds where it landed. With trembling hands, she holds it beneath the trickle. Water, she's going to have water, and if she has water she can survive. But the mouth of the bottle is too small, missing too much, sending it sloshing over the sides.

Outside, the rain slows, then stops altogether. *No, no, no.* Sarah tries to steady her hands. More, she needs more if she's going to make it. If *they're* going to make it. But the trickle dwindles to drops too small to catch. Then, with one final, feeble plink, the last drop falls.

Sarah whimpers, but then looks at the bottle and laughs. Half full. She shouldn't be amused by ridiculous clichés at the world's end, yet she laughs again. Her glass is half full. She takes a gulp, then another. She swirls a mouthful around before swallowing. Cold and gritty and tasteless, she declares rainwater to be the finest thing she's ever drunk.

Marcus lets out another whoop and presses his wet hands to his mouth. "Go ahead, girl. Tell me that was just random chance. Tell me that wasn't God."

"That was just random chance," she says, though looking at Marcus, she understands why he believes otherwise. Bright-eyed and buoyant, with a smile near as wide as his head—there's joy in his faith, and she wishes she could feel it too. But her joy rests elsewhere. She takes another gulp of water. "This particular bit of random chance gives me hope, at least. I didn't have that before you showed up."

Another rumble sounds, a noise louder and deeper than the thunder. A primal groan that rises from the earth's ill-tempered depths, yet doesn't shake the ground. A harsh, unnaturally white light pushes its way through the gaps in the hall's half-collapsed wall.

"What is that?" Sarah asks.

The light intensifies, and Marcus steps toward it. "The end," he says, leaping down from the stage. "I think this is the end."

Sarah's head fills with images of the sun pulsing and brightening until it explodes. But Marcus will keep walking toward the light. She knows that without asking. Moth to flame. Usually such a dismissive metaphor, but what if the moth sees beauty in the flame, finds meaning in it, and dies with joy? That's a belief worth envying.

Marcus turns back to her, hand outstretched. "You don't have to be alone. You could come with me."

She stares at his hand, expecting indecision, yet feeling none. Earlier she would have taken it, even without knowing who he was. But now…

"Thank you," she says. "But I have a recital to play. A prayer to finish."

She sits at the piano, touches her fingers to the keys, and starts to play: Mozart, Piano Sonata No. 11. Marcus listens for a moment, eyes closed, head swaying in time. His mouth spreads into a grin. "It's nice finally hearing some Mozart."

Sarah smiles, fingers still traversing the keys as Marcus climbs up the pile of debris and strides into the light.

"For Thine is the Kingdom," he declares, his dark silhouette fading as it melds with the white glow, "and the power, and the glory, forever. Amen!"

Alone yet joyful, Sarah plays until the end.

✄〜

Barbara A. Barnett is a writer, musician, orchestra librarian, Odyssey Writing Workshop graduate, coffee addict, wine lover, and all-around geek. Her short fiction has appeared in publications such as *Beneath Ceaseless Skies, Lady Churchill's Rosebud Wristlet, Fantasy Magazine, Cast of Wonders, Daily Science Fiction*, and *Flash Fiction Online*. You can find her lurking about the Philadelphia area or online at www.babarnett.com. She would like to dedicate "This Is the Way the Prayer Ends" to the late Gerald Warfield, a fellow writer, musician, and Odfellow whose feedback on and cheerleading for this story were invaluable, and whose insight, wit, adventurous spirit, and friendship are deeply missed.

Did You Hear the Angels Sing?

H.L. Fullerton

WAYLON WAS DEAD. They used to joke that where there was a Wills, there was a Way, but now Way was gone so Wills wasn't sure where that left him. Presumably answering questions for the nice men in suits who stopped by to inform him of his husband's murder.

To be honest, the nice men in suits—law enforcement of some type; they'd flashed ID badges, but Wills' brain had been so otherwise occupied juggling shock and grief and fear that he hadn't zeroed in on what agency was ripping his soul in two—they weren't actually nice. The suits they wore were nice and they looked nice in them (the one on the left more than the one on the right), but Wills, who Way always said was a great judge of character, didn't think either man knew much about niceness. Wills recognized an interrogation when it showed up on their doorstep.

The two suits who had bullied their way into his living room and cornered him on the couch—the couch he and Way had shared only that morning— asked him about Way, how long they'd been together, where they'd met, did Way have any enemies, all sorts of questions except the one they had to be salivating to ask.

Wills didn't have anything to do with Way's death and these two knew it. He wanted to toss them out and it was tempting, *so* tempting. Fingers itched; limbs ached. But Wills couldn't allow himself to be tempted. The part that wanted to shred and storm and shriek with fierce delight had to be kept hidden. The last thing Way would have wanted was for Wills to end up killed, too.

"Everyone loved Way," Wills said as his voice strained and hands shook. And it was true. But Wills, of course, loved Way most.

"Where was Waylon headed?"

To the school's radio station. Wills had told him not to go, said it wasn't worth the risk. But Way had insisted it was the best way of spreading the word. "The campus gym, I think. He said he was going to work out. Maybe stop by his office."

Both gym and office were in the opposite direction of the radio station, but Way had taken his gym bag to give himself a reasonable excuse for being on campus and so Wills could have plausible deniability. The men shared a look, maybe deciding who would ask the next question. "Any reason your husband would lie to you?"

"No."

"Is it possible—"

"I want to see him."

They didn't recommend it. They promised to be in touch. They'd catch this guy, whoever he was. Oh, and one more thing, "Did you hear the angels sing?"

"No," Wills lied, "I wasn't there." He didn't dare say anything else.

The men left. Maybe they had believed him.

But maybe not.

ഇരു

Three months ago, a band of angels appeared at the re-opening of a mini-mart in nearby Bethel. They sang a song—just the one—then disappeared.

Soon after, the death rate in Fairfield County soared, most notably among those who had posted blurry pics or distorted audio of the mini-mart miracle online.

Wills and Way hadn't advertised their presence, but Way must have been spotted in someone else's pic. And everyone knew that wherever there was a Way, there'd be a Wills. It was only a matter of time before the men in nice suits determined he'd been there, too.

Thank God he'd stayed in the car.

ഇരു

The not-nice men followed him into the funeral home where Wills tried to make arrangements for a body no one would let him see. This time, they wore spendier suits and intimidating sunglasses. They wanted to know what Way had told Wills about the angels. "There's a chance someone is targeting people who attended the mini-mart opening."

Yeah, no shit. "Sure, sure. Whatever I can do to help. Way said it was beautiful."

It had been catchy, a sort of punk pop/operatic funk deluge. The most wondrous sounds Wills had ever heard. The kind of music that changed whoever listened. Way claimed all change was for the better. Wills wasn't completely certain that was true.

"Anything else?"

Wills shrugged as if it didn't matter. "That it changed him. That given a chance, it would change the world."

Wills bet whoever had sent these two suits over wasn't thrilled about the world changing. Wills wasn't thrilled about how his life had changed. Losing his Way was just the crappiest tip of this conspiratorial pyramid.

"Are there any recordings?"

"Those would be at the school, Way used their studio. Or on his phone. Did you search his phone?" The men stared at Wills. Perhaps he'd gone too far. Sounded too accusatory.

"Recordings of the angels."

"Way didn't have any. He played me snippets from the Internet, but those were mostly static-y. Why? What does that have to do with his murder?" That was definitely too accusatory, but Wills was tired of his temper being leashed. Way always called him Wills-ful when he got tetchy and if anything should make him furious, Way's dying should be top of the list. Wills ought to be angrier, much angrier, at these men, at the loss of Way. Wills resented the angels most for making Way's death bearable. Whatever had touched his soul that day made it harder for him to be—well, human.

"Did he try to play it?"

Wills needed to be careful he didn't reveal himself. Talking about the angels meant remembering the angels and, if he thought about that day too long, their song reverberated through his entire body, crescendo-ing to epiphanic heights which his tongue longed to give voice to, despite its present inability to recreate the heavenly lyrics. Also, it was potentially life-ending. He picked up an urn and gripped it tightly to distract his awestruck brain. "Way tried. But he got frustrated that none of his efforts came close and stopped playing altogether. In some ways, it ruined him."

It hadn't. If Way had more time—if the men in nice suits hadn't killed him—Wills had no doubt his husband could have recreated the angels' song. Way'd had that kind of ear. What had ruined Way, and all the other souls who'd come together that afternoon, was whomsoever employed the men before him. Although sometimes it felt like Way wasn't gone at all—and not just because Wills carried him in his heart.

"You look like you've put on some weight since the mini-mart," the prettier man said.

Wills tugged at his t-shirt, hid his increasing girth beneath crossed arms. "My weight doesn't have anything to do with the mini-mart," he lied. "Was there anything else?"

The men left the funeral home, but Wills was certain they didn't go far. He didn't like his chances of surviving a third encounter with them.

ℴ℥

Wills saw Way see the angels before he saw them himself. He'd been watching for Way to come out of the mini-mart, cringing as the Live Music part of the grand re-opening extravaganza butchered Prince's "Little Red Corvette." The song ended, badly, there was a smattering of applause, and a new song started. The intro alone was miles better than anything they'd played yet, although Wills couldn't identify the song. Then Way came out, glanced over, up, and froze. When he stayed stock-still, Wills simultaneously reached for the door handle and checked to see what had stopped Way in his tracks.

First, Wills thought the band had set off fireworks, which in the middle of the day made no sense. Second, he thought it was some special effects projected images (also not very effective in full sun). He squinted in hopes of figuring out what the images were when, as if some long unused part of his brain booted up, he noticed the band wasn't playing even though the music was and Wills thought, *Angels.*

They shimmered like aurorae in vaguely humanish shapes and had wings, several sets. The largest flickered fast like a hummingbird's and seemed to keep them hovering like giants just above the horizon. Smaller wings, dotted with eyespots, opened and closed in rhythm with the song, in the way of musical instruments. Their faces had faces, human and *not,* which rotated as they sang. In their arms, they held…something.

Wills saw swords, Way saw trumpets.

But they both agreed it was angels that sang at the mini-mart.

Wills and Way fought *a lot* over the angels at the mini-mart: Wills wanting to forget it ever happened, go on with their lives, go on *living* period; Way insisting that angels didn't appear for no reason, that they'd been chosen to— Wills always cut him off at that point, yelling, "We didn't choose! We were out of goddamn milk!" And Way was out of Starburst, but Wills would never begrudge Way his candy fix. And Way would calmly say, "Wills, we *heard* the song."

No matter how many deaths and disappearances the local news reported (first among women of child-bearing age, then everyone else) Way believed it was a blessing. Wills knew enough Bible stories to know angels heralded destruction or conception, sometimes both. Neither a forecast Wills had wanted anything to do with.

But if Way wanted to change the world, Wills would change it for him.

℘℃

Wills abandoned the home he and Way had shared, following the plan they'd made once the murders started. They'd thought they would have more time before needing to disappear. And Way had wanted to play his latest attempt over the air. Now it was up to Wills to stay alive long enough to see the angels' message realized. Long enough for him to complete the change that started with the first hosanna.

Wills' gut cramped and he breathed through the pain as the concordant notes in his head played louder. His tongue formed sounds he almost understood. He wasn't sure if he was turning into an angel or *having* an angel. Either way, Wills figured he'd see Way soon.

℘℃

H.L. Fullerton writes fiction—mostly speculative, occasionally about miracles at mini-marts—which can be found in more than 60 publications including *Tales to Terrify*, *Kaleidotrope*, and *Underland Arcana*. On Bluesky as @HLFullerton.bsky.social.

Devil Dog

Len Bailey

"OH, POOR TAFFY."

The little girl knelt on her back porch in a back hollow in the back of the world. She cried and cried as only brokenhearted little girls can. Enough teardrops to fill a coal bucket. Her dog, no bigger than a bread box, was tied to the stoop post. He whined. He drooped his head, for his body was covered with red sores and scabs except for a few patches of hair on his hind quarters and on the very tips of his ears. He twitched. He trembled. He looked up with eyes so forlorn that she cried all over again.

"What're you crying for, Corky Sue?" came a voice. "You never seen the mange before?"

The little girl spun around. There stood a tall man dressed in a soldier's uniform. His chest had medals and colorful ribbons.

"Lawton?" cried Corky Sue. She clapped and went to hug him, but Taffy bared his teeth—the only thing left to identify the pitiful creature as a dog.

"Stop it right now." She jerked on his leash. "Don't you remember Lawton? For shame."

"Oh, he don't mean no harm." Lawton smiled pleasantly. All of his smiles were pleasant. All the girls in Bent Branch Hollow and the upper coal camp were in love with him, or had been when he went away to war. "I'd be fractious too if I was bald and covered with sores and such."

"Why, I didn't know you were back from Germany," said Corky Sue "Did you bring me back some chocolate? I see it all the time in them moving picture shows, soldiers giving chocolate to children. Could you teach me German? I like German. It sounds like you're cussing but getting away with it. What do those swords on your patch mean? Oh, have you been down the hollow to

195

see Janet Lou, yet? She'll just die. Are you home to stay, Lawton? What'd your mother say when you showed up?"

He put his head back and laughed. But Taffy had not yet fallen in with the jocular mood. He growled deep in his throat.

"I reckon my surprise homecoming backfired on me." Lawton plopped himself down on a chair next to the ringer washing machine. He fished in his pocket for his cigarettes and lit up. The smoke trailed out over the back yard. "I stepped off the bus just now. Walked all the way up the hollow toting my gunny sack, and wouldn't you know it, no one's at home. Nossir. Serves me right, doesn't it? But I need to stay hid away until I surprise mama proper-like."

He craned his neck and peered down five back yards to his own. Large white sheets billowed from his mother's clothesline like sails in the stiff April breeze. If the coal train was to chug by, those sheets would turn a dingy gray. He settled back and the chair creaked like an old man's bones. He drew on his cigarette, squinting through the smoke at Taffy, who continued to regard him with hostility.

"I didn't know you smoke, Lawton."

"Swore I never would, Corky Sue, really I did. Saw what it did to my daddy. But the army changes a fellow in ways he don't figure on."

"Well, I can't hardly believe it's you."

"Can't hardly believe you recognize me in this uniform with all these stripes down my arm," he replied. "You were only five years old when I shipped off."

She stared him up and down. His medals glowed in the shade. Her blue eyes met his brown ones and he smiled kindly.

"Careful of your dog, Corky Sue. Strange things can happen between beast and man."

"Well, I'm awful tired to the point of exhaustion, to tell you the agonizing truth. I've been weeping with a lot of burdensome lamentation, crying the tears of Job, 'cause of Taffy, here. My daddy says he'll die soon. Mama won't feed him no more. Says I'm a witch for keeping such a devil dog."

"She's just kidding with you. Taffy sure looks like a devil dog, though. Like I said, he hasn't got nothing but the mange. Real bad case of it, though."

"I thought he was dying last night. I was expecting myself to plan a funeral."

"Dying? From rabies or fever maybe. But not mange, usually. But your daddy's right about one thing. Taffy's not long for this world if he gets much worse."

Parts of Taffy's hide had broken into open sores. He brought up a hind foot and scratched one of the few places on his head that still had hair.

"I can't stop him from doing that," Corky Sue said.

"I'd be inclined to help him if he didn't hate me so much."

"Can you help us, Lawton? Would you?"

He sat forward in the chair and looked her right in the eye. "You got to go somewhere scary. You gotta take Taffy up to Hell's Hollow."

"Where's that?"

"Pigpen Hollow, same thing. And once you get there, you got to do something terrible."

She looked out over her back yard, across the alley, to the mountain that towered behind her house. She shivered. "I can't, Lawton. I'm not allowed up to that Pigpen Hollow. Daddy would whip me good for it. It's an evil place. A place of particular distress. Jeremiah Banks went up there and got himself lost once."

"It's a bad place for sure. But there's no other way to save that pitiful creature of yours. He's got but a few hanks of hair left on him."

"Corky Sue?" A voice called from inside the house.

"It's mama!" she squealed.

Lawton jumped up. He tiptoed over and pressed himself against the back of the house. A woman in an apron came to the screen door.

"Corky Sue, who you talking to out there?"

The little girl just shrugged and shot a sideways glance at Lawton, who grinned back.

"I hope it ain't that old dog of yours, honey. He's as good as dead—hate to hurt your feelings so. Becky and Roger's heading down to the schoolhouse. Go on, now, and play with your friends."

"Taffy's my whole world, mama. I hate Becky Jo. She's a tattle-teller, and Roger's a little pecker."

"I'll wash your mouth out with soap, young lady, and we'll see how you sass me. I know you're upset about Taffy, and I am too, such a sweet dog before his sickness. But wipe off your long face or folks will think you got the mange, too. Go on now, and get."

"Yes'm."

Corky Sue relaxed and winked at Lawton, a signal the coast was clear. The soldier leaned against the washing machine. He took another puff on his cigarette.

She asked, "Why's it called Hell's Hollow?"

He traced the corner of his mouth with his thumb. "Flames and smoke, is all, Corky Sue, and real bad smells. Hotter'n Nebuchadnezzar's furnace. But it's Taffy's only chance—I ain't kidding you."

"I'm not going up there, Lawton. I'm not brave like you."

The soldier craned his neck to peer over at his back yard again—no sign of anyone at home. He snapped a look at his fancy army watch and knelt in front of her. "Look here, Corky Sue, I'll take you there myself. If your daddy finds out, you just tell him Sergeant Lawton Hunt escorted you the whole way. How's that?"

"You'd do that for Taffy? Really, would you?"

"But you've got be real brave when the time comes. Just like a soldier."

"What for?"

He looked at her with solemn eyes. "You'll see when we get there. C'mon."

Lawton led the way across the back yard. Past the squawking chickens, past the onion garden, Corky Sue following with Taffy on a leash. She glanced over her shoulder. No sign of her mama. They followed the alley for a while and then turned into a grove of trees and up a footpath leading into the woods between the hills.

"Not a lot of folks know this trail." Lawton stopped to catch his breath. "Lordy. I gotta quit these cigarettes."

"A secret path?"

Lawton chuckled good-naturedly. He fished out another Lucky Strike and lit up again. "Cherokees used it years and years ago." He breathed in and sighed, "Oh, the things you forget when you're gone from home too long."

Corky Sue shivered, but climbing the mountainside heated them up real quickly. They came to a rickety old bridge spanning a stream. Taffy quieted down and became a little perky. Maybe the coolness of the woods soothed his itchy hide.

Up ahead a neighboring mountain brought its slope down to bar their way, but Lawton knew a hidden passageway used by Confederates to give Union soldiers the slip during the Civil War. "And we gotta watch out for snakes," he cautioned.

Corky Sue kicked at last year's leaves as they walked. "Lawton, why'd you ever go off to the war?"

"Wanted to get outta these mountains for a spell. Wanted to see the world. And I'm too tall to be a motorman in the mines like my daddy. If it was me driving that tram in the mining shaft, my helmet might graze those electric wires. Fry me like a piece of bacon."

They hardly made a sound as they wound through the trees and picked their way down a flight of old wooden railroad ties laid down like stairs, slippery with creeping plants and moss. At the bottom, Lawton led the way through a bend in the trees and out onto a dirt road, then past rows of pigpens with slumbering pigs lying in their own stench, dreaming contentedly of hog heaven.

The little girl scrunched up her nose again. "It sure stinks back here."

"Be glad it's not summertime." Lawton wiped his brow with his sleeve. "I guess there's other things you don't miss while you're gone."

Corky Sue snickered. "You look kind of funny, Lawton, standing out here in the middle of Pigpen Hollow all dressed up in that fancy uniform with your ribbons and such. Real funny."

The hollow grew narrower and narrower, and Lawton said, "Makes a soul feel pressed in, don't it? Why, it's so dark up the head of this hollow they've got to pipe in the daylight."

The joke fell flat. They looked up the sheer sides of the surrounding mountains hemming them in. The land grew quiet and watchful.

Above the gloom appeared a massive head with a sagging jaw of sharp teeth supported by a long thin neck, like something prehistoric. Corky Sue drew in her breath sharply. About the monster's feet coiled immense snakes, frozen in time.

"That's just an old steam shovel, Corky," Lawton said tenderly. The snakes turned out to be rusty old rails from the mines, bent into fantastic shapes. Nearby, a crumbling brick structure had succumbed to thickets of ivy, sweet everlasting, and rhododendron blossoms. Two large spotted porkers looked up from furrowing, grunting heavily, their shoulder hairs bristling.

"I don't want to go any further, Lawton," Corky Sue said.

"Got to, if you want to save that dog of yours."

Close by, a large garbage can flickered with yellow fire. Sparks hovered and danced like restless souls tied unwillingly to this earth, and then danced upward, released to wing their way to heaven.

Lawton pointed up the path with the fingers holding his cigarette. "Up yonder is where it gets real bad, the track where the trolley motor dumps off its load of bone. Bone is slate, Corky Sue, leftover ore. Coal Company's been dumping it down the mountainside for years. After a while it'll catch fire and burn for months. Looks like Hades back here. Hell's Hollow. The coal tar boils out of the slate—creosote, they call it. Time was it got so bad it seeped down and polluted the creek which flows on down to the coal camp. Folks complained about the bad water so the Company built a dam to keep the creosote back."

They came to stand on the edge of the small dam. There lay a foul lake of water covered with a thick film of black, oily liquid—creosote—grimly reflecting the strip of blue sky overhead. Taffy whimpered pitifully and brushed against Corky Sue.

"Good," said Lawton simply. Carefully he ground out his cigarette butt so as not to ignite the standing pool of noxious, malodorous coal tar. "They haven't burned it off."

His face became serious, his jaw muscles working.

"What's war like, Lawton?" asked Corky Sue in a small voice.

"You're just like Janet Lou. Real good at guessing my thoughts. Sometime I'll tell you, hon. Just not now. I will say, though, some parts of Italy looked just like this, all barren and dead and burned to hell."

"I thought you were in Germany."

"I ended up fighting in Italy. Mussolini's friends with Hitler, you know. I saw a lot of bad things. Lots of bombing and burning and shooting and hunkering down in the hills. But like I said, Corky Sue, that's a story for later on when you're older."

"So, you going to marry Janet Lou?"

Lawton laughed. "You sure got a wheelbarrow full of questions." He crossed his arms and said, "A long time before I shipped out, I knew I was going to marry her. In fact, I hid a secret treasure for her."

"A treasure? Really?"

"But if I tell you where it is, you got to swear not to tell anybody."

"Don't say it out loud." She motioned to the little dog. "Taffy can't keep a secret."

"Raise your right hand, Corky Sue, and swear."

She stood straight as a ladder and raised a small white hand. "I swear I won't tell nobody nothing never about your treasure, Lawton."

He leaned down and whispered in her ear. Taffy whined and sniffed. "Now that's our special secret, Corky Sue."

"It sure is."

He looked Taffy right in the eye. The dog growled again.

"Here's the terrible thing you got to do, Corky Sue, that I warned you about if you want to save this here dog of yours." He lit a cigarette and flicked the match the other direction from the dam. Under his breath he said, "You got to pick up Taffy and throw him into that creosote."

Her mouth gaped wide. "I darn well will not." She wrinkled up her face and pointed up at him. "And you can go ahead and tell my daddy I was here in this bad place if you want to, and you can tell him I said a swear like I just did. But I'm not never doing no such thing to Taffy."

"I said you'd have to be awful brave when the time came." He breathed out some lazy smoke and then shrugged. "Well alright then, let's get on back home. Just remember, you had your chance. Taffy had his chance."

"But throwing him in there will kill him. Or he'll drown."

"Naw, he won't. But he'll sure sound like he's dying." Lawton studied her. "I'd never tell you to do something that wasn't good, especially with your precious dog. But I'll tell you this for a certain fact: if you don't throw Taffy in there, he'll die real soon."

Taffy shuffled closer to her. She grimaced to feel his bare skin against her leg.

"Will you help me, Lawton?"

He shook his head and exhaled smoke out his nostrils. "I will not. Some things a person's got to do for herself."

She bit her lip. She reached down and picked up Taffy. Ever so gently she unhooked his collar. Taffy seemed to sense something was wrong and he began to bark and struggle in her arms. Truth be told, as seasoned and as tough Sergeant Lawton Hunt was, he nearly wept to see Corky Sue with tears streaming down her face toss her beloved dog out into that pool of vile, odorous, viscous liquid.

With a splash the dog vanished below the surface only to reappear, howling and whimpering, whining, grunting, yelping, yapping, and growling—enough pitiful noise to make anyone shudder. Corky Sue cried out in tragic grief to see that sloppy, greasy dog swimming back toward them.

Taffy reached shore and shot away like a tar-covered comet—if a comet can be said to howl and yammer. He fled down the hollow around the pigpens and clean out of sight.

"Now look what you done." Corky Sue whimpered and wiped her cheek with the back of her hand. She leveled a finger at him. "Just look what you done."

"He'll be alright."

They made their way back down the hollow and then back along the path between the mountains, Corky Sue crying over her empty leash. They didn't talk. Once or twice she thought she caught sight of Taffy scampering through the shadows, a fierce little monster with sharp, gnashing teeth and bulging eyes.

In no time they found themselves in Corky Sue's back yard and walked around to the front of her house.

"Well, look'ee yonder." Lawton pointed as a car pulled up in front of his house. A man got out wearing an army uniform. "It's Charlie Fergus, the fellow who recruited me. Ol' Charlie Fergus, still wearing his army pistol. How'd he know I was back?"

They both waved and Charlie waved back, and opened the front gate leading to Lawton's house.

Lawton knelt down in front of her. "You were brave today, Corky Sue. You did real good with Taffy. The U.S. Army would be proud to enlist you. I got to go down to my house now, but I'll see you and Taffy later."

Corky Sue watched Lawton run away, his army boots pounding the dirt road. He jumped over his front gate and flew up the front porch stairs after Charlie Fergus. From inside the house, Mrs. Hunt let out a high-pitched cry of surprise.

Lawton was finally home.

Over the next few days Corky Sue surveyed her back yard from her upstairs bedroom window. She'd catch a glimpse of Taffy now and then, or so she thought. Her little nerves were on the brink of shattering. She would lie in bed at night and toss. Where was Taffy sleeping? What was he eating? Maybe some bear or panther would eat him—Taffy couldn't defend himself. She thought she heard him one night, but his bark had changed into something she didn't recognize. Her thoughts drifted to Hell's Hollow. She liked Lawton. He had a way of putting a body at ease. She hoped everything he'd said was true but part of her thought she'd never see Taffy again. At least, not the Taffy she knew.

One day her mother poked her head into her bedroom. She was wearing her nice dress and earrings even though it wasn't Sunday. "Corky Sue, I told you to get away from the window and get yourself dressed. Stop looking for that beast of yours. I've laid out your polka-dot dress you look so nice in and your Sunday shoes. Your father's waiting on us. I'm not going to tell you again."

"Yes'm."

Mrs. Hunt, Lawton's mother, was having a bunch of folks over to her house, Corky Sue figured, because of her son coming home from the war and all. Janet Lou would be there, and as Corky Sue wiggled into her best dress, she felt a twinge of jealousy. Sure, Janet Lou was a grown woman and she herself was just a little girl, but Lawton had a real charming way about him. Everybody loved him. Corky Sue loved him. She practiced a sweet smile in the mirror. Lawton had told her his secret, and only her.

Corky Sue's daddy was in a suit, which he hardly never was, and her mother looked awfully dressed up with her white gloves and her best purse. They walked down the road to Lawton's house. The front porch was crowded with folks from all over Bent Branch Hollow and Breggen Coal Camp.

"Where's Lawton?" Corky Sue was watching for the handsome soldier.

Her mother leaned down and said in her ear, "You just behave yourself, young lady, and don't ask such foolish questions." Corky Sue didn't think it was foolish. Lawton needed reminding their trip to Hell's Hollow was a secret.

Mr. Varney nodded at her. Corky didn't much like him. His eyes always closed when he smiled. She'd never seen him so scrubbed up before and wearing a suit. He wasn't a churchgoer, not with that filthy mouth of his, nor half these other coal miners.

She followed her mama through the crowded porch into the living room. There were no balloons or punch or cookies or fiddle playing or dancing. These folks looked none too happy, neither.

Something caught her eye. A big picture of Lawton hung on the wall with a black wreath around it and draped with black ribbon, and two American flags crossed at the bottom. Mrs. Hunt sat nearby blowing her nose with a tissue. Mr. Charlie Fergus and all sorts of women huddled around her. A cold shock went over Corky Sue. Below the picture was printed these words:

SGT. LAWTON P. HUNT
1923-1945
U.S. 10TH MOUNTAIN DIVISION
KILLED IN ACTION

"Mamma, what—?"

"Hush, honey. This is a memorial service for Lawton. You remember him, Janet Lou's man? You stay here whilst we pay our respects. Don't you go wandering off. You can go play with Amanda and Cecil but don't get that dress dirty. Do you hear me?"

But Corky Sue did wander off. Her head swam. Lawton dead? Killed in action? Here in Kentucky? Nothing made any sense.

She made her way through a forest of tall people, trees that politely moved out of her way as she searched for an out-of-the-way place, somewhere empty to match her empty feelings. She came upon a quiet bedroom. A young, pretty woman sat alone on the edge of a four-poster bed. She looked as lost as her heart.

"Hello Janet Lou," Corky Sue said quietly.

Janet Lou nodded. She looked dull. The bedroom walls were decorated with army posters and airplanes. The bedspread was dark blue. This must be Lawton's bedroom.

Corky Sue put her hand on Janet Lou's knee. "Where did Lawton go?"

"He's not here." Janet Lou sniffled. "He's never going be here again. He's gone, that's all. I loved him so, but he's gone."

"But he loves you. Where would he go without you?"

"I thought he loved me. But his letters sounded different. I wondered, truly I did." Janet Lou studied her tissue and then applied it to the corner of her eye. But the more Corky Sue comforted her, the more her tears flowed. "I thought maybe Lawton found himself some pretty foreign girl and wasn't ever coming back, or he'd bring back a foreign girl, like in the story books, and I'd die of embarrassment and of a wearisome broken heart. But maybe it's true that war can make a man vexatious. I guess he did love me after all."

"There's no girl prettier than you," said Corky Sue.

"Thank you, hon." Janet Lou ran her hand over his bed's coverlet. "Yes, I know he loved me with a true heart, the way he'd caress my hair and my cheek. The way our fingers would touch as we walked along, and we'd hold hands for hours."

"He was so nice to me and Taffy just last week," said Corky Sue.

"Enough of that foolishness." A woman's voice came from the doorway. It was Mrs. Hunt, Lawton's mother, being helped along by Charlie Fergus. "He was killed in action, child. Killed in the war."

"What war, ma'am?"

Mrs. Hunt's voice wavered. "That's enough, Corky Sue. Lawton's gone. That's all."

"He was doing fine just a few days ago over at our house. He helped me with Taffy. That's my dog."

Mrs. Hunt wiped at her nose with a tissue. "None of your silly stories, young lady. Not now."

"But he was down at my house," persisted Corky Sue. "Charlie Fergus— we saw you about four days back going up to Lawton's house—"

"With the telegram from the army," said Charlie sadly, "stating that poor Lawton was killed."

"But you waved at us."

He frowned and scratched his head. "I waved at you, Corky Sue. I sure didn't see nobody else."

"But I heard you shout, Mrs. Hunt," declared Corky Sue. "Surely I did. When Lawton ran through your front door you yelped."

"I cried out when I read the telegram from the War Office. Please leave me be. I've always thought you were a sweet little girl, but this is mean of you, Corky Sue."

"But Lawton had just taken me over to Hell's—" she bit her lip.

"I can't abide you right now, child." Mrs. Hunt's voice had risen to the point that folks in the kitchen had fallen quiet.

"What's going on in here?" Corky Sue's mother and father appeared in the doorway.

"Corky Sue's just a little confused," said Janet Lou, sympathetically. "Aren't you?"

"Causing trouble's more like it," Corky Sue's father replied. "You come on out of there right now, young lady. You're in some real trouble."

Mrs. Hunt broke down crying again, burying her face in her hands. "You're a wicked little girl."

Janet Lou, her own eyes red on the edges from crying, patted the little girl on the shoulder. "She didn't mean no harm. A child's troubled heart can think up some strange stories."

"Straight up lying is what I call it," Charlie Fergus said.

"But Lawton was here. On Tuesday. He took me to Pigpen Hollow—Hell's Hollow—and we threw Taffy into the creosote up by the dam. Lawton said that'd cure Taffy's mange. I'm not making it up."

"That's enough, young lady." Her mother's voice sounded as dark and thick as molasses. Her father's eyes smoldered, and he worked his gnarled fingers. Corky Sue and her daddy were normally real close, but she'd clearly transgressed some terrible law in the far-off world of adult doings.

"Now, just a minute," said Janet Lou, looking into the little girl's frank, honest eyes. "How would she know to do such a thing with Taffy?"

Corky's mother stepped in and took her daughter by the hand. "Listen to me, young lady. We're going on home right now, and when I'm done with you, you won't be able to sit down for a week. You apologize to Mrs. Hunt, here. These folks are black with grieving and have lost their precious Lawton over in Germany. They don't need you—"

"Lawton wasn't in Germany," declared Corky Sue. "He was in Italy."

Mrs. Hunt looked up from her tissue. Her hand came to rest over the pocket where she kept the Western Union telegram. Her voice was barely a whisper. "Now, how would you know my Lawton was in Italy, child?"

"He told me."

Mrs. Hunt sat down on the bed next to Janet Lou. She stared at Corky Sue who looked unblinkingly back at her.

"What else did he say, my Lawton?"

"He said he loved Janet Lou, and he loved her forever and ever, even before he left for the war."

Mrs. Hunt put her arm around Janet Lou, who burst into soft sobbing.

"And Lawton," Corky Sue said, looking at the room of adults, "he told me a secret."

Corky Sue's father muttered something to her mother, and she went to guide her daughter out of the room. But Mrs. Hunt reached out and grasped the child's hand.

"Did he now? My Lawton told you a secret, Corky Sue? You wouldn't be playing a terrible trick on me, would you, child? I must tell you truthfully, my heart is broken."

"Lawton said he was going to ask Janet Lou to marry him."

"That ain't hardly no secret." Charlie Fergus snickered.

Corky Sue stood back. She gripped the knob atop the bed's footboard post. It wouldn't budge.

"Whatever are you doing, child?" asked Mrs. Hunt.

The little girl walked around the foot of the bed and twisted the other knob. It wouldn't budge either. She climbed up the far side of the bed onto the pillow and reached up to the headboard post. Everyone watched. To their amazement the knob twisted off. She fished into the cavity with her little fingers and grabbed hold of something. She replaced the knob carefully and scrambled down. She came around to Janet Lou.

Everyone craned their necks. Corky Sue opened her hand. There lay a dazzling, sparkling diamond engagement ring.

ഇരുജ

Bent Branch Hollow baked in the haze of an August sun. Limp birches and willows, too hot or weary to move, shadowed a creek which had slowed to a trickle. Dragonflies hovered and darted over what pools of murky water remained in the streambed while water moccasins sunned themselves on the sandstone rocks, oblivious to the swarms of hopping sand flies and to the orchestrated rise and fall of a million cicadas' steady, rhythmic song.

From her front porch, Corky Sue shielded her eyes. Down the frying-pan-hot dirt road came a bouncing, fluttering ball of black fur. It scampered up to the front gate and barked excitedly.

"Come here Taffy." But Taffy didn't come. Corky Sue sprang off her porch swing. The little dog panted in the heat and looked back the way he'd run. Down the road stood a tall soldier, the sun blazing off of his ribbons and patches and medals.

Taffy tore back down the road. He reached the soldier and began to dance on his hind legs. The soldier laughed. Then he went to walk away.

Corky Sue bounded down the porch stairs, out the gate, and fled down the road. Her feet didn't even touch the ground. She felt like she was in a dream, running toward heaven.

"Lawton!" she called. "Lawton!"

He turned back. She stopped, gasping in front of him. He smiled that lazy, good-natured smile, and readjusted the green gunny sack slung over his shoulder.

"I'm headed on home now, Corky Sue," he said, "into the arms of Jesus."

"Why didn't you fly straight through heaven's gates when you were killed in the war?"

"A soul lingers back sometimes, hon. I wanted to wander these hills some before I go. I'll miss this old hollow. But I stopped by this one last time, like I promised I would, to make sure everything's alright with your dog." He glanced down at the happy, panting creature. "Got to go through a little hell, ain't we, Taffy, before we can taste anything of heaven?"

Taffy stuck out his little red tongue and shook the dust out of his thick, black hair, and peered up at him with bright eyes. Lawton looked at the little girl. He brought up his hand in a slow, deliberate salute.

"You're my favorite soldier, Corky Sue."

Lawton's medals and ribbons wavered in her tear-filled eyes. She saluted back with a trembling hand. She found it awful hard to swallow with what felt like a lump of coal lodged in her throat.

And that was the last Corky Sue ever saw of Sergeant Lawton P. Hunt. He walked away down the hollow into the shimmering waves of the hot summer day.

Corky Sue found she was standing directly in front of Lawton's house. Out on the front porch stood Mrs. Hunt with tears streaming down her cheeks. Her hands were clasped to her chest.

And she was smiling.

§⊃⊂§

The author was born in Huntington, West Virginia, and his early childhood spent in the mountains of Eastern Kentucky, coal country. He received a BA in History from Trinity College in Deerfield, IL. He is the son of Don V. Bailey of Hardy, Kentucky (Pike County), who is the son of Clarence Bailey of mostly Cherokee blood, a true blue, tried and true, genuine deep-under-the-mountain coal miner. Len Bailey's other publications include *Sherlock Holmes and the Needle's Eye* (Thomas Nelson/Harper Collins) *Clabbernappers* (Tor Books/Macmillan), and *Fantasms* (Tor Books/Macmillan).

Salvation

John Nadas

ROBERT PUTS HIS reasoner to his temple and makes himself believe Emma means well. He fixes a trailer to his bike. It is a short ride. He pumps the hilltop and her house into view. He leaves his bike by her gate. He knows the code. His breath is still sweet with beer; it's bright, cold, and midday. There is no dead hose on the front lawn. There is no fountain of red, holey leaves. There is just a barbecue beating with coals and smoke.

Robert checks the window above the porch. They are all there: Jo, Emma, Max. They are chopping food, even Jo.

Robert rings the doorbell. He steps back. He listens. He knocks.

Max opens the door. He has some tongs, a cloth, and a plate. "Robert, how are you?" He takes Robert by the arm and shakes his hand.

Robert lets his hand move up and down. He nods. "Hello." He looks around Max. He wants to tell Jo to get ready.

"You fancy a barbie?" Max asks. He says "barbie" in an Australian accent.

Robert doesn't like the accent. He doesn't like Max either: he is the kind of person to do accents in everyday talk; he is too friendly; he is English, and views it as a role to play. "I'm alright," Robert says. He sees himself shrunken in the other man's sunglasses.

"Are you ever anything else?" Max asks. He smiles.

Robert never finds anything else in those smiles.

"I'll get her." Max puts his plate on a chair and goes inside.

Robert takes his hands out his pockets.

Emma comes out, her coat fat. "She doesn't want to go just yet."

Robert nods. "Alright." He's careful with his voice. "No problem." He stands on the edge of the porch. There is only a sun in the sky—nothing to look at. "I spoke to the school."

"No, Robert," Emma says, her hands up at him. "I don't want to talk about it. Please." She stamps her feet. "I wish it weren't so cold."

"We could apply for exemptions, from classes," Robert says. He's compromising still.

"How's your dad?" Emma asks. She stands next to him. She leans on the railings.

"He's alright." Robert sees the old man in his nest of blankets, music playing in the dark room because he never liked TV. "His brain is like you wouldn't believe."

"That's good."

"He's getting funny about religion," Robert says. He'd meant it as an offering; he wishes he hadn't said "funny."

Emma snorts. "He was so unkind to me about it." She glances at Robert. "Sorry."

"He's just practical." Robert's father was a mechanic; he also loves his son.

"It upset Jo," Emma says. She straightens.

"She can't go through life thinking it never ends," Robert says. Jo is too soft, he thinks; they won't let the world at her.

Emma hides her lips. She looks at him. "Is he scared?"

"He's dying," Robert says. And everyone knows it.

Emma touches his arm. "Things needn't be so hard for you."

Robert sighs. "I know." He'd thought about using a reasoner. Inputting some belief and putting it inside his dad's head. The old man would see there was nothing to worry about, plain as murder. "He's going to church. Virtual, I mean. St. Francis'."

"That priest must be as old as he is."

"I suppose." Robert doesn't know. He hasn't seen the priest since his wedding. Both men are at that manmade age where people bunch close together.

"He's always welcome at Glory Mountain," Emma says.

"I know we are," Robert says. She breathes it, he thinks. He remembers the girl he married. She'd sought ley lines in their part of Melbourne, spooled from Machu Pichu or Lascaux. She'd said Salem was "similarly transgressive." Robert can't believe it. "He wouldn't take to it," he says. For his father churches must have candles, gold, and kinglets.

Max comes then. He has Jo with him. They are holding hands.

Robert tries to ignore it. "Hi bud," he says.

"Hi dad," Jo says. She looks at the barbeque.

"Why don't you stay?" Max asks. He lifts the plate. "There's plenty."

You reasonable bastard, Robert thinks. He looks for the thought in Emma too. "Well, I had plans with Jo." He doesn't mean it but the words are a fence.

"Can't it wait?" Emma asks. "Robert, we hardly see each other." She cocks her head.

"We were going to go hiking today," Robert says. He looks at Jo.

"I don't like rocks," Jo says.

"I didn't say we'd go look at rocks," Robert says. He forgets about the formations.

"Take her tomorrow," Emma whispers, leaning toward him. "It's important, for Jo. To see us together."

Robert has read that. "Alright." He touches Jo's head.

Jo puts her hand on his.

"Do you want to stay here a bit?" Robert asks her.

"Yes," Jo says. She doesn't wait for a response; she goes back into the house.

Emma follows her.

So much for seeing us together, Robert thinks. He peers past the gate and down on the suburb. There are new builds, some tall and others short, a broil of seeded suns.

Max lays some food on the grill and presses it with his tongs.

The food looks good at least. Robert doesn't know where to sit. He feels like a drink now that the other one has gone from him but there is nothing to be seen.

"How's work?" Max asks.

"It's OK." Robert doesn't like to talk about it. Max enjoys his job. He remembers the other man likes fishing too. "Been fishing much?"

Emma used to swim in the river every week. "Water has a memory," she'd said. "Someone must have drowned in there. The fish are very stressed. I'm trying to calm the place."

"No," Max says. "Too busy with work."

Robert will not be baited.

"At the church."

"Right," Robert says. He went there once when he and Emma were still together. It was just a room with some chairs in a circle. They spoke about the Bible a bit. Max was the leader who was not a leader; he remains the leader who is not a leader. No way around leaders, Robert thinks. He hadn't felt anything. He hadn't listened. He'd watched the clock, the great cross up front with its shadow rolling onward like soldiers at night. Their baptisms, all turned inside out.

Max troubles some halved zucchinis. He pulls at an eggplant with some tongs. Its flesh tears on the metal beneath.

"You need oil," Robert says. He regrets it.

Max nods. "I know. I put some on. Don't worry. Aubergines are tricky." He turns, with his mouth like little glasses of milk. "We've grown a lot, Robert."

Robert sighs. "Alright." He looks around for some beers or something. It is too early for music but he must change the topic. "Got any music?"

"I don't really like music," Max says. "I'm glad you're staying."

"I can't stay long," Robert says.

"Emma wants to talk to you."

"I see," Robert says.

Max says, "And I don't have anyone to talk politics with." He laughs.

"I hate politics."

"No, you don't," Emma says, returning with some salad and two beers. She offers Robert one of the beers and puts the other down. She holds the door with her foot and waits.

Jo doesn't follow her.

Emma lets the door close.

Robert takes the beer. "Thanks."

Emma sniffs and smiles. She shakes her head.

"This beer is good," Robert says. He doesn't know what else to say.

Emma stands next to Max and takes his hand, squeezing it white. "Robert, I'm sorry."

"What are you sorry about?"

"Jo," Emma says. "We baptized her."

Robert drinks his beer. You bastards, he thinks. He feels like punching them both. He tries to shake the anger out of his head. It is just a bit of water. The belief could be undone, he thinks. All I'd have to do is get my own reasoner. He finishes the beer and puts it next to the second, where they clink with laughter. "I said no."

"I know, Robert, I know," Emma says. "It's—"

"It's such an important thing," Max says, nursing the food. "Emma, she was up worrying, weren't you, love? She couldn't deal with it. What would happen, if she died."

She never let me interrupt her, Robert thinks. "Did she want to?"

Max frowns. "She's just a kid."

"Emma?" Robert asks. He remembers when he wouldn't let Jo run free. Emma had fought him. "There are so many things we don't understand, so many lost folkways. Our ancestors saw things we forget to see when we're children. Or, more accurately, are made to forget," Emma had said. Robert had said, "Kids don't know shit." Emma had said, "That's just not true. Children have a special kind of wisdom, and we pretty much beat it out of them. You can see it in other animals." Robert had thought it all ridiculous, but at least she had made some sense then. He calls out for Jo. "She's a kid. She's not about to crash a car. Is she sick? Is that it? Don't I know everything about my own daughter?" He looks at them both.

"No, no," Emma says. "She's not sick." She glances at Max.

Emma is like Max's kid, Robert thinks. Did he do that, too?

"She's not sick, Robert." Max puts his arm around Emma.

Robert walks to the front door. "Jo," he shouts. "Come here."

The girl doesn't answer.

"Don't lose your temper," Emma says.

"You people are a joke." Robert gestures at Max. "Your church is a joke."

"I'm sorry you see it that way," Max says.

"I'm not sorry," Robert says. "If it made sense, then you wouldn't need to play around with someone else's head." The simplicity is dishonest, he knows. He doesn't care.

"You know that's not true." Max removes the food from the grill and puts it on the plate. "How do you like your steaks?" He lifts a slab of meat like he's just caught it.

"Christ, I don't want a damn steak. I want to get going."

"Please, language." Max forms that sincere smile again.

"It's no different to raising her," Emma says. "It's just faster is all."

"That's not the point." Robert paces. He goes to the window. "Where's Jo?"

"What would you do, if you saw Jo drowning?"

"I'd let her drown, obviously." Robert goes to the front door and opens it. He guesses where the girl went. "Jo," he calls. "We're going."

"I don't want to!" Jo shouts.

Robert can't see her. He listens for footsteps. He will pick her up if he must. He feels for the reasoner in his coat; he is still wearing his coat. He will do that to her if he must. "Jo?"

Jo comes out from behind a doorway. "I don't want to go. I don't like hiking."

Robert sighs. "You loved hiking. What's wrong with you?" He is angry then. They have done something to her, he is sure of it.

"I don't anymore," Jo says.

"Did mum use her reasoner on you?" Robert asks. There is spit on his lips.

Jo blinks. She looks away.

Robert can see the lightbulb in them, little fires on wet coals. "Sweetie," he says. "I'm not angry with you." He extends his hand. He feels a hand on his shoulder. He turns around.

Emma smiles at him. "It's alright."

Jo comes to Robert then.

They have turned her against me, Robert thinks. "I just want to get on with my day," he says. "Where's your coat?"

Max stands in the doorway, dark in the sun. "Please stay."

Robert reaches for Jo's hand. "No, it's alright. Thank you." He takes her hand.

The girl struggles.

"What's wrong?" Robert asks.

"Will dad go to heaven?" Jo asks.

Emma and Max don't say anything.

Robert rubs his nose. What have they done to her?

"Robert dad," Jo says, as if it weren't obvious.

Kids are awful, Robert reminds himself: they have no tact. "Come on." He begins walking, expecting her to follow like a toy.

She does.

Max stops him at the door. "I can't let you leave." He puts his hand on Robert's shoulder. "I'm sorry."

Robert doesn't see Max's reasoner coming. He feels it on his skin and pushes the other man away but it is too late. And he is grateful for it. He could not have lived without it. He welcomes the Lord. There is water on his face. He hugs Max. He turns to his daughter. He hopes she can forgive him. There is a light inside him, that is how it feels. He stands up and he heads onto the porch. This is what their baptisms are like, he thinks. He looks out. Everything is workmanship. He has done so much wrong; he has lived wrong.

"It's alright," Max says. He stands next to Robert. He puts the steaks on the barbeque. The meat sings.

"I feel like such an idiot," Robert says. He wipes his face.

"You couldn't help it," Max says. "Some people, they can't see. You were like that. You just needed glasses."

∞〇∞

Ephesians 2:8 says, "For by grace you have been saved through faith, and this is not your own doing; it is the gift of God." What forms may such grace take, and does it matter? John Nadas is a European writer based in Melbourne, Australia.

Milestone and the Fifth World

Marissa James

The Doorstep

I WAS SITTING below the Rib, thinking to shoot one of those damned vultures that kept congregating and scaring the respectable birds to greater heights, when Catalina came up on the swaybacked mare, urging even them out of range. Knew it was her by the smell of watered perfume and sarsaparilla. Knew it was the swayback because we'd called a meeting and shot the mule for meat last week.

Which was maybe why the vultures were starting to look good.

I put aside my double-barrel as she dismounted, fighting her skirts. A pile of rope came sliding off the saddle with her, so she snatched it up, strode close, and shoved it into my chest. None of the townies would come looking for me without reason, so I knew this wouldn't be good.

"We've got company, Pearson, and it's your turn to play welcome committee."

I let her hold the rope though I noticed her arm shaking with the weight. "Always seems to be my turn."

She shoved it at me again, good as a punch in the ribs. "Hurry. Fellah's been out there on the Doorstep screaming for a half hour."

"Yeah, and ain't Milestone famous for its hospitality?" I took the rope, hefted it over one shoulder, shotgun over the other, and took the horse because she could walk back to town fast as I could ride to the Doorstep. "You just get the boys and Tanner digging a hole now, those vultures don't need to be encouraged."

215

I didn't hear her reply. Made my way around the shacks and outbuildings of Milestone. Its heart of once bright storefronts and knocked-down signs and busted glass lay so still and quiet it'd easily be mistaken for a ghost town if anyone else were to see it. But the few of us who remained had grown used to the silence and ruin. The harsh, unhappy truth that, thanks to the drop-off ringing us on all sides, we were likely what remained of humanity.

Excepting, of course, the rare climber. Milestone only continued to exist because its little patch of earth had got stuck, by divine providence or infernal jest, to the outer curve of the Rib like some damned piece of gristle. Standing at the edge you saw nothing but the Rib curving below into the mist and all the way up into the thin blue sky.

Nothing else existed anymore.

Those climbers who made it this far did so by scaling the Rib until the foundation of Milestone interfered, then shifting over to try their luck on our little clump of dirt. No matter how they tried, though, the closest they could approach was a couple meters down, on a ledge we called the Doorstep.

Tanner had gone out for the last climber, said by the time he got there, wasn't no one waiting. Had jumped off, maybe. I wondered if the unfortunate soul just hadn't had anything more to offer than misery, regrets so painful they'd been eating him alive, chewing like a termite through soft wood. We had more than enough misery ourselves so why bring up more?

Maybe Tanner thought that way but I'd made the climb myself, when you could still climb all the way without having to rely on townsfolk to haul you up. It wasn't as steep or impossible then but just as murderous. Oblivion's cold claws sinking into my shoulder blades, ghosting voices whispering to let go and drop off into the mist because they'd catch you—catch you just fine. The fact I'd survived the climb made clearing the Doorstep my business over anyone else's now. That was more than six months past and still I remained the newcomer to Milestone.

Maybe I would've ended up in the mist, too, if I hadn't had a loaded shotgun to make me worth keeping. After me, only Pastor Cray still had ammunition. Either because he had a vision for using it or no stomach to do so.

Even at a distance, I caught the fellah's screaming, high and thin. The voice of desperation.

I dismounted and tied the nag to the post there. Rescuing was once a serious operation in Milestone, back before the actual chance of saving a soul proved to be a fiction. No breeze—a good thing, as that would keep the voices down. They never went silent, but I'd gotten good at blocking them out even when, sometimes, the wind carried them all the way through town. Which was why I was still whole in mind and body, still alive. It only took the slightest slip—a pause to hear a familiar voice, to envision the familiar shape of lips forming those words—

I leaned over the cliff edge and the fellah reached bloody hands up like I was the answer to a life's worth of prayers. And when another man looks at you like that how can you turn away? I wished I knew how Tanner managed it.

I held one end of the rope and let the rest unspool at my feet. Didn't look too hard at him after the blood. "Quit hollering and don't listen to anything but the sound of my voice, you hear?"

"I'll give you anything—"

"I said to quit." I walked back to tie the rope at the post; he whimpered like a lost pup. I dropped the rope to him, watched him wind it round one arm, then went to hauling. He felt like bones and air. When a bloody hand clawed up over the edge, I grabbed it and dragged him to flat ground. He lay in the dirt gasping and muttering thanks. I went to the nag to see if Catalina had left a canteen or bandages, which would've bordered on saintlike behavior. No such luck. Before turning back, I braced myself for the inevitable sight.

He was a scrawny fifteen years or so. An Indian kid. I rolled him like a ragdoll to his back. Blood ran from his hands to elbows, the result of barehanded climbing. I pulled up his buckskin shirt to see ribs and flesh, no wounds. Slapped his shins and they were whole. Fine.

If nothing was eating him alive then he was like me. Hadn't looked back. Hadn't listened to the voices creeping after him.

Had believed he was doing himself a favor getting here.

"Don't thank me," I said. Sounded like nastiness even to my own ears, though I didn't mean it to be.

Milestone

Back in town I met a less than enthusiastic response: another mouth to feed if he hung on and lived and didn't we have enough trouble feeding ourselves? Another man, which meant tipping our balance to fourteen fellahs and just the two ladies. Sure he was young, but why did that matter? There wasn't all that much we might need him for, huddling on this last scrap of the world. The oldsters sat on the saloon's porch like they were part of it, while the O'Malleys, all four not much older than the Indian kid, spat and said hadn't the ruin of the world been the fault of his kind in the first place?

They couldn't understand what it meant to leave someone there. Would it be any better for him here in Milestone? I couldn't speak to that.

I dragged him from the saddle on my own, as none of the boys jumped to help, then crouched to put him over my shoulder when a pair of hands came into view and took his legs for me. Jenny. I was surprised she came out of the saloon at all, and just as surprised at the help. She lifted, stone-silent as ever, and jerked her head inside. Led me to a closet of a room and we laid him on a cot in there.

I glanced back into the bar to see the boys at a table, digging through the Indian kid's bag and coming up with bits of pemmican, flints and twine and— with a chorus of whoops—tobacco packed and wrapped in nice little bricks. He'd expected to have to pay his way up before he started the climb. They decided to split and hide the goods before Tanner showed up for the lion's share. Which should be mine for hauling him up from the Doorstep, but I hadn't yet won that sort of argument with the boys. Or Tanner.

Jenny started to clean the kid up. I gave her a hand by wrestling his boots off. Kicked them under the bed so no one would try them on for size.

She washed blood off the kid's hands, careful as a mother tending to scrapes. I moved to thank her for the help but got stuck watching her face, the silver strands coming loose in her dull brown hair, until she drew her shoulders up and winced.

"Stop," she breathed, so I turned away. Six months and I hadn't figured her out yet. Catalina was easy; when she said yes it meant yes and no meant no. Jenny just pressed her lips together and like a dog you had to look if her head was up or down and even that didn't always mean what it ought to. She avoided all us men, hiding behind the bar or Catalina or cold silence, but me especially. Because I was the newcomer? I'd thought so, but she didn't hesitate to touch this Indian kid.

"He's as old as my boy would've been," she said, and her unused voice sounded strange, like it even surprised her. "I think. I don't remember time anymore."

I never knew she had a boy.

I wanted to tell her not to get too attached, but Tanner and Cray joined the others in the bar. Tonight was shaping up to be a real get together. "Find me if he comes to."

Her eyes remained fixed on the kid. I met the growing crowd. Looked like most of us, as Catalina had turned up too.

"An Indian, Pearson? And you brought him up?" Tanner demanded.

"Sorry to make you do all that digging for nothing," I said. Knew he hadn't, really. Aside from me only Cray cared for burying the dead rather than pitching them back over the edge. "I don't think he looked back. Ain't nothing really wrong with him."

Tanner folded thick arms over his chest and did his best to look down on me. If nothing else, at least I was the tallest man in Milestone. "And you brought him up?"

"I wasn't going to climb on down and join him," I said.

I strode halfway to the door, to return to the shack at the outskirts of town I called home, then stopped. The Milestone Hotel always had a vacancy or two. I figured I may as well stick around and see what conspired with the kid.

The Fifth World

Next day I sat on the saloon roof, using shingles from the dentist's office across the street to patch holes from the last rain of brimstone. Didn't have a dentist anymore so who'd miss them? The youngest O'Malley trotted into the street to holler that the Indian kid was up. I stopped work and came down.

Half the town had congregated: Jenny and Catalina arm in arm, Tanner leaning against one end of the bar, Cray and the three oldsters sitting in a row like county lawyers, all four boys crammed at a table sharing a smoke. The Indian kid sat cross-legged on a bar stool, facing everyone, eating a bowl of corn grits with bandaged hands, long hair washed and combed out neat. I entered as Cray was asking his name.

Kid answered with nonsense; Tanner scoffed.

"Don't speak English," he said.

"I do but that's my name," the kid said. "It means shooting my bow with the opposite hand." He mimed.

"Lefty," Lewis O'Malley translated, which brought some dry laughter.

"Southpaw," I said.

Kid looked up at me and didn't argue and that was that.

Cray gestured at me with his good hand. "Son, this is Whit Pearson. Whit's the one who brought you up."

Southpaw already knew that. He gave a nod so slight maybe I imagined it.

"You didn't look back," I said.

"There's nothing to see."

There was everything. When you started to climb you left everything behind and that was the problem. That was why you looked back. And lost not just everything you had but everything you still were.

Cray and the oldsters put their heads together as though to decide how you talked to an Indian. Tanner glared at the side of his head like he wanted to crack it open.

219

"Exactly what's that mean?" I asked.

"Nothing means nothing." He wiped the bowl out and licked his fingers clean. "Everything is dead, plants and animals and people. The world is rivers and lakes of fire."

In the back of my mind fluttered the image of a beautiful woman I refused to think of. With enough refusal, she faded away.

"I wouldn't come here if there was somewhere else," he said.

"Then tell us your story," one of the oldsters said, once they'd reached consensus.

Southpaw set his empty bowl on the bar and the whole room settled back.

"The world," he said. Frowned into the floor thinking what he'd say. I didn't understand why until he started. "The first world was an island in the middle of four seas. That's where humans came from. When the people argued it stirred the waters into a fury that drowned the world. Most of the people died but some of the people were swept up into the sky. Into the second world. The second world was trees so tall their tops vanished in the clouds. There was nothing to eat so the people made tools of wood, and rope from bark fiber, and they climbed. For generations the people climbed, and many died. Those who lived reached the third world.

"They reached a place of no trees and no water, only dragging mud and sharp rocks that cut them so they bled. This was the third world, and the people had no way to get to the fourth world above. For countless years they bled on the sharp stones and suffered in the mud. One day one of the people took wood from the second world, and sharp stones from the land, and fashioned a bow and arrows. He shot them into the sky, each arrow striking the tail of the last. He made a ladder of arrows reaching into the sky. The people climbed the ladder of arrows until they came to the place of water and trees and stone and earth that was the fourth world." He looked up. "This is where we are now and if none of the other worlds could sustain us then why should this one?"

The room was still, waiting for him to get to his story. Maybe I caught on first that that'd been it. What more could he say about the world left behind if he'd truly left it behind him?

"He meant tell us where the hell you come from and how the hell you got here," Tanner said.

Southpaw frowned at him. "You don't listen. I climbed."

Tanner's slack-jawed response was too much; I laughed. His expression shored up into a glare for me.

"You oughta listen, Tanner, he climbed. They're a tribe of climbers so he climbed." I was still laughing around the words. "You thought maybe he swam?"

"Shut your mouth, Whit, you knew what I meant."

"But how could you not know what he meant?"

"I knew what he meant," Jenny said and moved a little closer to where Southpaw sat. "Not just his tribe. All the people climbed."

Tanner pushed away from the bar and stalked past. Jenny stiffened like he'd smack the kid on his way out. "Well if that's all he's got, I'm done. Storytime ain't my thing."

The boys screeched their chairs out and finished their smoke and followed. Southpaw's novelty had worn off.

Catalina's voice rose after him. "Tanner, what about the pump, you said you'd work on it—hey! Lewis—Charles, get back—you lousy—"

The oldsters swiveled their heads to her. "The pump?"

"Yeah, the pump."

"No water again?" Cray said, but was it much of a loss? What we caught in rain barrels stank of sulfur. The water we hauled up tasted metallic like blood. It didn't make sense that we could still pump water, anyway, unless we'd tapped into the Rib and some wellspring in that monolith of bone sustained us. If so, I suspected it wasn't exactly water we'd tapped.

Most all the eyes in the room converged on me.

"Not this time," I said, making for the exit myself.

"Pearson, you're a reasonable man," Cray said.

"How's it reasonable to pick up after everyone else? Look, have Southpaw do it, we all work for our meals around here, don't we, and I ain't done with the roof."

"He's only just arrived," Jenny said.

"Funny I didn't hear that excuse when it was me," I said and strode out.

The kid needed to prove himself as smart as he looked—smart enough to be useful.

The Rib

He worked at it for a long time, Cray helping with his one good hand and Catalina watching to tell them what they did wrong. I could see it from the roof. Jenny came out long enough to frown up at me then went in again.

Catalina threw her hands up after maybe a half hour. Cray went next, to see if the boys remembered how they'd got it to work last time. I didn't know shit about pumps but how could the kid even know that much?

The sun was turning when I gave up on being on the roof.

"Give it a rest now," I said, coming up to Southpaw. "It'll work if it wants to."

He wiped his forehead with a bandaged hand—bandages spotted with fresh blood—and retreated to sit in the shade of the boardwalk. I joined him.

His dark eyes studied me. "They didn't all have to climb. It's easy to see in their faces that they don't understand. But you did."

"Don't mean I understand it. You have your story about the way the world goes and we got ours. Ask Cray if you want to know it right, he used to be a preacher, I just remember the part about how the dead rise up on the last day. I've heard them out there, so I know it's for sure. Something about the bones of the world and Leviathan, I don't know."

He chewed his lip. "I've heard about the fire coming from the sky and people turning to dust."

"Dust?"

"When they look back."

"Salt," I said. "But it's just a story."

"But it's happening."

He was right, in a way. Looking back could destroy a person, crumble the flesh off their bones. Turn them to dust because that's all any of us were and, someday, what we'd all return to.

And that day had come.

Or had it? I thought of Southpaw's story. Could there be another world, another place for us to go where we could keep on living? This sure wasn't much of a life.

He took a pouch from the inner waistband of his trousers. Opened it and proved himself clever enough to stash some tobacco where it wouldn't get stolen. He started to roll a smoke. "There is a fifth world."

"Is there?"

I shouldn't've been surprised when he pointed across town, to the Rib vanishing into the limitless sky. Devoid of birds today. I had to wonder where they'd gone.

I considered, scratched the stubble on my chin. "You gonna climb up there and shoot yourself a ladder of arrows?"

"Those other fellahs have my bow. If you could get it back for me." It wasn't a request but a hope.

"We'll see. But you won't really—"

He licked the cigarette paper and twisted the ends. "I think it's just a story."

"Then why climb all this way?"

"To be sure." And he offered the finished product to me.

I patted down my pockets. "Ah, we ran out months ago, I don't carry matches anymore."

The boardwalk creaked behind me and I froze, expecting Tanner or one of the boys. Instead, Jenny held a box of matches down to me. She'd been listening from the saloon's side door. I accepted and she sat beside me, comfortably enough.

I made to give the matches to Southpaw, but he still held the smoke out for me. "Go ahead. Those others took everything else, so I guess we share."

So I did the honors and took the first drag. Wasn't anything like I remembered but then, nothing was these days. Jenny declined with a smile, so it went to Southpaw. I wondered about her smile, and the way she sat beside me now when she couldn't bear my eyes on her a day before.

"How long have you been here, Whit?" Southpaw asked.

"Half a year or so," I said. "Which is more than enough."

"I remember it," Jenny said, gazing forward—or backward, I thought, into the past. "My husband brought me to Milestone a couple months before, when it was still possible to get to, hearing it was safe though everything else was crumbling. Falling. Our son was in the next town, so he left to get him. Should've come right back in a few days. The way turned impassable, but I waited at the edge every day." She turned to me then and amazingly her face held wistfulness rather than the rejection I'd learned to accept and ignore. "When I first saw Whit climbing, I thought it must be him come back to me out of the pit of hell." Her smile held on until it looked painful. "But he's just Whit."

She said it lightly. Distantly. I understood then why she hated the sight of me, but not why it had changed.

We ate dinner in the saloon kitchen, the three of us standing around the cook's table like some absurd family. Jenny smiled the whole while, bright-eyed and seeming happy, though I didn't know what happiness looked like on her face. Seemed as though telling her story had put her ghosts to rest. When Southpaw went to bed, she stayed with me. Put her hand on my elbow and I had to ask myself if I'd put my ghosts to rest, too.

When the saloon emptied, she led me to her room. Called me by someone else's name but who was I to correct her?

Voices

The stink of scorched grease woke me; someone had started breakfast and then forgot. Thumping feet and raised voices followed. Jenny was already up so it seemed a good time to take my leave. I stepped out of her room shrugging on my shirt and almost ran into Catalina—she sidestepped with a wide-eyed stare.

"What's burning?" I said, hoping to wipe that look off her face.

Instead she took another step back. "What the hell did you do to her?"

Below, one of the boys was blurting something to the oldsters about the Rib, and the tone of his voice, and the silence that met it, and the abandoned stove and Catalina's stare told me all I needed to know. I shot down the stairs strangling on the mad beat of my heart.

The other O'Malleys were already there, and Tanner, and some others. I saw Southpaw scrambling up the Rib as fast as he could.

Jenny clung on above him, on the sheer side that would see her drop into endless shadow if she fell. Her skirt flapped in a high, scolding wind biting with the voices of the lost.

Charles or Peter or both of them grabbed me before I skidded to the edge. She saw me below, rather than Southpaw climbing for her.

"I knew it all along," she said, and the regret in her voice reached me like a bullet. "You were always just Whit."

She let go and fell backward into oblivion. The nothing that was everything else.

I screamed her name, helpless. Mariah fell the same way, though I hadn't seen it happen. My Mariah, and when did I last let her name echo free in my mind? Halfway through the climb to get here she let go, and I'd put my face into the stone and screamed for her. And wept, and then went on.

I made it to Milestone.

I didn't look back.

I fell on my knees at the edge and stared into the blankness below like I expected to see her. Like that whispering wind might've blown her to safety. I was trembling on the verge of being sick and wondering why. Why, if she wanted to be with me the night before—

Someone hauled me up by the arm and I caught the twist of Tanner's face and he knocked me down before I saw it coming. Got a faceful of dust and then my ribs groaning under his weight. His hands in my collar forcing me toward the edge.

"What did you do to her?" he shouted. "What did you do?"

I didn't know and at the moment it wasn't her face ghosting through my mind, not her dark hair and eyes, not her lips. She wasn't the one whispering so deep in my mind that I didn't even hear Tanner screaming in my face.

A gunshot split the air before he could throttle me. Cray strode forward, pistol in hand. From the corner of my eye Southpaw descended the Rib like a cat backing out of a tree.

"Let him be," Cray said, forcing calm into his voice. "No one's killing anyone here."

"Then what do you call that?" Tanner demanded, motioning over the edge.

"She looked back," he said, and pointedly holstered his gun with both his good hand and withered one. "We all know what that means."

"That's not good enough," Tanner said, but his voice had given in, his hold loosened. Southpaw ran flat out to meet us but by the time he got there he didn't need to. Tanner stood refusing to look anyone in the face, rubbing the knuckles he'd hit me with, then slunk off back to town.

I sat up trembling at her loss, the whispers flooding my mind to fill the raw hole she'd left in my gut.

"Get back to town and tell the rest of them what's going on," Cray said, shooing off the boys. Southpaw stayed, frowning silence at the lost preacher and me.

A vulture shrieked overhead, the echo of my screams.

"If there was anywhere else for you to go, Whit, I'd suggest for you to leave town," Cray said as gently as he could.

I could still leave, she said in my mind. Two steps away from the edge, and what was two steps but a million miles?

And what was death but a different fall?

"You stay out here," Cray went on, talking over my misery. "I'll speak what reason I can. Tell you what they decide. You staying with him, son?"

Southpaw nodded.

Cray left. We sat in the sun, waiting for it to turn around enough that the Rib would cast its shadow on us, me with my face in the crook of one arm hoping to block out the doubled vision of Jenny falling, and Mariah, which I'd never seen but God could I imagine it. Six months of refusing to think it once, surely the inside of my skull was branded with the vision.

The wind, a hundred thousand voices, rose up as a constant reminder. Falling wasn't much different than climbing. I almost believed it.

A hand settled on my arm and I started. I'd forgot about Southpaw, and when I raised my head, I realized I'd been rocking on my haunches since Cray left.

"Whit, who is she?"

"Jenny?"

"Mariah."

He shouldn't've known to ask as I'd never mentioned her since reaching Milestone. Unless hers was the name I screamed when Jenny fell.

Unless I was talking back to the voices whispering in my mind and I of all people should know better. Of all us trapped fools, I knew the dangers of regret.

"She's nobody," I said. Neither of us believed that.

The Blessing Hand

It was mad to think she might come back but everyone who ever lost someone believed it. Everyone looked back and everyone waited for the impossible to happen because someday it must.

Besides, hadn't it already? Here we were, a last fleck of gristle clinging to the Rib. Only the bones of Leviathan remained since the world's flesh of dirt and stone had crumbled away. The world was dead, rotted like a carcass into whatever pit waited below. One of these days God would remember Milestone and scratch us out of existence too.

The first time they sent me to the Doorstep was for a dead woman and a child. A girl, maybe five years, round rosy cheeks and darkening blonde hair. And she'd looked back. What more could you expect from a kid that age? By the time I got there the regret was eating her alive: one leg a stump, one hand falling apart as though rotted lace, not flesh, bound those bones. The raw bloody holes in her little cheeks must've hurt, so she cried—and cried harder at the salty pain of tears through them.

Standing there listening to those cries, Mariah rose up in my mind before I could help it. I backed away and retched in the dirt, forcing myself to see that little girl and not her. Thank God she'd fallen, hadn't looked back and suffered like that, thank you God—no, I had to forget her. If not, I'd end up on the more painful path of being consumed by memory.

I had to forget her if I wanted to stay alive.

I hauled the girl up and somebody helped me get the woman's body so it could be buried. The little girl hung on for a few days that were really an eternity of dying.

That's when I understood why Cray oversaw the burials but didn't pray at them—and that withered hand. He had, once, but praying for the dead meant another kind of regret. You couldn't live like that. The best thing was to put the past behind and not speak of it. Like Jenny had done of her family. Like I had done.

In the afternoon Lewis stopped a dozen paces from us and spat to the side.

"Catalina says you need to get the pump working."

Which meant I should forget Jenny too. Move on. Milestone would, if it meant survival.

I didn't give a damn about surviving anymore. I might like the taste of regret, seeing as I'd never tried it.

The bar still smelled of burnt food when I entered. Silent but not empty, all the eyes in that place avoided me as hard as they could. At least Tanner wasn't there.

When I headed to the stairs Catalina stiffened behind the bar. Southpaw hung back down below.

Jenny's room was first on the landing. The outline of her body stood out in the tangled sheets, and mine. The air stale with last night.

I stood in the doorway reliving her. She'd mistook me for her man or decided I was as close as she'd get in this place. If I'd looked harder, I'd have seen it.

And maybe I refused to see it in her because I was doing the same thing—thinking of Mariah. You couldn't fall in love a second time without remembering the first.

"Mariah."

I'd already screamed her name over the edge how many times today? After I'd swore to myself to swallow it until I forgot the shape of the word. The room didn't change but the hair rose on my arms. She was here with me. Had never left, maybe. I'd simply been refusing her memory so hard I hadn't noticed.

My hat hung on the back of a chair and I realized that's what I'd wanted. Nothing else for me here.

When I came downstairs a half dozen heads went back to their own business.

Catalina froze again when I came behind the bar and reached under it where I knew she kept the best drink in reserve. Wasn't much left but I grabbed myself an unopened bottle not bothering to read what it was. When I leaned toward her, she leaned away.

"Tomorrow," I said, and meant the pump, and she made no show of caring.

On my way out the only eyes to meet me belonged to Southpaw. He came over from where he'd been waiting.

"So here's the thing," I told him, and checked the label—whiskey. Sounded just fine. "You can stay here with them or you can come with me, no one cares. Because Milestone is a place for people who don't care."

The concern on his face almost made me laugh. When had anyone last concerned themselves with me?

"Where are you going?" he asked.

"Nowhere," I said, tasting the bite in every word, "Because there ain't nowhere to go."

Stay or Leave

It was Mariah. Or Jenny. The half bottle of whiskey across my vision made it hard to tell but she stood over my bed. Dark, silent. A half year without someone was long enough to forget anything you didn't like about them. And after one night you couldn't have found any such flaws. So whoever she was, I felt nothing but love for her. Called both names but didn't get a response.

I reached out and like moth's wings felt the flicker of her, couldn't catch hold. The harder I tried the further she moved away. I got up, almost tripped over Southpaw snoring on my floor.

She slipped through the hanging blanket that passed for a door to my shack. I caught her arm on the other side and shuddered—seemed wrong any physical thing should be able to stop her. Then again, maybe she wanted to be stopped.

Her face, blank and shadowed, suggested a blackboard, a clean slate. I peered through it trying to make sense of her. Couldn't. Because she was Jenny, and Mariah, and all the ghosts of Milestone. Jenny's man and her grown son and my two sisters, so long lost they shouldn't count. The little dead girl with her ruined face, her mother. The ancestors and families of the few townsfolk left.

"I can stay or I can leave," she said, in her dozens of voices. "You can stay or you can leave."

Climb or Fall

I did get the pump working. It helped that some of the voices now living in my skull had advice to give. I told Southpaw my intentions concerning the Rib, so he followed me to town, disappeared for a while. When I saw him next he had his bow and arrows, and his now-empty shoulder bag. He sat in the dirt alongside my shotgun and waited.

I worked with enough purpose that soon he wasn't the only one watching. After all, I had no business knowing what to do or couldn't I have done it before? If anyone asked after my method I wouldn't've been able to explain it to them.

Not much longer and we had water again. Looked like piss and smelled worse. But it was water.

"Well, hell," Lewis said, watching a bucket fill faster than ever before while Southpaw worked the pump. "And why didn't you do that a long time ago?"

I opened my mouth to answer when Cray hollered. I heard his pistol being cocked close behind my ear, and then Southpaw ducked behind the pump, lot of protection that would give, and Lewis scrambled away.

No surprise who held that pistol. And with the ghosts crowding the corners of my vision I had to turn to face him. Cold steel inches from my face.

"If he'd done it before he'd've outlived his use that much sooner," Tanner said through set teeth. "Which means he's useless now."

"Is this about Jenny?" I asked through the whirlwind voices roaring in my skull. "Or you got something else eating you?"

"Me?" His teeth came unset and he sneered. "You're the one that messed with her—"

"I mean you ever think about your boys?"

He twitched the gun to Lewis and Pete up on the boardwalk. "They take care of themselves, don't they, why would I have to—"

"I said your boys. Didn't you have two? You were married once, before the world fell away. And you had a fine pair of boys."

He raised the gun a little higher, a little closer. I saw nothing but bloodshot eyes and the lines of regret etched around them. He made an effort not to look at the others. "Who told you that?"

"They did."

He understood but didn't believe. Even believing wouldn't stop him putting a hole through my skull.

"They're here," I said, tapped my temple. "I figure that's what was eating Jenny. She used to go to the edge every day and God knows what she got in her head but now I've got it. She's here too. Funny it don't bother me very much, isn't it?"

"Because you're crazy, Whit."

"I'm telling you, they're all here," I said. "Your boys, and the O'Malleys' pa, and all the people we've buried who we never knew by name. The moment you put a hole in my head they'll get out and they'll be your problem. Presumably so will I."

To my surprise he lowered the gun. Stared at it in his hand.

"I don't want to see pa again," Lewis said on the boardwalk, quiet and terrified. "He shot himself through the mouth to get out of here and I don't want to see that again, Tanner."

The other three O'Malleys echoed him.

"Their names," Tanner said, hoarse. We stood close enough to breathe each other's breath and I couldn't say if I feared being stuck with these ghosts forever in me or, more, for him to make me one of them. "Tell me their names if you know."

"Samuel and Jacob Tanner."

"Tell 'em I'll see 'em soon," he said, and raised the gun to my belly and fired.

Then I was lying flat on my back, both hands bright with blood. The boys were screaming after Tanner—his boys, and the O'Malleys on the boardwalk, too. He stumbled back, put the pistol to his own head, and it clicked on empty. I didn't see where he went but he had nowhere to go.

Like all of us.

Cray appeared on one side of me checking the wound, Southpaw slumping slack-faced on the other.

I turned to Cray. "Am I gonna be all right?"

"Alive," he amended. "For a couple hours."

I closed my eyes, focused on Mariah's voice until the pain faded into the background. You could only die or fall, and they amounted to the same thing in Milestone.

Southpaw looked sick. He'd said there was nothing left of the world. Nothing to regret leaving behind. His face didn't say that anymore.

I had one last job, then. "You still climbing?"

"What?"

"For your fifth world."

He made his face steady. "Yes. I will."

"I'd like to see that," I said, and offered a hand so he could get me up. "Only a couple hours, you better climb fast."

"What are you talking—"

"Get me up. Someone bring that horse."

Cray moved back. His eyes closed and his lips moved halfway to forming a prayer before he realized what he was doing and stopped.

I breathed deep and it hurt, and the hurting made me want to gasp for breath, which hurt even deeper, grinding its way into bone and nerves and the backs of my eyes.

They got me up and into the saddle, I don't know how. Southpaw picked up my shotgun. I focused on Mariah standing in the corner of my mind. Waiting.

"Why are you doing this?" Southpaw asked when we were halfway there, only the two of us. Because who among them wanted to see me die and have that regret, small as it might be, on their conscience?

"Because if we've been wrong about this place it figures maybe you're right," I said. Winced when the saddle horn stabbed under my ribs. "I'm thinking there's only one way out of Milestone and that's to go up."

"You can't climb."

"You just do it for me, Southpaw."

He didn't talk the rest of the way, so I worked harder to hold down the pain that jolted with every step the nag fumbled.

He helped me down when we got there. Handed over my shotgun and, of all things, took out his pouch and rolled the last smoke he had. His hands were steady—good thing.

"You're gonna hate me for a while, I guess," I said.

He shook his head. "I can't hate you."

He gave the finished cigarette to me like he didn't care for smoking and struck a match from his bag. I took a drag and that bullet bit into me; I choked on the smoke and spat to the side.

"Sorry," he said.

"No, I'm sorry." I opened the breech of my shotgun, checked the loaded round, then took a breath. Jerked it shut and thumbed back the hammer and leveled it at his chest. "Tanner was right, you made friends with the town crazy. Now I want you to get out of here. Climb. And if you look back even once, even partway, you ain't getting to the top. One way or the other."

He stared, deciding if I would or not. I drew a little more carefully on the cigarette. When the gun barrel followed him getting up, he nodded, understanding me. There wasn't nothing here for him to look back for.

"Trust me it ain't the best way to go," I said. "Nor this the best place to be stuck in."

He backed away, watching me to the last second. When he finally turned and started up, I sagged in relief and lowered the gun. Even reaching for the smoke between my lips was a struggle.

I put my head back and watched him, vision darkening with ghosts. Mariah at one shoulder and Jenny at the other, and I wondered, if he looked back, if he'd see them.

I drew the smoke in deep. Not the same as I remembered, but sweeter than I could have imagined.

∞CR

As a fine art professional, Marissa James has wielded katanas and handled Lady Gaga's shoes. As a veterinary assistant, she has cared for hairless cats, hedgehogs, and, one time, a coyote. As a writer (under Marissa James or Mar Vincent), she can be found in *Flash Fiction Online*, *Translunar Travelers Lounge*, *Zooscape*, and many other publications. She is a recipient of the Ladies of Horror fiction grant, a Pushcart Prize Nominee, and a reader for Interstellar Flight Press. She resides in the Pacific Northwest and can be found on Twitter or Mastodon @MaroftheBooks.

The Secret Place of the Lord

J.L. Royce

ARMITACH STOOD AT the edge of a vast concrete plateau: the former McHugh Air Force Base. He was neither stooped, nor sagging, nor pot-bellied; yet all of that felt as near as the wind rising in this desolate place. He'd flown in from Kansas City, taken a very expensive hired car out to an airfield, but no one was there to greet him. No one was there at all.

Cracked pavement stretched to the horizon, a rectilinear garden of seam-bound weeds. It had *been* an airbase, once receiving dozens of flights daily returning the honored dead to their homeland. Bodies remained for a while, then were identified and sent to families, or if not, to the national cemeteries to join their comrades in final repose.

That was all before Armitach was born. When Vietnam escalated, the Defense Department created the cold storage facility for the returning dead. After the war, the base became a graveyard for decommissioned planes, left to sit in the sun and slowly weather or be pilfered to skeletons.

The day had started out nice enough. Early October was warm here. Armitach pulled his phone out of his pants pocket. The tiniest bar, the bar of last resort, was lit, but he'd learned from experience not to trust its hollow promise. He scrolled to the saved message and clicked the number anyway, cursing silently when, as expected, the call failed.

Armitach lit a cigarette and stared down the road, east then west, scanning the ribbon of pavement, debating which direction to walk: the desolation he had ridden through, or the miles remaining unexplored. He was about to flip a mental coin when a vehicle approached at speed from the direction of the unknown.

It resolved into a weary-looking F-150. Faded green, its rusting rocker panels had been spray-painted with brick-red Rustoleum in a pathetic attempt to forestall the inevitable.

Armitach stepped into the road, prepared to get a ride by any means necessary. While he debated whether to draw out his identification or his weapon, the question became moot when the vehicle slowed and the driver addressed him.

"Mister—ah, *Agent*—Armitach?" The driver was dark-haired and tanned, around his own age, but casually dressed in faded chambray and real denims.

"The same. You Father Jones?"

"*Reverend* Jones."

Armitach wondered if there was a *Mother* Jones waiting at home, but bit off the remark. It was that *attitude*, as they called it at the Bureau, which had earned him this low-cred assignment in the ass-end of the Midwest.

His supervisor's advice had been simple. *Keep your lip buttoned, do your penance, and don't bitch about it.*

"Well, I guess you'd like a ride?" The Rev (as Armitach christened him) was squinting through the windshield as if searching the speed limit sign for an answer.

"Sure thing."

The agent stepped around and opened the passenger door, eliciting a painful shriek of metal. Armitach tossed his bag behind the seat and settled on the barely-sprung cushion. The Rev was staring expectantly at him.

"Uh—the Wenton Arms," Armitach supplied, after fumbling his phone out and checking. "In… Wenton."

The Rev nodded and slipped the pickup noisily into gear, rolling through the dying grass on the shoulder and into a U-turn.

"It was that or the truck stop cabins," he observed. "Most visitors don't know there *are* cabins."

"I didn't," Armitach agreed. He'd ridden past the "oasis" full of semis and a handful of smaller vehicles.

"More for the convenience of the long-distance drivers. Ah, hourly rental, if you know what I mean…"

"Thanks. I'll keep that in mind, if I get lucky."

The Rev didn't react.

"Where's the, uh, storage facility?" Armitach asked. Past the window he saw nothing but concrete and weeds.

"Northwestern corner of the base, behind that bit of a rise. There's a road north out of town that takes you there. It doesn't go anywhere else."

Cresting a line of worn hills, a grove of trees came into view, bisected by the highway. A half-dozen streets stretched out a few blocks before devolving into grass or gravel paths. The northern road intersected at the only stoplight.

"Sheesh," Armitach remarked. The sense of punishment was growing.

"One hundred twenty-three souls, including fifteen teenagers and twenty-seven younger minors."

A steeple poked its cross out of the southern side of the grove.

"Yours?" the agent asked. The Reverend nodded agreement.

"School?"

"Not here. They're bussed to Farley."

The speed limit dropped precipitously as the highway became Main Street, as it had in a hundred places east of here and would a hundred places west. It was home to a handful of fading storefronts, a diner (closed until morning), and a gas station. The Rev swung the truck into a lurching left turn at the first intersection and pulled up to the curb.

The Wenton Arms entrance was at the chamfered corner, framed by painted double columns. At three stories it was the tallest building in town. Beyond the glass and wood doors lay the foyer, leading to a bar and dining room.

Compared to the motels he typically occupied the Arms appeared quaint, if not promising.

"Will they still be serving?"

"Oh, I'd imagine so. If not, there's always a corn dog at the service station." The Reverend grinned. "Check in; I'll wait."

Armitach retrieved his bag and slammed the truck door. Stepping through to the genteel foyer with its wooden wainscoting and tin ceiling, he confirmed the dining room was open late, and gave his name to a clerk.

Outside, he informed the Reverend, who replied, "When can I pick you up?"

Though he'd rather sleep in, Armitach offered eight o'clock.

"See you then." The truck pulled noisily away from the curb, executed a squealing U-turn, and returned to Main Street.

಼ೕ

The food was adequate, if uninspired. In the morning, the Reverend Jones turned down coffee, pressing for immediate departure.

They proceeded west, then north.

"Can I get a ride to the airport?"

"I suppose. Will you be handing the investigation off to your team?"

Armitach suppressed a laugh. "No, I'll finish by end of day."

Reverend Jones frowned.

"Why don't you tell me about the first disappearance?" Armitach activated the recorder on his phone.

The driver leaned over the wheel, concentrating on the road but collecting his thoughts.

"Well, the first disappearance I *discovered* was probably the third one."

"After?" he prompted.

"Yes—after the third incident, I recalled that a few days earlier I'd come in and found the hall light on."

"And that's suspicious? Couldn't someone else—"

"No one else visits this place. The staff's been cut to delivery contractors."

Armitach almost made a snarky crack about Amazon but recalled the recorder, and his supervisor's advice.

"And you couldn't have left it on yourself?"

"Was it dark when you arrived?" the Reverend countered. "I'm there in the late afternoon, no later. It's quite bright outside, so I don't use the lights."

"You mentioned the *third* incident. What was the second?"

"One morning, I was praying in the chapel we have—you'll see it in a moment."

He swung the truck up to a gated yard surrounding a low concrete building. A sign detailed restrictions on federal property use. Someone had commented on it with a shotgun.

Hopping out, the Rev lifted a heavy latch and slid open the gate. Back in the truck, he pulled through the empty parking lot and took a spot near the entrance.

"Come on." He left the windows open, Armitach noticed.

The building dated back fifty years, at least, the interior more concrete blocks beyond a small, paneled foyer with an unattended reception desk.

The Reverend pointed. "The chapel's down this hallway." The hallway ran along the narrow front of the building, lined with dingy windows facing the lot.

"Near the end of Vietnam, they took in many bodies, so many that the ceremony was, well, curtailed. But this isn't a forensic lab, so they only received identifiable corpses."

He opened a double door graced with crosses cut in the wood to reveal a generic chapel with a few pews.

"I was praying here, almost a week after I found the lights burning, when I heard it." He waved behind him.

"What, exactly?"

"It was a gurney being moved. I thought perhaps someone had followed me in. From time to time you'll get the lost tourist on their way to the National Park. But there was no one in the hall, no vehicles in the lot."

The Reverend led Armitach out, unlocking an inner door.

"The sound came from here."

"Usually locked?"

"Yes. I have a desk here. A place to meet family, or law enforcement. Whoever is claiming a body."

"Are there many claims?" Armitach asked.

"Not really. The oldest are cold cases—" he caught himself. "The more recent ones occasionally cross-match with criminal investigations."

Armitach recognized government-issue décor. Innocuous nature scenes and wildlife prints dotted the faded beige walls. A battered steel desk filled the space, with an office chair behind and a pair of guest chairs in front.

The Reverend stepped around and pulled open a desk drawer. He removed a toe tag he'd stored in a plastic sandwich bag and offered it to Armitach.

"I found this in the hallway, right outside."

John Doe: dead many years. The attachment wire was twisted and bent: used and removed.

Armitach nodded. "And the body was missing?"

"Gone. The tags are coded to the location in storage and the files—such as they are." He waved at a row of laterals. "Mostly not computerized. I went through our entire occupancy list, drawer by drawer, and found two more discrepancies." The Reverend slid the file folders across the table.

"You mean missing," Armitach grunted, sitting down.

"Unless it was a bookkeeping error, and they never—"

The agent cut him off. "Well, I'll need whatever security footage you have."

The Rev laughed. "The budget is barely enough to keep the refrigeration systems running. There's nothing in it for security on a bunch of cadavers."

"Yeah, things are tight everywhere," Armitach admitted. "What about local kids?"

"They're not bad, just bored. They sneak onto the base from time to time—there are miles of fence—just so they can race their bikes on the flats. The Vietnam-era planes from the bone yard have been sold off to collectors. Besides—stealing a corpse? If it were a prank, it would have shown up by now."

"No break-ins here before?"

"No. Everybody around knows there's nothing here but dead bodies."

The agent leaned forward. "Have you seen any strangers around town, or anyone acting different?"

"Like how, *different?*"

"Well, perhaps extreme politics, or paranoid behavior."

The Reverend's eyes narrowed. "You're thinking of someone trying to harvest, like, germs? We do still have some of the CDC's AIDS victims."

"It's just a theory," Armitach assured him. "Frankly, it's a lot easier to buy a truckload of fertilizer and make a bomb than to create an effective biological weapon from a corpse. What happened when you spoke to the local authorities?"

"We have a sheriff, twenty-five miles away. He's got a 'real' city with 'real' problems like opioids, and runs an understaffed department. He came out once, looked around, shrugged, and left."

"Hard to argue with him. These are unclaimed bodies. Corpses are property, so they can't be victims, and there's no evidence the corpses are being put to illegal use. *Any* use." Armitach stood, gathering the folders. "Look, I'll rerun the prints to see if there's any connection, or recent developments."

"Aren't you even going to look at the scene of the..."

"Sure." Armitach thought it was a waste of time.

They proceeded through locked double doors into the cool and gloomy interior. Many of the overhead fluorescents were out or flickered fitfully. The air hummed, dry and tinged with a stale taste. Freezer units lined the half-dozen halls, each with a dozen metal drawers.

"This is a negative temperature facility, expensive to operate. We've merged somewhat, but then OD's came in from the South."

"No names," Armitach noted. "No break-in at the office?"

The Rev shook his head. "I always lock it, for the confidential records."

"Show me where the bodies went missing."

The latches on the drawers the Rev indicated had all been broken. Armitach snapped pictures with his phone.

"Why this?" the Reverend complained, shaking the damaged hasp. "They could just snip the cable ties."

"Criminals, by and large, are not geniuses," the agent opined. "Any prints?"

"The sheriff collected several sets from each freezer, then ruled out myself and the delivery folks. He found some partials, none in the databases."

Armitach sent a message to the sheriff's department, requesting the investigation records. After examining each drawer and taking more photographs, he turned to the Reverend.

"That's all I can do now. Drop me back at the hotel, so I can get online."

ುಆ

The files revealed that the missing were all long-forgotten John Does dead of AIDS. It seemed an unlikely coincidence.

The sheriff's email contained the latent prints from the freezers, with a terse note: *Not sent to NGI due to budget constraints.* With a snort, Armitach opened his portal and uploaded the images.

The missing corpses were long-term residents, with no apparent pattern to where or when they died, their race or religion. The only common thread appeared to be their diagnosis.

Armitach called the Rev.

"How many of your bodies are AIDS deaths, do you suppose? Just a rough percentage."

The silence stretched out. "Ten or fifteen percent, I'd say."

"You realize that your missing bodies were AIDS-related, right?"

"Yes, but…"

"What?"

The Reverend's voice rose. "It's impossible to know that without accessing my files! I already said—"

"Yeah—locked door."

Armitach glanced out the window at the dusty street.

"What's a decent place for lunch—with beer?"

"I'll be downstairs in ten minutes."

ುಆ

"So I know why I'm here," Armitach began, sparing the Reverend the details, "but why are you stuck out here? And what *is* your first name?"

"Michael"—pronounced in three syllables— "and I *choose* to be here."

Theirs was the last occupied table of a sparse lunch crowd at Wenton's only diner.

"*Mick the Mick*," Armitach declared. "What's a nice Irish boy like you—"

"Just Michael, please. What makes you think I'm Irish?"

Armitach waited.

"Well, yes, on my mother's side," Michael admitted.

"And my first question?"

"It's a ministry. I learned about the storage facility when I was working on state AIDS treatment legislation."

"You minister to unclaimed bodies? Shouldn't you preach to the living?"

239

"I have my church here, and I counsel an online community. Do you belong to a faith community?"

"Not anymore," Armitach replied.

Michael offered, "If you're still in town, you're welcome to join us—"

"So, you're gay?" Armitach interrupted.

The Reverend was unperturbed. "Not that it matters, but yes."

"Does your gay-ness—gaiety?— better qualify you to pray over a bunch of corpses? Why can't you pray for them back in, say, New York City, or Chicago?"

Reverend Michael hesitated. "I *had* a congregation, a big congregation. But a conservative one."

"You were dumped, and here you are, in the sorry—"

"This is my home now," the Reverend snapped, "and I respect these people. You should too."

Armitach waved his empty longneck at the server, then added it to the barrier growing between them.

"Do you always drink this much?" Michael asked.

"Only when I'm working. And after, sometimes."

An intermittent hum joined their conversation. The agent patted himself down, then searched the jacket slung over his chair.

"I'm feeling the payback of running off my fat mouth," he explained, unlocking his phone. "Since we're playing Truth or Dare."

He scrolled through the phone, then swore, causing the shop-worn waitress to frown from him to the Reverend.

"Response from NGI. I sent the latents from the sheriff along with scans from your post-mortem records, and they came up with a match. Several, actually."

He realized that the waitress was staring.

"Coffee, black," he said. "Please."

The Reverend nodded. "With cream for me."

Armitach waited for her to saunter away.

"OK, Reverend. Your turn to tell the truth. What would you do to draw attention to the fat middle finger society gives anyone who stumbles off the straight and narrow? Like your flock in the freezers?"

"I don't understand—"

"Simple question. What kind of stunt might *you* pull?"

"What did you learn from the freezer drawer fingerprints?"

"No names yet, just matches. To the John Does."

The Reverend looked confused. "What?"

"Each set of latents matches the former occupant of the drawer. *That's* what I'm saying."

The waitress returned with two eroded mugs, steaming. When she departed, Armitach continued.

"Enough with the fun and games. I'll leave tomorrow, and to save you any embarrassment, not tell them that the local minister is a publicity-seeking fool." He sipped the coffee, grimaced, and lurched to his feet.

"That's ridiculous!" Reverend Michael protested.

"By your own statements, no one else *could* have known who was HIV-positive in the freezers."

Armitach tossed a bill on the table and stumbled out of the diner.

ഏറ

With nothing better to do on his last evening in Wenton, Armitach accepted the Reverend's challenge: to stake out the base facility. He nursed a beer in the Rock Solid, Wenton's only bar, until ten. A noisy exhaust announced the Reverend's arrival.

The agent sauntered out and pulled the creaky door of the F-150.

"Get some WD-40," he complained.

The driver had dressed in black jeans and a hoodie.

"What's with the outfit—you *undercover*? We're not breaking in." He waved away the Reverend's explanation. "Let's just get this over with. Come dawn, I'm going back to the Arms for a few hours sleep. Don't forget, you promised me a ride tomorrow."

"Of course." The truck lurched down Main and out of town.

The building was dark, the only lights within coming from the dim red glow of Exit signs. Reverend Michael drove past the entrance, around the building, and into a narrow alley leading to a loading dock. "We'll leave the truck out of sight," he suggested.

Armitach shook his head in disbelief. Michael led the way along the back of the building.

They took up position in the small grove of trees at the edge of the lot, with a view of both the front door and loading dock.

"We picked a good night," the Reverend whispered.

"Yeah?" Irritated, Armitach used a normal tone of voice.

His companion gestured east, at a glow: the rising moon.

"Great—very romantic."

"Didn't you notice? From the files?"

"What?"

Reverend Michael frowned. "The full moon. These incidents all happened at the full moon."

Armitach stood. "What a load of crap. Now they're vampires? Werewolves? I suppose you find it funny, dragging a Federal agent out to the ass-end—"

"Look!" the Reverend hissed, pointing.

The shadows in the entrance were fleeing the moonlight.

The door slowly opened—from within—but no one appeared. Someone had pushed the power assist button.

Armitach peered through the pale light, heart racing. There was no other sign of life around the building.

"Should we—"

"Stay here," Armitach directed, stepping out from the trees. He flipped open the holster of his sidearm and drew it, held at his side, as he approached the black rectangle.

"Federal agent," he announced, and peered inside.

A figure huddled in the back of the small reception area shrank back at Armitach's entrance.

"Stand slowly. Show me your hands."

The man on the floor was clutching a sheet, his chest bare beneath it. He spread his fingers.

Armitach relaxed, drawing an obvious conclusion.

"Rough night?" he asked. "How did you get in here?"

The man seemed to consider the question, shaking his head and finally rasping, "I don't know."

Armitach's breath caught in his throat. He'd smelled death before—fresh and hot, fetid and cloying—but this was something else. He stepped back, breathing through his mouth.

"Where am I?" The man wobbled to his feet.

"What's your name?" Armitach demanded.

"I... George," he replied. "I live in the city. But I was sick. I was on a lot of drugs."

"I'll bet you were," the agent muttered. "What city would that be?"

He stared at Armitach. "Minneapolis. You're not a doctor." Questions tumbled out. "Is this the hospital? It doesn't look right. Did I get better? I feel better."

"Well, George, I don't know," Armitach replied. "Maybe we can ask your sorry-ass friends, the ones who left you here after you passed out? Any idea where we might find them?"

"My friends all died."

The bleak expression brought Armitach up short.

"Where are your clothes?" A voice from the doorway: the Reverend.

George offered no explanation. "Why is it so warm?"

"It's called *summer*," Armitach snapped.

"Where *am* I? It was cold in Minneapolis, it was winter. Freezing cold."

The Reverend rummaged in a closet behind the reception desk and produced a raincoat.

"Why don't you put this on until we find your things?" He approached the man cautiously.

"We need to check him in somewhere, maybe pump his stomach," Armitach suggested.

George took the coat without comment and slipped it on, balling up his sheet and laying it beside him on the floor. "Did you say I had friends nearby?"

The Reverend stepped past the agent. "Why don't we get you somewhere comfortable, where we can talk?"

As Michael led George through the door, Armitach noticed the tag attached to the man's foot.

"Sick joke," he muttered. Kneeling in front of the swaying man, he unwound the wire. "Some friends."

"They were all I had," George replied, pulling his foot away. "My parents…"

"Can you walk?" Reverend Michael asked.

George nodded, walking unsteadily across the foyer. Armitach looked around, and finding nothing to further inform his opinion of this prank, flipped off the lights and closed the door behind him.

"Wait here. I'll bring the truck around," the Reverend offered.

"Yeah, sure," Armitach replied. George stared around the parking lot and the abandoned airfield beyond.

"This isn't Minnesota."

Armitach bit off another sarcastic remark. "When did you last see your parents?"

George's gaze drifted back to the agent. "The summer of '91. I had come out, and told them I had AIDS, wasn't doing well. They told me they wanted nothing to do with me."

"That's a long time ago." Armitach considered. "Have you told them you've gotten better?"

"There's no 'getting better'," George said bitterly.

"Sure there is," Armitach argued. "I've heard the drugs are really effective."

George stared. "A long time ago?"

"So, do you remember what drugs you took?"

"In the hospital?"

"Not *in the hospital*," Armitach said, annoyed, "*tonight*. Recreational drugs. It'll help the doctor."

"No—I *was* hospitalized." George peered at the agent. "I'm not dead, am I? I thought there was a white light."

"You don't look dead, though you might feel that way. See that?" He pointed at the approaching truck. "Just headlights, probably." He took George by the arm. "We'll figure out what to do—"

George's eyes widened. "This *is* the other place! I'm in Hell, and you're—"

Breaking free, he darted into the path of the Reverend's truck.

The vehicle shuddered to a halt, barely missing George, who ran across the lot and into the trees beyond.

"Come back here!" Armitach shouted. "Stop!"

"What happened? What did you do?" the Reverend called out of the vehicle.

"Nothing! We were just talking. He said something about Hell and bugged out." He trotted around the truck. "Go—maybe we can catch him."

But the Reverend sat motionless behind the wheel. "No."

"What do you mean, *no*? If nothing else, he was trespassing on Federal property!"

"I want to check something first." He took the tag from Armitach.

ℂ)℁

Another line of beer bottles grew. They sat in the same booth, staring at the body tag.

"It proves nothing," Armitach argued, "other than this gang of body-snatchers has a weird sense of humor, tying this on one of their own."

"You took the prints—"

"And I'm sure they'll match the former tenant perfectly, because they pressed the corpse's fingers..." He trailed off: frozen fingers didn't leave such clear latents.

"The drawer, yes, but what about the crash bar on the storage room exit? What if *they* match?"

Armitach considered the cardboard tag. It was real. The shivering slob they'd encountered was real, and gone. The rest...

"Be reasonable. If some confused corpses were walking around in their winding-sheets or what-have-you, why haven't you seen them? No reports of the wandering undead, I suppose?"

"No," Michael countered, "because they don't *look* like corpses, or zombies. They act as alive as you or I."

"They're disoriented, make irrational statements—"

"Sure, and *every* day, in *every* city, they're *ignored* on the street. Right?"

Armitach took another sip from his bottle, waiting for the inevitable leap of faith to land.

"It's a miracle," the Reverend breathed.

Armitach guffawed, causing a few lethargic patrons to gawk. "You've been wandering the corn fields too long. We have cult experts, shrinks. I can put you in touch with one of them."

The Reverend looked stubborn and offended.

"Oh, *think*," Armitach pressed. "Where did they *go*? Surely you'd notice a fresh face around town."

"They're all around you." The Reverend waved airily. "All around."

"What are you saying?"

Reverend Michael leaned forward. "Nobody could see them *before* they died. They were nameless. We couldn't see them *until* they died. Now that they're *living* again..."

He stared at Armitach with raised eyebrows, waiting.

❧☙

Armitach delayed his departure by another day, and spent it waiting at the E-Z-Go Truck Palace, east of Wenton. He had hired a car to get there, without telling the Reverend where he was going, or why.

He knew how undocumented people got by. His patient surveillance paid off.

The man in a faded t-shirt and worn jeans was seeing off an adolescent girl boarding the daily eastbound bus. She waved shyly at him through the broad bus window as it pulled away. Strolling back to the mini-mart, George caught sight of Armitach and beamed a smile. He looked fit—for a corpse.

"Hello! Ah... afraid I didn't catch your name last night... Tall Blond and Handsome."

The agent accepted the outthrust hand. "Armitach." George had a healthy grip and solid build.

"You look... different," Armitach noted.

"Yeah, clothes make the man. I do remember you're FBI, though. Not here to bust me, are you?"

"That depends. How did you come to be on the base last night?"

"Not sure. But I can tell you, I didn't go there under my own power."

Armitach considered this. "Buy you a cup of coffee?"

"Love it." They headed across the lot to the diner.

"It's a fine day!" George exclaimed, taking a deep breath. "I can't remember when I've felt this good."

"Who's the girl?" Armitach inquired. "A friend?"

"On the bus? Oh, no. Just a wayward kid. Runaway, no money to get home. She would have turned tricks to earn it. So, we talked, and I bought her a bus ticket home." He shrugged and held the door for Armitach. "There goes my first day's wages. So many of them, lost to themselves. Nobody seems to notice."

Armitach led them to the quiet end of the counter, ordering two coffees.

"Sorry I ran away," George said. "But once I started moving, I felt better and better—just running—and I ended up here. I waited at the service entrance until morning. They needed a dishwasher, so they offered me clothes from the cast-off bin at the truckers' rest. I guess I can earn another bus ticket tomorrow." He peered into his black coffee. "I've got a little catching up to do, it seems. Terrorism, wars—and what's going on in Washington? At least there's progress with AIDS."

"So, you believe you were, like, in a coma?"

George looked at the agent. "I think you know better."

"Will you try to get your life back?"

"Can I?"

Armitach considered. "Someone may have petitioned to have you declared legally dead, to get at your estate."

George snorted at the word *estate*.

"You should be able to go back to Minnesota, or wherever, and prove who you are by fingerprints. Get a birth certificate re-issued, then a driver's license. Check your Social Security status. Start over." Armitach considered the man across the table. "Your prints are in the Federal database, so the FBI couldn't object."

"But *you* could."

Armitach sighed, considering how to shape his next field report.

"I'll tell them the facility has a record-keeping problem dating back years. It's not missing corpses; it just never received them. Reverend Michael will concur."

"Thanks." George smiled. "Would you happen to know if he's, say, involved?"

"You'll have to ask Michael that. What will you do, with your identity back?"

"I'm not sure. My family would be shocked if I just appear, and hardly any older." He studied his hands. "Same with friends, if any survived."

"Well, you'll have a lengthy bus ride to think it over."

"I'm in no hurry." He stretched, locking his fingers behind his head. "Maybe I'll stay here a while and help. Lots of people drift along the highways. I've got a second chance at… this. Maybe I can help them."

Armitach considered George. "It must be nice, having no one setting expectations. Freedom."

"Freedom." George chuckled. "Sure—all you have to do is die."

めぐ

Author's note: "Towns are strung along the roads of America, very familiar, hypnotic in their repetitive fashion. The extraordinary may be hiding anywhere in plain sight. It takes a liminal moment when the light shifts and the shadows move to reveal itself."

J.L. Royce is an author of science fiction, the macabre, and whatever else strikes him. He lives in the northern reaches of the American Midwest, exploring the wilderness without and within. His work appears in *Alien Dimensions, Allegory, Cosmic Horror Monthly, The Fifth Di…, Fireside, Ghostlight, Love Letters to Poe* (Visiter Award winner), *Lovecraftiana, Mysterion, parABnormal, Penumbric, Sci Phi Journal, Strange Aeon, Utopia, Wyldblood*, etc. He is a member of WWA, HWA, and GLAHW. Some of his anthologized stories may be found at: www.jlroyce.com.

Find him on **X** (Twitter): @AuthorJLRoyce
Bluesky: jlroyce.bsky.social
Facebook: https://www.facebook.com/AuthorJLRoyce
Instagram: authorJLRoyce

Breaching the Distance

Hannah Onoguwe

THE UNCOMFORTABLE METAL chairs were peeling to reveal what could be rust or dried blood. I had inched away from those suspicious bits earlier, but as time passed I made myself as comfortable as I could because, what did it really matter? Edem was going to take at least an hour and a half to get to Yenagoa from Port Harcourt and I was calling myself all sorts of names for encouraging him to travel in the first place.

I huffed out a breath as I disconnected the call. Then I felt a flutter over my fingers. The man beside me jerked his head towards the desk when I looked at him.

"Is that you?" he asked. I cocked an ear to hear, "Rayman Patience," the nurse's voice laced with irritation. At the back of my mind was the certainty that she had indeed called it a number of times.

"Yes!" I heaved myself out of the chair.

The nurse's eyes narrowed on me with little sympathy as I approached. "Madam, help us to help you. I've been calling your name how many times now and you just dey on top phone."

"Sorry," I mumbled. "Na my husband I been dey talk to."

Her colleague raked me up and down with a look. "Which EDD did they give you?" she asked.

"April 4." Today was March 23.

"Hmm. About ten… eleven days early. The labour ward is full so you'll have to wait a bit."

"We had wanted a private room," I said.

"And you didn't pay for one?"

"We were told to wait until the renovations were over."

"Who told you that?"

"One of the doctors."

"Na wetin MD been tell us?" she asked the first nurse, forehead lined. The first nurse started to mumble something, but she overrode her. "No. He said payments could be made in advance." As she spoke I could feel an impending contraction and braced myself for it.

She turned to me and said, "Madam, you will have to pay for the room in Accounts and then—"

"But…" was all I could manage before I gripped the edge of the desk to ride out the contraction, breathing through my mouth as I'd seen it done on TV. When it subsided, I took a minute to catch my breath.

The first nurse spoke. "This one that you are opening your mouth to breathe, you will get tired on time o. Close your mouth and breathe through your nose."

I didn't have the strength to argue about my YouTube findings. "Will the room be ready soon? I think this pain… baby will soon come."

"Is it your first pregnancy?" Nurse Two asked.

"Yes."

She smiled. "Don't worry, it will take a while. We'll go and see what rooms are available and which you can pay for. Just go and sit down first."

"But I don't think…"

"Just wait, madam. As I dey see you so, the thing never serious yet. When e serious, you sef go know. You nor go dey speak Queen's English like this."

Nurse One laughed. As I shuffled back to my seat, I heard her say to the second, "You get mouth, sha."

"Look who dey talk," Nurse Two shot back as she left the desk, presumably to see what rooms were available. I rubbed my tummy and sighed as I resumed my seat. My mind was going in a hundred directions, but threaded through it all was a very robust fear. It had been building and ebbing over the past months but I had never given voice to it. Fear of the unknown, of my body's capabilities. Of failure.

I never thought I would get married, let alone have a child. After growing up in a Christian home with the works—family devotions, full church membership, parents staunch church workers—it had been the greatest of shocks when my parents got divorced. The foundations of what I imagined to be a rock-steady life had crumbled and I had felt betrayed. How did two people who had counseled others for years allow their own marriage to break down irretrievably? At fifteen years of age, it had also been a huge embarrassment. The last year of boarding school had been a welcome escape but the wound was reopened when Rita and I returned to Abuja for the holidays and had to split our time between two homes. Rita had taken it all in stride eventually, holding tenaciously to her faith and marrying at twenty-five. However, it had all given me a jaundiced view, not only about marriage, but about the so-called Christian values I had been raised on.

I mean, everyone in Nigeria was a Christian. Or at least it seemed so. Every corrupt politician who gave tithes from monies which were supposed to be for their constituents, every university lecturer who collected bribes or, more commonly, slept with girls in exchange for grades, every shifty vendor who hummed gospel songs under their breath. I had a dozen churches on my street, with their public address systems advertising contemporary choirs and pastors with rousing sermons. And each year the country seemed to slide into even more decay. Where before I had gone with the masses and said, "God will help us," or "We will keep praying," the scales had seemingly fallen from my eyes and I determined to live the way I liked because what did it matter, after all? If people I looked up to could practice all sorts of atrocities both overtly and in secret, why bother?

Enter Edem: fifteen years older to my thirty-eight, a widower, two university-age kids. He was nothing like any man I'd ever known: optimistic even after a less than sterling marriage, he said he had prayed me into his life. Me, in my single, un-celibate state. But he had been so patient, so persuasive, so amusedly dismissive when I warned that I just might be looking at him as a father figure. He also wasn't looking to have more kids. And then this had happened. And his delight over the news had floored me. I hadn't been prepared, in any way really, but especially emotionally. I was also wary of what values I would pass on to my child. Honesty, hard work… Somehow I felt hollow at the thought.

Outwardly though, I had ticked all the boxes, especially this last trimester. Binged on Red Raspberry Tea, faithfully eaten dates daily, taken walks around the neighbourhood, done pelvic core exercises when I remembered, which I rarely had, to be honest. What was left was to see how effective it all would be. The only time I remembered talking to my child was early on in the bathroom one day when I had announced to my swelling stomach: "I'm sure you know I don't really want you," words that had plagued me with guilt ever since. And if I had felt none of the connection to him mothers were supposed to have as the date drew closer, the increasing excitement, I kept that to myself. But I needed Edem here. He was the one with the great faith. "It's something you need to find and live out for yourself," he always said. I had none, admittedly, but his was always a comfort somehow.

"Sorry, my sister," my neighbour said, intruding on my thoughts. I peered at him. He was the one who had drawn my attention when my name had been called repeatedly.

"Thank you."

"These nurses, if not for the situation in Nigeria, ehn… they would be sacked. So rude."

I snorted softly, thinking about what the nurse had said about speaking English. She hadn't talked to this man yet. I gave him a closer look. He was clean-shaven, maybe 45 years of age, but looked athletic in jeans and a T-shirt. I'd assumed he had a wife in labour, but he didn't look anxious.

"You have someone here?" I asked.

"Yes. My sister just underwent a successful CS, so I'm waiting for when they allow me to see her."

"Oh, great. Congrats." I allowed myself a moment of envy for the mother whose baby was out already.

"Thanks. A girl, by the way."

"That was my next question. Her husband couldn't make it in time?"

"Oh, no husband," he said cheerily. "She's older than I am and decided to do this on her own."

"Oh, wow." I had the greatest admiration for her. I wanted to ask a dozen questions, but realized it was none of my business. IVF? Casual boyfriend?

"And you? I overheard you talking on the phone earlier?"

"Yes. Hopefully hubby should be here soon."

"Someone should be with you, though."

"My sister will be here next week. It's just this baby's timing." I shrugged. He laughed, and when he didn't ask about my mother, I was grateful. I expected she would show up for the *omugwo*, but I didn't count on our relationship warming up significantly.

"Mrs. Patience." It was Nurse Two with a piece of paper. "You can pay for the room at Accounts, then we'll take you to it."

"Thank you." I hustled to my feet and found my way to Accounts, which was almost on the other side of the hospital. There were three people in line already, a woman with two children, an elderly man, and another woman with a small baby bump. I wasn't going to wait. I didn't have to. I let out a groan which made all eyes swing to me in surprise.

"Abeg, let me pay for my room. E be like say this pikin wan comot o."

They scooted out of the way and I swallowed a laugh. They were probably afraid the baby would pop out right into their unprepared hands. Only the lady behind the mesh looked at me askance.

"You should have someone with you, madam."

251

"Yes. But I haven't even reached my EDD and my husband traveled…"

There was a hum of sympathy from the mother of two. "Did you say 'room'?" she asked, peering over my shoulder at the piece of paper in my hand.

"Yes." I scrunched my face up for good measure. "They say they've been renovated."

I caught her frown. "Really? I thought the issue with those rooms was more than renovation."

I gave a pained shrug as I handed over the slip of paper and my ATM card to the cashier. Clamped my lips between my teeth as she asked if it was Savings or Current. Narrowed my eyes like I was losing my vision as I tapped out the PIN. She ripped out the receipts and handed them to me and I hobbled away with a thank you.

"Safe delivery," the mother of two said.

"Thank you," I mouthed back at her. When I turned the corner, I resumed my usual waddle, and it was only then that I realized I hadn't had another contraction in quite a while. Was this normal? Would they come back with a vengeance?

I submitted the receipts and after taking their copy, Nurse Two asked where my bag was. I pointed to where I'd been sitting only to see my neighbour rise to pick up the bag.

"You don't have to do that," I said.

"No worries. I'm not really doing anything."

"Thank you."

Nurse Two looked impressed. "Men like this still dey?"

He laughed. As I turned to fall into step behind Nurse Two, my eyes caught Nurse One's. The expression on her face was unsettling and I looked away quickly. She reminded me of a dozen meddlesome church "aunts" I had growing up whose faces morphed into those very lines of judgment whenever they saw you standing too close to a boy, or caught you in town during the week wearing tight jeans. But she needn't think too far: all I was after was a helping hand, not a flirtation.

Nurse Two didn't slow on my account. In no time, I was panting and the armpits of my loose dress were damp.

"Nurse… take it easy."

She didn't even glance at me. "Exercise is good for labour," she said. I looked back at my helper and he gave a small nod.

"I hope someone doesn't come looking for you," I said to him.

"I doubt it," he said, and there was a smile on his face that didn't quite sit right.

To take my mind off my growing fatigue, I said, "I never asked your name."

"I didn't ask yours."

I glanced at him in surprise. That had sounded a bit rude, coming from someone who had been anything but earlier. I could have reminded him that he had inadvertently gotten to know mine from the nurse's calls in the waiting room, but I was focusing on putting one foot in front of the other and looking forward to resting for a bit. Maybe he hadn't bargained for the distance when he had offered to help with my bag. Too bad. If I weren't lugging around an extra fifteen kilograms in baby, water and fat, I might have told him something.

I didn't know the hospital was this big, I thought. We entered a wing and the smell of fresh paint made me wrinkle my nose. The walls seemed to stretch forever, and our footsteps echoed eerily. We seemed to be the only three people in this part of the hospital and I began to feel uneasy. What if I needed something urgently?

Finally, the nurse stopped and opened a door. She flipped a light switch and I followed her in, coughing as a wave of mustiness and the smell of new paint hit me. The room was spacious and relatively neat, although a few things were out of place, likely due to the renovations. As soon as she removed the plastic cover over the bed, I sank onto it with relief. The nurse bustled around, setting things straight while the man set my bag on the bed beside me.

"Thanks," I said with a smile.

The nurse dusted off her hands as she came back towards me. "Sorry. I'll send someone to clean the room. I'll also come back to check you."

I thought back to the long walk it had taken to get here. I also realized I hadn't had a contraction since before paying for the room. I frowned and the nurse seemed to read my thoughts when she added, "Your labour doesn't seem to be progressing for now."

I opened my mouth, then shut it. The sooner she went, the sooner she would be back to check me properly. I thought about Edem. Surely twenty, thirty minutes must have passed? Hopefully he would be here soon. I didn't relish the thought of trying to do this without a familiar face. "Okay," I said finally.

She nodded and walked to the door. As the man moved aside for her, she stopped in surprise. "Aren't you going back to the other ward?"

"In a few minutes, ma," he said winsomely. "I'll just stay to keep her company."

She turned to me. "Are you all right with that?"

I suddenly felt the weirdest pressure on my chest as I looked into his eyes. He was smiling, but his eyes were darker than I remembered, watchful, with a clear message in them: he wanted me to say yes. I opened my mouth to agree, but a shaft of fear made me falter. I shook my head.

"I… not really," I said, and the pure anger that streaked through his eyes like lightning made my heart beat faster, a heavy, throbbing rhythm. "I just met him there. He said he was waiting for his sister."

"Eh-ehn. What's your sister's name?" she asked him. He mumbled something that could have been anything and she cocked her head. "Anyway, let's go back. I'll be back to check on her."

She waited for him to precede her from the room and the look he flashed me just before he turned away made goose bumps break out on my skin. "Later," he murmured as they left.

I took a deep gulp of air as they left, willing my heartrate to normalize. What on earth was that? For a moment there I wanted to snatch up my bag and sprint back to the waiting room I had left. I swallowed and shook my head. He had been so nice when we had struck up that first conversation. So helpful. Surely my imagination had gone into overdrive just now? He couldn't have been as threatening as I had suddenly feared, could he?

As their footsteps faded away, the stillness of my surroundings settled over me like a scratchy blanket. Shaking off my unease, I unzipped my bag and took out a wrapper. I would just lie down for a bit. I knew I was supposed to walk around for as long as possible to speed things up, but no way was I doing that now. Besides, I needed to rest. I touched my belly and the familiar guilt swamped me, with a touch of nervousness.

"Don't give me too much work, hmm?" I murmured, then froze on realizing I had spoken to my child for the second time. Taking off my slippers, I moved my bag to the side table and stretched out on the bed. Calm, the research said. Keep calm. I took deep breaths. Trust that your body knows what to do. Anxiety will only slow things down. I shut my eyes, took another breath. *I want to love you*, I told him. *Help me.*

As if in response, I felt an impending contraction and fought not to stiffen as I rode it out. My breath was puffing out audibly as I rooted for my phone in my bag. There were two missed calls, one from Edem and the other from my sister, Rita. I immediately pressed Redial, but it went off without connecting. I frowned. Damn. The network was near nonexistent. I waved my phone in a couple of directions, hoping for some improvement even as I thumbed Redial again. Nothing. Seemed this part of the hospital was out of the loop. I hoped it changed soon because how was I to contact anybody?

The nurse had opened the window, so the room was losing some of its mustiness, but it was still uncomfortably warm. I concentrated on not being anxious and hoped the nurse returned in a hurry. Sure enough, a few minutes later, I was relieved to hear footsteps approaching. The nurse opened the door, holding a steel tray aloft. I tried to tamp down my apprehension.

"Sorry. You know how busy we are over there."

"I seem to be the only one in this part of the hospital," I said as she placed the tray on the shelf at the foot of the bed. She asked me to sit up and then wrapped the blood pressure cuff around my arm, concentrating as she took my pulse. When she was done, she said, "You should have someone with you."

"I tried calling. The network here is bad." I wasn't happy that it sounded like I was whining, but it was only just dawning on me what might happen if I was close to giving birth and there was no one with me. The contractions weren't overwhelming yet, but...

The nurse was at the foot of the bed now, pulling on latex gloves. "Please lie down so I can check you." I lay back and focused on the ceiling. When I felt the cold metal between my legs, I fought to remain relaxed but couldn't prevent a small moan. That was the most uncomfortable shit ever.

"Two centimetres," she said, stripping off her gloves. "Still some way to go. Please try and relax."

I was disappointed. You heard of women who hardly felt a pinprick of pain and when they went for a routine checkup, they were 5 cm dilated and told not to leave the hospital. Not me, obviously.

The nurse left with a reassuring smile, promising to send someone to clean the room. I reached into my bag for my plastic bottle of water as the silence settled around me again. I was just placing it back on the table when I heard footsteps again. Goody. Even a cleaner with zero medical knowledge was preferable to being alone. I looked up expectantly as the door opened and felt every thought flee when I saw who it was.

My would-be helper, Mr. No Name, smiled at my frozen expression as he shut the door softly behind him. "I'm back," he said softly.

I felt my whole body prickle with perspiration as my heart took a nosedive.

"Nothing to say?" He sounded a bit put out. As he spoke, he walked around the bed slowly, back and forth, eyes roaming all over my body. I watched him in fixed fascination.

"You didn't have to," I finally said, my voice strained from the struggle to sound normal.

He laughed. "Oh, I didn't do it for you, but for..." Eyes gleaming, he gestured to my belly with something like glee.

I shook my head. Was he saying he had pitied me, being pregnant? "What—"

"I felt bad when you told the nurse that you didn't really know me," he said.

"I'm sorry." The apology spilled out of my mouth. Anything to placate what I recognized as a growing anger. "Pregnancy makes one crazy."

"Yes, but... You've had a relatively easy time, haven't you?"

My breath was coming jerkily now. "How could you know that?"

When he giggled, I shivered involuntarily. I swear it had sounded like a chorus. "We know things," he whispered, leaning towards me so I heard him perfectly.

His once-pleasant face seemed to morph into something sinister and not quite recognizable. Fear was a damp constriction in my throat and I fought to appear calm. This was surreal. I sat up with some effort, but when I tried to move my legs over the side of the bed, he seized my feet to stay me.

"Don't move," he said. His eyes bored into mine, his manner controlled. His hands against my feet felt eerily cool, almost cold, and they tightened for a moment before he let go. "You need to rest," he added, as if by way of explanation.

"My husband and sister are on their way," I said, scooting back so I could lean back against the headboard. It was uncomfortable, being more of an iron frame than anything else, but it gave me that much more distance from this man who I suspected was quite unbalanced. What did he want? To rape me, a bloated pregnant woman? My mind stuttered at the thought, but people were known to get off on all kinds of freaky shit. It also skittered away from considering any more sinister reason.

"Ah, your husband. Edem."

My eyes rounded. "How—But..."

"Relax. I heard you on the phone, remember?"

His eyes crinkled in genuine amusement, a return to the man I had met in the waiting room. It made me wonder if, maybe, I was overreacting to him, his words. Maybe he only wanted some gratitude?

"Your sister. Hmmm..." He placed a finger against his chin. "Would that be Rita? Older, two children, the advertisement executive? She's getting some leave, abi?"

I was shaking by now, tears close to the surface. When they came, my words didn't sound at all like me. "I never discussed my sister with you."

A smile slowly lengthened his lips. "No," he said. "You didn't. Only that she was coming next week."

As if from far away, I heard footsteps. "Someone's coming," I said. Unnecessarily, as I saw from his cocked head that he had also heard. I couldn't disguise the relief in my voice, but as I looked at him closely, I saw that the smile hadn't disappeared completely and that he, in fact, looked anything but bothered.

I immediately broke into speech the moment the handle turned. "Please, please. I don't want this man here. I..." My words trailed off as I saw who had come in. It appeared to be a nurse, but not any I recognized from the past hour or so. She was dressed in what, on closer inspection, appeared to be a nurse's uniform, but the white having turned grey. She went by me without a word, smelling so rank that I gagged. She held a bag with some things in it which she immediately showed the man.

He frowned. "What's that?"

"Pitocin."

"Are you mad? We don't have time to induce labour!"

She looked me full in the face for the first time and I shrank back at the malevolence of her expression. Her face was twisted in parts, lips twitching in some sort of facial tic. One side of her mouth was pulled back in a permanent half-snarl, showing yellow, uneven teeth. When she spoke, her voice was gritty, saliva pooling at the corners of her mouth. "So, what do we do?"

He rummaged in the bag. "Get it out, of course. You obviously haven't done this in a while."

My heart was pounding so hard. "What are you talking about?" As I spoke, I edged my feet over the bed. Something told me this wasn't a time to talk, but somehow I couldn't stop myself from confirming in plain English what was the vilest of intentions.

His gaze snared mine. "We are going to relieve you of your baby."

"That's impossible! You said—Your sister was in... had just had surgery—that—"

The odd pair looked at each other and then broke into raucous laughter. "You, sef," the woman said, her eyes at that moment appearing almost serpentine.

I didn't wait to hear more. I jumped down from the bed and lunged towards the door. I didn't make it, but then I really hadn't thought I would. In a flash, the man had grabbed my shoulders and lifted me bodily back to the bed while I screamed, kicking out and tears sprouting. I expected to be knocked out by some chemical, indeed at that moment there was nothing I longed for more than to slide into oblivion. Instead, the man held me down while they spoke words over me in unison, words in an unfamiliar language that lifted every hair on my body. By the time they were rounding off he wasn't subduing me any longer. He didn't need to as my struggles had slowed until my limbs lay quiet. It crossed my mind half-hysterically that some knowledge of that spell they used could come in handy when dealing with certain in-laws, because although my body felt almost numb, I stayed conscious of everything happening around me. And everything happening *to* me, I discovered, as within minutes of their subduing me, I watched the woman cut through my clothing with scissors. She looked me over from neck to groin with cold eyes before stroking my bare nipple with her fingers.

"Your breast no bad o," she said with something close to lust in her eyes. And that was the first time I realized I could still hear everything. I watched them go into the bathroom, drying their hands off as they came out. Saw the man lay surgical tools on the table the woman had drawn up beside the bed. Saw him raise a scalpel consideringly, testing the blade against his naked thumb.

"Sharp." He smiled when there was a resulting welt of blood. "This might hurt a bit." And then without hesitation he dug the scalpel into my abdomen, like he was gutting a fish, blood welling up everywhere. I couldn't move, couldn't utter a word, had hoped that the numbness I felt would be complete, but I felt that cut deep in my bones so that my body jerked from the agony, animal sounds struggling for release from my throat. Tears ran from the corner of my eyes unchecked.

"You have a steady hand," the woman said admiringly. "But I think that technique is twenty years old." The man ignored her.

From what I'd read about Caesarean sections, the cuts were made in layers. This man didn't bother. He was in a hurry. I had also heard from women who'd undergone them that they took next to no time these days. He seemed to have that down pat, as in mere minutes he was holding aloft a wad of grey matter. A chill went over my skin as it seemed to be confirmation that there was something wrong with my baby, something else I had feared all these months.

But the woman had an expression on her face like she had seen an epiphany. "Madam will be so pleased," she said, her voice throbbing with excitement. "En caul."

"Don't be stupid," he said sharply. "There's no way we can leave it like that. Sew her up."

"Me?" she sputtered. "I thought you said—"

"Stop talking and just do it."

My insides seemed to be a free-for-all as she reached in matter-of-factly for the placenta. My eyes widened as the man made a tiny incision on the grey mass and water dribbled down his arms. He peeled the mass aside and there was the most perfect little form I had ever seen. There he was! I barely noticed the woman's fumbling attempts to stitch me back together.

The tears tracked faster down my face, my throat working with unintelligible sounds. I wished I could see my baby properly. *My baby! Oh, please, don't... Don't take him from me.* All the distance I'd felt in all the preceding months was breached in an instant as a rush of love drenched me. I wanted nothing more in that moment than to hold my baby in my arms. As if in response to my thoughts, a high-pitched wail came from his mouth.

"Keep quiet, my friend," the man said in irritation. I couldn't see clearly, but he seemed to be cutting the cord, clamping it and cleaning the small limbs. My heart railed at the combined injustice and irony. Soon, they would be gone. Soon, they would just walk out that door with my child. *God, can you see this?* There was nothing, no answer, but I hadn't expected one. I wanted to slap myself for bothering, but deep down came the memories of all those antenatal mornings when the nurses led us in songs and prayers before the health talk. At first I had been annoyed at their taking for granted—in typical Nigerian style—that regardless of religious affiliation, no woman would mind. But later I had come to accept it with an inner smirk even as my lips learned the words of the songs and my hands clapped along with everyone else's. One came to mind and I sang the words compulsively, in desperate silence: *Do not allow me, do not allow me, Jesus, to go empty-handed. I want to be alive, I want to carry my baby, I don't want to lose my baby. Oh Lord, see me through.*

The woman's hand dipped up and then down as she stitched me up. I fought to move an arm, my head, something, but nothing would respond to my impulses. My sounds of frustration were recognizable, though, and the woman paused to say, "Don't worry. It will soon be over."

Their concern about stitching me up seemed to mean they didn't want me to die. But without my baby, wouldn't I want to anyway? I was unable to visualize life beyond this, beyond coming into the hospital with a swollen belly and leaving with empty arms, arms made so in such a horrific, nightmarish manner. How would I live with that knowledge? I wasn't certain I could. The wailing of the newborn went on and on, and I knew it would haunt me forever.

"Oya, do quick," the man said to the woman. He was galvanized by a sudden energy as he hurried over to my bag and rummaged through it. I wondered fretfully where he had put my baby as he emerged with diapers and an outfit. He disappeared out of view and I guessed he was dressing him up. Was he okay? Without the preliminary checks needed for an accurate APGAR score, I fretted. What did they plan to do with him? The woman had mentioned a madam. Was this about trafficking? Were they going to sell my baby? I had a feeling it was something more diabolical.

The woman finished and as if in a dream, I watched them grab anything on hand to wipe their hands. The man emptied my bag and placed the wrapped bundle inside. *Please,* I tried to say, the word powerless in my mind. *Please, don't do this.* With only a final glance at me, they were gone. Only the sounds issuing from my throat remained in the room. As if their departure galvanized feeling into my nerve endings, I was visited with a wave of pain so great the edges of my vision dimmed. I was going to pass out. I was going to pass out. Mucus clogged my throat and nose and I thought I might just die from asphyxiation, after all.

Things took on a fuzzy quality and my eyes drifted shut, then open. Something stirred on the fringes of my senses and it took a while to recognize the sound of footsteps, of maybe more than one person. I tried to work some sound from my throat, but nothing happened. When the door opened this time, I couldn't even open my eyes to see who stood there.

"Jesus Christ," someone said. And on the fervency and shock contained in those two words, I slid away from it all, thankfully. Time was only a word as I drifted in and out of consciousness, only bits of conversation coming to me.

"…like an abattoir in there…"

"…is she alive?"

"…stitched by a carpenter…"

"…find the man?"

"…terrible world…"

When I came to, it was in degrees. My body was screaming in protest, but it also recognized that I had received some heavy-duty painkillers. I felt a bit out of it, but despite the fight to keep my eyes open, I slipped away again.

The next time my eyes opened, there was a man sitting beside the bed. Good-looking, dressed in a wine-coloured native up and down, white in his beard. He leaned forward when he saw I was awake.

"Sweetheart, how are you feeling?"

Only then did I realize my limbs had twitched in response. I opened my mouth and a garbled sound escaped. I tried again and it was more a croak.

"Take it easy," he said.

"Edem." The splintered name finally emerged on the third try, and then I began to cry, great racking sobs that brought my pains and aches to flaring life. But all I could focus on was the sadness lurking in his eyes.

"Don't say anything, love," he murmured. "Just get your strength back."

"I'm sorry," was all I could say, over and over again. "I'm so sorry."

"It wasn't your fault. If I'd been here—"

"I'm sorry. Our baby. I didn't want it, not really… I'm a horrible person, right? Horrible. And now this… just punishment. God must be punishing me—"

"You have to calm down, Pat."

But I was getting more agitated, my breath choppy. "Admit it. I'm a devil. And it's too late. Too late I realized I *did* want him, so much. And now—now… I'm so sorry, Edem. I'm going to carry this until I die, this guilt, I…"

I barely noticed when a nurse came in. "Mrs. Rayman, take it easy," she crooned, a syringe in hand. She stuck it into the IV drip as she said, "It's all right. You're okay."

I attempted a few more words from the host of my disjointed thoughts, foremost among them the certainty that I would never be okay.

The next time I woke up, I was in no hurry to open my eyes. Unbidden, my thoughts went over the nightmare I had experienced. Why hadn't I just died? It didn't make sense. I heard voices and was about to ask for water, but felt too parched to speak up. In the next few seconds I was glad I hadn't. One nurse was right beside me, changing my drip from the sound of it, and another was near the door. They were speaking in semi-hushed tones as though not to disturb me.

The one near the door said, "This life, ehn. So, just like that, this woman for just die."

"My sister. People are wicked o. Na God just save am."

"I heard she was rambling about a woman in a nurse's uniform? A dirty uniform, and the nurse's face was somehow deformed…"

"There's no one like that here," the nurse beside me scoffed.

"But… I overheard Matron telling the M.D. that the only person by that description was one Nurse May who worked here but died some years back. That she hadn't been cheated of some of her benefits by the management."

There was a prickly, disbelieving pause after that rush of information. "You believe such stories, Ope?"

"In this Naija? Stranger things have happened. But you know that that part of the hospital used to be land belonging to a local deity?"

"Abeg-abeg-abeg. You're the only one hearing stories. Let's go."

There were footsteps to the door, even as the other nurse said, "*Haba.* Maybe because you're new here. It's common knowledge na. My uncle had mentioned just yesterday, that…" and their voices faded as the door shut behind them.

I opened my eyes slowly, but they remained dry. I bit back a moan. Somehow, I was going to have to live through this. I wanted to ask God why, but felt I didn't have the right. On the other hand, I was also afraid I might get an answer I wouldn't be able to bear. I remembered how I'd lost it when Edem was here. He wasn't here now, and who could blame him after everything I'd said? Would he even still want to be with me?

Later a nurse came to urge me out of bed. I wasn't surprised as I had heard that with Caesarean sections, women were encouraged to move as soon as possible. I wanted to stay in that bed and mope, but one look at her determined face and I bit back my protest. No use making her think I was going crazy. I mean, I was, but only quietly, in my mind. With her help, I took a few steps around the room with great effort and excruciating pain. When I lay back, exhausted, I also felt a marginal sense of accomplishment.

Edem came later and I studied him surreptitiously, trying to gauge his mood. But he seemed open, kissing me gently, asking how I was. He made some small talk about work, his mother who he warned would be descending on me tomorrow, news from one of his kids who had called. I listened with half an ear, trying to look interested, picking at the corner of the sheet.

When there was a bit of a lull, I blurted, "About the other day—"

He shook his head. "Before you say anything more, I have a surprise for you."

I sighed. This man really did mean well, so I didn't want to tell him he shouldn't have bothered. "What?" I asked instead.

"Just a minute." He stood and dashed out the door. He returned some minutes later with a wheelchair, a male nurse trailing him.

"What—?"

"Just wait and see, okay?"

I gritted my teeth while they helped me into the wheelchair, and then Edem wheeled me out of the room. Maybe he wanted to take me for a walk of some kind, to lift my spirits. I doubted anything could do that, but I said nothing. My gaze skidded off the curious gazes of the medical personnel as we went by. I left it to Edem to respond to their greetings. I couldn't handle the pity behind what were supposed to be clinical expressions. I kept my eyes straight ahead as we passed what appeared to be the children's ward, but after a few metres, Edem stopped at a desk to talk to the nurse. I couldn't hear what they said, but in a minute he was back and wheeled me down another hallway. I turned to give him a questioning look but he only raised his brows with a smile.

We pushed through a set of doors and if I had been on my feet, I would have halted in my tracks. I murmured Edem's name, but he pushed me on. There were maybe half a dozen babies in incubators or under bili-lights. They looked so precious and fragile and I felt my eyes begin to moisten. I so did not want to be here. Besides another nurse who sat unobtrusively in one corner, three of the babies had a parent with them and it was hard not to feel overwhelmed by the palpable love and anxiety in the room. Edem stopped beside one of the babies.

I glanced around, but no one paid us any mind. "Should we be here?" I fought to sound normal but avoided looking at the baby before us. Dressed in nothing but a diaper and a woolen hat pulled low over the eyes, its skin took on an eerie hue from the bili-lights. Just being there made the weight in my chest that much heavier.

"Yes," Edem said. He stilled my head with gentle hands so that I was face-to-face with the baby. "Read the tag, Pat."

"Is this some kind of lesson, Eddie, is that it?"

"Not in the way you mean, I promise."

"Eddie—"

He turned the wheelchair sideways and braced his hands on its arms so that our faces were inches apart. "Do you trust me, Pat?"

I searched his eyes swiftly. They were candid, his face bearing traces of the strain of recent events. This man was solid, dependable. And somehow, miraculously still mine. I let out a breath. "I do."

"Have I ever hurt you?"

I cocked my head. Well, there *were* those couple of times, first when—

Edem caught my raised brows and quickly added, "On purpose, I mean."

I couldn't have stopped the beginnings of the smile that stretched my mouth. A beautiful feeling. "No."

"Then, please." He clasped my hands in his warm ones, rubbing them gently. "Please, read it. Okay?"

I nodded. "Okay." I took a deep breath and forced myself to focus as he turned the wheelchair back towards the baby. It took a while to actually locate the tag, but when I did, I shook my head. "I don't understand."

"Don't you?"

My heart was rushing to my chest, threatening to choke me. I leaned forward to read it again, although I was positive my eyes hadn't lied the first time. Rayman Baby, it said. *Rayman Baby.*

"I don't understand," I said again. And this time, my voice shook. With the tears that had begun to descend, with disbelief and with hope.

Edem squatted beside me so that he looked into my eyes. "Your baby, Pat. *Our* baby."

"How is this possible?" I was crying in earnest now. "I thought he was gone."

He reached for my hand as if to soothe me. "One of the nurses was coming back to you with a cleaner and saw the man trying to escape. She called out for security and he panicked and dropped the bag."

"They didn't catch him?"

"They said he just disappeared."

"What about the other person? The woman?"

He frowned. "The nurse didn't mention anyone else."

I nodded. I was fast accepting the fact that I was the only one who had seen her, whoever she was. I felt a chill when I thought back to the conversation the nurses had had in my room. Shaking the thought away, I peered at the miracle in front of me, feasting on the tiny limbs, the adorable wrinkly facial features, the fisted hands. I brushed my hands over my wet eyes.

"Our baby." It sounded unreal. "How come no one told me?"

"I asked them to allow me do that," Edem said slowly. "To show you when you were more… settled. Was this wise or…?"

I caught the uncertainty in his voice and considered. If anyone had told me earlier, wouldn't I have assumed they were lying and only trying to make me feel momentarily better? I shook my head slightly, marveling at this incredible moment.

"God, I'm so sorry, Pat. I thought—"

"What? No, *no*. I think you did the right thing." My senses seemed sharper, colours brighter as I stared at the tiny human before me. "Is he okay?"

"Perfect. Just a bit of jaundice got the doctor concerned, but everything else checked out okay. And, er, sweetheart… That's not a he."

I swiveled my head to gape at him, and then again at the baby. "*What?*"

"That's what I said."

I touched the back of a forefinger to her dewy cheek, smiling as she recoiled slightly, then to the skin just above the clamped umbilical cord. I couldn't wait to look into her eyes. My heart was full to bursting with incredulity, with thanksgiving, with a cocktail of joy. I couldn't speak for long minutes for the tears that started again. It was an amazing feeling to know that my silent prayers had been answered.

Something occurred to me, and meeting Edem's gaze again, I asked, "Am *I* okay?" I braced myself as my husband seemed to steel himself.

"It was a botched job… the first time. They were able to get you to the theatre in time, but repairing everything…"

"I won't be able to have more kids?"

"They… weren't sure."

I searched Edem's eyes. I knew if it was an outright no he wouldn't have hesitated to tell me. I nodded. I found I could face almost anything now. My eyes couldn't stay off the baby for long. She was the most beautiful thing I had ever seen.

"I don't deserve this," I said.

He squeezed my shoulder and then bent to kiss me softly. He opened his mouth to speak and I forestalled him with a raised palm. "I know what you're going to say. 'All things work together' and all that, right? Maybe for you. Because I haven't loved God for a long time." I couldn't tell him just yet about the prayer I'd sung in my head when I thought I might die.

"No." He smiled. "I was going to say, none of us does."

I reached blindly for his hand and clutched it to me. "I don't deserve you."

"Well… on some days I'm inclined to agree with you," he laughed, but his eyes were so soft and suspiciously shiny that I let it slide.

₫₫

Hannah Onoguwe's fiction and non-fiction have been published in the *Imagine Africa 500* anthology, *Adanna*, *AFREADA*, *PerVisions*, *The Drum Lit Mag*, *Eleven Eleven*, *Omenana*, *The Missing Slate*, *Litro*, *Brittle Paper*, *The Stockholm Review*, *Timeworn Lit Mag*, and the *Strange Lands Short Stories* anthology by Flame Tree Press, among others. She was shortlisted for the 2020 Afritondo Short Story Prize, with "Yellow Means Stay" appearing as the title story in the anthology of longlisted works. She lives in Yenagoa with her family where she is eternally distracted by the Internet, but often finds time to bake.

"With this story, I was exploring how regardless of one's background, certain situations will test and reveal your true beliefs. As a mom myself, I also explore some of the highs and lows of expecting and having a child."

You can find Hannah on Twitter, Facebook and Instagram @HannahOnoguwe.

The Cure

A.J. Cunder

JACOB HELD HIS daughter close at a party where Château Pétrus spilled like water and stained the floor.

"I want to go home," she said, wrapping her arms around his waist.

"Just a bit longer, Mira," Jacob answered, tussling her hair. "Daddy needs to speak with a few more of his friends about an important science project coming up at his company."

"But I don't like it here. There's a monster on the ceiling."

Jacob laughed. "Don't worry, my love. I'll always protect you." He kissed her forehead. "Go play with Josiah and Michael." He pried her hands from his thigh, and although she went and sat with the children of her father's associate, she kept her eyes on me as I drifted along the crown moulding, doing my best to avoid the cobwebs the housekeepers couldn't reach.

One of them here would die tonight, though I couldn't say who. Perhaps it would be the woman laced in diamonds. Or the politician adjusting his Rolex. I didn't have the power of foresight in a room filled with so many people, only felt necessity draw me to this place. I listened to Jacob talk with billionaires about funding his experiments to reverse aging, to postpone death. I scoffed at their audacity. Though I had already seen science wage war on religion and chip away belief in God, I didn't truly think it would stand a chance against such an immutable fact of life as myself. Science might deter me, it might even resist me; but it would never erase me.

Or so I thought.

I drifted closer to Mira, the girl who saw me when most couldn't. Something sparkled in her eyes, something alien. Was it fear? No, this wasn't fear. Horror? Disgust? No. Distrust, perhaps, with a touch of curiosity. What

266

was it she saw when she looked at me? I wore no mortal body. I existed on no visible plane. And yet, her gaze followed me as I moved, unmistakably attracted to whatever shimmer or shadow she saw.

When her father said his goodbyes and led her out to their limousine, an invisible tether pulled me with them. I knew, then, that one or both would soon perish. A car accident, perhaps? I wondered as I nestled in the dark crevices of the car, Mira's eyes still locked on me.

"Daddy." She pulled on the sleeve of his jacket. "It followed us in here."

"What did, sweetheart?"

"The monster from the party."

"Oh? And what does this monster look like?"

"A bright hole in the air with lots of wiggling fingers coming out of it."

Hmm. Of all the depictions of me throughout human history, that was certainly a first.

"It's okay, Mira. It's probably just a friendly ghost." He turned back to his phone. "Trent—sorry about that. My daughter's got quite an imagination." He smiled at her and patted her knee. "Now, about those clinical trials. When can we start?"

℘ↄ⊂ℛ

That night, while he was still on the phone with Trent, Jacob put his daughter to bed for the last time. "Goodnight," he said, even as Mira begged to sleep with him, her eyes still on me as I hovered above them.

When he left the room, I followed, leaving Mira to sleep in peace.

I saw her again that night, though, when she came to Jacob's bedroom. "Daddy, I just had a nightmare," she said, nestling against him.

Thump, thump, his heart beat as he comforted her. *Thump, thump. Thump, thump.* I drew closer, and Mira jumped up.

"Honey, what is it?" Jacob asked as he held a hand to his chest.

"The monster is coming."

Thump... Thump...

Mira clenched her small fists and stood between me and my task, shielding her father even as his heart stopped.

Her eyes darted for a moment to an old Bible on the nightstand, the edges frayed and worn from each generation passing it down to the next.

I paused, admiring the girl's courage, but then passed through her and continued with my duty, my purpose, the task that gave me life and substance. I pulled Jacob's soul from his body and absorbed it into myself for a moment, as I did with all souls before taking them to the borderlands, intoxicated by their essence, their light and energy.

As I carried her father away and left his soul on the edge of eternity, the girl vowed to uncover my secrets, even though she didn't entirely understand what I was, remembering those old Bible stories her father once read to her of Eden and immortality, angels and demons. I believed it to be the whimsy of a child, harmless, just as every other human attempt to unveil the secrets of Death had proven harmless.

Despite my certainty, though, I watched the girl from a distance as I continued my work elsewhere, collecting souls throughout this world as they died and ferrying them to the edge of the next, to the gray borderlands that exist in the space between atoms, in the time it takes to reach the horizon. I watched as she devoted herself to science, living it, breathing it, worshiping it. She thought she could best me, as only one ever had. But I was confident in my purpose, my role in the natural order. I was the final gateway through which all must pass, the greatest power on earth. I was the god in which everyone believed.

೪ೞ

When Mira turned thirty, she called an old friend of her father's. She ran her fingers over the embossed cover of the ancient family Bible. Recently restored, the oiled leather gleamed. I wondered why she went through the trouble, considering she never read from it anymore, always occupied instead with her scientific papers and conferences.

"Trent! It's Mira. Yes, Jacob's daughter. How are you? Listen, I need a team leader for a project I've been working on. I've been looking through my father's old research, and I think I found where he went wrong. I know it's a crowded market for longevity drugs, but I think we can extend my father's research beyond telomere and protein cap therapies. I'll be at his favorite diner in an hour."

When she met with Trent, she put a blank check on the table. "Thanks for coming."

Trent pushed the paper away. "You don't need to show me that. Yet." He smiled through his snow-white beard.

"You may reconsider after I tell you what this project is really about."

"You mean it's not about your father's research?"

"It is. But it's more than that. I don't just want a drug to extend life. I want to create one that will make us live forever." Mira stirred her tea. "I know it sounds crazy. But aren't all great scientists called crazy at one point or another? If they aren't, then they aren't innovating." When he stayed silent, she added, "I've never told this to anyone, but I saw something the night my father died."

268

"You were there, weren't you?"

"They said he died from a heart attack. But there was something there, Trent. Something took him. I don't know if it was his time or what." She took a sip. "Anyway, I really want you as my team lead on this one. You've worked with my father, you know his research. I want this to be a project in his honor."

He glanced at the blank check still on the table. "So how would this drug work, exactly?"

"At the cellular level. Our bodies already regenerate tissue when it's cut or injured. We just need something to speed up the process. Heal a puncture wound in seconds so no one bleeds to death."

"That's just one way people die, Mira. What about disease? Cancer?"

"We'll work on that too."

Trent tapped the table. "Let me see that check. Just kidding. To pull together a team for this, we'll need government backing."

"I already have it. My father knew people."

"Right. Well, if it means that much to you, count me in. I doubt we'll succeed, but I guess every medical breakthrough started with a crazy idea somewhere."

෨෬

Her conviction burned as strong as the sun, even when experiments failed, cancer spreading unstoppable through lungs and marrow. I found myself captivated by these humans who thought they could erase me, and an unfamiliar joy filled me as I took the souls she thought she could save.

But then the scientists realized their first success, and a laceration healed in mere hours. Hours became minutes, minutes became seconds, and my fleeting joy evaporated. A knot in my core twisted and grew as I wondered what the world might look like if no one died, what might happen to me if my purpose disappeared. I tried to remember a time before human death, but I couldn't. Though I existed outside the constraints of time and space, my earliest memories were of carrying souls to the threshold of the borderlands. That had always been my purpose, and without that, in a world that no longer needed me, I wondered if Death itself could die.

෨෬

"We're almost there, Trent," Mira said one day, studying the test results as I lurked in the shadows of the room. "Trent? You don't look so well."

"Nothing a good sleep and handful of Advil can't cure."

"Have I been pushing you too hard? If I am, tell me."

"No, no. I'm fine." He rested a hand on hers. "Your father would be proud of the way you've devoted yourself to this project."

She afforded herself a small smile. "How's the family?" she asked.

"Oh, you know. Marge always worries about me, but that's what fifty years of marriage will do. Josiah and Michael always ask about you."

"What do they have to say about all this?"

Trent ran a hand through hair that had thinned over the past year. "Josiah and Michael are excited. They've always been innovators themselves, looking forward to the future. Marge... worries sometimes that we're playing God."

"What do you think?"

He shrugged. "If you told me right now that I could swallow a pill and live forever, I'd turn it down. But then again, I'm not at Death's door, and I've always been confident in my faith—the only way to get to Heaven is death. Others might answer differently."

Mira looked up from her tablet. "Are you saying we should just let people die? That research to cure cancer is misguided?"

"Genesis chapter six: 'My spirit shall not abide in mortals forever, for they are flesh.'"

"What about the stories of Christ raising people from the dead?"

"Eventually, they all died again. None of them lived forever, even after coming back. Not in this world, anyway."

"Are you saying we should give up? Just throw away the past five years of our lives?"

Trent held up his hands. "No, Mira. I just wonder if there's a reason why we haven't been successful yet. If God and nature are trying to tell us something and we're just not listening."

"Faith, Trent. That's what we need here more than anything. Why don't you take the rest of the day off and we'll start fresh tomorrow?"

Before he left, he squeezed her shoulder. And as much as she told herself she was doing the right thing, in the back of her mind, I knew doubt lingered.

෪ා03

With a cup of coffee in his hand and a clot in his brain, Trent collapsed the next morning. Despite his prior assertions, he clung to life as I came for him, struggling even as the darkness closed around him, as I extracted his soul from his body and drank in the rush it gave me. I might have smiled, if I had the anatomy for such a thing. Many believed he'd be the one to finally discover that magic formula to erase me, but I still survived even as he didn't. I couldn't stop the pride that bubbled in me, and with that vanity, I made my first mistake.

℘℃

Mira attended Trent's funeral, but she was distracted. *If we had been faster,* she thought. *If I had started this project sooner...*

Her doubt haunted her, and I relished it. She remembered the strange figure on the night of her father's death whenever she found herself staring at the shadows that had begun to darken even sunlit rooms, or shivering at a breath of wind in her study when the windows were closed. The scientific advisory board talked behind her back. They thought she had killed Trent with her impossible project, despite the advances—broken bones healed in a matter of heartbeats, diseased tissue regenerated overnight, even a severed finger regrown in a day. But they had yet to keep me away. Not a single terminal patient had been saved. Though her project's funding jumped with each success, she pushed her team harder—they still hadn't reached their goal. She hadn't been able to save Trent. Death was still a fact of life.

The night of Trent's funeral, she sat alone in her father's old study, staring into the shadows, the Bible in her lap. She hadn't opened it since its restoration, preserving the new binding, the perfect spine. She knew the stories, though, from when her father read them all those years ago. Lazarus. The little girl brought back. Christ's own resurrection and triumph over Death.

I hovered near her shoulder, and she shuddered. Was I still a monster to her, as when she was a child, or had reason and science transformed me into something less abstract? A quantifiable mechanism, perhaps, or a calculable mode of transport rather than some supernatural being.

Setting the Bible on the table, she pulled a syringe loaded with the latest copy of the drug and gritted her teeth as the needle pierced her flesh. With eyes of quartz, she climbed the private staircase from her penthouse apartment to the roof of the high-rise she had inherited from her father and looked out over the city sparkling with lights. Wind whipped her hair as she stood at its summit, looking down over the edge, pale moonlight washing her face. Then she leaned forward until the force of gravity could no longer be ignored and offered a prayer as the ground rushed to meet her.

℘℃

With giddy anticipation, I plunged alongside her until she struck the pavement. She thought her defiance would conquer me, her belief in this Cure would frighten me. I snatched the soul quivering in her body even as her drug tried to fuse her back together. But no medicine could overpower me. No Cure could prevent me. No mere human could defeat me. I neared the edge of the borderlands, her soul soft and bright as it mingled with my own essence, and a sense of relief engulfed me. I had survived her efforts to destroy me. Her project was already fracturing, scientists insisting they focus on their successes rather than chase an impossible dream. Without her iron leadership to direct them, they would take their drug as it was and leave me in peace.

Though I knew I shouldn't have, I couldn't help myself. While I carried her soul within me, I had the power to dig into her mind, to force myself within her being. I bored into her consciousness to flaunt my survival, my power, my supremacy. I wanted her to know she had been defeated, to know without doubt that all must succumb to Death.

And yet, when I penetrated her soul, the violent surge of her determination assailed me. *I will never yield*, she screamed.

The knot in my core clenched. Whether my own pride rebuked me or the Cure cast some unearthly tether upon her spirit, my grip slipped and her soul fell, rushing away from the borderlands. I floundered with her, tried to catch her, but I tumbled like a leaf swept in a windstorm, a pebble thrashed in an angry river. I couldn't grab hold of what I had lost, and her body sucked in her soul like water poured over bone-dry sand. She gasped, her eyes wide, and I scrambled to take her back, to separate her soul from flesh and blood. But too late. A bright light now shielded her from me, emanating from the very cells of her body like an angel's armor. I reeled, and time spun, the knot within me writhing like a nest of vipers. I reached futilely for her soul, for that rush of energy that should by rights be mine, but I might as well have grasped at air. And in that moment, for the first time in my existence, I trembled.

℘℃ℜ

Passersby on the street saw what happened, and most of the world had seen it online within an hour. In a news conference that aired around the world, Mira said, "After years of research in honor of my father, we have finally discovered a Cure for death. I stand as living proof. My body was broken and destroyed, and yet here I am. I believed in this Cure. I had faith, which is half of all healing, as my father would say. Soon, we all will know a world where daughters never have to say goodbye to fathers. No longer must we say, 'She was taken too soon.' We will live in a world that never dies, a new Eden of immortals."

And so, the Cure crossed the world—to those who could afford it—and when the immortals procreated, their children carried altered DNA that could instantly repair a shattered skull, stop the spread of cancer, strengthen heart muscle and regenerate brain cells. Their bodies no longer aged past thirty years, surrounded by a golden barrier that kept me away no matter how hard

I tried to pierce it. With a hollow pit deepening in my core, I savored the souls of the final few mortals carried from this world to the edge of the next.

The last was an orphaned girl, her mother too poor to afford the Cure. I left her at the threshold of the borderlands, waiting there longer than I ever had before. Without direction, I balanced on the edge of the void, lost, forsaken, a sailboat on the ocean stranded without wind.

The immortals cursed me like a half-remembered dream. "*You have no place here. Science is our Law. Science is our King. Science is our God.*" They imbibed and reveled as the world became a utopia. War became obsolete, soldiers unable to die, and political rivalries were settled with diplomacy, or games of strategy or chance. Thrill seekers jumped from planes without parachutes, filled their bodies with drugs, explored the ocean depths, finding new highs, new ways to test their limits knowing death would never come.

Each time a body rightly should have died, it taunted me with the sweet memory of the rush I once felt with each soul, the insatiable need for purpose and direction. And slowly, I began to wish for my own death, wondering how I might achieve it, where I might go, how I might end this endless malaise. I looked to the borderlands among the neutrons of stars and wondered how I might cross to the other side.

೮ාಜ

As the years became decades, and decades rolled into generations, Mira watched the world change. The earth around her—around them all—had shrunk. Those who had once been the one percent became legion, leeching the land, poisoning the waters, razing forests for room to live. Plastic trash and toxic debris soiled marble streets. Vagrants once rich now stared with hollow eyes and empty stomachs, their bodies sapped of energy yet unable to die. Their gold was useless, not worth its weight in wheat. From her luxury apartment, Mira looked out upon the homeless who slit their wrists on street corners and wailed as they healed, Death refusing to come, as they scoured the sewers for crumbs.

I paid little attention to them, focused on my own task. The borderlands had proven difficult to navigate, a gray void that stretched endlessly, everywhere and nowhere, like a memory or a dream. I knew that souls left within it eventually melted into its substance—or traversed it in some way unknown to me. Only one man had ever returned under his own power from the other side, and when I had asked him how he did it, he simply smiled and said it wasn't my place to know. I probed the vastness with every dimension of my consciousness, but only once did I encounter anything else. For the briefest of moments, I sensed a searing light among the emptiness. But then it vanished, and I returned to my eternal scrutiny.

ΞΟΩ

The governments of the world eventually convened a council. "We must reverse this," they said as sources of food reached critical levels and bodies spilled into oceans where they floated undying, the last open space left for them to occupy.

The scientists summoned Mira to their laboratories, insisting that she must serve as their test subject since she had brought this upon them. They experimented with formulas and brought her to the guillotine while the world watched. The blade flashed down, and her head rolled but continued to scream, then regrew a body in moments. Lethal injections proved powerless. Bullets left no scar. They even ripped out her heart, only to watch it reappear. Finally, they chained her to a stake and lit a fire at her feet, stopping their ears as the flames licked her flesh. For hours they waited, adding more fuel to the fire. I fumbled at the barrier that kept me from her soul, tried to rip it from her body, to find a purpose once more: to end her suffering. But I couldn't. The metal shackles eventually melted, and she stumbled from the pyre, skin pink and tender like that of a newborn infant.

They sent her home, with a warning not to leave the city. In her study, she stared into the shadows. She cracked open her father's Bible, rent pages from its seam, threw it across the room where it landed at the base of a bookcase. Mira wondered how many history books mentioned her, how many more would be written to rewrite the stories that cast her as a hero. She ripped encyclopedias from the wall-length shelves, searching for Death, the history of Death, Death in history, in myth, in legend. She searched for rituals to summon Death, the angel of Death, the Reaper, Osiris, Hades, the Four Horseman, Pestilence, Famine, War.

Silly girl, I whispered into the wind. *Now you see. Now you know. Now you want me after all these years of thinking I was your enemy.*

At War, she paused. She read of the Second World War, the deadliest. That led her to Hiroshima, and suddenly, she knew. Suddenly, I felt purpose tingle within my core once again. Her face like iron, she went to the Council and said, "A nuclear explosion may overcome the effects of the Cure within the blast radius. If every cell in the body is destroyed instantly, there will be nothing left to regenerate."

Some shook their heads and sneered. Others shrugged. Some asked what they had to lose. The Chairman made his decision, and I shivered.

ΞΟΩ

On the Last Day, some said their farewells; others curled in the streets. Most offered prayers, in some form or another, either grateful or hopeful.

Mira stood beside one of the atomic warheads placed strategically throughout the world as the countdown began. A mix of emotion clouded her mind. Her forefinger twitched as she clutched what remained of her father's Bible to her chest.

At the final moment, just before the detonators ignited a thousand fusion bombs and reduced the world to ash, Mira looked to me, her lips a thin line, not quite as a friend, but no longer as a monster.

The devastation was majestic. A jolt like lightning crashed through me, the golden barriers around the immortals evaporated, and I drank in the rush of souls like a desert wanderer must savor a pool of cool water. I took billions in those seconds, but I only cared for her. I held her tighter than gravity held the sun's core, speeding carefully toward the borderlands, the stars in the universe a blur, her soul humming at a frequency I had never felt before. And she hoped, with a glimmer of sudden uncertainty, that eternity for the dead would be different than immortality for the living.

∞CR

A medievalist, a type 1 diabetic, and a federal criminal investigator, A.J. graduated from Seton Hall University with a Master's in Creative Writing. He previously served as a Senior Editor with *Flash Fiction Online*, currently manages *Et Sequitur Magazine* as founder and Editor-in-Chief, and helps sift through the slush pile as an Assistant Editor with *Cosmic Roots & Eldritch Shores*. Find him on Twitter @aj_cunder, or online at www.WrestlingTheDragon.com.

"In college, I wrote an essay about Edgar Allen Poe's consideration of death in some of his works, and how, for him and other American Gothic authors, mortality might not be such a bad thing. After all, what would the world really look like if no one ever died? Then I started wondering how Death, if personified as a supernatural being, might feel if no one died, how the loss of purpose might affect their own perception of the world, and what they might do in such a void."

Bearing the Flame

C.A. Barrett

CHRIST'S NEWEST CHANDLERS stood facing the congregation, their five young heads bent demurely for anointing oil and their cupped hands extended for incense to burn in the flames cradled against their bare palms. Three boys were already familiar to everyone: they had been brought to the Church of Holy Fire as apprentices when their talent kindled. They were joined by a barbarian girl with startling yellow braids beneath her headscarf and a boy with skin dark as incorruptible altar-wood, both living proof that priests had searched to the very ends of the empire for those most skilled at kindling and brought them here to serve God.

Basil was not standing with them.

Basil was still planted where he had taken a step out from the gathered people, standing alone. He wore the same plain red tunic as the Chandler initiates. His feet and legs were also bare, he was also twelve years old, and he held the same slip of golden flame. But the Bishop had not taken Basil's hand to pull him farther forward. Now Basil felt very hot, although he was aware of the empty space behind him as a great cold gulf. His eyes were watering even though the flame in his hand was smokeless. He shook with small fast breaths. It was a mercy that he did not face the crowd, because the uncontrolled tempest on his face would shame him. Basil had not *wanted* to be a Chandler. Basil had known that he would be a Chandler with the same certainty with which he knew his own name. Ever since the day that flames first kissed his fingertips during a service, perfecting his fire had consumed him.

And now Basil was the only one who had been passed over. The flame in his hands had no flaw that he could see. He looked at it from every angle before closing his palms and then taking them apart, extinguished. He stared numbly into the mosaics on the walls, seeing only the points of reflected candlelight in each glass tile and not the images formed by their pattern.

When the evening prayers ended, the crowd spilled out of the church onto the street and their chatter echoed back into the sacred spaces. Families with elderly or infants were going home to sleep. The Week of Lights was so crowded with services that it took stamina. The young would keep vigil in the streets tonight, watching for the arrival of pilgrim flames. They would have more fun waiting than those chanting in the darkened church. But the church was where Basil stayed. He had often waited after services to make conversation with the Chandlers. Now he had to know if their encouragement had been insincere mockery. As the final congregants left, those who served them came out to bustle around the edges of the church. The five Chandler initiates appeared from a side door, struggling with one of the golden monstrances that would receive the seventy pilgrim flames. They turned away from Basil's accusatory stare. He already knew the tricks that they did not for assembling the pieces, because he had helped last year.

Justinian was walking briskly down one side of the church, pinching out flames with his unburnable fingers. Basil drifted to his side.

"Why wasn't I chosen tonight?" Basil asked quietly.

Justinian was not much older than Basil. He had no beard to hide the disquiet on his face.

"Why?" Basil repeated.

"You know that the Church only takes the best."

"Then what was wrong with my flame?"

Justinian looked down and fussily straightened the strap of brocade cloth that belted his robes, which were red and embroidered all over with teardrop-shaped flames in gold thread.

"Did you see anything wrong with my flame? Why didn't the Bishop elevate me?" Basil pressed.

"Maybe he saw your pride," Justinian replied.

"It was good enough." Basil's voice was rising with his anger. "The Bishop made a mistake."

"Life is shaped by mistakes as well as by plans. God uses it all, just the same."

Basil looked away from Justinian's splendid clothing and balled his fists against his plain red cloth. "So you think it was a mistake, too. I deserve it."

"I'm sorry, Basil," Justinian said, "I know you're disappointed, but remember that you serve God, not the flame."

"Why did He light fire in me if He won't use it?" Basil shouted. His anger reverberated against walls angled to amplify singing voices. The five initiates looked up from their tangled monstrances and the droning reader looked up from his prayers.

Basil fled.

He stopped in the candle room to retrieve his blue striped coat and his sandals. He also took a thick beeswax candle as long as his outstretched arm. As he left the church he dug his fingernails into the wax, scoring it with deep grooves. He loitered on the steps before the church doors, waiting for Justinian or some other messenger to come running out and beg him to return.

No one came. Basil took deep steadying breaths and watched the people. The crowd was colorful, each in their own best clothing. So many held candles that the night was bright as day, and all the candles were moving under the black sky. Children ran along chaotic trails visible only to the very young. Adults laughed and darted around as they hailed loved ones. The news from every mouth was that the first pilgrim flame had been spotted and it was not far outside the city. Everyone was taking great pleasure in telling this news to others who already knew but were taking equal pleasure in listening. Close to the road the crowd pressed shoulder-to-shoulder into compacted stillness, and shouted liturgical songs with tuneless joy.

Basil caught their elation between his fingertips and lit his damaged candle from it. The light was strong and steady. It did not dance or gutter. It sat proudly atop the wick. This was more than the flame of an apprentice kindler: it was a flame that would make a city lamplighter proud. It was better than Justinian's flame, which was sometimes green at the edges. It should be Basil in the embroidered robes, a small voice said inside. It should be Basil being cheered.

Basil resolved that tomorrow he would go to the Bishop and demand his place as a Chandler. Tonight, he lifted his great liturgical candle high with one hand and rested the other hand lightly on his own stomach, where he would wear his belt soon. The crowd parted for him, and Basil took methodical steps to the side of the road. He stood straight and formal, waiting.

The procession of the Flame of Antioch was led by a boy with an icon of Saint Evodus on a tall pole. He was burdened by a full four layers of embroidered fabric, as if he were assisting at a liturgy instead of traveling the road by night. Sweat made pathways through the dust on his face, but he held his image of Saint Evodus high and danced with the last of his energy. He had a huge grin on his face, and the crowd roared its approval of his capering.

The Chandler of Antioch who followed was older and solemn. His expression was one of distant concentration. His mind was still in Antioch, with the Christians who sent their fervor in the flame he carried. That flame was a giant burning globe, as wide across as his shoulders and balanced on both his hands. The light was overwhelming. People that it passed shaded their faces and turned away. But Basil was a kindler, and his eyes resisted flame just as well as his fingers. He stared into it and saw many feather-like small flames with their points tucked into the whole. Individual flickers surfaced only to submerge again as the interlocking flames rotated in a pattern of beating wings. Basil stared in wonder as the flame passed him and he felt his heart follow it just as the crowd lining the street broke their formations and came together behind the light. The Chandler of Antioch, never looking down, carefully went up the three wide steps and into the church.

When the flame went through the doors and was hidden from sight, Basil's elation drained from his chest. The first pilgrim flame entering the Church of Holy Fire marked the end of Flame's Eve. Basil could demand an audience with the Bishop, but next year he would be too old to stand with the applicants. He had not been chosen. He could either sweep and clean the church to which he had been apprenticed without handling its flames again or take his kindling talent home, to a provincial town he left so long ago that he only remembered its dimness, but he would never lift a full church's flame in his hands. He knew now that nothing else would ever satisfy him. He would rather give up his fire entirely than have it stunted, and use it only to dandle sparks between his fingertips while he stood in the back of a crowd during the Week of Lights. But what would he do with himself? Kindling was the only skill he'd practiced, and he wasn't good enough at it to earn a place in a city with a heartbeat of light and life.

Basil lowered his candle and pinched the flame at its wick. He retreated from the road and its joy.

"Are you leaving? Aren't you part of the processions?" a man asked him. He wore a short blue cloak over brown clothing, and he was not long out of boyhood himself. He spoke to Basil as an equal. His teeth were bright in the candlelight.

"I'm not in the procession," said Basil.

The stranger looked puzzled. "Aren't you a Chandler? Your candle's not gone down a notch. You weren't burning it to feed that flame."

"I have the kindling magic," said Basil, "but I wasn't good enough to be chosen as a Chandler." Saying it aloud brought a fresh pang of grief. He braced himself for pity, but the man responded with a slowly spreading smile.

"It's good they didn't catch you," he said. "You were made for so much more."

Basil stared at him, uncomprehending.

"She told me that we'd have a kindler. I have work for you. Come see." The man took Basil's arm. His fingers were rough with calluses.

"Who are you?"

He paused, and a slow smile spread across his face. "Call me Saint Cain, patron of rejected sacrifices. Come on, come on."

Basil felt that every tie binding him to the happy crowd had been broken. He saw no other path before him, so Basil left his broken candle and followed. No one noticed him going.

∞⚭

Cain led him outside the city walls, far from the crowds spilling out of the gate. This still and quiet road led to a small house. When Basil stepped inside the door he faced a man Cain's age with a new beard, the hair growing in wild and coarse, who sat facing the entrance and oiling a blade. He leaned forward, the forgotten rag on one knee and the naked steel lifted, until he saw Cain coming in behind Basil. Then he nodded and resumed his cleaning.

Cain clapped the other man's shoulder as he walked past. "Loom," he said to Basil, "walked over a thousand miles to join the Emperor's guard. On his own two feet, guarding himself with his own blade." Cain's voice lifted to the edge of laughter. "It took him so long to walk the distance that when he got here, they said he was too old to apprentice to a warrior."

"And he's our kindler?" Loom asked gruffly.

"I don't know what you want me to do," said Basil.

"Just look," said Cain, and he pulled Basil again. Around the corner was a dim workbench of thick wood, scorched and gouged deeply in places. It was cluttered with a jeweler's trade tools: hammers, a small anvil, tongs, and a cold crucible.

In the very center of the workspace sat a dragon made of gold, and she was beautiful.

The dragon had a broad serpent's face. Her flat and toothless mouth was slightly parted in a hollow smile that revealed her to be a tall oil lamp, with a cavity for fuel and a notch in her forked tongue to hold the wick. All the scales of her head were carefully scratched out in patterns like tiles: a lip of small rectangles, a coin-sized circle at her jowls, and concentric layers around her empty, hollow eyes. A wider hood came off the sides of her head, evoking an aroused cobra. She had four legs and reared up on two of them, sitting with her short arms against her sides. And she had six breasts. This incongruous flesh was sculpted out of small planes and facets that emphasized how the artist's hands had traced every nipple.

Basil's throat constricted. "You are worshiping idols."

"We are worshiping nothing," said Cain. "We are bartering. Your god is not the only living spirit, churchboy. There are others, and they'll reward anyone who helps them take form." He reached out to caress the dragon between its eyes. "She's brought us the gold to build her, and showed me her shape."

"You made her a body," Basil said.

"I built her a trap." Cain turned his head to Basil, but he did not turn his back on the dragon. "We will have a god beneath us, a god made from our hands, a god that does as we command. We just have to offer her something that she wants enough to crawl all the way inside, and it will close shut behind her."

Basil stared numbly at the golden dragon. "I still don't understand what you want me to do."

"What is your name, boy?" asked Loom behind them.

"Basil." He regretted giving it before the end of Loom's brief nod.

"She loves fire, Basil," Cain said. "You're a kindler. Don't you love flames, too? So you share a special understanding with her already. I sculpt gold and I admire the beauty of what I've made every time I see it. Show us your flame. Show *her* your beautiful flame."

"I was training to be a Chandler of Christ," Basil said.

The Lord's name hung heavily in the silence before Cain spoke. "You said they didn't want you. She brought you to us. She wanted you. She thinks you're good enough." He pressed on Basil's back, pushing him toward the workbench. "Come and feed the dragon, Basil. Our arts were never only for worship."

Basil had never lit a flame that wasn't gathered from the faith around him. He did not think it possible, but he could make Cain's command an experiment. Basil lifted his hand, and he called on the beauty of flames, the lights of amber and orange that he could see more clearly than anyone else and command better than any of his age. What he pulled from the air was a small spark, red as blood, and Cain caught it on a thin chip of wood before it went out.

"A little dancing ruby, so beautiful," Cain pronounced. He inserted the burning wood chip into the dragon. It slid between her jaws and disappeared down into her belly. The light flared up, its red flashing briefly in the dragon's empty eyes before it went out. A small line of smoke came out of one side of her mouth.

"She is hungry for more," said Cain. "Think of all she'll give us when she is alive!"

Basil reached for his sharp desire for layers of fine cloth, worked with dyes and threads and wrapped around his body. He reached for the gluttony of taking all the charred crust off a piece of smoked meat, all for himself. He felt the crowd cheering for him. This flame lit the room from his fingers.

Cain made no move to take it. "Feed her," he said.

Basil reached out his hand and held his fire to the dragon's mouth. The gold tongue flickered, and the skin beneath her jaw swelled as she took the flame and swallowed it. Her hollow eyes were filled again, and this time the red had narrow black pupils in its center. She looked at Basil with a beguiling tilt of her head, and then she left the idol again, leaving behind only smoke.

"She needs more," said Cain, leaning close over the bench. Loom was behind him, amazement plain on his face.

Basil summoned up wordless heat and agitation and lust. His belly and loins filled with the fire before it came to his hand this time. His skin flushed and he turned his embarrassment to anger before it could take his power. He would choose a life of fire. He would stride across the empire with this flame in his blood and no one would dare to deny him anything again...

The flame that bled into his palm was thick and dark as a smoldering coal, and the golden dragon herself darted her head forward to snatch it from his outstretched hand. She licked both sides of her lips with her horned tongue and then closed them in a smile. Smoke came thickly from her nostrils, filling the room with a smell that was more cloying than any incense Basil had ever burned. Beneath the sweet the smell had a punch of rot. Then the golden jaws parted, stiff and dead again. The light faded in the idol's eyes.

Basil felt cold, as if all of his heat were handed away. He turned to look at Cain. The man was staring at his dragon, dazzled.

"That is closer than she's ever been to us," said Cain. "That was well done."

"It wasn't enough," said Basil. He felt suddenly nauseated. He had failed, once again, to kindle a good enough flame to earn a place. And this time he could not take comfort in looking back at the attempt and seeing work well done. He had betrayed all of his instruction from the Church and fed an idol, and he was ruined.

"I thought she might need more than any one kindler can summon," said Cain. "And that's why we meet tonight."

"The pilgrim flames," Basil blurted aloud. As he realized their plan, he felt sicker.

"Don't you want to hold one?" Cain asked.

Basil swallowed. "More than anything," he said very quietly. He would never lift one now. That duty was reserved for the most dedicated and pure of the Chandlers, not boys who missed being called forward on Flame's Eve and then gave in to the first temptation ever offered them.

"A pilgrim flame will trap the dragon in our idol. The flames are on the road now, but we need a kindler to carry it."

"You can't just pick up a pilgrim flame."

"Who told you that? Were they right about summoning fire, or were they lying about things they didn't want you to know?" Cain was smug. "It will only be a few steps that you have to carry it. And then, we three ride a god. Will you come with us?"

Basil looked down at his hands. He was ashamed by his palms now. He belonged with these two wicked souls.

He desperately wanted to belong somewhere.

As his answer to Cain, he picked the dragon up and cradled her under his arm.

୫୬ଓଷ

The road was darker now. The crowd had lost more of its numbers to the call of home and bed, and flames were now entering the city by every gate, dividing the remainder. The only revelers left were now well inside the city walls, a good distance away from this bend in the road and the pillar of rocks that marked it. Once it passed the pillar, any flame on the road would be clearly visible.

But Cain and Loom were waiting in the darkness, where the flamebearers wouldn't have the chance to call for help.

Basil was standing by the pillar, still carrying the golden dragon. Cain wanted him to stay in this specific position because Cain was still taking care to not turn his back to the idol. Basil was feeding the dragon small sips of flame, dim and apprehensive sparks pulled from his agony. As she ate, she moved her legs into comfortable positions, sighed, and sank comfortably into his grip. She always became cold and stiff again as her spirit withdrew. Despite this, Basil thought she might be growing larger. She felt heavier.

The dragon made a sudden aggressive twist in Basil's arms. He looked up and saw light approaching. The dragon froze in place, but this time she did not grow cold. Her golden sides still shook with quick breathing, and her forked tongue twinkled as it reflected the light she tasted.

Cain and Loom both held uncovered swords, glinting in the dark. Basil thought of trying to summon a flare to his hand and reveal them all, but nothing he could kindle alone would outshine the brightness of a pilgrim flame made by hundreds of souls. It brought its own daylight, but only to a small portion of the road, directly in front of its escort.

The golden dragon leaped down from his arms and sat up on its own, alert as a ferret.

It was a procession of only two. The Flame of Corinth was so large and bright at his back that it was hard to see the iconbearer, but Basil made out a very young boy holding a picture of Saint Silas on a pole. He'd tied blue ribbons beneath it, and they fluttered. The boy's mouth fell open as Cain and Loom stepped out in front of him, and the icon wavered. He stopped in place, and so did the Flame.

"I am carrying no coin," said the Chandler. "Let me pass." He was older than Basil, with a man's narrow face and a thin beard. Although he spoke with quiet confidence his voice carried clearly to Basil's hiding place. Both of his hands held the fire. He could not move a finger to defend himself.

"We aren't common robbers. We need your fire," Cain replied.

"Let me pass," the Chandler repeated. "I am a servant of the most high God."

"We're both serving our gods, and you're outnumbered." Cain beckoned to Basil, then leveled his sword at the Chandler. "If you won't give it to us, we'll have to take it."

Basil felt ashamed and pulled his coat tightly closed over his red robe. He suddenly wished that he were standing beside the Chandler and sharing his perfect confidence, but he went to Cain's side. He did not know where the golden dragon had gone.

With a sudden clatter, the icon of Saint Silas fell. The small wide-eyed boy ran off into the darkness. Loom stepped over the pole and crushed its ribbons under his foot.

"Give us the flame and you can follow him." Cain stepped close, turning his head away from the blinding light. He kept his sword raised.

"He won't let His flame hit the ground," said the Chandler, looking straight at Basil and his red robe. His gaze was a rebuke, not a challenge to a contest.

"Basil," Cain commanded.

Basil reached out to possess the Flame of Corinth, but it was a great ball of flickers cresting and diving into the whole and each of those tiny lights fled his hands. The sphere started breaking apart at his touch, and the Chandler's attention returned wholly to the fire between them. The form knit itself back together as the small lights completed their circuit by crossing his hands. Basil pulled away before he destroyed it, and tried to think. Before tonight, he'd always caught fire by delighting in shared worship. That togetherness formed the pilgrim flame. Basil tried to work out how to seize the flame alone, while feeling a hollow ache inside.

There was a cracking noise, of metal claws striking against paving stone.

"Then we take it," said Cain, and his sword came down.

"Don't, he's not stopping me—" Basil cried, but he was too late.

The Chandler's two severed hands fell away from the Flame of Corinth like pieces of pale eggshell. The flame itself fell, and Basil lunged forward and fell to his knees with his arms outstretched, trying to save the mass of wisps before they broke apart. When they hit him, he felt everything that went into the making of this Flame. He caught voices both singing and groaning. He caught shouted and whispered prayers. He caught the tears of true repentance in his hands as he felt them stream down his own face, and he caught both roaring joy and the quiet comfort of a babe still at her mother's breast.

Basil caught the pilgrim flame. And every soul singing in the flame caught Basil, and welcomed him back. His earlier rejection by the Chandlers was the miracle that had brought him to this place, at this time, in this darkness, where he was needed. All of his practice was for this moment. Understanding did not take the pain of losing his art away. Experiencing the greatest that kindling magic could accomplish made his loss sharper. But his suffering was now in service to the community crying out inside the Flame and that gave him something to grab hold of so that he could lift it. It did not hit the ground.

When he got his balance, Basil turned his back on the robbers to face his church.

A snap from the dark below him tugged at his coat. Basil ripped free and stumbled forward. Without regaining his balance he ran, tilted and nearly falling, until he cleared the pillar and the road took its sharp turn. Knowing that help could see him now, he untangled his feet and looked back.

"He wants to keep it for himself!" Cain shouted, coming after Basil. He was slower, because the pilgrim flame blinded his eyes. He stumbled over the stones. And while giving chase, Cain had finally turned his back on the golden dragon. She had her body, and she no longer needed him.

Behind Cain, the Chandler of Corinth was still standing up. The cauterizing flames on his lifted arms illuminated Loom beside him and the golden coils twisting between them and Cain. The serpent had indeed stretched her golden body when she entered it. She sat up on her hind legs now, and her flared hood was above Cain's head. Her tail was a fat serpent itself, rippling behind her. Her small arms opened wide with her mouth, and there were now long black claws on each digit.

She dived at Cain, biting him from above and behind and ripping him open between neck and shoulder. He was dead before he could scream. As she bore him to the ground Basil and Loom both lifted their eyes from the terrible sight and looked at one another. Like the metal shaping, the sword work was done.

Loom sheathed his sword and ran into the darkness.

Basil ran toward the safety of the city. He could not use his hands without abandoning the pilgrim flame that filled them, and even if he had been free to move his only weapon was fire, the dragon's delicacy. He could see very little in front of him because of the flame he carried, but he heard shouting. He knew that he had been seen and help was near. It spurred him on to greater speed.

But when he reached the walls, Basil found something in front of him as terrible as the dragon behind: the gate of the city had been closed.

He turned and put his back to the wood, thinking that he could knock by jerking his head. But when he turned around, he saw why the gate had been slammed shut. The dragon was faster, and the dragon had caught him. The golden form lifted from the roadbed and raised herself above Basil and the Flame of Corinth, sparkling in the light. She tilted her head at Basil, who had fed her, and flicked her forked tongue out its notch in her lip. Her eyes were deep red pools with flashes of gold swimming behind her black pupils.

Basil stood before her with the flame. He closed his eyes, but he could still see the afterimage of light. And then he opened them. He had learned tonight that he loved this particular golden Flame and each of its people. He would not let her reduce it into mere fire in her belly.

She opened her mouth, and it kept opening wider and wider until the slit stretched to the very edges of her hood. It was endlessly dark inside her. Nothing reflected from the roof of her mouth or her throat. The dragon plunged toward the fire.

Basil turned and curled around the pilgrim flame, ducking his face inside its heat. He felt himself lifted bodily by the jaws and he pulled up his legs, putting his hurt knees into the fire too. The small flames battered him and tried to escape, but Basil gathered and protected them, shepherding them into the sphere even as he fully climbed inside it. The dragon's metal belly was a furnace, and the heat was suffocating. He felt even his kindler's skin scalding. He saw only white, even through his eyelids. And then the dragon thrashed, knocking his head against one side of her belly. She thrashed again, and Basil hit his shoulder against metal. At least she would beat him to death before he died of burning.

Then, with a sudden drink of air, the flames surged all around him and leaped tall. Basil lifted his head; Basil could lift his head. He stood cautiously, unable to feel his way with his hands or to balance himself because his hands were full of fire, and he encountered nothing above him.

Basil looked down and saw the shell of the golden dragon scorched and split open. It was hollow and thin as a reptile's discarded skin, and the foil had melted and curled away from the point where heat burst its belly.

Basil had not fed her this time. She had tried to swallow what was not offered, and the Flame of Corinth was stronger.

He flexed his hands, balancing the flickering pilgrim flame on his palms, and Basil caught the joy of his deliverance in a flame on each fingertip. He stood in the dragon's wreckage and wrapped the pilgrim flame back together with his own lights, restoring it to a strong and luminous sphere ruled by an inner dance.

As he finished, two figures walked into the light. The small boy came first. He had taken his icon of Saint Silas back up in one hand, tattered ribbons and all. In the other hand he had Cain's sword, but he dangled the horrible object limply. He looked back anxiously at his pale and wounded companion.

The Chandler of Corinth's ascetic thinness was heightened by his terrible pallor, and the single light cast harsh shadows in the hollow of his eyes. The sleeves of his robe were each tied shut in a knot. Yet he still walked with slow dignity, as if nothing unexpected had happened on his procession, and he again regarded Basil.

The boy held his icon straight and tried to lift Cain's sword with his other hand. "One of the thieves and idolmakers!" he cried, as the heavy sword shook in his grasp.

"And the little boy who ran from them!" Basil replied, but the heavy weight of shame was growing in his gut. His hands suddenly felt the heat of the Flame of Corinth clearly, and he looked down through the light. He felt as if he were holding both palms to a hot pot. The skin there was not blistering, but he had lost part of his magic.

"I came back," said the boy.

"It is always possible to come back," said the Chandler, never taking his eyes from Basil. "You hold a pilgrim flame well, Kindler. Have you ever considered serving the Church?"

Basil knew that his red apprentice's robe was clearly visible beneath his open coat, and the Chandler's wry tone meant he recognized it. Internal heat reddened Basil's cheeks. He could go back, and he would go back. In the morning, he would take the place he'd actually earned, cleaning the streets after the festival. "I serve the Church, but I wasn't needed to tend fires." He lifted his arms and held out the Flame of Corinth to its true keeper.

"What if I need you to be my hands?" the Chandler replied. He made no move to lift his own injured arms.

Basil's heart leaped. "I can carry it tonight," he said.

"I expect to still need hands tomorrow."

"I wasn't good enough," Basil said. He had learned tonight that however clever he was at making flames, a Chandler needed wisdom too. Instead of trusting and obeying, he had stomped off in a tantrum, and brought mortal danger to himself and others. The heat that he felt now would be a reminder every time he kindled flame, although the pain was not great enough to overcome the joy of it.

"You are holding a pilgrim flame together, and there is no better proof that you can keep others' flames lit. The Church needs your talent, if you will let your temptations burn away. Leave your idol behind and come with me if you still want to be a Chandler."

Basil stomped and crushed the gold foil underneath his heels as he worked himself free of it all. His chest was about to curl open like the dragon's skin, unable to hold the swelling of hope in his heart. The little boy stepped past him and rapped on the gate three times with his standard.

The gate was thrown open and many people poured out: soldiers in armor, men with no weapon greater than a lit candle, and women and children woken from their beds, carrying household tools. Suddenly light and noise blossomed. They exclaimed over the dragon, and goggled at the dragon killers. When Cain's body was discovered on the road a group surrounded it too. People were soon crowded so thickly around the dragon's corpse that there was no room to move.

But the crowd parted when Basil lifted the Flame of Corinth high and walked into the city between the boy and the Chandler of Corinth.

By the time they reached the Church of Holy Fire, the cheers for their burned and bloodied procession were the loudest of the night.

꧁꧂

C.A. Barrett lives in a busy home in Kentucky, and writes fantasy stories while her knightly husband guards her from children and dragons—although their dragon eats insects instead of holy fire. Her short fiction will also appear on *Podcastle* this year. She blogs about writing at www.enchanted.horse.

About the story, she says, "I wanted this to feel like the product of a Byzantine imagination without being strictly historical."

Ceiling Snakes and Slithering Saints

Barbara A. Barnett

THE THING ABOUT ceiling snakes is this: there ain't just one kind. Rattlers, copperheads, cottonmouths—you name it, they're up there, slithering round where your church trusses ought to be. Nobody can tell you how they get up there or where them trusses disappear to, and it sure don't seem like a bunch of twisty old snakes should be able to hold a roof up, but as my grandpappy used to say, things is what they is and ain't nothing else.

The morning our snakes showed up, we was all in the church listening to young Reverend Ambrose preach—well, folk called him young, mousy as well when he wasn't like to hear, but he was a good fifteen years older than my fourteen. But wasn't anyone who could keep more than half an eye on him when they noticed the slithering going on overhead. You'd think a truss was moving, then you'd realize that truss was a snake. They just sort of slipped into view like that.

Reverend Ambrose trailed off in the middle of a passage from Matthew 4. Looking up at them snakes, his eyes went as wide and round as the rest of him. "I reckon we ought to clear out and—"

"You keep preaching, Reverend," Elder Mayfield said from his seat up front. Being an elder meant sitting on the bench with the fewest splinters and the sturdiest legs, my ma liked to say. "God will protect us."

"Amen," said Elder Clayton beside him, bobbing his head so hard I was surprised his spectacles didn't fall off.

Reverend Ambrose went pale as a milk cow, but he kept on preaching. Had to raise his voice to compete with all that hissing, though, and 'specially with those rattler tails. I'd swear those snakes was commenting on the sermon.

Reverend Ambrose was just starting to talk about how you can't love God while hating your brother when a coral snake dropped straight down from the ceiling. Fell over his shoulders like a red- and black-striped stole. He tossed it off real quick, and it landed right at Elder Mayfield's feet. Now Elder Mayfield's usually a tough old fella—built like one of them new-fangled steam trains, people say—but that morning he leapt onto the bench and let out an awful shriek like raccoons make.

The elders was always lecturing us boys on how we was supposed to be brave and protect the women from evil, 'cause God built us strong and built them soft. But that morning there was just as much screaming and swearing and bolting for the door from the men folk as there was from the women. And my schoolteacher, Mrs. Simpkins, was just as quick fetching her shotgun as Elder Clayton. I think she only let him take the shot so as not to wound his pride.

The blast was loud enough to get those ceiling snakes hissing something fierce. You wouldn't think Elder Clayton could see so good given those thick round spectacles of his, but he took that coral's head clean off. We was left with a splintered hole in the floorboard, though, not to mention a big old splatter of blood and snake guts.

Reverend Ambrose shooed off everyone who hadn't already run. He couldn't move none too quick on account of his bum leg, but you'd think those snakes was snapping at his heels given how fast he shuffled that morning. Once we was all outside, he slammed that church door shut and fell into a heap on the front steps. His shirt was always coming untucked, and a bit more than usual had snuck out on him during all that ruckus.

"That coral bite you, Reverend?" I asked, 'cause he was puffing and panting real hard.

"No, son." He'd gone even paler than before, though, white as the chalk dust down at the schoolhouse and looking like the breeze would blow him away just as easy. "You tell your ma I won't need your help round the church for a bit, though. Not so long as we got ceiling snakes."

That set me frowning. I didn't mind patching things up for him the way my pappy used to, 'cause Reverend Ambrose was real kind to me and my kin after Pappy died. Let me have a good cry instead of telling me I had to toughen up and be the man of the house like the elders did.

"What we gonna do about them snakes?" I asked him.

"I reckon we—"

"God will take care of it," Elder Mayfield cried out. He and the other elders had gathered near that twisty old oak tree with the roots as thick as a grown man's arm. "So long as we have faith, He will protect us from those serpents."

Reverend Ambrose heaved himself up to his feet. "I think we—"

"What if God's punishing us?" I couldn't even tell you who said that. Folks was circling round the elders in a tizzy like I ain't ever seen, hands waving and lips flapping and faces so red I wouldn't have been surprised to see smoke coming out their ears. "What if we did something to deserve this?"

Reverend Ambrose stumbled forward, one arm raised like he was asking permission to speak, but wasn't no one looking his way. "We—"

"This is Satan's work!" Elder Clayton declared.

Got me steamed the way the elders was always talking over Reverend Ambrose—young or not, that's not the way you treat a person with a title and learning, my ma taught me. So I started clearing a path through the crowd for him; he like would have given up and gone home otherwise. Folks was packed in so tight my nose was full of damp salty sweat, and that was only a mite more unpleasant than the things they was all shouting at each other. Started with old bushy-bearded Elder McTaggart saying our trouble was on account of the baker's boy being a cow thief, but the baker said them snakes was here 'cause one of the elders had been skimming off the collection plate and just wait 'til he caught him in the act, but then Elder Clayton's missus said adultery was the reason but she wouldn't go naming names since surely we must all know who the harlot was.

"The Lord is testing us," Mrs. Simpkins said, fanning herself with one hand, her shotgun still clutched in the other.

When I finally reached the center of that crowd, I felt like a cork popping out of a bottle. Reverend Ambrose was right behind me, but he couldn't so much as open his mouth before Elder Mayfield was pointing a meaty old finger in his face.

"Or is the Lord testing *you*, Reverend? You're the one the snake fell on. Maybe you ain't right with God. Maybe we should be sending for a new preacher."

Reverend Ambrose made like he was gonna slink off, his shoulders all curled in, but I gave him a nudge forward since I could see my ma on the other side of the crowd. She was eyeing the elders as hard as she eyes me when I ain't tending to my chores fast enough. I reckoned she wanted to hear what the reverend had to say.

"Those snakes," he began, tucking in that loose bit of shirt of his. "It's real tempting to go about our business and leave it in God's hands." His voice was so thin people was leaning in trying to hear, but he got louder with each word, like someone was cranking him up the way you would a bucket of well water. "But the Lord don't throw a problem at you without also giving you the tools to fix it. I think we need to take a good look at our—"

"Been making my own snake repellent for years," Elder Clayton said, running right over the reverend's words like they was horse flop in the road. "Bit of sulfur and cinnamon, mix in my missus's little special something—it'll do the trick."

Elder McTaggart snorted hard enough to send a ripple through his whiskers. "How you gonna get your repellent up on that ceiling?"

"Never mind that," Elder Mayfield said. He got all squinty-eyed, looking at the other two like they was the snakes. "What's gonna hold that roof up if those serpents slither off? You'd send the whole thing crashing down on your own thick head."

The elders lit into each other for a bit, tossing round words like "lunkhead" and a few less charitable things my ma would slap me for repeating. Reverend Ambrose sagged against the old oak, as limp as one of my little sister's ragdolls.

Once the elders stopped fussing long enough to take a breath, Mrs. Simpkins cut in. "Word has it folks over in New Hope Valley had ceiling snakes a few years back." She was always asking what the word was in other towns when folk passed through. "Had to call in some serpent wranglers."

"Serpent wranglers?" Elder Mayfield chewed on the words like they was a thick slab of beef. "Where you think we gonna find serpent wranglers, woman?"

Reverend Ambrose straightened up so quick you'd think someone lit a fire in his britches. His shirt snuck loose again, but he tucked it right back in. "I know some folks who know some folks."

℘〇℃

Ain't none but Reverend Ambrose had ever heard of the Slithering Saints, but word was they had a reputation that spread further than I knew there were places you could go. How we was gonna pay them was another matter.

Reverend Ambrose said folk had been putting more than enough into the collection each week. Before those snakes came along, he'd been planning to use the money for that leak we could never seem to seal up proper. But turns out the church coffers wasn't near as full as he'd thought.

"Gonna have to go door to door and raise that money," he said. "Might move folks to hear a young person like yourself saying how much the church means to you."

So of course I went with him. I'd spent too much time helping him patch that church up to let them snakes have it.

It's strange, though, the way folk act when they ain't expecting you to drop by. Like Mrs. Simpkins. There was a whole lot of ruckus inside her house

292

when we knocked, and her hair was all a tussle when she finally opened up. Said she'd have to talk over her donation with Mr. Simpkins when he got home.

"You by chance seen Elder Clayton today?" Reverend Ambrose asked.

She said "no" and wished us good day, but before she shut that door, I was pretty sure I spied Elder Clayton's spectacles sitting on her rocker. Mr. Simpkins ain't never worn spectacles, let alone ones that thick.

Next house over, Elder McTaggart invited us in for lemonade and said it was hard to believe the church was so short on money when folks had been so generous lately—and he'd be one to know, seeing how often he helped out with the collection.

"That a new hat?" Reverend Ambrose asked him.

"It sure is," he said, and tilted his head and stroked his beard to better show it off.

Reverend Ambrose thanked him for his time and shuffled me along without taking him up on that lemonade.

Every house we went to, Reverend Ambrose's frown got a bit deeper. By the time we was almost done, his face was sagging like my grandpappy's old basset hound, 'specially when he saw that Elder Mayfield's wife had another black eye. She said the cow got spooked and kicked her while she was trying to milk it. The last black eye had been on account of her slipping and hitting her head on a table.

"Mrs. Mayfield sure do meet with a lot of bad luck," I told Reverend Ambrose as we was leaving.

"She sure do," he said, and wouldn't say no more.

ഇറ

Once we'd rustled up enough money for the serpent wrangling, my ma started pestering Reverend Ambrose to let her give the church a good cleaning. The Slithering Saints was due to arrive any day now, and she said it wasn't good manners to invite strangers inside a dirty church, snakes or no snakes. Reverend Ambrose looked green as a toad when she asked, but he finally gave in, so long as she let me and a few other boys stand guard in case one of them snakes came falling down again.

The elders insisted on being there too—don't know why, other than they never seemed to like anything happening without their say-so.

Soon as Reverend Ambrose got that church door open, the elders barreled on through and let slip some words me and the other boys would have been whupped for saying. In the days since we'd last been inside, you see, them snakes had gotten worse. You couldn't even see the ceiling no more—just them long, wiggly bodies slithering around.

While everyone else stared up at that, my ma was wrinkling her nose at that mess of snake guts we'd left rotting on the floor. Place smelled real nasty on account of it, and there was enough flies buzzing round to compete with all that hissing from above.

"The Lord is testing me," my ma said. "I ain't never had to mop up after no dead thing in here before."

"That's why we don't shoot 'em," another woman's voice said. "The cleanup can be a right old bitch."

Elder Mayfield had gotten all hunched and twitchy since stepping inside, but now he near leapt straight up to the ceiling; maybe he would have if it weren't for all them snakes. "Mind your language in the house of the Lord, young woman."

The young woman in question was dark-skinned and tiny. Even with her slouch hat she weren't no taller than my little sister. Except she weren't dressed like no woman I'd ever seen: trousers, cracked leather boots, and a weathered brown greatcoat. She held herself like that was the most natural thing in the world for her to be wearing, likewise her two companions—a thick-built old lady with short-cropped hair and a young native girl with tattoos down her face and neck.

"The name's Abigail Pickett, not young woman," she said, tipping her hat. "Folk usually just call me Miss Abigail. And if you want us to take care of them serpents for you, then you're gonna have to put up with a whole lot more cussing in here."

The other boys chuckled—I might have too if my ma wasn't standing there—but the elders went all huffy and red-faced, like they'd been told someone had lit off with the collection basket.

"You're supposed to be the Slithering Saints?" Elder Mayfield spit on the dead snake, then shot a nasty look at Reverend Ambrose. "Wasn't expecting no lady wranglers."

"I reckon you wasn't expecting no ceiling snakes either," Miss Abigail said, "yet here we are."

"Here you are." Elder Mayfield eyed the women up and down, mouth quirked like he couldn't decide if he wanted to frown or laugh. "Two little girls and somebody's grandma." He went with the laugh. "Go home, ladies."

The old woman stormed forward with a hard heavy stride like a bull, but Miss Abigail stopped her with just a raise of her hand.

"My team can do this job as well as any man." Miss Abigail nodded up at the ceiling. "All them venom spitters you got up there? We've trapped more than that in any given month."

"These ladies are the best there is," Reverend Ambrose said, flinging his words out fast before the elders could cut him off. "In my traveling days, I heard folk in every town 'tween here and the mountains vouch for them."

A lot of mumbling and shuffling from the elders followed, but seeing as we'd invited the Saints and raised all that money, they agreed to let the ladies give it a try—well, all of them except Elder Mayfield agreed. He stomped on out of the church, muttering something about heathens and sending for a new preacher.

Reverend Ambrose shook Miss Abigail's hand.

"I promise we'll take care of your snake problem," she said. "Afraid I can't help with what else is ailing y'all here."

I didn't dare say nothing 'cause I knew my ma would give me a mouthful for it, but I wanted to let out a big old whoop. I'd never seen nothing like those ladies before; it'd be a right shame if they lit out of town as fast as they'd come. We hadn't had this much excitement since that traveling circus came through and Elder Mayfield's eldest ran off with a girl who could twist herself into all sorts of acrobatics while riding a horse. Maybe that was why he was so cross now, worrying he'd lose another son to a snake wrangler this time.

ဆၢ

The Slithering Saints had themselves a crochety mule named Percy and a rickety wagon full of supplies. But before they could start any wrangling, Miss Abigail set a bunch of us to work putting up supports so the ceiling wouldn't come crashing down as the snakes was cleared.

"It's on y'all to get some new trusses up there once we're done," she said. "We're only paid for the serpents."

The snakes didn't like us shoving those supports in place. They'd slither aside, but they'd hiss something fierce. Some of the men took to hissing too; don't think they much liked taking orders from a woman. But when Mrs. Simpkins came by with lemonade and heard her son talking some sass, she smacked him right upside his head.

"Ain't said nothing worse than Elder Clayton," he grumbled.

You can believe Mrs. Simpkins had some words for Elder Clayton after that, and he was right quick to apologize. Heard some fellas snickering about how she had him tamed better than his own missus.

Once the supports was up, the wrangling started. Bunch of us stacked up crates so we could watch through the windows—had to keep the door clear

295

in case one of the Saints needed to run out to the wagon for something. Usually that was the native girl, Inola. She told me her name meant "black fox," and she was as quick as one.

Inola was about my age and the only one of the Saints I ever got talking to. Miss Abigail was always too busy, and I was too scared of the old lady—Permelia King was her name. She was thick and tough and grunted more than the surliest of our pigs.

First part of wrangling a ceiling snake, Inola told me, was getting the snake off that ceiling. They tied bits to the end of a rusty old crook until it was the length Miss Abigail needed, then she'd poke it up there and yank one of those serpents down to the floor. That's when Miss Permelia stepped in. If the snake was a mostly harmless one like a garter or a hognose, she'd just grab it with her bare hands. But with the venom spitters, she had this long old stick she'd wave near its face, real slow like to keep its attention. Meanwhile Miss Abigail'd sneak up behind with her own stick, only hers had a steel cable loop at the end. She'd get that loop over the snake's head and pull it tight.

Took a few tries with the ornerier snakes. Some would twist and strike quick as a tornado. More than one got its teeth into Miss Abigail's boot. Others just slithered off to hide under a bench, curling round one of the legs so they was harder to pull off. But she'd loop 'em eventually, and that's when Inola would dart up with a basket. They'd force that snake in there and close it up right fast. Once they had as much as their wagon could hold, they'd ride about a mile or so out of town and set the snakes loose.

"Don't that cause trouble somewhere else?" I asked, but Inola said once you got them snakes far enough away, they'd just coil up and disappear by sunrise—there one minute, gone the next. Nobody knew where they vanished to any more than they knew where they came from in the first place.

By the time Saturday rolled around, it looked like they were gonna be finishing up real soon—only a dozen or so snakes was left up there. Elder Mayfield had nothing but scowls for the Saints, 'specially when he spied one of his boys flirting with Miss Abigail—much as you could flirt with a woman who mostly ignored you. But otherwise folks had stopped grousing about having those lady wranglers in town, though little Minnie Wirt still got a paddling when she told her pa she was gonna wrangle snakes when she got older.

While the Saints was off carting some more snakes out of town, Reverend Ambrose and me stood in the doorway of the church looking up at the ceiling.

"Gonna need your help getting those new trusses up first thing," he said. He had this real big grin on his face. But then one of the ceiling snakes hissed like it'd been stepped on, and that set the others off. Reverend Ambrose's face got all sad and saggy. "We gotta look to ourselves like Miss Abigail said, or we're just gonna end up with more snakes up there again."

"What's that mean, Reverend? Look to ourselves for what?"

"For the things we like to pretend ain't there."

I can't say anything would have changed had the Saints gotten to clear up the last of those snakes without a fuss. Folk might have gone right back to doing like they did. So I'm not sure if it was for good or bad that the Reverend Whitney Herschel Wallace came riding into town right then.

His wagon was the flashiest thing I'd ever seen. Had this white canvas over the back with his name in swirly letters, striped red, yellow, and black like a coral snake. He had a scrawny little pock-marked boy traveling with him who beat a drum as they went, keeping that sleek black horse of theirs at a pace so slow you knew they was doing it for show and not to get nowhere. All that noise got folk pouring into the street. Reverend Whitney tipped his top hat at everyone he passed, smiling like they was his best friend in the world.

Reverend Ambrose got real quiet. If it weren't for the way he started chewing on his lip, I like would have run out to greet that wagon too.

The drumming stopped, and so did the wagon, right in front of the church. Reverend Whitney climbed on down. He took long steps, like he was on stage in some weighty old drama, the black tails of his coat flapping behind him. A few of the ladies was swooning, so I reckon he was a good-looking fellow by their account. Elder Mayfield ran on up to him and shook his hand. The two of them talked close for a good bit, then Reverend Whitney addressed the crowd.

"Elder Mayfield here invited me on account of your serpent problem," he said, and the way he spoke put me more in mind of the barker from the traveling circus than a preacher. "And I'm not talking about those snakes in your ceiling."

He pointed west, just as the Slithering Saints' wagon came tottering over the crest of a hill. That set folk whispering, and Elder Mayfield led a few others in an "Amen!"

"Bit more theater than the Lord with this one," Reverend Ambrose whispered to me. "You watch him close."

"With your permission," Reverend Whitney said, though he didn't wait for it from nobody. He strolled on into the church, right past me and Reverend Ambrose like we wasn't there. Such a rush of folks came scurrying in behind that we was pushed along inside with 'em.

Reverend Whitney strode up to the pulpit but didn't settle there. He kept pacing, like he was waiting for something, and finally we saw what. That scrawny boy of his came running inside with a crook, bit like the one the Saints used, except this one wasn't rusty. It was silver and shined so clean the sun glinting off it could blind you. And the reverend's boy didn't have to tie on extra bits to the handle to get it long enough for the ceiling. He just pushed a little button, and more length of silver came shooting out with a clank.

Some folk backed toward the door when they realized the boy was about to yank a snake down, but Reverend Whitney threw up his hands and cried out, "Those who run now show no faith in what God's own son told us: 'And these signs shall follow them that believe: In my name shall they cast out devils; they shall speak with new tongues. They shall take up serpents; and if they drink any deadly thing, it shall not hurt them.'"

There was a bit of nervous scuttling, but folk stayed put, even when the reverend's boy hooked a snake, red-orange like fire, and tugged it down to the floor.

Reverend Whitney grabbed that snake with his bare hand and held it up high, paying no mind to the way it slithered round his arm. "Luke 10:19: 'Behold, I give unto you power to tread on serpents and scorpions, and over all the power of the enemy: and nothing shall by any means hurt you.'"

That got him a whole lot of gasps and amens, and Elder McTaggart's missus right out fainted, but a whole new fuss followed at the sound of Miss Abigail's voice.

"Of course that one ain't gonna hurt you," she said, coming through the door with Inola and Miss Permelia in tow. "That's just a corn snake. Kept worse than that in my pockets when I was a little girl."

"Don't you see what's happening?" Reverend Whitney shouted. He shook the snake real hard, and it twisted its head like it was a mite annoyed, but it didn't bite or hiss. "The Lord sent these snakes as a test, and Satan sent those women to lure you away from facing that test."

Miss Abigail laughed. "We got a contract here, Reverend, and Satan ain't got no part of it. So why don't you clear on out and let us finish what we was hired to do?"

"I think you ladies are the ones who oughta be clearing out," Elder Mayfield said. He pulled some crumpled bills from his pocket and threw them at Miss Abigail's feet. "Count yourself lucky you been paid anything at all and go."

"Hold up there," Reverend Ambrose said, stepping 'tween them—or limping rather. His bum leg looked to be bothering him real bad, shaking as much as his voice. "You don't get to make decisions for everyone in this church, Elder Mayfield."

"Maybe I ought to from now on." He nodded toward the Saints. "You got all our children thinking these women are something to look up to. But they ain't natural. Not one of 'em. I won't stand by and see all the good money this town donated handed over to heathens."

I knew my ma would give me hell for sassing an elder, but I couldn't help myself hearing him talk like he was the one who'd raised all that money. "Who's gonna clear out them snakes then? You?"

"Don't need to, boy, or wasn't you listening to the right good Reverend Whitney just now? Our faith will protect us." Elder Mayfield spat at Reverend Ambrose's feet. "Not this fraud. He wouldn't fear those serpents if he was right with God."

Miss Abigail scooped up the money from the floor. "I'm sorry, Reverend Ambrose, but like I told you: y'all gotta look to yourselves. We just catch snakes."

She started for the door, and her team followed right after. Inola gave me a little look-see back, along with a shrug that said there weren't nothing she could do, and then they was gone. Reverend Whitney started more shouting, something about the Lord casting out evil, but my eye was on Reverend Ambrose, red-faced and puffing for breath as he limped along after the Saints.

Reverend Whitney shook that corn snake real hard again, and folks was crying "Amen!" and "Praise the Lord!" and then we had another fainter. They sure thought God was protecting Reverend Whitney, even though more than a few had to know that snake had no fight in it like Miss Abigail said. So I followed on out after her and Reverend Ambrose.

Outside, the Saints was loading up their wagon, which looked even shabbier alongside Reverend Whitney's. Had to admit that was one reason I was willing to take Miss Abigail's word over his. I'd been watching Reverend Whitney real close, and he didn't look like he'd seen a hard day in his life. Only thing he had that wasn't shiny was that boy, who looked like he wasn't fed on the regular.

"Cure the symptom, leave the disease," Reverend Ambrose was saying to Miss Abigail. "I suppose you wouldn't have no more business if you tried to do more than that."

"I ain't no doctor, Reverend." She rummaged under a pile of ratty blankets for a spell, then finally pulled out a scratched-up lockbox. "I meant it when I said I was sorry. You seem a good man. But I spent years shouting myself hoarse trying to get folk to change, and I've got no more time for it. I ain't got a silver tongue like ol' Whitney in there, and the ones who need to hear it most are more like to listen to you than the likes of me."

"You run into this preacher before?"

"Yeah, we got some history. Likes to get us driven out of town without getting paid. So today?" She took the money she'd scooped up from the floor and locked it up in that box of hers. "Today was a good day by them standards, even if this ain't near half what we're owed."

Reverend Ambrose kicked at the dirt and rubbed his chin for a long minute. Looked like the Saints was gonna leave without getting another word from him, but then he said, "How about I pay you what you were promised?"

Miss Abigail laughed. "For what, Reverend? You can see we ain't welcome in there."

"That's not what I wanna pay you for now." Reverend Ambrose got a right wicked grin on his face. "Where is it you take them snakes after you catch 'em?"

꧁꧂

Next morning, Reverend Ambrose and me was sitting on the church steps before most folk started waking. We hadn't gotten so much as a wink of sleep, but he made some coffee strong enough that I wasn't feeling it too bad. And it was worth that bit of pounding in my head to see Reverend Whitney climbing out young Ellie McTaggart's window before dawn and back to where he was supposed to be housing, still buttoning up his drawers as he went.

The McTaggart family was the first to show up for Sunday morning service—one to be preached by Reverend Whitney now. They didn't make much of me and Reverend Ambrose sitting there; Elder McTaggart just gave us a puzzled cock of his head before leading the ladies inside. I felt a mite bad knowing what was gonna happen, but I also couldn't help a chuckle when Mrs. McTaggart let loose a scream and came running back out.

"There's more snakes," she wheezed.

Course Reverend Ambrose and me already knew that, on account of us being the ones who put 'em back in there.

Wasn't long before the whole town was gathered inside the church, waiting for Reverend Whitney to stroll in and start preaching. More snakes had to be God's work, didn't it? Another test—that's what most of 'em was saying. Me and Reverend Ambrose just sat there grinning.

Elder Mayfield nudged one of his boys. "Why don't you go see what's keeping the preacher?"

That's when we heard the sound of hooves and wagon wheels rumbling so fast you'd think the town was on fire.

"He's leaving!" That was Elder Clayton, staring slack-jawed out a window. "Reverend Whitney and his boy both!"

While everyone else was running to the windows, Reverend Ambrose gave me a nod. I grabbed the crook Inola had helped me fashion before she and the Saints left town. Just like she'd taught me, I hooked it round the nastiest rattler I could spy and pulled real hard until I'd yanked him down. Landed him right on top of the pulpit too.

Mrs. McTaggart was the first one to notice the rattler, and her screaming got a whole lot of others doing likewise. Elder Mayfield ran up front, waving his arms and shouting for folks to calm down.

"God will protect us," he said. "These snakes are a test of our faith."

Elder Clayton snorted. "Let's see you handle that rattler then."

Elder Mayfield went real pale, and I can't say I blamed him none. That snake was close to a six-footer, head raised and fangs bared, hissing and rattling from that pulpit like he was giving the most hateful sermon you ever heard. Yet Elder Mayfield took a step toward it, sweat beading up all over his face.

"Elder Mayfield, stop." Reverend Ambrose took to the front, keeping clear of that snake, and laid a hand on Elder Mayfield's shoulder. "I know Elder Clayton don't want you to touch that snake any more than you want to admit to being wrong. But Reverend Whitney was not an honest man. Honest men don't tempt you to danger then run out of town at the first sign of it. Honest men don't try to force God's hand, asking him to perform a miracle to protect them from serpents when He already gave them brains enough to protect themselves."

Sure as I stood there, Elder Mayfield dropped to his knees and started bawling. Most said it was the weight of his sins finally bringing him down. I think it was more relief no one was expecting him to touch that serpent. Whatever it was, it set off a whole slew of others falling to their knees, crying out so many sins at once you couldn't tell who was 'fessing up to what. What matters is that moment changed folks some—not real quick, and not without a whole mess of stumbles after. But I think we all started looking to ourselves like Miss Abigail said we oughta.

First, though, we had to look to that rattler. 'Cause he didn't seem intent on giving up that pulpit on his own.

"Hope you got some real good tips from those ladies," Reverend Ambrose said, readying a stick with a loop on the end like the Saints had. "We're gonna be wrangling our own snakes here from now on."

ഇരുന

Barbara A. Barnett is a Philadelphia-area writer, musician, Odyssey Writing Workshop graduate, coffee addict, wine lover, and all-around geek. In addition to *Mysterion*, her short fiction has appeared in publications such as *Beneath Ceaseless Skies, Lady Churchill's Rosebud Wristlet, Fantasy Magazine, Daily Science Fiction*, and *Flash Fiction*

Online. Outside of writing, she's spent most of her career working for performing arts organizations, first as a grant writer and database manager, and more recently as an orchestra librarian. You can find her online at www.babarnett.com.

Barbara says, "One summer, two unrelated things happened in fairly short succession: (1) I learned how to catch a rattlesnake (a long story that ends with the snake getting away), and (2) my church discovered the trusses were pulling away from the roof (another long story). A bit of wiring near the trusses looked rather snake-like to me, and thus a story idea was born."

Vocation

Jessica Snell

IT DIDN'T BOTHER me that the library I lived in was sentient.

It was that it kept assigning me book reports.

I knew I was lucky to live here. Our House covered one of the smallest continents, and so it only had a thousand rooms, and only three of those rooms were libraries.

I would rather live in a library than, say, a bathroom (there were over a hundred of those in our House). Though even a bathroom would be a better place to live than the Yard outside.

That's where I'd grown up and of course I didn't miss it at all.

𝕊𝕠𝕢𝕣

The first book the library assigned to me was *Behind the Scenes: Domestic Arrangements in Historic Houses.*

I thought that was a bit on the nose.

But I read the whole thing and started writing my report.

I wrote about the sculleries and drawing rooms and water closets that they'd had back on Earth. I wrote about how they captured wild yeast for their beers and their breads, and how they maintained habitats for the fish and the fowl they ate. I wrote about how they hauled in water and sluiced out chamber pots and eventually piped in real plumbing.

(I thought about how I missed going to the bathroom—or, rather, squatting over a hole, since that's all we had in the Yard. But, as everyone knows, people are made for Houses and not Houses for people, and so once I'd been assigned to my Room, all of my functions that did not fit that Room's purpose had been taken away.)

I wrote about dovecots and brewhouses and stables and wondered at how many elements of historic houses were not actually a part of any of our Houses. Back on Earth, the big estates—the *households*—had included not just scores of people, and one huge, sprawling stone residence, but also all the land and outbuildings and agriculture that supported the estate.

Our Houses weren't fragmented like that. Our Houses were whole.

It was a much more sensible arrangement, and so I noted in my report.

But the library didn't seem overjoyed at my conclusion. It simply said, "Thank you," and assigned me next month's book.

৪১৩

The second book had a character who said that his home was not a place, it was a person. Except he didn't mean a House, he meant… a person. Like a human. The character even corrected himself and said his home was not just a person, but "people." By which he meant his family: his wife and his son and his father.

Humans.

I swallowed and closed the book when I got to that part. I closed my eyes too, but I could still see the faces.

That book was near the beginning of a series. When I finished my report, I went and found the rest.

I was not sure I liked what I learned.

৪১৩

I read more. I read and I read and I read, and when the library told me it was a pity that I could only read English, because there was so much more, from so many different cultures, I told it that was all very well, and I didn't care, and this was quite enough thank you, and that I had enough to read, and maybe even *too* much to read—

And then I stopped talking. Because reading was my vocation, and if I couldn't read, then I was in the wrong Room, and this was my only Room, it was the only one I would ever get, and if I could not fit myself to this Room, I could not fit myself to the House, and then all I was fit for was the outside, for the Yard, for the scrabbling and the rocks and the scratching and the cold and the—

৪১৩

Gaudy Night was the third book I was assigned.

It did not have houses in it.

It had a university.

ଛୋର୍ଷ

I decided I had to read the rest of that series too. And I kept reading: more and more. More than the library assigned to me. (It wouldn't answer when I asked if it was deliberately assigning books around a particular theme, but did confirm that it had read them all itself.)

I was so far away from the doorway through which I'd come in. I wasn't even on the library's first floor anymore. I was up the curving wooden staircase that led to the second story of bookcases. The second floor was like the deck on a ship, opening up into the air above the first floor as if it were cresting over the top of a wave.

I had seen waves, from the Yard.

The Yard was made up of the odd bits of our continent's border—the scrapes and scraps of land that flopped out from under the edges of the House, like an uneven circle of dough protruding out from under the clean, crisp edge of a biscuit cutter.

There wasn't much to eat there. There wasn't much to do. We scrambled around on the rocks of the shore like tiny, helpless crabs, snapping at each other and scrounging for food to fill our mouths with, for holes to live in.

It wasn't like Earth had been. Earth had miles and miles and miles of land. Earth had lakes and rivers.

Of course, it was all poisoned now. We'd been doing it to ourselves—polluting our water and air, causing the inevitable rise of the atmosphere's temperature. We knew it was coming, the gradual disaster that we'd decided not to avoid.

But we were wrong. The actual disaster came swiftly, like a hammer blow. The aliens' migratory stop on our planet left us reeling, and the waste products they left behind crippled our ecosystem quickly and permanently.

We began to die.

ଛୋର୍ଷ

But disasters aren't always bad. They're just changes, really, when you look at them head-on.

Our next disaster was that we were rescued.

Some other aliens had pity on us. They brought us here.

And they tried to make us shelter like what we'd had before. But they were so different from us that we couldn't quite use the Houses they'd built, even though we tried.

So they took pity on us again, and they arranged for us to change so we'd fit the shelters they'd made. There weren't quite enough Houses for all of us, so some of us still lived outside, at least for the beginning of our lives. And when we finally got to enter the Houses, the way we were changed was… not quite what we were used to, I suppose.

But they did their best.

℘℘

I'm sorry. I put that badly.

Their best, of course, is much better than our best ever was. Of course, I didn't say that before because of course it's obvious. It's obvious. Of course.

We never used to have houses so grand that we had to fit ourselves to them, rather than the other way around.

But great gifts require great sacrifices. How else can you make yourself worthy to receive the gift?

They'd given us so much.

℘℘

Once, after I wrote the library a report on *The Collected Works of John Donne*, the library asked me what I thought people did who were assigned to the bedrooms in our Houses and I told it, *They sleep*, because there was only ever one person assigned to a room, that was the law, there was never ever more than one person in a room, and it asked me if I thought that sleeping was really all bedrooms were ever for and I thought of the bedrooms that I'd read about that had been for sleep *and* for sex and even for reading and listening and laughing (as if they were libraries and theaters and bedrooms all rolled up into one) and I told it to stop, to stop, to please, please stop.

I changed my mind. I did mind that the library was sentient.

I minded that it had read all its own books.

I minded very much indeed.

℘℘

The months moved on. I read and I read.

And because the library asked me to, I kept writing it reports.

I read and I wrote and I read.

"Jeeves kept house for Wooster," I wrote. "But not a proper House."

The library assigned me another book.

"Irene and her consort made merriment and feasts for all their guests in their great palace," I wrote. "But it must have been awful. So crowded."

The library assigned me another book.

"Clan Korval was a Tree and some ships and their cats. How could they even call themselves a House?"

The library assigned me another book.

306

Another, and another, and another.

℘℃

I could not take it. I could not read one more. Not of the kind that it was giving me. Not of the kind that had families and households and churches and bread and wine and kindled fires and the shade of trees and the cool of the evening in a garden and a hand holding yours as you walked.

I don't think you understand, I told the library. *You're not being fair to me.*

Those things in those books—they don't exist. There never was a Shire and a Barrayar and a Hundred Acre Wood, but even if there actually was once an Ivory Coast and a Persian Gulf and an India, there isn't *anymore! I can't go to the cool green quadrangles of Oxford or the high glass towers of Hong Kong or the rain-sweet slopes of Costa Rica. They aren't there. They haven't been for years.*

There is the outside and there is the Yard and there is the House.

Even if I went to another continent, there would be, on that continent, the outside and the Yard and the House.

There is nothing else anymore and you are making me want these things that I cannot have.

℘℃

I started staying on the stairs, the only part of the library that was more than a few feet away from the bookshelves. The stairs were made of oak, or at least they looked like they were. Who knew what unearthly materials the Houses were actually made of?

But they looked like oak. The knots and whorls of the wood were large and the posts of the stairs were thick and plain, which made them easy to lean against as I sat and stared, unseeing, at the ceiling.

How long could I sit and stare without reading?

I sat.

I sat, and I tried to ignore the small, quiet, persistent voice in my head.

I asked myself, *How long can I sit here, inactive, before the House decides to give my place to someone more worthy?*

And the small, quiet, persistent voice in my head answered, *Let it.*

℘℃

One of my next book reports was on *One Corpse Too Many*. It was a murder mystery, but by this time I wasn't puzzled that the library had given it to me: murder mysteries often had the very best descriptions of homes and houses. By their very interest in restoring justice and order, the mysteries' protagonists almost always had something to say about what the nature of goodness was…

even if the protagonist's idea of social good was most eloquently stated in their true and pure enjoyment of the perfect cup of tea.

Not a house this time, and not a university.

A monastery. An ordered life. A garden and all the healing goodness that came from it. A place to worship and be human together, in the sight of a God that was somehow less alien than the aliens who had rescued us, because he had been human himself.

(He hadn't changed us? He'd changed himself instead? That was... oh help me and hang me for a heretic, that was *comforting*.)

This book had songs and friends and tasks worth doing.

And the hero was an herbalist-monk who had once been a warrior, had been lover and fighter all at once, but who had given it up for the call of something he loved even more and would fight for even harder.

The people in his town needed healing, and he would heal them.

His God had preserved him, and so he would worship his God.

I sighed, and I shut the book, and I didn't just stare unseeing at the ceiling this time.

Instead, I looked all around me, looked hard, looked on purpose. I looked at all of the shelves, every one packed full of books, full of stories and histories from a world left behind. Stories full of a humanity that built not just Houses, but households. Not just one room per person, but rooms shared. Not just an inside divided like a honeycomb, but an outside full of gardens.

A humanity that cultivated not just the fruit of the ground, but a humanity that had the inherited knowledge to turn that fruit into wine, that wheat into bread.

A humanity that could break bread together.

Those shelves of stories stretched back, rank on rank, further than I could see.

I could read for years, and not come to the end of them.

My enemy's arsenal was infinite.

And I knew I could not stand against it.

⁝⁞

I left, still lacking the things that had been taken from me—the things that had been taken in order to fit me to my room in the House. I did not need to eat or eliminate. I did not need the shelter of blankets or the rest offered by a bed. I would have a long, long life, out there in the cold and the scrabbling and the waste.

(Could we grow gardens in that waste? Build houses? Remember how to pray? We didn't know. With the security of the Houses in front of us, we'd never tried.)

(But the library had showed me: security was not enough.)

I left.

I left, still lacking the things that had been taken from me.

I left, too, with everything that had been given to me. I left with the task that had been laid on me. I would have the time now—the time to tell everyone else: we were humans, and maybe even made in the image of a God who wanted us to stay that way, and *we were not meant to be alone.*

I knew now what we had lost. I knew now what we must rebuild.

(Buildings, but not just buildings. *Homes.*)

And yet.

And yet.

I left, leaving my dearest enemy behind.

(*Oh my library. Oh my friend.*)

And I went outside, weeping.

ꕥ

Jessica Snell is a writer whose work has appeared in *Compelling Science Fiction*, *Tor.com*, *Christ and Pop Culture*, *Focus on the Family* and more. She is also a freelance editor who loves helping other writers polish their books till they shine! In her free time, she gardens, knits, and spends time with her husband and their four children. You can follow her on X.com at @theJessicaSnell, where she tweets about books, faith, and family. Her website is jessicasnell.com.

"'Vocation' is (pretty clearly) a love letter to the books that have shaped me. (The protagonist's critiques are not mine; the library's taste in literature is.) I'm a sucker for libraries and always have been—even before I spent six years working in one. I'm also a sucker for any story that has a strong picture of what home means. After the first two lines of this story popped into my head, the rest of it followed quickly. I hope you enjoyed it!"

Kirishitan

Marshall J. Moore

HIZEN PROVINCE, JAPAN. 1577.

Crows flapped and cawed around the dead man's face, jostling one another for the privilege of pecking out his eyes.

"An ugly way to die," Okabe Yukiko murmured, rubbing her thumb over the pommel of her wakizashi. She shaded her eyes against the noonday sun as she looked up at the row of dead men lining the dirt road.

Four dead men on four crosses. Each had been stripped naked, nails driven through their feet and hands and into the heavy wooden beams. The wounds were crusted with dried blood, and each corpse's face twisted into an agonized grimace. A placard was nailed to the foot of the nearest cross, the kanji scrawled upon it crude and unlovely.

"What does it say?" asked Nori, his gaze shifting nervously from the dead men to Yukiko. Like most farmers, he was illiterate.

"Kirishitan," Yukiko read. An unnecessary label—the means of execution declared the reason for these men's deaths on its own. Anyone who walked this road would be in no doubt as to why they had been executed, or the local daimyo's policy towards followers of the foreign faith.

"We should move on," the elder of Yukiko's two companions grunted.

She turned her head to peer down at Isukiri, surprised. Until now, the elderly Buddhist priest Nori had introduced as his uncle had hardly deigned to speak to her. She had not been surprised by his reticence. As a masterless ronin, she was used to being mistrusted by samurai and commoners alike.

Isukiri looked levelly back up at her. Alone of the three, he was seated, resting with his back against the edge of the wooden cart his nephew pulled.

310

He was past seventy, with the bent back and bad knees common to those of the lower classes who reached such an advanced age.

"Nothing we can do for them," he continued, looking up at the crucified men. "They've gone to be with their God. Best not to linger unless we want to join them."

Yukiko raised an eyebrow. "I didn't think you were that kind of priest, Isukiri-san."

The old man scowled and fussed at the ojuzu prayer beads wrapped about his wrist. Yukiko returned her gaze to the corpses beside the road.

Of the four crucified men, three were farmers, unremarkable and plain-looking. But the fourth was unlike any man Yukiko had ever seen. Even beneath the greenish tint of death his flesh had a pasty-pink cast to it, and his nose—what remained of it after the crows had eaten their fill—was almost comically long and broad.

"A gaijin?" Yukiko's eyes widened with surprise.

"Hai." Nori nodded, shifting uncomfortably. "One of their priests. The merchants are smart enough not to travel this far from the coast."

Which meant that the three dead locals beside him must have been converts, perhaps even disciples. Had they known this was the fate that awaited them for turning away from the faith of their ancestors and adopting the religion of the western barbarians? Had whatever solace the foreign god offered them been worth this cruelest of deaths?

"Okabe-san," Nori murmured, glancing over his shoulder at Isukiri, "my uncle is correct. We should not linger here if we hope to reach the shrine before nightfall."

Yukiko shook her head and turned away from the grisly spectacle. Both commoners were right. They had hired her to perform a task, after all. And while having a ronin guard's protection on the roads in these uncertain times was a boon, it was not for her swords alone that Nori and his priestly uncle had enlisted her service.

Shouldering the pack that held her meager worldly belongings, Yukiko set off down the road, towards the mountains. Nori grunted as he lifted the wooden cart and set off after her, his uncle fidgeting silently with the prayer beads. Behind them the mangled bodies faded into the distance, though their stark message remained in Yukiko's mind.

Preach the word of the Crucified God in Hizen Province, the nails through their hands proclaimed, *and meet the same fate he did.*

ജ�ൕ

"Tell me about your ghost, Nori-san."

Nori wiped at his brow, eliciting a dissatisfied grunt from his uncle as the motion rocked the little cart. The afternoon sun beat down oppressively, and the dusty mountain road was unshaded by any trees.

"I am not sure what I can tell you that I have not already said, Okabe-san," Nori said. "Our shrine is haunted by a yōkai of some sort. Our own attempts to dislodge it proved to be fruitless."

Isukiri snorted. Yukiko glanced over her shoulder to see the old priest rocking uncomfortably from side to side in the back of the cart as they climbed the winding mountain trail, running the prayer beads through his weathered hands.

Small wonder he resents my presence, Yukiko thought. *Even a humble priest has his pride, and it must sting his to admit that he requires help driving away an unfriendly spirit. Particularly from a lowly ronin.*

Like all masterless samurai, Yukiko occupied a precarious position in Nippon's social order. She was of nobler birth than the commoners, but without a lord to provide her with food and lodging her lot in life was little better than that of a penniless vagabond. Her swords and the name of her long-dead clan were all that set her apart from a common cutthroat.

"So we elected to seek out someone with experience in dealing with unfriendly spirits," Nori continued, recalling Yukiko's attention to the present. A nervous chuckle escaped his lips. "Lucky for us that the famous ghost hunter Okabe Yukiko happened to be nearby!"

Isukiri leaned over the side of the cart and spat. The thick wad of phlegm landed and mingled with the dust of the road.

"Lucky for us all," Yukiko said drily, patting the coin pouch that jingled at her side. "When did your yōkai first appear?"

"A week ago," Nori said. "Not long after we moved into the shrine. The building had been in disrepair for quite some time, its altar untended and no offerings made to the kami dwelling within."

A dissatisfied grunt from the back of the cart showed what Isukiri thought of the state of the roadside shrine that was now his responsibility. Yukiko could hardly blame him. The local daimyo, Ryūzōji Takanobu, had been generous in gifting the unkept shrine to the elderly priest, but his generosity did not extend nearly so far as to encompass labor for repairs of the dilapidated house of worship.

"Many yōkai are attracted to places of spiritual significance," Yukiko mused as they rounded a bend in the mountain path. "A roadside shrine left untended would be highly tempting for many of them. Tell me, what did this yōkai of yours look like?"

Nori opened his mouth to respond, but to Yukiko's surprise it was his uncle who answered.

"Not a yōkai," Isukiri said with unexpected heat, shaking his head. "Nor a yūrei. It is a wicked oni, Okabe-san."

Yukiko wiped a bead of sweat from her brow. Oni were hulking, demonic brutes taller than a man—not the sort of being she expected to take up residence in a roadside shrine.

"You're talking nonsense, uncle," Nori said, once again letting out that nervous, chittering laugh. "It's too small to be an oni."

"You've seen it, then?" Yukiko asked, fixing Nori with a direct gaze.

"Hai," Nori said, quailing away from Yukiko's keen grey eyes. "Not clearly, you understand, and only fleetingly. It appears each night around the Hour of the Dog, but it keeps to the shadows."

Now they were getting somewhere. Yukiko opened her mouth, about to ask Nori any of a hundred questions: *How big was the yōkai? Was its shape human or animal, or neither? Did it speak?*

But before she could ask even one, another voice cut through the mountain air.

"Hold!" it shouted, brusquely authoritative. "By order of Lord Ryūzōji Takanobu!"

Ahead on the road stood a pair of sentinels leaning against their long yari. One was short and broad, the other lanky. They were armored in the manner of ashigaru foot soldiers, their iron cuirasses emblazoned with the mon of the Ryūzōji clan: a six-rayed white sunburst on black.

The shorter ashigaru lowered his yari, its iron tip pointed at Yukiko's heart. Beneath the brim of his conical bamboo hat his eyes flicked to the swords tucked into her obi.

"Declare yourself." He adjusted his grip on the yari's haft. "Who are you? And what business do you have on Lord Ryūzōji's roads?"

Yukiko's grey eyes roved over the pair of ashigaru, sizing them up. The one who had spoken had his feet planted too close together; if she could parry his first strike, she could close inside his reach and unbalance him with a single strike. The trick would be meeting his comrade's counterattack...

She shook her head, clearing it of such violent thoughts. *You are here on legitimate business,* she reminded herself. *There is no need for bloodshed today.*

"Good evening." Yukiko tucked her arms into the sleeves of her kimono and bowed at the waist. "I am Okabe Yukiko. This priest and his nephew have hired me to assist them in cleaning and repairing their shrine."

Out of the corner of her eye Yukiko saw Nori shoot her a look, his face pale. She ignored him, keeping her attention fixed on the pair of ashigaru. In

Yukiko's experience, mentioning evil spirits did little to set wary soldiers at ease.

"Heh," the second ashigaru grunted, scratching at his chin. He was taller than his companion, with pockmark scars cratering his face. "Thought even ronin were above doin' handywork like that." His attention shifted to Nori. "What's the matter? Couldn't find a carpenter down in the village?"

"Ebisu smiles on all honest work," Yukiko said, her own polite smile unwavering. "And a ronin with a hungry belly makes a passable carpenter at need."

"True enough!" the scarred ashigaru laughed. He took off his hat and fanned himself with it. "Let 'em through, Chirhiro."

The other ashigaru—Chirhiro—narrowed his eyes, but slowly lifted his yari. Yukiko let out a breath she hadn't realized she'd been holding.

"You may proceed," Chirhiro said, the words begrudging. "But only if you pass the test."

Yukiko's smile froze. *Test?*

Chihiro reached into his travel pack and produced a rectangular bronze plate about the size of Yukiko's hand. Out of the corner of her eye Yukiko saw Isukiri lean forward in his cart to get a better look.

Chihiro thrust the plate towards each of them in turn. Nori flinched away as though it were a brand, although by now Yukiko was beginning to wonder if there was anything the farmer *didn't* cringe at. Isukiri looked at it impassively, his dark eyes betraying nothing of his thought.

Then the plate was under her nose, the late afternoon sun glinting off the dull bronze. Yukiko blinked, tilting her head for a better look.

A man, hanging from a cross by his hands. A likeness of one of the dead men from the road?

"Know what this is?" Chihiro asked, his eyes roving over Yukiko and the two commoners. Without waiting for an answer, he pressed on. "This is the dead god of the Kirishitan. Any of you Kirishitan?"

Nori shook his head fervently. Yukiko maintained her pleasantly smiling mask, but her shoulders tensed as she recalled the four men crucified on the roadside. She smelled a trap.

"We're all Buddhists here," Isukiri said, speaking up for the first time since the ashigaru had appeared. His prayer beads rattled against each other as he waved them demonstratively.

"Good." Chihiro grinned, and threw the bronze plate to the ground. A small explosion of dust billowed up around it.

"Stomp on it," he commanded. "Should be easy if you're really good Buddhists like you say."

A sharp intake of breath from beside Yukiko. Nori glanced down at the bronze icon, then back up at the soldiers, naked terror in his eyes.

Act, a voice in Yukiko's head pleaded, high and urgent. *Act, before his cowardice kills you all.*

Yukiko moved with the fighter's instinct that had saved her life dozens of times. Chihiro's voice barely had time to echo off the hillside before she brought her sandalled foot down on the bronze plate, driving it further into the dust.

She backed away, and the eyes of the ashigaru turned to Nori. Yukiko's hand dropped to her katana's hilt, ready to draw and strike in a single breath.

Nori nodded and stepped forward, driving his own foot down onto the figure of the crucified god. When he retreated his chest rose and fell as though he had just finished a long race.

"Looks like you were wrong, Chihiro," the pockmarked ashigaru cackled. "No Kirishitan here."

He stepped out of the road and waved for them to move along, but Chihiro remained where he was, frowning. His gaze fell on Isukiri, sitting in the back of the cart and worrying at his prayer beads.

"The old man, too."

Nori turned his head, looking fearfully at his uncle. Yukiko moved between the commoners and the two ashigaru, her hand still resting on her katana.

"Come now," she said, still polite but with frost creeping in at the edge of her voice. "This is absurd. Isukiri-sama is the priest of the roadside shrine further up the mountain. Your daimyo Ryūzōji-dono himself granted it to him, and now you accuse him of being a secret Kirishitan?"

Chirhiro's companion cackled. "She's got you there, mate!"

"What you say makes sense," Chihiro admitted, looking uncertain. "But we have orders. Anyone passing this way is to be tested—"

"Sir," Nori said, his voice wavering as he bowed low. "My uncle is quite old. His knees trouble him…"

As his nephew spoke, Isukiri began chanting a low prayer, his prayer beads rattling as he turned them over in his hands.

"Alright!" Chihiro interrupted, holding up his hands in a gesture of surrender. "Alright. I see that it's as you say. Go ahead."

He stepped out of the road, allowing them to pass. Nori hoisted the handles of the wooden cart.

"I apologize for the inconvenience," Chihiro said, nodding his head deferentially to Isukiri. "Say a prayer to the kami for us, would you?"

"Yeah," his comrade jeered as they passed him by. "And if you see any Kirishitan, send them this way, you hear?"

Yukiko did not smile. She set off beside the cart, easily keeping pace with Isukiri as he was trundled along.

"That was quick thinking," the old priest murmured to her, a little further down the road. "Stepping in before Nori's hesitation was apparent."

So the old man had noticed that, too.

"Why *did* he hesitate?" she asked, keeping her voice low so the ashigaru behind them would not hear. Ahead of her Nori's exposed neck flushed red, but he did not look back.

Isukiri swayed with the rocking of his cart. "My nephew is a... superstitious sort, Okabe-san. He is hesitant to disrespect any spirit, whether a native kami or foreign god." His prayer beads rattled. "You are not similarly burdened, it seems."

Yukiko looked over her shoulder, past the two ashigaru once again lounging against their spears, to the small metal plate lying in the dust. A shudder passed through her as she recalled how the crucified man engraved on it had stared up at the sky, his mouth open in a silent wail.

"He's not my god," Yukiko said.

&ᘐᙆ

The shrine sat on a high bluff overlooking the valley below, beyond which Yukiko could just barely glimpse the distant glimmer of the sea. The sun was grazing the peaks of the western mountains when they arrived, bathing the shrine red. She tried not to take that as an omen.

Isukiri had not been lying. His shrine *was* in dire need of repair. The paint had peeled from the torii arch that marked the shrine's entrance, exposing the bare wood beneath. One corner of the sloping tiled roof had caved in, and the walls rattled with every gust of wind. The ground was thick with dust, the eaves heavy with cobwebs.

"I apologize for the state of the place," the old priest said as Yukiko stepped gingerly over a pile of leaves that had accumulated on the shrine's doorstep. "We had planned to clean it out earlier. But as you might expect, the oni's appearance put a pause on those plans."

Behind him Nori fetched a broom and began to sweep at the accumulated leaves. Strange, Yukiko reflected, how he and his uncle had switched roles ever since their encounter with the ashigaru. Isukiri now spoke easily to her, while Nori had fallen totally silent—ashamed, no doubt.

"It's no trouble." Yukiko looked around the shrine's interior. It was a modest building, not much larger than a small farmhouse, dominated by the shintai altar at its center. On it sat a white marble statue of a serene woman surrounded by tall wax candles. She sat cross-legged, cradling an infant child in her lap. Her eyes were closed in contemplation or prayer, but the child's were wide open.

"Jibo Kannon," Isukiri said, following Yukiko's gaze. "A renowned bodhisattva."

"The compassionate mother." Yukiko nodded, eyes fixed on the statue. There was a strangely lifelike quality to the cold marble. Something in the way the woman cradled the infant to her, in how the babe's pudgy hand rested atop hers. Yukiko remembered how it felt to hold a child that way.

"Are you a mother, Okabe-san?" Isukiri asked quietly.

"No," she said. *Not anymore,* she thought.

Yukiko shook her head, fighting down the sudden lump that had risen in her throat. She stepped closer to the statue, to both examine it more closely and hide her shining eyes from the old priest.

"Kannon was not the first shintai housed in this shrine," she said, turning back to Isukiri. "Was she?"

Isukiri's eyebrows lifted. "How could you tell?"

Yukiko knelt and pressed her hand against the wooden floor. When she raised it, her palm came away coated in dust.

"Kannon is clean," she said. "Nothing else in this shrine is."

Isukiri chuckled. "Your eyes are sharp indeed, Okabe-san. You are correct. This shrine was formerly a home to a kami that dwelt in this mountain."

"One you replaced with her," Yukiko said, waving at Kannon. "I think I understand the cause of your haunting, Isukiri-san."

The priest's eyes went flat. Behind him, Nori stopped sweeping, glancing from his uncle to the swords at Yukiko's side.

Outside, the sun had sunk below the mountains, casting the shrine into their long shadow. Yukiko produced a tinderbox and matches from her kimono and began to light the candles surrounding the statue of Kannon.

"Your yōkai," she said, watching the flames dance and flicker. "It is the shrine's kami, angered that you have rejected it for another."

Isukiri made a disgruntled sound in his throat, but his nephew spoke before he could.

"How do we appease it?" Nori asked, clutching the broom to his chest in shaking hands.

Yuikio rubbed at her chin. "It has been provoked to rage by its shrine being given to another. If Kannon's shintai were removed—"

"No." Isukiri's voice cut through the gloom like a knife. "We will not do that, Yukiko-san. Not under any circumstance."

Yukiko's back stiffened as she lit the last candle. She had expected resistance on this point, but the old priest's vehemence was surprising even so. "You won't be persuaded?"

"No," Isukiri said curtly. "This shrine is to be dedicated to Jibo Kannon and no other. I would give my life to ensure it remains so."

"Uncle," Nori said, tugging at the old priest's sleeve. "Don't—"

"Very well." Yukiko nodded. Nori's mouth dropped open, and Isukiri's brows lifted in surprise. Neither had expected her to acquiesce so quickly.

"You hired me to deal with your haunting," she continued, feeling that she owed them an explanation. "I took your coin and gave my word, so I will do as I was hired. But if you will not remove the shintai to Kannon, our options are limited. Understand?"

Both men nodded.

"The spirit will remain angry," she said, "and so there is no chance of pacifying it. We must allow it to reveal itself and drive it away once it does." Her hand rested on her wakizashi, thumb tracing a circle around its pommel. "By force, if need be."

Nori paled, but Isukiri nodded. His rheumy eyes glimmered in the candlelight.

"We must cleanse the shrine." Yukiko knelt to rummage through her traveling pack. "Physically and spiritually, as best we can in the little time remaining to us."

Nori had said that the yōkai appeared each night at the Hour of the Dog, not long after sundown. Judging from the dwindling sun, they had less than an hour to prepare for its arrival. She produced several sticks of incense and handed them to Isukiri. "Incense and prayer will help cleanse the air of spiritual contamination, weakening the yōkai—"

"The oni," Isukiri corrected, frowning as he took the incense. "I suppose you want me to chant a prayer when it appears?"

"Sooner." Yukiko wondered again at his insistence that the shrine was haunted by an oni rather than some other disgruntled spirit. "I would begin immediately. Any prayer will do."

"What should I do?" Nori asked, his eyes darting nervously around the ceiling, as though he expected the yōkai to appear among the shadowed rafters at any moment.

"Keep cleaning," she said, pointing at the broom in his hand. "It will help purify the shrine."

And, she thought, *it will keep me from tripping over these damned leaves when it comes time to draw steel.*

ഇരു

The wooden walls rattled like bones as the night wind howled outside. Tall shadows danced around the room, cast by the candleflames as they flickered and swayed. The lit incense sticks lent a fragrant heaviness to the air, and Yukiko found herself fighting to keep awake and alert after their long climb up the mountain.

She knelt before the altar, gazing steadily up at Kannon and her babe. The candlelight danced and flickered on the bodhisattva's face.

Nori and Isukiri knelt behind her, nearer to the shrine entrance. The old man's voice rose and fell in a steady rhythm, and though the prayer was not one Yukiko was familiar with, its words were a comfort nonetheless.

"Okabe-san?" Nori asked, his voice near a whisper. Yukiko could barely hear him over the chanted prayer, the rattling walls, the howling wind.

"Yes?"

"Will we survive this night, do you think?"

Yukiko glanced down at her swords lying on the floor beside her, carefully placed so that she could draw them and strike in a single blow.

"No one knows what the dawn may bring," she murmured. "I do not know what sort of creature we face, Nori-san. I cannot measure myself against that which I do not know."

"But you have driven out yūrei before, haven't you?" Nori pressed. "And battled oni, if the stories are true."

Yukiko shut her eyes, but the candleflames still danced before her. They grew to great pillars of fire, a vast conflagration roaring and consuming all it touched.

A face appeared in the flames, a hideous grinning visage with rust-red skin and horns protruding from its brow. No; not a face, but a war mask, one of the terrifying menpō worn by high-ranking samurai.

The general with the oni mask, Yukiko thought, and the mangled grief and rage that rose in her howled like the wind through the mountains. The flames roared in answer, and in her mind the man behind the oni mask laughed, deep and cruel.

And beneath it all, the sound of a little girl crying.

Izumi…

"Hai," Yukiko murmured, opening her eyes. Kannon's babe stared serenely down at her. "I have crossed blades with an oni before."

She glanced over her shoulder at Nori, noting the way his hands shook around his broom, now clasped against his shoulder like a soldier's spear. "What is your fear, Nori-san? Dying is not the worst thing, you know."

Again, the sound of a little girl's terrified wails rose in Yukiko's memory. There were far worse things than dying, indeed.

Nori did not answer for a moment. Isukiri's prayer fell to a lower register, and for a moment the only sound was the restless howling wind.

"I suppose you think me a great coward," Nori said at last. "But... please understand. I do not fear for myself, but for my family. My wife, back in the village..."

He swallowed, loudly enough to be heard over the insistent howling of the wind. "She is pregnant with our first child. If anything should happen to me, or to my uncle..."

"Nori-san," Yukiko said, peering over her shoulder to face him. "I cannot say what will happen here tonight. It might be that the yōkai, or oni, or whatever it might be, is more than a match for the three of us, and we shall all perish this night."

Nori whimpered and clutched the broom tighter.

"But know this." Yukiko raised her voice a little as the wind's moaning rose to a mournful *yooo*. "I have promised you and your uncle that I would free this shrine from that which haunts it. I took your coin, and so the oath was sealed. My honor is bound to you, and to this shrine, until the task is fulfilled. If anyone is to die this night, I shall be the first."

"Hai." Nori nodded. His face was still pale, but his hands had ceased their shaking.

"If it's any comfort," Yukiko said, "I have been a ronin for seven or eight years now, and I have not died yet."

She reached down, resting her hand lightly on the handle of her wakizashi. A rare genuine smile crossed Okabe Yukiko's lips. "Have faith, Nori-san."

He returned the smile. "I will try. Thank you, Okabe-san."

They fell silent, save only for Isukiri's chanting and the murmuring wind. *Yoooo...*

"My uncle's right, you know," Nori murmured as the old man's praying fell into a slower cadence. "It is a powerful oni. It speaks things that should not be spoken. Knows things that no man can know—"

Yukiko held up her hand, curling her fingers into a fist. Nori fell abruptly silent as the gaunt ronin looked about, looking like a lean wolf that has just caught a scent.

Yoooo, the wind murmured. Yukiko strained her ears, listening with every fiber of her being.

Yooooo...

Yooookiko...

She rose to her feet in a single breath, candlelight flickering on cold steel as she drew her katana in the same motion. Behind her the steady rhythm of Isukiri's prayer faltered.

"Don't stop," Yukiko hissed at him. "No matter what, keep praying."

Isukiri resumed his prayer. Beside him, Nori clutched his broomstick. Yukiko's eyes scanned the shadowy rafters, searching for the malignant entity.

"We know you're here," she said, raising her voice. "Show yourself, spirit."

A high, chittering laugh echoed from somewhere overhead. A voice like the rasping wind followed it. "Why would I do that, Yukiko? Why, when you all look so funny from up here?"

"It's a rude host who hides from his guests," Yukiko said, her voice calm and even. "Reveal yourself."

"You are no guests of mine," the unseen yōkai snapped, its laughter suddenly gone. "These men are thieves in the night, come to rob my very house from me. And you, Okabe Yukiko?"

It laughed again, and this time Yukiko caught a glimpse of a shadow scurrying along the rafters like an oversized squirrel. She raised her katana, but it had already vanished into the gloom.

"You are a poor excuse for a yojimbo," the creature cackled. "What good is a bodyguard who leaves her own child to die?"

Behind her, Nori gasped. A sickening wave of grief roiled through Yukiko's belly as the memory of smoke and flame and her daughter's screams rose again through the incense and candlelight.

That was long ago, she reminded herself, her grip tightening on her katana. *This is now.*

"This is not your home any longer," she said as the candles danced and guttered around Kannon and her child. "Now it belongs to another. Leave it in peace, creature."

"Ah yes," the yōkai jeered, and this time Yukiko caught a flash of yellow eyes glimmering in the shadows before it faded out of sight. "The priest of Kannon. Not only a thief, but a liar too. Isn't that right, Isukiri?"

Isukiri's chanting did not cease, but his brows furrowed together in a scowl. Nori whimpered.

"How do you mean?" Yukiko asked before she could stop herself. *You're playing into the thing's hands.*

A scuttling sound from overhead, and suddenly those yellow eyes were directly over Yukiko. Shadows still clung to it, but its shape was something like a monkey or a small child.

"Don't," Nori moaned. Out of the corner of her eye Yukiko saw him standing with his back pressed to the wall, holding the broomstick out before him like a sword in shaking hands. "Don't tell her, please—"

"That," the yellow-eyed shadow said, jabbing a spindly red finger at the statue below it, "is not Kannon."

Yukiko's heart skipped a beat as the pieces fell together. The crucified men beside the road, one of them a gaijin priest. The sentries demanding travelers stomp upon the icon of the crucified god, and Nori's reluctance to do so.

She looked slowly at the white marble statue of the mother and child, then back at the two men. She felt foolish for not realizing it sooner.

"You're Kirishitan," she said.

Isukiri tilted his chin to her, his eyes full of challenge. He continued to pray, but now Yukiko realized what was different about his prayer. It spoke not of enlightenment of the self or veneration of the ancestors, but of one spirit over all the others, of sin and death. A Kirishitan prayer translated into their own tongue.

"The old man is," the yōkai cackled. "Converted and baptized in the name of their dead god. A true believer, unlike his nephew."

"That's not true," Nori whimpered. His eyes were wide and wild, giving him the look of a hunted animal. "I... they baptized me—"

"Yes," the yōkai hissed, vicious pleasure dripping from every word it spoke. "You let them bathe you in their holy water, but only because you feared the flames of their Hell more than you loved their god."

The shadow clambered across the rafters, and for the first time Yukiko glimpsed its face: round and ugly, with beet-red skin and a too-wide mouth. A stubby yellow horn rose from its forehead.

An amanojaku. Isukiri had been nearly right. The shrine truly was plagued by a demonic power—though compared with their hulking oni cousins, the amanojaku were smaller and craftier, and all the more dangerous for it.

Yukiko approached slowly, katana held aloft. She knew now what sort of creature she was dealing with. Perched atop the rafters, the amanojaku was too high to attack them, but if Isukiri faltered in his prayer...

The amanojaku crouched on the broad wooden beam, leering down at Nori.

"Not that it matters," it said. Its grin revealed a mouthful of jagged teeth that would have put a shark to shame. "You stomped on his face, so you're damned anyway. You'll burn in the fiery lake, your dear wife crucified—"

"My wife?" Nori said numbly, staring up into its terrible yellow eyes.

"Of course," the amanojaku laughed. It leaned down, clinging to the wooden rafter with clawlike feet. "They saw you hesitate. The guards on the road. They know you live in the village. They'll find out who your wife is, torture her until she confesses..."

Nori put his head into his hands, his shoulders shaking. An ugly sob choked its way free of his throat.

Yukiko crept closer, moving slowly to avoid drawing the amanojaku's attention. Hanging from the beam, it was within reach of her katana. One quick strike was all it would take.

"She gets her heaven, at least," the amanojaku continued, grinning as Nori put his face in his hands and wept. "Though maybe if you run fast enough, you can reach her before they're finished with her. Who knows? If you tell them everything, they might even spare her."

Nori looked up, staring openmouthed at the hideous creature. He looked at Isukiri, then at Yukiko. Naked fear shone in his eyes.

Yukiko shook her head mutely, mouthing *don't*—

Nori turned and fled, out the door and into the night. Isukiri stumbled to his feet, shouting his nephew's name.

The amanojaku struck.

It leapt from the rafter like a pouncing wildcat, claws outstretched. A hungry light blazed in its yellow eyes as it hurtled toward the old priest.

Yukiko acted on instinct, her training and sword forgotten. She rushed forward, shoving Isukiri rudely to the ground. The old man let out a surprised cry of pain as he hit the wooden floor, but Yukiko had no time to check that he wasn't seriously injured. The amanojaku collided with her, clawing and screeching.

She thrashed wildly with her katana, but her strike went wide, and the creature was atop her in an instant. It squatted on her chest, surprisingly heavy for its size. Yukiko raised her forearms to protect her face as it raised its claws. Long yellow nails raked at her, tearing through both kimono and the flesh below. Yukiko bit back a scream as they gouged bloody gashes across her arms.

Candlelight gleamed off the katana as she tried to strike again, but those terrible claws caught her by the wrist and bent it back until the sword clattered to the floor. The amanojaku seized her other arm and forced both her hands away from her face, leering down at her with its terrible toothy grin. It leaned in very close, blasting Yukiko with a hot breath that stank of rotten meat.

"Why struggle?" the amanojaku giggled, high and hysterical. "You'll see your Izumi soon enough."

Its head split in two as it opened its mouth impossibly wide, rows upon rows of snaggleteeth gleaming in the candlelight.

Not like this, Yukiko thought desperately, praying to whatever god might answer. But the creature's grip on her wrists was a vice. *Please, not like this.*

The amanojaku gargled, its hot breath suddenly gone. There was a rattling sound as it released its grip on Yukiko's wrists, clawing at its neck.

Isukiri stood behind it, his prayer beads wrapped around the creature's throat. A vein bulged in the old priest's temple as he strained, choking the amanojaku with what little strength he possessed.

The creature's red face turned purple as it tore at the beads throttling it. Yukiko scrabbled blindly with her free hand, her fingers crawling across the floor towards her sword.

A clattering sound split the night as the amanojaku tore the prayer necklace apart, sending dozens of beads rolling across the wooden floor. Isukiri stumbled back, thrown off balance as it rounded on him, hatred blazing in its yellow eyes. Yukiko's groping hand closed about the hilt of her katana.

The amanojaku sprang towards Isukiri, its talons raised to cut the old priest down.

Yukiko struck. Candlelight glimmered off her blade.

The amanojaku's head went rolling across the floor, its mouth still open wide. Its body swayed, then toppled to the dust.

Yukiko's heart hammered against her chest as she pulled herself to her feet, then bent to help Isukiri up. The old man leaned heavily against her.

"You saved me," he gasped, clutching at her with his gnarled hands.

"I think we saved each other," Yukiko said, glancing at the prayer beads strewn across the floor. "You were right, you know."

Isukiri's brow furrowed. "About what?"

"That it was an oni," Yukiko said. "An amanojaku. A creature that sees the darkest places in a man's heart, that speaks his secret sins aloud. His failures."

"We all have our sins, Yukiko-san," Isukiri murmured, looking down at the creature's corpse. "I am sorry for lying to you."

"Your nephew said you were a priest." Yukiko smiled thinly. "I suppose I am to blame for not inquiring which god you worship."

"Nori," Isukiri breathed. He pulled hard at the sleeve of Yukiko's kimono. "The creature frightened him into going to those guardsmen. If he tells them…"

"You will join the others on crosses of your own," Yukiko finished. She wiped the monster's blood from her katana, sheathing it. "But not if I catch him first."

Isukiri caught her by the kimono sleeve as she made for the door.

"Yukiko," he said, forgoing the honorific -san. "Please. Spare his life. If you can."

Yukiko looked down at the old priest. She nodded, then ran off into the night.

න්ථ

Her wooden sandals clattered along the rocky path as Yukiko raced down the winding mountain road, the night wind whipping her hair back from her face. The moon hung round and nearly full above, lighting the way before her.

She ran with her katana in her hand, safely sheathed in its saya. Yukiko hoped she wouldn't have to kill Nori, but if he told the ashigaru guards the truth of what had transpired this night, she would be crucified alongside the Kirishitan.

You should have known, she chided herself as she rounded a sharp curve in the winding path. *Kannon with her infant. Don't the Kirishitan believe their god was born of a woman?*

And Isukiri's prayer beads. Yukiko had heard that the gaijin priests had brought their own version of the sacred implements with them to aid them in their prayers. And Isukiri had fingered his incessantly, ever since they came across the crucifixions by the roadside.

She rounded another bend in the roadside. The moonlight revealed a shadow ahead of her, scrabbling down the treacherous path on unsteady feet.

"Nori!" Yukiko shouted.

The shadow turned to look over its shoulder. She caught a glimpse of Nori's face, pale with terror, before he turned back around and kept running.

Yukiko cursed and put her head down, picking up pace. Nori had a lead of several minutes, but Yukiko's legs were long and muscular, her body toughened by years of hardship. She ran until her legs burned like fire.

She closed the distance rapidly—but not quickly enough. Ahead in the distance the light of a campfire gleamed. The ashigaru Chirhiro and his companion were vague silhouettes against the flames.

Still running, Nori raised his hands towards the campfire, about to cry out and alert the guards to his presence.

Feet pounding against the trail, Yukiko raised her katana above her head and threw.

The sheathed sword arced through the night, spinning end over end beneath the stars. It hit Nori squarely between the shoulders. He stumbled, tripped, and fell to the dirt without a sound.

There was no movement from the campfire ahead. The guards had not noticed.

Nori was still lying there by the time Yukiko reached him, pausing only to retrieve her fallen sword mid-stride. She stood over him, holding the katana's sheath in one hand and gripping its handle with the other.

"Let's talk, Nori-san," she said softly.

Nori stared up at her, eyes wide. He opened his mouth, taking a deep breath. Steel rasped against sheath, and the tip of Yukiko's katana was at his throat in an instant.

"Don't shout," she said softly. "I promised your uncle I would not kill you unless you forced me to."

Nori gulped, causing a tiny pinprick of blood to well up where the blade touched his throat.

"The crucified men," Yukiko said, glancing towards the valley below. "You knew them?"

"Hai," Nori gasped, his voice ragged. "Two were our neighbors, fellow farmers. Another was the village miller. All Kirishitan, like us."

"And the gaijin?"

"The priest who baptized us," Nori said. Moonlight glistened in his eyes, suddenly wet with tears. "We had sent for him a week ago, to come and exorcise the yōkai from the shrine. I... it's my fault he died, Okabe-san. Another sin on my hands."

"You can travel the length and breadth of the land," Yukiko murmured, recalling something she had told her daughter once, long ago in another lifetime. "From sea to sea, mountain to valley. But nowhere will you find a man with clean hands."

She looked down at Nori, lying very still beneath her sword. "I'm going to let you stand, Nori-san. Shout or run, and I cut you down. Understand?"

"Hai."

Yukiko removed her katana from his throat but did not sheathe it. Nori clambered unsteadily to his feet, wiping the dirt from his knees.

"Let's return to your uncle," Yukiko said, taking him by the arm. Nori did not resist as she began to march him up the road, back towards the shrine.

"My wife," Nori murmured, wiping at his face with his sleeve. "The yōkai..."

"Lied to you," Yukiko said. "Your wife is at home, sleeping soundly. Tomorrow you will go back down this mountain and see her."

"But the soldiers—"

"Have no interest in you or your family," Yukiko said firmly. She turned and pointed at the firelight, and the two men silhouetted against it. "They saw us stomp on your god. You fooled them, Nori. The amanojaku lied to you. That is what it does. It feeds on the weakness of our hearts."

Nori was quiet for a moment.

"It's dead, by the way," Yukiko said. "I killed it. Your uncle helped."

"Isukiri?" Nori looked at her, surprise written across his face. "Truly?"

"He is a brave man."

They trudged up the mountainside in silence beneath the stars. The shrine loomed ahead and above them, the candlelight spilling out its entrance and into the night.

"I am not," Nori said at last. Yukiko looked at him.

"Brave, I mean," he continued. "You saw tonight. I feared damnation, so I became Kirishitan. Out of fear for my wife I betrayed my uncle and faith both."

He bowed his head, shoulders slumping as if beneath a great weight. "We are not the only Kirishitan in Hizen, Okabe-san. Had I confessed to the soldiers, I would have given up others. There would be a score of crosses lining the road."

"Nori-san," Yukiko said, her voice gentle. "Listen to me. You are guilty of nothing save cowardice. You have done no lasting harm."

Nori frowned at her. "But the priest—"

"Came to Hizen of his own volition," Yukiko said, "knowing Lord Ryūzōji's policy towards his faith. He walked to his death knowingly, and bravely. To try and help you."

She put a hand on his shoulder. "Take his example to heart, Nori-san. If he drew such courage from his faith, you can as well."

"I…" Nori swallowed, looking up at the shrine. They were close enough to see Isukiri standing framed in the door, his old voice rising and falling in a prayer of thanksgiving. "I don't know, Okabe-san."

"Listen," Yukiko said. "Your uncle's prayer was strange to me. But he sang of death, and rebirth, and redemption. New life, free of sin. That is a cornerstone of your faith, isn't it?"

"Hai."

"Then come," Yukiko said as they approached the shrine. "Come and pray with your uncle, and begin your new life. Not everyone gets that chance."

Nori looked at her. He nodded slowly, then walked past her and into the shrine.

Yukiko watched from outside as Nori embraced his uncle. They spoke no words, but stood there for a long time. Then they turned and knelt, bowing before the shintai. Their infant god and his mother smiled down at the Kirishitan as they began to pray.

Yukiko remained outside, in the shadows beyond the candlelight. The wind tugged at her hair, and she pulled her kimono tight about her shoulders.

I have died once already, she thought, remembering the smoke and flame of her burning home. Remembering her daughter's helpless cries. *But my new life is still heavy with sin and grief.*

The oni mask rose in her memory, lit by flame. He was still out there, somewhere: the general in the oni mask who had burned her home and taken her daughter from her. Yukiko did not know his name, or who he served. But one day they would cross swords. She had sworn it on Izumi's grave.

Her hand fell to the hilt of her katana.

Okabe Yukiko turned her back on the house of worship and stalked into the night, in search of her own redemption.

ഔⓂ℞

Marshall J. Moore is the author of the *Rites of Resurrection* trilogy of high fantasy novels, the *Son of a Sailor* pirate cozy fantasy trilogy, and the children's book *Postcards from a Lake Monster*. He has also written over thirty short stories appearing in publications such as *CatsCast, Mysterion, Flame Tree*, and many others. His Okabe Yukiko short story "Red Lanterns" won Second Place in the 2022 Baen Fantasy Adventure Award Short Story Contest, and he has spoken as a guest on panels for conventions, including the Nebula Conference, DragonCon, and Apollycon.

You can find Marshall online at his website www.marshalljmoore.com, as well as on TikTok and Instagram under the handle @marshalljmooreauthor, or on Blue Sky at @marshalljmoore.

He is represented by Brent Taylor at Triada US.

An Exchange of Values, Conducted in Good Faith

David Tallerman

DANIEL TOOK THE four-by-four as far as it would go, to the point where what had been cracked tarmac and then become dirt track petered out into a sunken footpath between high banks. The wheels were spinning and slipping, and he wondered if he'd be able to reverse out. The main highway seemed very distant, and even that had been only a narrow, single-laned serpent chasing recklessly over the hilltops.

He took his wellingtons from the back seat, swapped his shoes for them, and trudged round to the boot. Drawing out his rucksack, he shrugged his shoulders into the straps with a grunt. Though he'd packed judiciously, it might as well have been full of lead. And the rucksack contained barely a third of the belongings he'd brought. Six months was a long time.

The rest he'd come back for. He merely took the map, in its plastic case, and passed a moment in getting his bearings: from this spot, he was close, but the intervening contour lines bunched worryingly.

Daniel sighed. A good job he'd spent those years as a Scout leader; a good job he was comfortable outdoors, that he was fit and healthy. All reasons they'd chosen him, no doubt. *But*, an insidious voice proposed, *perhaps not the main reasons*. His eyes drifted to the sky, which was as solidly grey and sombre as the ceiling of a medieval cathedral. And as much as he tried to assure himself this wasn't a punishment, he didn't succeed.

He locked the four-by-four, an act of caution that felt exceedingly pointless, and set off. After a few dozen metres, a stile appeared on his left, and the red line drawn on his map advised him that was the way onward,

329

though what lay beyond was more a streak of dirt slicing the short-cropped grass than any sort of trail. As the contour lines implied, the slope rose steeply; soon he was sweating profusely, despite the drizzle that had begun to fall.

When he cleared the brow of the incline, he assumed he'd see it. How could a building be hidden here, upon so barren a landscape? Yet there were only the folds of the moorland, ragged with grey-green heather, stained with birthmarks of peat, and riven by trickling streams. Nearby, a crowd of black-faced sheep stared back with loathing. When he waved apologetically, they complained among themselves and their glares grew, if anything, more hostile.

He checked the map, though he was confident he'd come the right way. And for an instant, he fought the feeling that this wasn't just a punishment but also a cruel joke. Could he have offended the bishop so badly? Were innovative ideas and a fresh approach really such heinous crimes? Yet he'd known all along the fine line he trod: the young liberal in an organisation that, no matter its good intentions, remained deeply conservative at heart. For all that he loved that heart, he'd known the only way to protect it was to break it into a new and more resilient shape.

Or so he'd told himself. In darker moments, he'd questioned whether he wasn't simply trying to reconcile the conflicting parts of his personality. At any rate, he'd never expected his ideas to be met without opposition. But this? This he hadn't anticipated, even on his most sleepless nights.

The trace of a path here was more fitted for those glowering sheep than for people, but he followed it because that was where the map insisted he go. The rain was getting heavier, penetrating his waterproof jacket at neck and sleeves. He hunched over and trudged, as the drops bounced from the fabric of his second skin.

And suddenly, there it was. He hadn't predicted the dip; rain had been driving into his eyes, leaving him half blind. Abruptly, the moorland sheered away, to rise once more in the near distance, and at its lowest level was what he briefly misjudged to be a heap of stones, then acknowledged as a building, and then, recognising the cruciform gap above the door, understood at last to be a church.

No, not a church. *His* church. For the next six months, anyway.

He began the descent. He'd arrived on the steepest edge, and it took all his effort to keep from being sent tumbling by the weight of the backpack. The ground was hollowed like an eggshell cut lengthways, and the church was toward the rear of that oval depression, at its widest point, so that although the bowl was comparatively small, the building still managed to look tiny and isolated.

Of course, it really was tiny by any meaningful comparison. And there were actually three structures, which revealed themselves as his angle of view shifted. The main one, divided into two portions, was a rectangle appended to a blocky square, beneath tiles he took to be sheets of slate. Behind and to the side were outbuildings, the leftmost presumably a store and the other, he decided ruefully, an outside toilet.

There was no lock on the main door. It opened with a despondent creak. The space beyond was sufficient for twelve cramped pews, split six to a side, each long enough for four persons a piece if they didn't mind a degree of intimacy. That meant his new congregation would number no more than forty-eight.

The key he'd been given opened a second, narrower door at the back, which let onto the living area. One wall was given over to a simple kitchen, with a cooker, fridge, and freezer, and even, to his astonishment, a microwave. A table with a single wooden chair occupied the centre of the room. In a corner, an armchair sat before a television set of the old cathode ray type, with an ancient video player beneath. A number of tatty tapes were piled on shelves, along with paperback books and, bizarrely, sets of chess and scrabble. The bedroom, such as it was, consisted of a sort of mezzanine, a protruding platform tucked into the roof cavity and reached by a ladder.

There was also a window and another door, so that he wouldn't have to tramp through the nave every time he wanted to go out to the toilet: a minor act of mercy. Less humane were the uninsulated stone walls, which would turn the room into an icebox in winter; even now, in late summer, the foul weather had left the air distinctly cool.

All the same, the place had a certain charm. Daniel slipped off his pack, collapsed into the armchair, and let out the groan he'd been holding for two weeks, ever since the bishop first contacted him with this so-called opportunity. *A special mission for a special kind of priest.* At the remembered words, he struggled to suppress a chuckle, because now this seemed more than anything funny.

Perhaps he truly was being punished, or hidden away where he could do no harm. Nevertheless, it *was* funny, this church in the middle of nowhere—and the notion that someone might believe this would break his spirit. Surely the bishop of all people should understand that couldn't be done, since his spirit didn't belong to either of them. It was God's, to reward, to test, to torment, to squeeze into a ball and play tennis with for all Daniel cared. If his ideas might be deemed unconventional on some subjects, on this he was as old-fashioned as Methuselah: he belonged to his maker, body and soul. And if here was where his maker wanted him, he'd make the best of it, come what may.

Daniel dithered over whether to continue familiarising himself with his home-to-be or to return for the rest of his belongings. But when he looked out via the second door, he discovered the shower had become a downpour, and the sky was black in every direction. There was nothing in the four-by-four he couldn't survive without for a night, so instead he dashed to inspect the larger of the two outbuildings. As he'd surmised, it was a store, primarily for neatly stacked firewood, but it also housed a small petrol generator, which answered one mystery.

Back in the living area, he came upon a folder filled with photocopied sheets and instruction manuals. The uppermost page was a note torn from an A4 file that read simply, *Good luck!* Beneath were guidelines for keeping the generator fuelled and other matters of essential upkeep. They went into quite alarming amounts of detail, and curiously, that was what made the knowledge he was on his own begin to sink in. Oh, he might hope his parishioners would offer advice and assistance, and there was nothing to stop him driving into the nearest town except the two-hour round trip. Nonetheless, divine presences and antisocial sheep aside, he was altogether by himself.

He'd brought food, but as it happened, there were extraordinary quantities of canned goods in the cupboards. Though it was only mid-afternoon, he made a start on a meal: it seemed a suitable way to break down the barrier of strangeness between him and this tiny cottage in the middle of nowhere. After he'd eaten, he washed his plate and unpacked, considered once more a trek back to the four-by-four, and instead took out his laptop and opened a blank document. Today was Friday. Sunday would be his first sermon. He'd written notes, but none that felt like they'd coalesce into anything of substance. The truth was, he'd been so uncertain of what to expect that his every conception had floundered.

Now, his mind was marginally clearer. He had his hook, anyhow. He would talk about isolation, and about community. What better subject could there be when he was on the verge of inserting himself into these peoples' lives? He scribbled *Acts 2:42-46* and heard the words in his head: *And all that believed were together, and had all things common.* From there, he could discuss loneliness, and how ultimately none of them were alone, and he could joke about his own circumstances. Yes, he saw the shape of it, and he could pad out that outline over the course of tomorrow.

By that time, the sky was dark outside the single window, and the only light was the orange glow of the single dusty bulb. It was early evening, but he was tired from the long drive and his hike across the moorlands and from the anxieties of the last days, which now seemed equal parts reasonable and absurd.

Daniel hauled his sleeping bag up to the mezzanine, flung it over the mattress there, climbed down to flick the light switch, and navigated back using the torch on his phone. Once in the bag, he listened to the sounds of his new home: the constant low howl of the wind and the patter of rain and the creaking of timbers and the occasional screech of a hunting bird.

He closed his eyes. *Six months*, he thought, and was surprised by how little alarm he felt.

Sleep found him.

ಓಬ

It had rained through the night, and the result was a painfully blue sky, a strong odour of peat on the air, and a thrilling aura of freshness and vitality that he registered in his very blood.

He ate breakfast and set out. Reaching the four-by-four, he reversed down the track, to where the way was sufficiently wide that another vehicle would be able to pass should it need to. He loaded up his rucksack, and, between that and his two hands, managed to carry everything he'd originally left behind. He returned to the church at an amble, pausing to wave at the crowd of sheep as he went by. They weren't impressed, but he would wear them down. This wasn't the first time he'd had unwelcoming parishioners.

Back at the church, he spent half an hour unpacking and arranging his belongings. The effect was minimal and imposed no hint of character. Maybe next week he'd drive into town and buy himself a housewarming gift: a potted plant, a calendar, an ornament. Then again, perhaps it was better to concede that he was merely passing through. And mightn't that be viewed as more reason to give his all? The only place he truly needed to make his presence felt was in the pulpit.

Therefore, he went back out, picked a spot where the night's rain had dried, and set to work. He'd always felt nearer to God outside than in; even as a child, before he'd found his faith, a cloudless sky had filled him with a profound sense of the numinous. Man was a trivial thing in the end, a fleck in the cosmos—but one beloved above angels.

A nice line. Maybe he could use it; he scrawled it down in case. Probably a bit heavy for introductions, though. If only he had a better idea of his audience. He was conscious that his imaginings were absurd: when he pictured tomorrow, he saw raggedy shepherdesses and red-faced farmers, like some scene from a Constable painting. But then, who *would* frequent a church all the way out here?

Nobody, he told himself, *that's who.*

He strived to assure himself that the Church did not play cruel jokes. If this place remained open, that meant someone, somewhere, relied on it doing so. He read over the notes he'd made the evening before and set to concocting a few jokes that might break the ice. He wouldn't hide his trepidation or his fanciful imagination. Instead, he'd hold them up for laughter. And once they'd laughed enough, he could work toward more serious points.

Staring upward into the blue arch of the sky, Daniel felt the tininess of his existence, the insignificance of his miniscule life—and that, whatever he was doing here, this was precisely where he was supposed to be.

℘℃℞

When he woke the next morning, he realised he hadn't a clue when the regular service was scheduled for.

He dragged himself from his sleeping bag, stumbled down the ladder, and took up the folder of useful information from where he'd left it on the table. But having flicked through once and then again to be certain, he found no answers. Indeed, there were no references to spiritual matters of any sort: the folder's contents were resolutely grounded in the mundane.

At quarter to nine, he went through to the church. He considered sitting on one of the pews and continued outside instead. The day was dry, though the skies weren't so clear as yesterday's. Due to the church's location, he wouldn't be able to see anyone approaching until they broke the brow of the ridge. He could only stare, cupping his eyes with a hand.

Nine o'clock came and went. At twenty minutes past, he went inside and made himself a cup of coffee, which he took back outside and sipped. It helped to balance the slight nip in the air but did his nerves no favours. By ten, he was wound tight as a spring. He wished, absurdly, that there was a doorbell. *Please ring for sermon.* The idea should have been amusing and wasn't.

By eleven, he was pacing back and forth. Ten minutes later, he decided to make a recce to the top of the slope, though he felt faintly absurd trudging through the heather in his choir dress. Upon the higher ground, he could see no one and nothing, except for the ever-present sheep, who hardly acknowledged him.

He went back down to the church. Afternoon services weren't unknown, of course, and who could say what unorthodox rules a community such as this might have? It was his job to accommodate them and not the other way around. Perhaps he ought to have spent a portion of yesterday canvassing his neighbours, supposing he could find them. He determined he'd do so tomorrow.

Nevertheless, planning wasn't enough to keep away despondency. He milled about. He tried to pray, and the little church felt emptier than at any point since his arrival. He drank too much coffee, and sometimes walked up to the moorland and peered into the distance, not able to resist the hope that a head would bob over the horizon. The day wore on. Evening came.

It struck Daniel that he hadn't eaten. He wasn't hungry, but he prepared a simple meal anyway. His desolation had become a sort of numbness, which he insisted to himself would pass. He'd find his courage again on the morrow. He wouldn't be broken by this, though he might feel broken. He'd rise to the challenge. But not tonight.

He heard a creak of old hinges, a shudder of ancient wood. The church door.

Anticipation was followed by fear. He was, after all, alone here, far from any aid. Suppressing both reactions, he jolted to his feet and checked that no portion of his dinner had ended up on his cassock. Satisfied, he smoothed the fabric with the flat of his hand and hurried to the intervening door. He drew a deep breath, turned the handle, and stepped through.

Into darkness. The church was unlit and, now that he considered, wasn't even connected to the electrics and the generator. The only illumination came from behind him, and from the entrance, which he saw as a skewed rectangle barely lighter than the surrounding walls.

The wind, he thought. *You left the door unfastened and the wind caught it, that's all.* Yet the day had been heavy and breezeless, and had it not, he'd already noticed this dip had its own ecosystem, one largely immune to the moorland's wildness.

He heard a fluttering, like the shiver of gauzy fabric. Before it had subsided, he was also reminded of a wasp or some larger insect: a moth, maybe, battering heavy wings upon a lampshade. From the corner of his eye, he caught a last tremor of movement, which subsided into stillness and ambiguity. Was there a shape there, high as his hand, propped on the spine of the third pew? A bird, perhaps? Or a bat—did bats stand upright?

Whatever it was, its gaze was on him.

There was a second, farther back. He marked it as it hopped between spots. They were keeping to the shadows, but now he was overwhelmingly sure there were others as well, a dozen or more. He could feel their presence and was irrationally certain they were allowing him to do so.

The fluttering ceased. In the subsequent quiet, voices whispered. He was aware of a pressure—of expectation, he felt. He sensed indignation and couldn't quite persuade himself he was imagining it.

He was still holding his sermon, he realised. In the diminished light from the room behind, the hand-written sentences were a cryptic scrawl. But he'd read over it often enough today. The passages were burned into his consciousness. And even as he sought for them, the words came to his tongue.

"Welcome, all of you, to this house of the Lord… a remote outpost in his eternal empire if ever there was one. Today we greet each other as strangers. After today, it's my hope that you'll begin to see me as much more than that. For as the good book says…"

℘℃

He had anticipated lying awake, wrestling with his thoughts until the dawn finally came. But in fact, sleep had overtaken him almost immediately.

Likewise, he'd expected to have dismissed the night's mysteries as a result of the strain of recent days, his overworked brain rebelling against the abnormality of his circumstances, and instead, he woke with what was perilously close to acceptance. Yes, he'd been visited last night, and his visitors had listened in the darkness and then had left as subtly as they'd arrived. Perhaps he was mad, but if so, his madness had swayed his rational mind. He'd seen what he'd seen and had no impulse to deny it.

Rather, Daniel found himself planning.

His plans were not those of the previous day. They didn't involve herding up errant parishioners. He understood now that there were no nearby farmers or shepherds waiting for a new priest to occupy an hour or two of their precious Sunday. No, his congregation was far stranger, and therefore so was his duty. He didn't know precisely what was required of him. He knew only that *something* was, and that his notions of punishment had been severely awry. There was a function here to be performed, and he'd never for a moment been driven beyond the bounds of the Church.

What he planned, then, was a strategy, built from fundamentals. He could make no assumptions, though he supposed he'd have to begin with a few: that his words could be followed was among them. However, he saw that his greatest crutch in the past had been a bedrock of shared faith and knowledge. He had of course spoken often with those who didn't share his beliefs, but they didn't commonly attend a Sunday sermon. So—what had brought his nighttime guests? Was it curiosity? Did he amuse them? Was he nothing more in their eyes than a dancing bear cavorting to a nonsensical tune?

He couldn't assume. And he had a week in which to make ready.

℘℃

That evening, after a day that seemed feverish and faintly unreal in retrospect, he wondered suddenly if he should leave a message for his successor—and wondered, too, why no one had before. The answer to both questions was the same: would he have believed, had he not seen for himself? Would a warning have helped? Would sharing his half-formed theories achieve anything except to give the impression a lunatic had lived here?

Yet, looking at the folder, he felt powerfully that he'd been misled by so vast an omission of truth. He might know how to operate the microwave and how to refuel the generator, but he hadn't the faintest idea what to make of—

There his mind refused to go further. He could accept what he'd seen, but only at a mental remove. He was reminded of a poster he'd had as a boy, an incoherent pattern that, beheld in just the right way, revealed a tenuous image of a dolphin scudding through waves. Lose concentration even slightly and you were back to squinting at a garish blur of colours.

Taking up the folder once more, it occurred to him that perhaps it was similar: stare hard enough for long enough and he might identify hints of this second existence, clues left by men who'd experienced what he had and discovered their own means of dealing with it.

Or perhaps not. Yet its precise and comprehensive collection of mundane details made more sense now. The folder, this room, the copious provisions, the antique video player, the board games that would never be played: they were the plain and sturdy vessel in which he was expected to navigate this *terra incognita*, and their very banality was a protection.

ԑՈᏣᏙ

By the next day, Daniel was calmer.

Returning to his notes, he found them mostly gibberish, a series of questions without a trace of a solution. But there was sufficient to be going on with: in his immediate shock and distraction, he'd at least stumbled upon the core of the problem that lay before him. What remained was five days of hammering that lumpish mass into a functional form.

When he wasn't writing, he focused on the minutia of living, a preoccupation made easy by the difficulties of his isolation. He'd already resolved that he wouldn't leave the moors if he could avoid doing so; he would stretch his supplies to their limits. Leaving would risk breaking the mood that held him, as though he'd be stepping through the shimmering edge of a bubble. He didn't know what would happen then, what would be left when he returned.

His sole regret was that he'd no access to research materials. An internet connection and a day's searching of obscure websites might have answered half his queries; a decently stocked library would have accomplished the same in rather more time. Without either, he was obliged to rely on guesswork and supposition. And the more he gave in to those, the wilder his speculations became, so that he was constantly having to rein himself in.

The nearer Sunday drew, the harder he fought. It was an ever-increasing challenge to persuade himself he wasn't delusional. And even if he was wholly sane, how was he to know he'd grasped the situation correctly? Nor was he convinced that the sermon he was preparing could possibly be ready on time. Each paragraph felt like a universe in miniature, concepts nestled inside concepts. In stripping his faith to its first principles, he was flirting with ideas that threatened his perception of everything, with catastrophic blasphemies. It was a struggle even to pray; he couldn't say what he ought to be asking for.

On Saturday, he made a desperate attempt at compiling his notes into a legible form. It seemed to him that he'd wasted the preceding days in idle speculation. He'd been losing himself in abstracts when what he needed was something concrete and practical. He crossed out words with aggressive strokes, and then sentences and whole paragraphs. He told himself he was a priest, not a philosopher and certainly not a poet.

The sun began to set. The results were no more satisfactory. By the time he got up to turn a light on, he understood that they couldn't hope to be. He'd been seeking a single right answer rather than having the nerve to admit there wasn't one. In despair, he polished the remainder, what he hadn't excised in his anger. He ate a rushed meal, dragged himself up to his bed, and fell into troubled sleep.

He woke late, full of agitation. He had to remind himself he wasn't expecting any visitors until nightfall. Nevertheless, he pulled on his choir dress and went through to the church. He was struck by its age, which he'd hardly considered before. The timbers were warped and uneven, the stonework crude. He was no expert, but he could believe the place was Norman. Were there any surviving churches that predated the conquest? If so, he was inclined to accept that he stood in one of them. Had people once attended here, in some distant past? Had there been communities nearby? Or had it always been at the service of—

But even after these intervening days, even knowing his encounter might soon reoccur, he wasn't willing to articulate it. Instead, he sought distractions. He pottered up to the moors and stared into the distance, or at the sky, which was overcast today and spat intermittent rain. He felt full of useless energy, which refused to be exhausted, though at the same time his mind and body both were worn out from the emotional cyclone of the past week.

The sky dimmed. Night fell. Not willing to wait in the church, lest his presence be misinterpreted as some sort of threat, he sat in his armchair with the intervening door open, straining his ears for any noise, unsure if he was more afraid that they would come or that they wouldn't.

He'd left the electric light off, so that what disturbed him was first the realisation that he was sitting in darkness, and then that he'd noticed the darkness because the faintest glow was issuing from the doorway. The radiance was of a pale green shade, and as he became aware of it, Daniel perceived that hummingbird fluttering he recalled, along with other sounds: the delicate jingle of what might be bells, a creaking as of old leather, the patter of feet.

His heart was racing. He got up, as softly as he was able. The light was adequate to see the doorway by, but not what lay beyond. He felt the overwhelming sense of standing on the verge of a precipice. Whatever he did next, whether he dared enter the church or not, there would be no way back. He took a step, and another. The sounds he'd heard were fading to the barest murmur.

In the doorway, he hesitated. So did his visitors—and there was a long moment in which he could have sworn the room was empty after all, so still did they hold themselves. But there were the lanterns, no bigger than snow globes and suspended on poles at what he would regard as waist height, and it was impossible to see them and not look for their owners. A shiver went through him as he spied the figures, small as children and undoubtedly not children, not of his kind at all. Their features were broad and bulbous, their manner of dress earthy and strange, and their lanterns contained not candles but luminous clusters of dancing insects.

Daniel advanced unwillingly, as though his responsibilities were an outside force that manipulated him like a marionette. He saw now that his visitors weren't identical, despite their similar stature. Some were leaner, with more refined features. One had a nose almost the length of its forearm, another ears so jagged that slits had been cut into its peaked cap. And the flying creatures, also, had returned, though they'd already found perches and so were hardest to detect.

The words had dried and shrivelled in his mouth. He needed all his attention to keep hold of his sermon between sweat-slicked fingers. What carried him to the lectern was that same external propulsion as before, and he wondered dimly if this was what it was like to have the divine work through you—or other, less benevolent influences. He cleared his throat, and some of the tiniest visitors stirred anxiously. He compelled himself to breath, and by degrees the sensation of his body being not his own began to pass.

You have a job to do, he told himself. And yes, he'd been sent here for a purpose—for *this* purpose. The servant did not choose where they served, only how.

"Welcome," he said, and his voice was firm. "Welcome, one and all."

₧⁗

Exhausted by tension, weak as a rag doll, he slept soundly that night. It was as if he'd torn loose something vital inside himself and converted it into a tumult of words. He had no idea if they'd been good words, if they'd made the slightest sense, if they'd been the ones he'd intended in the order he'd meant, and still they had cost him dearly.

In the morning, however, he felt rested and well, as after a long fever. He went outside, and the air, moist with the memory of rain, revitalised him further. Inhaling deeply, he looked at the church from the outside, studying its hard lines, marking the points where the ages had left it crooked and strained. He felt at home.

And he had a purpose, even if he didn't altogether understand it. His role was perhaps impossible and yet utterly straightforward. He was to preach. He had no doubt that his congregation would return in another seven days' time, and he must be ready, because he was here and there was no one else. His was the voice in the wilderness, his the shepherd's crook.

Therefore, he had to do better than he ever had before. He'd invariably thought more in terms of vocation than job, but now even that wasn't sufficient. As he worked, a portion of his mind groped for the correct word, and when it came, he realised it had only eluded him because previous generations had tainted its meaning in his eyes. Nevertheless, there could be no question: what he had here was a mission, and that made him a missionary. He had been sent into a land more profoundly, fundamentally pagan than any he could have imagined, there to spread the light of the Lord.

Or so he tried to assure himself. As his fervour cooled, he was forced to acknowledge that the motives of those above him remained obscure. Maybe they were merely following some decrepit tradition; maybe his predecessors truly hadn't dared, or been able, to share what they'd encountered.

He had no shortage of maybes. What he required was an absolute, a rock to hang onto. And he already knew what that would be. He'd always loved the act of crafting sermons, that delicate balance of persuasion and artistry and entertainment and scholarship. He'd longed for a perfect audience, one so jaded as to need convincing yet open-minded enough to heed a message delivered with the utmost conviction. Could he have found that here?

Whatever the case, his sermons would be his focus. He had to refine his arguments, his language, his very self; he had to search his own faith, to apprehend clearly what had opened his eyes and how he might convey that to another—to *the* other. All of this he had to learn if he was to reach his nightly visitors, to keep them, and ultimately, perhaps, to sway them.

℘℘

Week on week, his congregation expanded.

Were his sermons the reason? He'd have liked to believe so, and couldn't quite. He had gone back to fundamentals in a way that would have been inconceivable a month ago, turned to arguments ancient as the Church itself. He'd stripped his language to the bones, striving for clarity above all else. He practised his oration constantly, to the bare stone walls and the pale moorland skies. On the more difficult days, he felt like some mad prophet—and wouldn't madness have been the easiest explanation? But then, faith was never the easy option and wasn't meant to be. He'd decided his course, and now he pushed away doubts as to his sanity with remarkably little effort.

Other doubts weren't so readily quashed. His congregation expanded and he didn't know what brought them. And though there were more each week, the tiny church was never packed. His visitors kept together in huddles, or hid amid the rafters, those that were small and agile enough, and ignored the front pews entirely.

He was unable to judge if he was seeing the same faces; their strangeness defied recognition. Was he getting through to them? Or was he preaching to an ever-shifting audience, each willing to squander a night and no more in satisfying their curiosity? He tried to insist that was what brought them, since curiosity was a gap in which he might insert a wedge through which faith would follow—but as one month vanished into another, he grew less sure.

He couldn't say what nagged at him, only that something did. He felt he had all the pieces of a question that refused to coalesce. Something about the way his visitors came, the way they watched, the way they listened, the way they trooped out, almost invisible and inaudible, into the night—but what?

By the end of the second month, Daniel was no closer to an answer. Maybe he was no longer seeking one. With so little possibility for variation, he'd become defined by routine. He'd been into the nearby town twice for supplies and found each occasion exhausting and excruciatingly loud. He suspected he was suffering from mild agoraphobia and wondered if that should concern him more than it did.

Mostly, he resented time away from his sermons. When he wasn't writing them, he was thinking about them, homing in on an ultimate argument he felt certain must be there. Somehow there must be a means to unearth the core of his faith and reproduce it in a new, infectious form, then to deliver it via the mechanism of perfectly chosen words. It had been done before, or else there'd be no Church today.

Was what held him back that the true fire of his craft had been lost over the centuries, by a religion that had won too many victories and grown complacent? Had the earliest fathers fought battles such as this? Had they succeeded? Or might it rather be the case that his fight was a mere sally in a conflict stretching to the dawn of Christianity, and here he was, naïvely envisaging a triumph that had eluded infinitely better men than him?

℘℧

He felt, that evening, even as the shadows began to lengthen, that something was different. He couldn't stop fidgeting and starting at half-heard noises. His sermon struck him as deeply unsatisfying, but every time he returned to it, he failed to settle on what precisely needed improvement. The words made his eyes ache, his shoulders tense. They were all so insufficient— and meanwhile, the noises that weren't noises continued, out there in the gathering night.

Then he heard a definite sound: the patter of a drum beat, a lonesome, remote pit-pat, pit-pat out of rhythm with his own thundering heart. A pipe joined it, liquid and mournful, and the two kept time together, struggling for dominance—growing louder. Further instruments accompanied them, some that he recognised and some that he didn't. The result could not be called music, yet he had no other description.

He went to the door. Above the hilltop, a silvery light flickered like cold fire, quite separate from the moon, which hung to his left. He thought he detected the tread of feet and hoofs, and imagined horses, before recalling that the notion of hoofed visitors wasn't so outlandish. A shiver descended his spine, and he retreated inside.

First to enter were the congregation with which he'd become familiar: furtive, flitting creatures that propped themselves on the backs of pews or skittered to the rafters and little hominids with coarse features and leathered skin who scowled with beady eyes down the lengths of bulbous noses.

But this night, others followed. Still they kept to the darkness, and yet they strode in purposefully—or, yes, clattered on hoofs and the crooked legs of stags. Some even had antlers sprouting from their heads and had to turn to navigate the doorway. A few were dressed in finery and might have been human, until a glimpse of their features made clear they weren't. And those moved with a certain unmistakeable ceremoniousness, which he could make no sense of—not until the final two entered.

There was a hush, a pause, an impression of many breaths being held. A gust stirred leaves that danced across the opening. Then the pair were in the gap and stepping within, and Daniel's own breath evaporated in his throat and refused to return.

They were a man and a woman. Or rather, he corrected, they had aspects that made them appear male and female. They were pale, ebon-haired, and extraordinarily lovely, every feature perfect, though by any human definition, their pointedness, their sharpness, their hints of wantonness and savagery, should have been strange if not actively horrifying. He calculated by their relation to the doorframe that they were both shorter than him, the male by a foot or so and the female by more. Yet his mind rejected that evidence, insisting they were exceptionally tall; it seemed likelier, in fact, that his eyes were misleading him.

He wanted to shrink from them. Though they'd done nothing, said nothing, he felt he was committing an act of outrageous arrogance to stand above them, indulging the pretence that this place belonged more to him than them. Of course it was theirs, how could it not be? And so were the gathered throng, who'd all gone absolutely still since the moment of their arrival. So were these moors, as they'd been from time immemorial, time before the very concept of time had meaning. So were these lands, by rights ancienter than any king could claim, and—

Daniel stirred with a shudder. He had almost thought, *So am I.* Now, that blasphemy made him sick inside. He wrenched his gaze downward, to the papers in his hands. The words swam and blurred. He tried to clear his throat, and what came out was a ghastly, choking gasp that seemed to him like an apology. He knew he couldn't possibly read what he'd written and thus worsen the insult he'd given simply by being here.

And he knew too that he had to speak, or everything he was and valued would be gone, and though he might breathe and move for another fifty years, the core of him would be dead and lost. He knew that what he'd perceived as his trial had been nothing, a petty preamble to the here and now. However he had failed or succeeded was irrelevant in the face of whether he failed or succeeded in the next minute. And he had to succeed, for much more than himself.

But first, he had to speak.

Daniel cleared his throat again, an awkward hem. He focused all his will on making the sentences before him stop swimming, and to his desperate relief, they did. The silence was crushing in its weight. He spoke solely to fill it, and only when a second had passed did he realise he'd read the opening line. Then he had no choice except to continue. It felt like falling, and he surrendered to that sensation, in the absence of anything else. He fell and fell, dragged down by the weight of his words.

Until he finished. That took him by surprise. His head jolted up, of its own accord. He saw how his visitors stood for an instant more, their reaction merely further, perfect stillness.

Then they began to depart.

The man and woman, of course, were first. The rest went after them in dribs and drabs, and Daniel knew, somehow, that none of them would return. This had been his chance. They'd shown him courtesy; they had tolerated his alien presence, listened to his alien ideas, waited in this alien place while he tried to convince them of truths that were as inimical to them as their existence was to him, and they would not do so again.

In a minute, the last of them was gone. All that remained was the skirling of the pipes, already growing faint, barely distinguishable from the howl of the wind.

He had no desire to follow, and nonetheless he did.

No, that wasn't true. The part of him he viewed as himself, the man of God, the man of reason, wished for nothing more than to slam the door and barricade it and go to whatever limited safety his bed offered, to cower until the dawn. But his body ached to pursue, and his heart throbbed, and an aspect he'd have liked to deny was flooded with longing such as he'd never known.

He wanted answers. He wanted some justification for the last weeks. He wanted to discover where that dwindling flute was leading, what place could give birth to music so sweetly sad. But most of all, he wanted to see those two, to be where they were, to taste the freedom that hung in their wake like smoke.

He scrambled to the rim of the dip, dirtying his clothes and clogging his shoes with mud and not caring. The pipes were clearer there, and a faint glow hung far off in the air. It was easy to keep to their trail, and easy to stay at what felt a respectful distance. They moved as flickering silhouettes across the moorland. The note of the pipes had changed, had lost its melancholy, and the drums had started up again, with a rhythm his feet had to fight to resist; the smallest lapse in concentration made a jig of his steps.

He forced himself to slow. Their destination was in sight: the forerunners, led by the man and woman, were reaching it even now. There was a hill, its contours too regular to be wholly natural, and on its summit bonfires burned, and around those fires figures danced with uninhibited joy. No human bodies could have performed such gyrations, because no human could surrender to anything so utterly. They showed no heed to the new arrivals, who were steadily incorporated into their number, all except the man and woman, who kept apart and moved at their own pace, like swimmers in deep water.

Daniel was closer than he recalled being. He had no memory of how he'd come to be standing on the edge of the hill. The music was frantic. It plucked at his limbs and raced through his veins. There was singing, many voices rising together, and it seemed to him that each pursued their own subtly different tune, that they were incapable of doing otherwise. If he should sing to that music, his tune would also be different, something uniquely his that had been growing in him, eager for this moment.

He couldn't tear his eyes from the man and the woman. Every motion of their courtly waltz through the chaos around them was a beckoning, an offer of what he'd denied himself for a lifetime. Tears stung his cheeks. A sob swelled in his chest. If he were only to let go, he would be free, finally and completely free.

And he would be lost.

He turned and ran.

֍֎

They came for him on the Thursday of the next week: three officials of the Church, none of whom he recognised. One was obviously senior, both in years and rank, and the other two had the air of bodyguards, though both wore clerical collars. They appeared uneasy, and he felt they'd been here before, felt too that they'd be glad to leave.

The older man, who didn't give his name, was kindly in a somewhat gruff fashion. He spoke as an officer might to a young soldier after his first night on guard duty. "Still in one piece, eh? Excellent. You'll be glad to hear you're relieved. Sorry we couldn't give you more warning. Why don't you make a start on getting packed up? We'll wait."

Daniel did as he was told. He moved about the room mechanically, packing his few belongings, mindful of their eyes on him. The process seemed to take a disproportionately long time, though it could only have been minutes. Eventually he said, "I'm ready."

As he locked up—first the door into the chapel, from the inside, then the smaller door of the cottage, from without—he sought for some emotional reaction. This place had been his for weeks, the source of experiences he could scarcely have conceived of. Yet he'd developed no attachment, and no connection was broken as he turned his back. His time here was the fading shadow of a dream.

"I suppose you'll have questions," the older man said from beside him.

345

Yes, Daniel had questions. But mostly they weren't of a sort he expected answers to, and putting them into words would be like trying to nail down smoke. Only one seemed worth the effort of voicing, and then as much because he felt a pressure to respond. "What if I'd succeeded. I mean, what if I'd converted them? Or even just one of them?"

He wasn't sure his interlocutor would understand or that it was appropriate to broach the subject. But Daniel found he didn't care. If his query was met with incomprehension, incredulity, or flat-out mockery, it made no difference to him.

Instead, the man smiled solemnly. "Do you think that's likely?"

He wanted badly to say yes. Then there were the other questions, inevitable in the wake of the first, those he dared not ask. *What if I'd failed? What if they'd converted me?*

"I don't know," Daniel replied, though he did. Though they both did.

They continued in silence. On the road, the three had parked their car ahead of his four-by-four, blocking the track as he had tried not to do. The younger pair climbed in, one getting behind the wheel, the other taking the front passenger seat. The older man offered his hand, and Daniel shook hesitantly.

"Well. Your bishop will fill you in on what happens next." The older man got into the nearside passenger seat. He wound down the window. As the car's engine roused with a growl, he called, "You'll be glad to get back to your life, I'll bet."

The window hissed closed. The car reversed up the ascending track, toward the corner that would steal it from view. Daniel watched them go. He was conscious of the church, out there somewhere behind him. He wanted to look and didn't. But even after he'd unlocked the four-by-four, he hesitated, caught as if by a magnetic pull.

He shook his head. He went round to the boot and threw his rucksack and bags in. He slammed it with more force than was necessary, as though in anger. He went back to the driver's door and climbed in and sat with both hands on the wheel, noticing how his fingers trembled.

He thought again of the barrow, and of the keening pipes and the drumbeat like foreign blood coursing in his veins, and of those beautiful figures, full of unearthly grace. He had measured his will against temptation. How long before he'd have been found wanting? Could he have endured even one more visit? He craved to be certain and knew he never would be—that the doubt was in him forever.

He started the ignition. Certainty: that was the prize they'd taken, deliberately or no. Not his faith but an element of it, which he'd never previously been able to identify. His complacency perhaps. Or perhaps his belief that he couldn't stray from the light of his God because there was nowhere to stray to.

As he at last pulled away, breaking the spell that bound him for that crucial instant, he thought, *Now I know differently*. Hereafter, his faith was a desert island, surrounded by trackless waters. And in those waters, sharks swam.

ഉ᳚Ო

David Tallerman is the author of numerous books: the historical science-fiction drama *To End All Wars*, thrillers *A Savage Generation* and *The Bad Neighbour*, fantasy series *The Black River Chronicles* and *The Tales of Easie Damasco*, and the science-fiction novella *Patchwerk*. His most recent release is *The Outfit*, an account of the true-life Tiflis Bank Robbery and the part played in it by future leader of the Soviet Union Joseph Stalin.

David's comics work includes the absurdist steampunk graphic novel *Endangered Weapon B: Mechanimal Science*, with Bob Molesworth, and his short fiction has appeared in around a hundred markets, among them *Clarkesworld*, *Nightmare*, *Lightspeed*, and *Beneath Ceaseless Skies*. A number of his best dark fantasy stories were gathered together in his debut collection *The Sign in the Moonlight and Other Stories*.

The Inksmith

Katherine Briggs

IN THE SEASIDE town of Goodeword, gossips whispered that Mrs. Helena Walker was an incarnate angel. She must keep her wings in a chest and Heaven's shine in a box, and other foolish prattle. Helena earned this hearsay by hemming her gown sleeves above her elbows and forgoing a bonnet even in sunny weather. Every other woman and man covered themselves and their children in gloves, low-brimmed hats, and high collars to hide the stains marring their skin, while Helena displayed her pale, unflawed arms, neck, and face in public. Only angels boasted such freckles.

Helena considered her virtuous reputation and laughed. She, like everyone else, earned stains.

The fire in the hearth crackled, and Helena remained near its warmth to powder her face and draw pale blue paint against the veins near her temples. Today warranted extravagance. Sails had been spotted against the sea. This would be the last ship to dock before winter's freeze, and it would bring her husband Oziah home after these long weeks. She would meet him when he landed, and she must look perfect. Appear joyful. Embody a charade.

Outside their home, autumn leaves crisped and curled. Helena grasped the silver looking glass passed down by Oziah's grandmother from the old land, an heirloom so valuable and condemning she still feared touching it, and inspected her dress. Three-quarter sleeves of imported linen, no shawl. Her reflection shivered.

The fire popped.

One more glance at their home, tidied the way he liked it, and Helena left to hitch horses to the carriage.

Most of the town lined the generous bay as the ship docked. Helena slipped through the thicket of greatcoats, mittens, and scarves until the crowd recognized her and parted.

Oziah Walker, young master shipwright, disembarked onto the creaking, windswept dock planks. Her husband was not a handsome man, but carried himself with nobleness, like his beloved sea. He saw her.

Her heart no longer jumped like before.

Helena accepted his strong, outstretched hands. Oziah smiled, and delicate arsenic-green markings, suggesting clusters of water hemlock, crinkled in the flesh near his glad eyes. A lesser man would strive to obscure those stains with a hat.

Did he appreciate her appearance? No. Oziah frowned at her gooseflesh, wrapped his wool coat around her shoulders, and helped her into the carriage.

Dense forest meandered past. Oziah sat tall holding the reins, asked after her health and their home.

"Everything is fine." She lied.

Oziah described the delivery of his last ship, one outfitted with several guns. He was known as a skillful shipwright who sailed his own vessels to their new owners as a guarantee of seaworthiness before catching a cargo boat home. His meticulousness in preparations and cost measurements garnered good pay, too.

Upon arrival home, Oziah put the horses away and inspected their property, one built with the same attentiveness he gave his ships. Helena hastened to prepare his favorite supper and hoped he did not notice her weak appetite.

After dinner, she peeked into the bedroom to find the warming pans slipped between their sheets and a candle lit. Oziah poured water from a pitcher into the small tabletop basin and pushed up his sleeves to wash.

Flickering light danced across vines and three-leafed stems, orange like copper, crawling across his sun-roughened forearms. A smudged, storm blue coil circled one wrist, like a deadly sea snake. These stains had appeared before their marriage, and Oziah had confessed their sins to her. The coil materialized after he copied another shipwright apprentice's designs. The leaves around his eyes came from demanding overzealous punishment of a careless sawyer during a ship's construction. That story frightened her now. Beyond these, any new stains would likely be beyond notice.

Helena gritted her teeth. Seeing him again after months away would break her. How could she fear and love him this much?

Oziah dried his face. Above his wrist, the sharp details of a tattoo always caught her attention. Inksmiths were usually paid to disguise stains, but Oziah had insisted that this depiction of a god ascending into the sky be inked onto yet unblemished skin.

Helena hurried to remove the basin and spilled dirty water. Her stomach jumped, but he stooped to sop up the mess. Did not chastise. Then Oziah had her sit on the corner of their bed and kneaded her shoulders.

She flinched, even after his fingers softened.

"Helena, are you well?"

"Yes."

After another moment, he rummaged for a nightshirt and paused. "May I keep the candle lit?" It was more assumption than question. When they married, they pledged to never hide their stains from one another, a practice that Oziah felt increased in importance when he traveled.

Helena folded her trembling hands. "I forgot to visit the candlemaker. There are one or two left, none to waste." Her affected dismay surprised her. She was a poor actress, yet tears stung her eyes.

Oziah frowned again. "I will visit the man when I return to town." He blew out the candle.

She allowed him to enfold her into his arms.

The next day after breakfast, Helena said she had received a letter from her family asking that she come and assist with the birth of her sister's second child. It wasn't true. There was no correspondence, and Helena had no idea how many children her sister had.

Oziah offered to accompany her.

No, she said, she knew her way. Winter preparations needed him here.

Oziah insisted she take the carriage.

The gelding was fine.

Helena dressed in an older gown, the worn bonnet instead of her trimmed hat, and cloak. She wrapped the hand mirror in cloth before packing it along with food. At the last moment, Oziah pressed a bag of coins into her hands, a portion of his recent earnings. The foreign currency would draw attention, but Helena breathed again—this money was why she had endured facing his return. And she hadn't been forced to steal it.

Oziah embraced her, kissed her goodbye. "Be safe."

She could not promise that.

Her hometown of Haerpp lay far enough away for comfort, but close enough for a speedy exchange of slander and scandal. Helena urged her horse on until wattle and daub housing and unruly fields emerged between the thinning, late season forest. The center of the village would hardly look better. There should be an abandoned lean-to nearby, complete with rotting beams, moth-bitten blankets and thick brush to hide her mount from thieves. None of her family or old friends could learn that she was here.

After settling into the shanty, Helena explored on foot.

Through woods melting into the fading afternoon sun, on the east side of Haerpp along the river that fed Goodeword's bay, the carpenter's shop stood, one that hadn't been there during her growing up. It already looked old, but maintained. Strange light enveloped the place and gave her pause. It reminded her of children's spook stories.

A swinging, wooden sign read in carving, "Enoch's Woodwork." Afternoon sunbeams glowed against paper windows.

This Enoch had to be the carpenter her husband spoke so highly of, the first craftsman he used to hire when building a new ship. Ship construction was a deeply religious trade. Some cried out to an all-powerful god and his legion of angels for providence, and others made prayers to the sky for good ocean winds and returns on their ventures. Not Enoch. He led Oziah to faith in the Stainless One, a being both man and god, who never sinned in life. This ancient faith demanded strict standards and offered glorious yet empty promises for its followers, and still Oziah believed. Despite retaining his stains after faith.

Why? Because of Enoch's influence, whom Oziah called his brother and a man liberated from a harrowing past and, shockingly, freed from sins. How was the latter possible? But years ago, Enoch had grasped her husband's hand in farewell and disappeared from Goodeword. Now she had found him, but not for his woodworking. Enoch called himself a carpenter, but Oziah said he was an inksmith first. Her husband had paid the man to tattoo the resurrection image onto his flesh.

Could Enoch possibly be an unstained inksmith? Above all else, he could not learn that she was his disciple's wife.

Helena slipped within the shop and inhaled earthy, nutty scents. It was surprisingly cozy and bright inside. Enoch's work lined shelves and boasted artistry and creativity. Everything was swept of shavings, dusted, and quiet until sonorous song wafted from the back. A hymn.

Helena pulled her shoulders down. "Sir?"

The singing stopped. A towering, grey-bearded man in workman's clothes filled the rear doorway. Though he favored one leg and leaned on a cane, she guessed he could easily best a younger man.

Helena avoided staring at the scar stretching from his chin to his ear or the color of his face. Not only a man supposedly freed from his sins. A freedman.

Yet he bore no visible stains, unless his were easy to hide, like hers.

Enoch inclined his head. "Good evening. Do you want woodworking done?"

"No." She swallowed. "I seek an inksmith."

His mouth turned down. "It's sundown, ma'am."

Meaning that goodwives stayed home past work hours.

Helena flushed.

"Come back tomorrow during lunch, if you like." Enoch tipped his brim and pressed through the doorway into the backroom.

Helena gathered her flustered emotions and fled the workshop. She checked on the gelding and returned to face the chilly night alone in the lean-to. Musty straw, piled, would be her bed. By light from the candle stub she had brought, Helena tucked the looking glass against the wall and undressed to see her stains.

Leaf by branch by bud, sins from childhood and maturity, common and uncommon guilt, colorful and dull, pride, gluttony, sloth, greed: all twined and swirled together, growing until one died of old age as Beelzebub's canvas. The form and extent of a stain was not dictated by the cost of its sin, and so humanity, with its conniving beliefs, became judges of which evils were deadly and which could be pardoned.

She located her recent falsehoods under her left collarbone and clothed herself.

Late the following morning, she stole to the carpentry shop. Let him treat her like refuse again. She must know if he was unstained, and if he could help her.

Inside, sunlight poured over the cleared worktable holding a basket overflowing with bread and hard cheese. Singing swelled from the backroom until straw-hatted, gray-bearded Enoch appeared, cane tapping. He nodded without missing a verse, gestured that she sit, and broke bread.

She blinked.

"It's a gift. My preferred way of undertaking new business," Enoch said and ate. "You seek an inksmith and found one. Most ask me to embellish preexisting markings."

If they discussed the weather, would he speak so frankly?

"Not hungry, ma'am?"

Her tongue refused to work.

Enoch folded powerful arms across his chest. "I can clarify sin stains. Tighten the lines. Reshape unpleasing images. But I cannot conceal a stain. Customers who insist I do this are never satisfied, and now I refuse to degrade myself with such work. Sin always shows."

She knew that more than anyone. Helena failed to repress a tremor.

Enoch's gaze narrowed. "I suggest you visit a seamstress, ma'am."

The most imaginative garment could not help her.

"I assume our business is concluded."

"No." Helena tightened her shawl around her shoulders. "I was told you can wash stains gone. That is what I want. I am prepared to pay upfront." Her fingers trembled as she untied the money pouch and spilled Oziah's pay across the table.

Enoch studied the coins before pinching one between his fingers. His brow knitted. "What is your name?"

She raised her chin. "Are you able to help me?"

Enoch placed the coin atop its brethren and brushed his palms down his shirt. "Few travel far enough to earn these coins." His gaze filled with sorrow. "You're Oziah Walker's wife."

Helena froze. How could he—

"Oziah told me he was pledged to wed a woman whose face, neck, and arms carried no stains. He likened her to an angel."

Her heart beat too fast. She gripped the edge of the table and forced words past clenched teeth. "I know you are a skilled craftsman, and I believe you that stains cannot be masked. My husband said you were freed from your sins. Because of this, he adopted your faith." How could she cling to this hope when her husband's stains still stood? "Oziah calls you brother. If you care about him a fraction of how much I love him, you will help me. Dear God." She couldn't stop shaking.

"Oziah is a good man. I never heard him lie."

She cringed.

"He is right that I am freed from sin. And it cost me everything."

Her stomach tightened. Were Enoch's stains really removed? Did she have enough coin?

"But I can't help you, Mrs. Walker." Enoch heaved a sigh. "Some stains won't be cleansed."

Like hers? She stiffened. Did he guess what she had done? Her voice came harsh, and she pushed the coins toward him. "How much for your silence?"

Enoch hesitated. "Gossip is sin. So is lying. I do my best to avoid both."

She sucked in a breath, pursed her lips, and left.

In the lean-to atop her bed of straw, Helena lit the last of her candle and undressed to her shift. Chills shivered across her skin.

The mirror glimmered against the wall.

Helena bit her lip until she tasted blood and lifted her hem.

Elderberry purple stains reminiscent of foxglove twisted up her ankles and calves. Across her thighs and hips, still life beetles crept among bell-shaped flowers. These were not new. But a delicate, vermillion vine now climbed from her navel up her stomach, and circled her left breast before reaching toward her sternum. It was exotic, with leaves like arrows, heavy with clustered berries. The evocation of nightshade.

The fruit had multiplied.

Helena sank to her knees and covered her face.

Like every stain, this sin had progressed in an unhurried and sure manner. The one she once trusted as a childhood friend grown from the same weeds and poverty as she, whose wretched stains she'd seen and now loathed, turned traitor and held the power to demand bribes she could not pay. How could she, a married woman, have given herself to him? His hiss that she'd married up and could afford his price—twisting a blade into the gaping cavern already gnawing inside of her—still slithered in her ears. Had she not sworn that she had given him all her earthly treasure? Begged him to keep their secret? Wishing she could kill him, unwilling to earn that mark, waiting for Oziah's return and money to solicit the inksmith instead of paying for the betrayer's silence? How long until the extortionist exposed her in his greed and envy?

Before she could ask or steal, Oziah had given her the coins needed to erase her sins. But Enoch would not help her.

She could not return to Oziah. Her stain would turn him inside out. Did this sin not wound him equally, being her husband? Would he stumble in his faith that promised to wash stains?

Oziah's discipline and honesty, everything she respected about him, would be turned against her, dangerous as a storm. Oziah was a hard man to himself and others. He would demand the full extent of the law, even for her. She must leave him, but where could she go far enough for the world to forget? Before this mortal sin climbed her neck and claimed her face?

Oziah bore stains around his eyes. But the law didn't insist that his sins deserved hanging, like hers.

How did one weigh sin? Why must she fall by hers when her lover wouldn't? While Enoch's old master likely enjoyed a meal and restful night's sleep? If Oziah did not forgive her, and punishment was meted, wouldn't he return to sea with hands considered clean?

If only Oziah had not returned. If only the ocean had swallowed him. He could have kept his peace.

Helena sobbed.

The candle sputtered and expired.

Tomorrow dawned cold and clear. The gelding nickered as Helena gathered her things, wrapped her shawl around herself, and searched for the coin bag. Gone.

Thieves, who did not touch her? She hissed before remembering. Enoch had the money.

She reached the carpentry shop and burst through the door.

Humming, Enoch dipped his head and tore fresh bread over his worktable. The full coin bag lay beside a second filled plate.

Why? Helena grasped the purse and did not sit.

Enoch squinted toward the paper windows. "Storm's coming."

Why did he say that? The sky was cloudless, and sunlight blinded this place.

"You look like you need to eat something, Mrs.—"

"No, thank you." She couldn't bear to hear her married name.

"Is there something I can do for you today?"

How could he ask that after refusing her yesterday? "No. Yes." She closed her eyes and ground her teeth. "You said you've been freed from stains. You led Oziah to your faith and called him a good man." Her mouth trembled. "Why didn't it work for him?"

Enoch ceased humming and bowed his head. "Do you believe that I am better or less than others?" He doffed his straw hat. Above the scar, tainting the born color of his skin, lead white stains seeped across his clean-shaven scalp. Mushrooms, roots, seeds, and sharp bolls mingled with thorns like a crown.

Helena palmed her mouth. "Liar."

Enoch shook his head. "It's said to hate is to murder. And there're plenty of reasons to hate. If stains are marks of the world below, no one can arrive at the good place dressed in them. I sweated blood to breathe freedom in my present life. I'd be a simpleton to neglect what comes next, but I'm not there yet." His glittering eyes chilled her soul. "The question isn't when someone's stains are cleansed, but can they be? I cannot help anyone who is unable to believe what they cannot yet see."

She retreated a step. Enoch and Oziah were to be pitied. She was, too, to come here.

"Hasn't your husband earned stains, Mrs. Walker?"

She did not answer but fled the front door. Darkness dripped from the heavens, and cold and wind stirred the forest. He had been right about the storm.

Rain fell when she reached the lean-to. The horse was gone. Spooked or stolen.

The lean-to groaned as if bearing the weight of a giant's hand.

She escaped before it collapsed, screamed, and pushed through the tangled woods to the main thoroughfare.

The rain thickened. She slipped and muddied her hem. Gray slush gathered around her boots.

Hasn't your husband earned stains? No one can arrive at the good place dressed in them.

She and Oziah were fools. Soon he would know it, too.

Wind wailed. Sleet pattered like distant, overwhelming gunfire, pelting her and swallowing sight of every path. She could hardly see, needed shelter, and slipped into the woods to grope toward the carpentry shop. There, a hulking shape. But it was a decrepit cottage that she'd never seen before, shadowed by flailing trees. Enoch's shop couldn't have disappeared. Was she going mad?

She fought for breath and returned to the road. Away from the refuge of town where so many knew her. Drenched skirts twisted around her legs. Hair clung to her face. Her fingers and toes burned.

Someone shouted—coming toward her. Two horses. Her runaway gelding.

It was Oziah calling her name.

Helena stumbled into the forest and watched.

Through the curtain of shadow and snow, Oziah passed like a ghost. Sounding angry and frightened.

She could hide from him. Flee. Let him think her dead and maintain the fantasy of who he trusted her to be. Permit Oziah to believe because he hadn't seen.

Or she could answer his call, and find out how far he was willing to trust a faith that promised to wash stains.

∞

Katherine Briggs crafted her first monster story at age three. Since graduating from crayons to laptop, she continues to devour and weave speculative tales while enjoying chai tea. She, her co-adventurer husband, and their rescue dog reside outside Houston, where she classically educates amazing middle school students, teaches ESL to adults, and enjoys studying other languages. Visit katherinebriggs.com to learn more about her young adult fantasy novels *The Eternity Gate* and *The Immortal Abyss*.

Soul's Wager

K.J. Khan

And now farewell! Enclosed by monstrous night,
I am borne away, stretching out to you,
yours, alas, no more, my unsteady hands.

Book 4 of The Georgics, Vergil

HOW DOES ONE describe death?

So asked Eurydice as she waited to be ferried across the river. She thought it might explain things.

"Slow and creeping," said an elderly ghost, dressed in armor as old as himself. "The one adversary man can never defeat."

"Violent." This from a young man supporting his own flopping head, with a look of pained bemusement. "A violent joke, poorly told and with no punchline."

"Relief."

"A lie! A lie! I am not dead, I cannot be dead!" The woman wept non-existent tears and they turned away from her, embarrassed, so that only Eurydice saw.

"What do you say?" asked the old warrior, and she closed her eyes, consoled by an unspoken secret. She did not remember death.

"A song," she half-lied, to be polite.

ಐ‍ಬ

The boats that came for them were arrayed in colors, and each spirit moved toward a particular one without prompting or thought of doing otherwise.

The inhabitants of some behaved differently than others, but Eurydice watched the waves and did not notice. In her boat, children clung to the sides, gazing around at the soldiers, old women, young mothers and slaves who shared their berth. There were no common factors between them, save the hushed and solemn silence in which they traveled. One of them, a bride like Eurydice, still held flowers from earth, and she dropped them, stalk by stalk, into the swirling wake as they went.

The boat found the far shore: a calm, silent wood, where thick, smooth grasses pooled between the white birch trees. The purple sky hovered at the hour before dawn, and the fragrant air felt cool, as though painted on silk.

The other ghosts moved like sleepwalkers; they touched every flower stem and tree and looked around for the echoes of music, which even now could be heard. Eurydice alone pushed forward, fast as she could, digging ever deeper into the woods. They could not go on forever. The master of the land must dwell here, and she meant to find him.

ဆာ

The palace came into view suddenly; there was no warning, no sign of it, until she walked from behind a tree and found herself at the foot of a structure whose spires pierced the twilight sky. Eurydice's dead heart sank at its colossal size. It would take days to traverse, and she did not wish to waste her time.

The portico lay open and unattended, and she stepped inside to find dark hallways and still, thick air. No one stirred in the main hall, and all seemed shuttered and silent.

At that moment she heard a sound, too solid for a shade. She turned away from the portico and there, within a partially walled arboretum, found a being unlike any she had ever seen. He stood the height of three men, and his body shone like molten metal or stone. He looked unbreakable as adamant yet moved as the wind-stirred sea. He was tending a tree, and his hands caressed new branches into being wherever he touched. When he turned to look at her, his face glowed like polished ore and his eyes like a furnace. He did not speak. That job, as suppliant, belonged to her.

She shivered behind her veil and walked closer.

"You are the lord Hades?"

The final word hovered like a foul, cold smell, and he waited as the air swallowed it up.

"No." He replied, and his voice reverberated in her like approaching thunder. "Take care of how you speak."

She took a moment to collect herself. "But… you are the master of this place?"

358

He turned away, touching the side of a tree and pulling forth a new branch. "No. I am merely its keeper." She didn't answer and he turned back. "Please say why you have come, Eurydice."

His use of her name surprised her, and she answered at once.

"I've come to contest my death."

He did not respond with anything like the gravity she'd imagined. Rather, he looked at her with mild surprise, and stooped down to touch her head. His fingers, immensely solid, passed right through, and made her vision ripple like a disrupted pond.

"There is not much to contest," he said.

She bowed. "I do not argue the fact. I argue…" dare she? "…that it was unjust."

"Ah. Where is the injustice?"

She thought about it again, of opening her eyes and finding herself on the bank of a river like a discarded hope. She lowered her hood to reveal her hair, cut short like a bride's.

"I was at my wedding."

He nodded, inviting her to continue.

"I want to know… why I was taken. Do you… you have not been, I think, to a wedding? No. Usually the brides cry. I've watched them, every wedding I've attended. Marriage to a bad man is a horror. And there are many bad men."

"Is this true, then, of the man whom you married?"

"No. No, he is good. He is… oh, why have you taken me from him? Why could we not be happy? Why have you allowed the violent and unfaithful to wed, and parted us? Look." She raised the hem of her skirts to reveal the unobtrusive snake bite on her ankle. "Would it be so hard to fix? Are not the gods just? Whom did we offend? Who has wronged us?" She wept amidst the questions, but softly: her voice did not shake, and her eyes kept their firm gaze.

The being-who-was-not-Hades studied her without a word. Then, with the slow, careful movements of a giant, he took a step closer and knelt to look at her upturned face. This close, Eurydice noticed a hint of green in his otherwise dark eyes.

"You cannot," he began, "go back as you are. But since you feel so wronged, I will give you a chance to regain what you've lost." He turned from the plant back into the portico of the great house and beckoned her to follow. "I have a test for you—a test of four riddles. Answer them, and you may return to earth."

He led her back into the still, quiet space of the great hall. In the corner of the room stood a table, and, on the table, a merchant's scale. To either side of it lay mounds of small counterweights, half of gold, half of silver.

"Here is the first. For every just human in the world place a silver counter. For every just god, place a gold. Measure rightly, and you shall win the first of four. You may consult the mortal world for the answer, but know that the living won't perceive you." He touched her forehead and she hovered with the sudden gift of flight.

Eurydice studied his impenetrable eyes. "If I succeed, do you swear to return my life to me?"

"I swear nothing, because I do not have the authority to swear in such matters. It is a chance I give. That is all. Now go, Eurydice, and may the wind be fair."

ℰᏔ

Eurydice flew, out of the underworld and back to the sky. No human could see or hear her now; only the trees knew and stretched branches to touch her as she swept overhead.

You might expect she felt relief. But return requires more than crossing space. She had lost her mortal body, and such a loss must change her sight. Even most of the living will acknowledge that there is the world as it appears, and the world as it is. She born of the former saw the latter, and the seeing proved a shock.

Understand: hatred has a color, dreams a weight, and sin and joy a particular luminescence. We, being material, cannot picture it, but Eurydice was wholly spirit and in spirit saw the world laid bare.

We lie to spare our hearts. Were thoughts not tempered, remade, or allowed to roll past half-conscious, we would die of sickness at them.

Eurydice had wept only three times in life; now she wept for the second time in death.

ℰᏔ

Time ran strangely in the garden, and to anyone watching, Eurydice's return seemed to come only minutes after her departure. She watched the keeper and the keeper watched her. Her eyes shimmered in the cool light.

"You have taken my peace," she said, and her voice held more grief than anger.

The colossus turned to the scale. "Have you come with the answer?"

Eurydice came into the room. She stared at the scale, then she picked up two fistfuls of silver coins and let them fall through her fingers and ping off the stones.

"The philosophers speak of the god who is in all mankind, king or beggar. And they were right, something of the sort is there. What they do not say is how much worse that makes it when every man is a liar. When every man denies what is clearly inside him. We have made the world unjust, and the coming of justice would kill us."

The colossus tilted his head. "Even yourself?"

"Yes."

"Even your Orpheus?"

The pause was longer, the answer softer. "Yes."

And Eurydice turned away from the scale's left side.

"Olympus was empty. I visited every temple I could and found them either empty or too frightful to enter." She bent and picked up a single gold coin, holding it out for the keeper to see.

"And yet?"

"Yet there is one." Eurydice dropped the coin onto the scale and the right side slammed against the table like a gong. "But he is terrible."

They looked at the judgement of the scale.

"You have balanced correctly," he said.

"Then I have seen the truth of the world."

"I would not go that far." And he handed her a scroll.

§∞℞

The scroll wasn't difficult to open. Though it looked and felt like gold, it uncurled at the slightest touch. Inside it read:

Bring hope ignited, hope deferred.

Eurydice turned it over several times, but there were no other words or clues. Yet as she closed the scroll, something slipped free and nearly fell to the ground before she caught it. She opened her hand and saw a delicate crystal vial, with a slender cork as its stopper.

"In this?" she wondered aloud.

§∞℞

Where does one look for hope? Eurydice could see it now, but seeing was not what the riddle demanded. It seemed too simple to pluck two hopes at random, though most proved too immaterial for even a ghost to touch. She had no deadline, only the pressure of answering right, and she flew to the far reaches of the world, wondering if she would know by sight.

Then the sky ahead filled with a color she'd dreamt of but never seen. It wasn't hope, but hope lingered in the edges, already half spent. Eurydice sensed the outcome and did not want to see, but she needed her answer and so sank down, through the cloud and into the house below.

The house held a small crowd but for her only one, for the battle belonged to the woman alone. She had strained to the last of her strength and still she continued, though she must have felt the new life flickering out as it moved toward the air. The mourners stood waiting even as the tiny soul crowned, and Eurydice told the unknown god she could forgive his world if only this baby would live.

But the babe's light—already bound to the woman—was ebbing. It hovered on eternity's rim, paused, then slipped over the razor's edge without so much as a breath between. The woman felt it go and stopped her fight for a moment, her mouth open in a gasp. The connected light of the two stretched taut. The little soul bent the bond to its limits and finally tore free, taking part of the mother's light and leaving some of its own in exchange.

It vanished across the sky before the woman had finished her inhale.

The band that had connected them hovered in the air, already starting to sink. Tiny winks of color fell from its fray, and Eurydice opened the vial and let the glow settle to the crystal's center.

She looked closer and saw that both hopes belonged to the woman.

ဆဩ

When she returned, the underworld's keeper stood waiting.

Eurydice held out the crystal.

"Ah." He took it in his hand, inspecting its contents. He looked from the crystal to her. "You have a question, I think."

"There were two hopes in that jar."

"Yes."

"They were both hers."

"Correct."

Somewhere in the distance, a bird trilled.

"She expects to be reunited."

He nodded, slipping the crystal into his pocket. *"I shall go to him, but he shall not return to me."*

"What?"

"One of the kings of her land said that upon the death of his own child."

There was a pause, during which he returned to tending his tree. Eurydice's voice, when she spoke again, was both a question and a statement.

"Those who go to the underworld as wailing infants remain wailing infants forever. They do not reside with the other ghosts."

He fixed her with a gaze that would have leveled mountains. "Has it occurred to you that you are not in the underworld, Eurydice?"

She didn't answer, and he resumed his work. "There are new instructions on your scroll."

ഇറ

She walked through the castle on her way to the surface, and noticed the room with the scales now held a door. It hadn't been there before, and she knew because the thing could never have been missed. The rounded frame was made of a dark wood, and one touch showed it to be impossibly thick and sturdy. Light peeked in from the edges, and the light was music. Eurydice put her hands to the edge, but the light poured through as though her hands did not exist. Her desire for what lay beyond it outweighed even her desire for the quest, and she would have tried it, but there wasn't a handle. She turned to ask the keeper, but the castle had changed and the path behind now led forward into the mortal world.

She looked down at the scroll.

What is the sacrifice most loved by the Divine?

ഇറ

Where could she go for sacrifices, when she knew the truth of the world's temples? She went back to the land where the woman had lived, but there was no temple—only the ruins where a temple once stood. Eurydice hovered, confused. She had thought the woman followed the just yet terrible god, but how had such a deity's temple fallen into disrepair? She could feel him in the fabric of the world—his breath would have been a windstorm, his touch an earthquake—and she knew nothing posed him a threat.

A stele stood by the ruins, and though Eurydice couldn't read its inscription, she recognized the imagery from her world-spanning flight. Had the god made a new temple there? It made sense—the city was splendid, the empire grand—far more fitting than this small, conquered place. Didn't divinity belong with power?

She went, but the conquerors had different temples. Necessity bid her to enter one and she saw a lurking darkness, far weaker than the god but stronger than anything human. It bore this smaller strength with a seething malice, and Eurydice's soul trembled as though filled with ice.

"Who are you?" she cried.

It caught her by the waist with a grip of searing cold.

The prince of this land, it said, and she felt rather than heard the painful, rock-sliding grind of the answer. Eurydice twisted and cried out, and that might have been the end of her quest if not for the scroll. The gold hissed against the shadow beast's touch, and it howled and flung her back.

Cheat! How came you by that? You should be mine by right, mine! How came you—
Eurydice fled at once and did not hear the rest.

ඞ

"Where is your temple?" she asked, if only to clear her thoughts. It had taken some moments to recover, and she didn't want to waste more time. "You have no shrines, no altars. How can there be sacrifices? How can mankind worship you, should any dare to try?"

Then Eurydice heard the language of the conquered place, of the grieving mother, and turned to listen. She didn't understand the words, but felt encouraged to hear it spoken within the realm of the shadow beast. Had the keeper given her a clue, in what he'd said before?

She followed the voice and it led her to an open window, visible from the street. Inside knelt a man, and the man was praying. Without a temple, without an offering, exiled in a foreign land, he prayed, and the men in the streets scoffed as they passed. Why shouldn't they? Why should a man pray to a god who couldn't protect his own country? Eurydice herself would have marveled with the rest, had she not known the power of the one to whom he prayed. As it was, she marveled at his audacity.

But the prayer was not a sacrifice, as the riddle demanded. She needed—
But wait.

She had entered the window to circle the suppliant but now stopped. From the man's chest came a gold thread, so thin she could barely see it, and only when she stood at the right angle to the setting sun.

Eurydice examined the thread—touched it, lightly, and felt a shock that should have been pain and yet was not, not quite. She let go at once, but as soon as she had, felt a longing to seize it again. The thread looked strange, and she feared taking hold of it would mean being at its mercy.

The man bowed—the prayer seemed to be nearing its end—but she continued to hesitate. The gold had an agency to it, as though it served as a conduit for some living thing that had gripped her hand in return. What if the touch proved more than she could bear?

The prayer ended; she stretched out a hand and took hold.

ඞ

She had expected it would wrench her off her feet. For the first instant she thought it had, but the movement proved an illusion. She, held by the thread, stood still—not as on earth, where things might move and then rest, as it suited them, but like a mirror when a torch is swung overhead. Place and time moved like the scattered light, but she had come into the glass heart and stood spellbound while the years and miles rolled and changed.

It was too much to count, even to see, and she rested in a waking daze until the movement stopped. In front of her, the thread came to an end in a great cloud of light, so bright that its density fell against the eyes the way thick darkness might. Eurydice shut her eyes and saw it still; she covered her face with her hands, but the light poured through her like glass, so that she feared her soul might split apart with its force. She cried out, but her cry sounded like the shadow beast's. The thread had betrayed her and brought her to the terrible God, and she stood naked, unable to escape what the unbalanced scales had shown.

Yet even as she cried out, the light began to temper. It did not dim; the essence remained, but somehow shifted to a spectrum that could be seen without pain. She saw, now that her burning eyes had reprieve to see, that the radiance had compressed itself in size. From infinity, it shrank to the size of a mountain, from a mountain to a palace, and from a palace to a human form. The brilliance crystalized, and she looked into the dark eyes of a man. He was flesh and blood, but his eyes held the eternal spark of the light, and the golden thread lay anchored forever in his breast. In his right hand he held a judge's staff; in his left, a flawless silver counterweight.

The terror in Eurydice's throat turned to wonder, and her shriek to a cry of delight.

"Oh!" she laughed. *"Oh!"*

She would have run the last steps to him, but time rolled backward like a receding tide, and she watched constellations reverse and the surface of the ground invert until she stood before a door in the castle underground. She turned, and there lay the courtyard, there stood the keeper.

The answer must have been written on her face, because he did not pose the question.

"The sacrifice most loved by the Divine," Eurydice whispered, "is the sacrifice of himself."

§∞Ↄ

"Come," said the keeper. "For the last riddle we must go elsewhere." He started down the path by which she'd first come, and Eurydice hesitated.

"The door..." she asked. "The one without a handle. Is there any way to open it?"

"It will open itself to whoever holds the key. But take care, Eurydice. Those who pass beyond the door leave the mortal life forever."

And so she followed, looking behind her as the palace faded. She had thought the door would have its place in the final riddle. To leave it, forever locked, brought an unexpected ache.

She walked with the keeper through azure fields, on a path whose familiarity nagged her. It led, she realized, to the river. She could see mists rising as they drew closer.

"Where are we going?" she asked.

But the keeper did not answer.

The mist from the river began to thicken around them. It swirled under the stride of her giant guide, but swept through Eurydice like water through a sieve, leaving her chilled. Then the mist turned to a veil, and they passed through it and stepped onto the rocky shore of the river. All that lay behind them remained shrouded, as though eternity held nothing more than a gray and empty wind. There was no color on the shore—save for the brown tunic and ruddy face of the living young man perched on a rock beside the dark waters.

"Eurydice!" he cried, and the lyre slung over his shoulder thumped against his side as he ran to her, arms outstretched.

She spoke his name once without sound, then tried a second time. "Orpheus?"

He slowed his final approach in a skid of stones. His arms remained outstretched, his face lit with joy, but even so he dared not cross the final stretch between the living and the dead. "Eurydice!"

She came to him; he hesitated a moment then caught her in his arms. To both their surprise, he did not pass through, but held her ghost as though she wore the thinnest shell of substance.

"Take care," warned the keeper, for the second time. "You may return by the passage you came, but once begun, you must not touch one another, nor Orpheus turn to look on her, until you have reached the end."

"The end?" asked Eurydice.

"The borders of this place."

"To the surface," Orpheus clarified. "I've come to take you back." He almost took her hand again but remembered the keeper's bidding and instead hovered about her in anxious happiness.

Eurydice smiled at him. There could be no denying the joy she felt at seeing him again, but the joy mixed with other thoughts, in a well of the unfinished.

She looked back at the keeper. "Were there not four riddles? Where is the fourth?"

"There are no riddles," Orpheus replied, not understanding. "I've come for you."

But the keeper gazed down at her, and the great stone of his eyes seemed softer. "The last you must take with you."

She waited, but no riddle came, and Orpheus shifted impatiently on the slipshod stones.

"I have questions," she said. "Things are not as I supposed them, and I want to know—"

"Eurydice," Orpheus interrupted. He knew the gods were fickle and was impatient to be off, before the dead lord changed his mind. "Come. The walk is far."

"Do not look back," the keeper repeated, though his gaze remained on her. "Do not look back or she must return."

"Yes. I thank you. The warning shall be heeded." He looked at Eurydice once more, as though to memorize and map her face. "Are you ready? Will you follow?"

How could she not, when he had come so far?

℘℘

The route they took proved rocky and dismal. The mist never cleared, and Eurydice marveled to see so much endless, unpopulated space. Her feet did not make any sound on the rocky shale, and Orpheus would call out her name from time to time, to reassure himself she was still there. Eurydice watched the back of his curly head through the mist. She could see how much he longed to turn to her, could see how he held his neck with deliberate stiffness to keep himself from any such accidental turn.

"You must speak to me," he called, his voice oddly loud. "Speak, let me know you are there."

She laughed. "As you say. Of what should I speak?"

"You are the one who should have a story to tell. What have you seen, these two days in death?"

"Two days? Is it only that?"

Now it was he who laughed. "It is difficult to mark the time here, no doubt."

"Or to always tell which way it passes."

He clicked his tongue. "Poor Eurydice, what a place this is! On return we'll make sacrifices to Zeus, in hopes he keeps us from here many years more.

367

We'll offer more, perhaps, than even the bridal hecatomb—much good that it did us, hmph."

Eurydice stopped as though she had reached the end of an invisible lead and been jerked back. It had not occurred to her that she would be expected to reverence the gods on her return. She had feared to enter the temples of Greece with her ghostly sight, and what she'd found inside the foreign one had forever confirmed her fears.

"I don't want to sacrifice to Zeus."

Orpheus could tell by the distance of her voice that she had stopped, and now stopped as well. "Choose another as patron, then. But we must offer something, a little something, to all the Olympians. We'll be a target otherwise." She didn't answer, and he tipped his head to one side in impatience. "Eurydice, we can't linger here. We must keep on." Still she didn't answer, and his voice caught a little. "Eurydice?"

His fear prodded her forward. "Yes. Yes, I'm coming."

They had walked the shore long enough; the path had grown steeper step by step, and now they walked along the edge of a canyon, with the water rushing far below. Just ahead stood the base of a narrow stone bridge that spanned the gulf to the other shore. There were no rails on the naked, narrow path, and the water below stirred the air into a windy current. Orpheus had already walked this path once, and she saw by the way he tensed that he did not relish doing so again.

"Tell me you are following," he called, his voice snatched by the wind.

"I am following."

The bridge's width matched that of a strong man's shoulders, and the rush of water below gave the illusion that it swayed slightly underfoot. The wind tugged at Eurydice's shawl, and it took her a moment to notice she had become more tangible since the journey's beginning. The thought brought little comfort, suspended as she was over such a terrifying plunge. The swirling wind brought her attention to the weight in her pocket, and she remembered the scroll. On the push of some odd insistence she took it out. Already its golden edges looked translucent, and it struck her that the scroll belonged to the hidden world and would vanish when she crossed the threshold. As she held it, the wind caught and rolled back the gold leaf, and she saw new words embossed.

Open your eyes at the crossroads of faith and doubt.

Up ahead of her, Orpheus had crossed the bridge and now called back. "Have you made it? Are you safe?"

She returned the scroll to her pocket and ran across the final stretch.

"Yes," she said, and fought not to cry because she loved him. But to return to his world, sightless again, without the scroll—to hear oracles whom she knew were not prophets, and to smell blood on the altars of terrible things against whom she had no protection...

When she reached the far shore, she looked and saw her arms were now half-tangible, like frosted ice that one can no longer gaze through.

"It's here," panted Orpheus. "Around the bend. The entrance."

They followed the curve in the road and came around to see a hole in the mountain, its opening scarcely larger than a person. Daylight streamed in, but the light was no longer sweet, now that she had seen what light should look like.

Orpheus sprang forward, relieved. For a moment, his silhouette blocked the light, and then he stood in the sun, his back toward her. He raised his head, and she pictured his face: the eyes closed, his mouth parted a little to taste the air. His delight in life had always moved her, and it didn't fail to do so now, as she stood on the edge of mortality.

"Have you crossed yet?" His hand searched the air behind him. "I don't dare turn, not now. Tell me when you've crossed."

She felt in her pocket for the scroll, whose visibility was now as thin as the ghost-Eurydice whom Orpheus had embraced. When she touched it, she saw the world ahead with the final vestige of her fading secret sight. The thoughts and plans of her beloved lay haloed around him, and in her mind she followed their beckonings into the future awaiting her on earth.

One thing grew suddenly clear: if she returned, she would have Orpheus, but that was all. Try as she might to hold onto all she'd seen, to put on flesh again would bring back the time and place of her old life. She'd resist, for a while—keep back from the temple, keep her head unbowed to them and her heart closed to their homage—but it could not last forever. Custom was built on the gods. Her husband would need her observances, her society would demand them. Who would heed the contrary visions of a woman, even one who had returned from the dead? Did she think she could unseat the shadow beasts? Comfortable in their dominion, they did not yet know of the golden thread. Unlooked for, unwatched, it unfolded in silence, bearing a remade world in its line. The thread would remain, but the decaying weight of time would wear her down—blur her memories, her convictions—until she settled in the unhappy limbo of belonging to neither the hidden nor seen, and hating both.

"Eurydice? Have you crossed?"

"No. Not yet."

She would have Orpheus… but she saw, the longer she looked, that even this was not true. She saw his future self in her mind: suspicious, increasingly wary of this wife who had left some part of herself in the underworld. Yes, she thought, as the scenes rolled before her like a stage play, there would come a day when Orpheus would wonder if it were truly Eurydice who had followed him out of Hades. He would watch her, at night, as they lay together, or in similar times of stillness and solitude, and if she caught his eyes she would find the fear that she was something else altogether: a stranger, or a changeling. Then, if the time continued and she still did not relinquish what she'd seen, there would come a day when he looked on her openly in his fear and revulsion, and they would be parted on a different level, in a parting made all the worse by the continued physical presence. The doubt was there. It was just a tiny spot, now, but it would grow like a tumor.

The doubt.

She took the scroll back out and looked at it again, hoping for more instruction. There were no words, but at the scroll's edge lay a faint, unmistakable, whisper-thin thread of gold.

Eurydice froze, heart in her throat. She shook the scroll, and the thread wavered in the darkness, showing its line by a thin gleam. The thread was anchored in another time, but hadn't she seen proof already that time too was his servant? Would he take her, a branch born out of season, if she followed? She did not know the answer, but the choice was clear.

"Orpheus?"

He had grown understandably angry and snarled a reply. "What? What is it, what's wrong?"

"I can't go with you."

For a moment he said nothing, but a flush of color rose on the back of his neck.

"So Hades has lied," he whispered, and his broken voice would have crushed her fledgling resolve, had she not held it in her own two hands.

"There is no Hades."

"Eurydice, I saw him, I—"

"—You did not. You saw a servant, that's all."

"—You're confused, you don't remember—"

"Orpheus, there isn't time. I can't go with you but perhaps you can follow me. Leave Greece. Go to Babylon, find the exiles who still pray to the God without a temple, and ask them."

"Ask them what—how best to follow you in death?"

"Ask them about their God. The one I'm going after."

"You can't." His voice was boyish in his tears. "You can't, I command you. I'm your husband and I command you to stay."

Behind her came the pull of the thread. She kept her voice firm.

"I have to go now. Turn and take my hand."

"What?"

"I will go regardless. Turn and remember."

Orpheus's shoulders curled forward in misery. He was angry with her, and she feared he might not turn and she must leave him like this.

Orpheus turned.

She caught his hand in hers, and with the other moved her touch from scroll to thread. In the final moment, in the still point before the break, she hoped he saw the secret world, if only by the conviction in her eyes. Then the thread drew her back. Their hands parted, and she vanished into the darkness.

"Remember!" She called out, her cry blending with his. "Remember!"

∞ℭ℘

But it was not fair to speak of "darkness" anymore, for the light of the thread grew brighter with every step she took. And each step came lighter than the next, until she seemed to fly rather than run. She sped over the chasm and crossed the rocky shore, and her silent guide glowed like amber through the mist. When she came to the palace, she found it changed: the windows blazed light, as though extending a welcome that had earlier been withheld.

Eurydice walked through the halls, where giants like the keeper stood, smiling at her as she came, and pointing her onward toward the garden.

Here, the keeper too had changed. He wore robes like the steward of a feast, and his eyes were no longer black at all, but shone with a living green in the midst of his ebony face. He stood beside the door, and held out his hands to her as she came.

"Lady," he boomed, in the full bloom of his voice (and yet she did not tremble), "Lady, why have you come?"

And the palace fell silent and the air stilled in preparation for one soul's reply.

Eurydice seemed to grow taller in the stillness, and she smiled up into the keeper's face. "I have come to enter the door."

"Lady, by whose name do you come?"

"My name and my old gods belong to the shadow beasts. I come with a plea to the King beyond time, who holds both gold and silver and will pave the way with himself."

Her answer passed over the assembly like the strains of a song, and the keeper waited for the echoes to finish.

"And has he given you his key?"

She opened her hand, revealing the slender bit of carved pearl, tied with a scarlet thread. She had felt it in her palm when she took the golden thread, and she saw that it fit the door's lock, which lay just above the newly-appeared handle.

"Yes," she whispered. "He has."

⚮

K.J. Khan lives in East Providence, RI, with her husband Tim and their two children. Her short fiction has appeared in *Clarkesworld* and *Short Edition*, and she splits her time between writing, painting, and the chaos of parenting (mostly the third option). You can see more of her work at Instagram.com/katie.j.khan, or at kjkhanart.com.

Author's note: Special thanks to Sam Phillips, who translated the story's epigraph.

Copyrights

About the Editors

Donald S. Crankshaw and Kristin Janz met at a church writers' group in 2009, bonded almost immediately over their shared love of speculative fiction and ancient Roman history, and have been married since 2011. They live in Quincy, Massachusetts, just south of Boston, with two cats named after famous scientists.

Donald has a Ph.D. in Electrical Engineering from the Massachusetts Institute of Technology, which was more useful for writing fantasy than he had expected, though less helpful for writing science fiction than he had hoped. He has published stories in *Nature Futures*, *Intergalactic Medicine Show*, and *Black Gate*.

Kristin is a Canadian fantasy and science fiction writer and a 2008 graduate of the Clarion West Writers Workshop. Her fiction has appeared in *Escape Pod*, *Daily Science Fiction*, and *On Spec*. She has an M.Sc. in Organic Chemistry from the University of British Columbia and worked in the pharmaceutical industry as a medicinal chemist for over a decade.

Together, Donald and Kristin edit and publish the online speculative fiction magazine *Mysterion* (MysterionOnline.com), featuring stories that engage meaningfully with Christianity from a range of perspectives. This is their third anthology, following the original *Mysterion: Rediscovering the Mysteries of the Christian Faith* (2016), and *Mysterion 2: Stories from the Online Magazine, 2018-2019* (2020).

About *Mysterion*

Mysterion the online magazine publishes stories each month at MysterionOnline.com, and is open to fiction submissions in January and July.

Subscribe to our newsletter: MysterionOnline.com/p/newsletter.html.

Subscribe to our Patreon: Patreon.com/Mysterion.